A Good
Catch

By the same author:

Fern: My Story

New Beginnings
Hidden Treasures
The Holiday Home
A Seaside Affair

The Stolen Weekend (short story)
A Cornish Carol (short story)

Fern Britton

A Good Catch

HarperCollins*Publishers*

HarperCollins*Publishers*
1 London Bridge Street,
London SE1 9GF

www.harpercollins.co.uk

Published by HarperCollins*Publishers* 2015
2

A catalogue record for this book
is available from the British Library

ISBN: 978-0-00-756294-7

Set in Birka by Palimpsest Book Production Limited, Falkirk, Stirlingshire

Printed and bound in Great Britain by
Clays Ltd, St Ives plc

MIX
Paper from
responsible sources
FSC™ C007454

To my darling Goose.
Thank you for making me laugh so much.
Love you, Mum.

PROLOGUE

Greer Behenna had never felt so drained. Relieved to be alone at last, she closed her front door and leant her head on its cool, solid wood.

The inquest had been conducted with meticulous precision. The courtroom, even with its lights on, couldn't pierce the gloom of the winter's day hanging outside its windows. The warmth from the old-fashioned radiators filled the air, right up to the high and corniced ceiling, with a density of heat that had left Greer drowsy and with the beginnings of a headache. She had listened to all that the witnesses had said and heard none of it. When called to the stand she gave her own evidence, but remembered little of it now.

So separated were her mind and body she almost floated up the stairs and into her room, where she pulled off her black Armani dress and carefully hung it up in the wardrobe. She found her jeans and a warm jumper and put them on. In the kitchen she filled the kettle. Tom was outside, sitting on the windowsill and mewing crossly. As soon as he saw her he jumped down and clattered in through the cat flap. She fed him. The kettle boiled and she wondered what she'd put it on for. She couldn't face another cup of tea that day. She went to the fridge but there was no wine. She'd drunk the last of it the previous night. She drifted through into the

drawing room and then the dining room, where they'd
had so many family celebrations. Back in the drawing
room, she reached for the remote control. The television
came to life with a rather camp man talking about
antiques; she switched the TV off again. Restlessly she
got her coat and warm boots from the boot room, picked
up her keys from the console table in the hall and left
Tide House for the only place that felt right: the cove.

Greer had found herself seeking the solace of the cove
more and more of late. The tide was out and she walked
down to the water's edge. She found a patch of smooth
rock to sit on that was otherwise covered in mussels.
She closed her eyes and breathed in the scent of ocean
and seaweed. She saw him in her mind's eye. He was
standing in the surf, casting his line to catch the sea bass
that were lurking beneath the waves. His back was to
her but she knew that he'd be frowning slightly, concentrating on the fish, his fingers feeling for a bite on the
line. She watched him turn round and, when she saw
his face, it wasn't the man that she saw, but the boy. His
blond hair, almost white from the heat of summer, plas-
tered around his face, his eyes the colour of the sea,
looking at her coolly with that familiar mix of curiosity
and indifference. Remembering his face as it was then,
Greer was suddenly taken back to the long hot summer
of 1975, when she was almost five, and she first saw Jesse
Behenna . . .

*

He was sitting on Trevay quay, loading a crab line with
a mackerel head. His tousled blond head was bent closely
to the task and, when he was happy that the bait was

secure on the hook, he swung the line to and fro before dropping it into the deep, oily water.

He drummed his dangling feet over the slimy sea wall in concentration. For a few seconds he watched the line sink to the bottom. Satisfied that it had, he shifted his face to the horizon and screwed up his eyes, as if hoping to bring into focus something that he couldn't see. He rubbed the back of his hand across his nostrils and then turned his attention to a bucket by his side.

''Ere you go, lads,' he said, putting a hand into the bag of chips by his side before dropping one into the bucket. Greer saw the quick scuttle of pincers through the opaque of the plastic.

'Move up, Greer.' Her mother, Elizabeth, sat down next to her on the sun-warmed, sea-roughened wooden bench, checking for seagull mess. 'Your dad's just bringing the ice creams. Don't get any on your dress.'

'Can I do some crabbing?'

Greer's mother looked almost offended. 'Whatever for?'

'It looks fun.'

Her father sauntered up, carrying three dripping 99s. ''Ere you go, my beauties.'

'Can I have a go at crabbing, Daddy?'

He looked at her sideways. 'What does your mother say?'

'I say she's in her best dress and I have quite enough laundry to do,' said her mother.

'She can take it off,' replied her father, Bryn, winking at Greer. 'Lovely day like today.' He ignored his wife's horrified stare. 'Eat up your ice cream and we'll nip to the shop and get you a crab line.'

'And a fish head.'

'Yeah, and a fish head.'

'And a bucket.'

'Of course, can't go crabbing without a bucket.'

The sun was warm on her bare shoulders as she sat, in just her vest and pants, on the gritty, granite sea wall, just a few feet from the boy. She dangled her legs, thrillingly and dangerously, over the sea wall, just as the boy was doing.

She had seen him pull in several crabs and drop them in his bucket and was desperate for the same success.

'Right. There you go. Mind that hook, it's sharp.' Her father passed her the baited line.

She looked at the lump of fish stabbed through with the large hook and nodded solemnly. 'I will, Daddy.'

'Do you want me to show you how to feed the line out?'

'I can do it.'

'Well, keep it close to the wall. The crabs like it in the dark. The tides comin' in so they'll be washed in with it. 'Tis no good crabbing on an outgoing tide.'

Greer was getting impatient. All the crabs would be in that boy's bucket if she didn't hurry up.

'Let me do it, Daddy.'

She took the square plastic reel from her father and slowly let the line out. She leant her head as far forward over the edge of the wall as she dared.

'It's landed, Daddy.'

'Good girl. Now sit on the reel and it won't fall in. If you lose it, I ain't buying you another.'

She lifted her thigh, already growing pink from the sun, and wedged the sharp plastic of the reel firmly under her buttock.

'Can I pull it up now?'

'Give it a couple of minutes.'

She looked over at the boy who was again wrinkling his eyes and staring at the horizon. Her father surprised her by talking to him. ''Ello. You're young Jesse Behenna, aren't you?'

The boy reluctantly turned his gaze to the man talking to him. 'Yeah.'

'Watching for your dad's boat, are you?'

'Yeah. 'E's been out three days.'

'Has he? That'll be a good catch he's bringing in then.'

'Yeah. As long as the bastard at the market gives them a good price.'

Greer's father laughed. 'Is that right?'

'Yeah.'

'I've got one!' Greer was pulling up her line and, as it broke water, her father and the boy could see that she had three fat, black, glittering crabs clinging greedily to the bait.

'Bring 'em in slow, Greer.'

'Get the bucket, Daddy!' she called excitedly.

'That's it. Nice and slow. Now drop 'em in.'

Greer watched as the three crabs plopped into her bucket.

'Mummy! I got three in one go!'

'Did you?' responded her mother from the safety of the bench; she was still not looking up from her magazine. 'Well done, darling.'

'Do you want to feed them a chip?' The boy passed over the bag.

She picked up the fattest chip she could see and dropped it into her bucket.

'Thank you.'

The crabs, which had been scrapping with each other, now started scrapping with the chip.

'Want one yerself?' asked Jesse.

Greer darted a glance at her mother, who shook her head. 'You've already had an ice cream, Greer. You don't want to get fat.'

Greer looked back at Jesse. 'No, thank you.'

'Suit yourself,' he said, shovelling a handful into his mouth.

'What bait you using?' he mumbled, standing up and wiping his hands on his cotton shorts. He ambled over, with his hands in his pockets, to look at her catch.

'Fish,' said Greer.

'What sort of fish?'

Greer's father replied, 'Mackerel, boy. But I reckon 'tis bacon that's the best. When I were a nipper, I always used bacon.'

The boy looked at him, nodding his head slowly, weighing up the pros and cons of mackerel versus bacon. 'I prefer mackerel. It's what Dad says is best and he's the best fisherman in Trevay.'

'Then he must be right,' smiled Greer's father.

The emptying of the crabs back into the water was a serious business. One by one they were counted and Greer had a pleasing sixty-four to Jesse's eighty-one.

'Not bad. For a beginner,' he told her.

'Bryn,' called Greer's mother, impatient to get home to a cooling shower. 'It's time to get Greer back.'

'Stop your nagging, woman. We'm 'aving a good time.'

'I've got to get tea on and it's getting late.'

'I told you to stop nagging,' he said, and silenced her with a look.

The children said their goodbyes and Greer's father said, 'Send my regards to your dad.'

'What's your name?' asked Jesse.

6

'I'm the bastard at the market who never gives him a good price.'

*

Greer snapped her eyes open, remembering Jesse's straight talking as being so typical of him, even as a young boy. He always seemed so sure of himself; he didn't ever seem to care what anyone thought. But had she ever really known him? Had any of them? She continued staring out into the churning, dark sea and pulled her coat closer around her, though she knew that it wasn't the winter chill that was making her shiver.

The sea in front of her was devoid of boats, reflecting the emptiness she felt inside.

*

Loveday Chandler knocked and waited for several minutes. She pulled her mobile phone from the pocket of her fleece and dialled Greer's number. She heard it ring out behind the closed front door. Snapping her phone shut and putting it back into her pocket, she turned away from the house and headed towards the only other place where her friend could be.

'Greer,' Loveday called as she jogged breathlessly down the beach. 'Greer!'

Greer hung her head and blew out a stream of warm breath into the cold wind. Why would no one leave her alone?

Loveday reached her, panting. 'Greer, darlin', you OK?'

Greer dragged her eyes from the horizon and focused on her oldest friend. 'I'm fine,' she said flatly.

'Only we was worried. You left so quickly.'

'I wanted to be home.'

Loveday sat down on a bunch of mussels next to Greer. ''Twas a tough day.'

Greer nodded, grim faced.

'Brings it all back again,' said Loveday, picking up a small pebble and throwing it into the lapping water.

Greer turned her gaze back to the horizon and again nodded. 'I can't believe he isn't coming back,' she said quietly.

Loveday put an arm around her friend's shoulder. 'I know.'

Greer turned her white and stricken face towards her friend. 'And I can't believe that you'll soon be gone too. My oldest friends are leaving me.'

Loveday felt the tightening belt of guilt around her chest. 'You've got lots of friends . . . And as soon as we're settled, I want you to come out to New Zealand and spend long holidays with us.'

'I haven't got lots of friends. I have clients, I have acquaintances, but there's no one who knows me like you do.'

Greer found an old tissue in the pocket of her coat, blew her nose and took a deep breath, trying to calm herself. 'I'm sorry. It's just self-pity.' It took a supreme effort for her to plaster a tight smile on to her face. 'I'm happy for you. I really am. And, anyway, I can't leave. Not yet. I must be here . . . in case . . .'

Loveday pushed a strand of her corkscrew hair behind her ear. Once such a brilliant copper red, it was now faded to a rust colour and flecked with white. She thought how lucky she was to have this opportunity of a fresh start. Looking at Greer she felt lucky that she had made the right decision all those years ago.

Awkwardly, she fumbled for Greer's hand and gripped it hard.

Greer said softly, 'Do you think he ever really loved me?'

Loveday pulled Greer towards her and hugged her tightly, but couldn't answer.

The dice had been thrown a long time ago.

Part One

1

Greer's mother had planned on sending her daughter to a small private school in Truro but her husband had soon squashed another of her dreams. 'Trevay Infants' was good enough for you an' me, and it'll be good enough for Greer.' Which is how Greer was to meet Jesse again.

It was early September. Trevay had said goodbye to all the holiday-makers and could get on with being the small Cornish fishing port that it was.

Greer was in her uniform of grey pleated skirt and navy-blue blazer, with dazzling long white socks and shiny buckled shoes. She walked between her parents as they covered the five-minute stretch from home to school. She was nervous. She had never been left anywhere on her own before. As they got closer to the school, more and more children filled the narrow pavements around her. Some of them she recognised but barely knew. Her mother had few friends herself, having always put them off with an extreme shyness which was often interpreted as an unwarranted air of superiority.

In the playground, Bryn bent to kiss Greer. She might not be the son he had wanted, but she was everything to him. His sun and his moon. He would – and did – give her everything. 'You be a good girl, mind.'

'I will, Daddy.' She put her arms round his neck and hugged him tight. 'Will you come and get me when I'm finished?'

'Aye.'

Her mother kissed her too. 'Have a good day, darling. See you later.'

Greer watched as her parents walked out of the playground. Her father striding out and nodding at acquaintances, her mother trotting to keep up with him and turning to give one last wave to her only child.

Greer's legs started to move towards the school gate and her parents and away from the school building. She was picking up her pace and tears were pricking her eyes. I don't want to be at school. I want Mummy, she was saying to herself.

She was getting closer to the gate. She took a breath, ready to call out to her mother. She could see her father chatting to man in a fishing smock. Her mother was surreptitiously wiping her eyes while her father was laughing at something the man was telling him.

Greer's lungs were now full and ready to shout to them. She opened her mouth but, before she could get any sound out, a small but firm hand caught her round the waist.

'Where you going?'

The air in her lungs escaped soundlessly at the surprise pressure on her diaphragm. She struggled but was held even more tightly.

'Hey. You're going to get into trouble if you go through the school gates.'

Something in the voice made her stop and turn to see who her captor was. It was the crab fishing boy from the quay.

A woman carrying a handbell was walking through the playground. She began ringing it loudly.

'Come on,' Jesse said.

He took Greer's hand and ran with her into the school.

*

A male teacher was standing inside the building, at the door to the school hall, identifying the new children. 'New boys and girls, walk to the front of the hall, don't run, and sit on the floor, cross-legged, facing the stage, please.'

Greer was feeling anxious but grateful to have Jesse's hand in hers. Once they got to the front he let go of her and sat on the floor.

'Are you a new boy too?' she asked him, settling down next to him.

'Yeah, but I know everybody 'ere. My brother comes 'ere too.' He was looking over her head and smiling at someone. Greer followed his gaze and saw a fat, plain girl with her flame-red hair in pigtails, also sitting cross-legged, showing her knickers and waving at him.

'Who's that?' Greer asked, feeling sorry for this unattractive-looking girl.

'That's Loveday.'

The fat girl bum-shuffled her way towards them.

'All right, Jesse?' she smiled.

'Yeah.'

'What's your name?' the girl asked Greer.

'Greer. I am named after a famous film star who was very beautiful.' Greer couldn't help herself.

'Oh,' said Loveday, her smile pushing her fat freckled cheeks up towards her eyes. 'That's nice. I'm called Loveday after my dad's granny.'

Jesse's eyes were darting around the gathering faces. 'Seen Mickey?' he asked Loveday.

'He's there.' Loveday pointed at an open-faced, tall and very skinny boy standing on the other side of the hall.

'Mickey,' Jesse called. 'Mickey, come 'ere, you beggar.'

'Who's he?' Greer asked Loveday.

'Jesse's best friend. Do you want to be my best friend?'

Greer had never had a friend and thought that she might as well start with this poor fat girl. 'Yes.'

'Can I tell you a secret then?'

'Yes.'

'I'm goin' to marry Jesse.'

Greer frowned. 'Has he asked you?'

'No. But I am going to marry him.' Loveday smiled, then had a thought. 'You can marry Mickey! That way we'll all be best friends for ever.' Greer looked at Mickey, who winked at her. She frowned back. Loveday was tugging at her sleeve and saying something. 'Do you like Abba?'

It was a long day. The new children were introduced to their teacher, Mrs Bond, who took them to their classroom. Loveday grabbed two desks next to each other for her and Greer. Jesse and Mickey were a row in front. Mrs Bond called the register, explained a few school rules – spitting and swearing were not to be tolerated, hard work was to be rewarded – and lessons began.

Greer already knew her numbers and most of her letters. She wrote her name quite clearly on her new exercise book.

Loveday was impressed. 'What you written there?'

'My name.'

'Really?' She leant forward and poked Jesse in the back.

'Ow.' He turned round. 'What did you do that for?'

'Greer can write. Look.' She showed him Greer's book.

He looked at Greer, 'Did you write that?'

'Yes.'

'Clever.'

With that one word, Jesse's fate was sealed. Greer decided it was she who was going to marry Jesse. Not Loveday.

2

Spring 1987

'You'd do a lot worse than to marry that girl,' Edward Behenna told his son.

'Shuttup, Dad.' Jesse Behenna ducked out of reach of his father's hand as he tried to ruffle his son's hair.

'It would be a dream come true for your granddad,' continued Edward as he pulled out an ancient wooden chair, scraping its legs across the worn red tiles before seating himself at the kitchen table opposite his younger son.

'If he were still alive,' murmured Jesse.

Jesse's mother, Jan, slid the tray of pasties she'd been making into the top oven of the Aga; she banged the door shut and swung round. 'Edward, don't start all this again,' she warned him, irritated.

But Edward hardly seemed to hear her. 'I promised my dad, as he promised 'is father afore 'im, that I'd do all I could to build the business and make Behenna's Boats the biggest fleet in Trevay.'

'And you have, Dad,' Jesse assured him. 'Behenna's is the biggest fishing fleet on the north coast of Cornwall.'

Edward nodded, but a frown marred his lined face. The pressures of running the business were very different from those of his father's day. This year, the European

Union had really become involved and laws were being passed governing fishing quotas for member states. Cornwall and Devon MPs had tabled questions in the Commons about their impact on their fishing industry. How could they all hope to keep going in this climate, when the government was impounding vessels and fining their owners? This interference, along with upstarts like Bryn Clovelly screwing them for every penny down at the fish market, were driving some fishermen to the wall.

The old ways were dying. Small fleets were struggling to remain at sea and Edward knew that it was the likes of Clovelly who represented the future. Edward's father had fished these waters for fifty years, man and boy. Sometimes his fish would be bought by a fishmonger from somewhere as exotic as Plymouth, but Clovelly saw the swollen wallets of the flash London City boys as rich pickings; he was buying monkfish for restaurants in Chelsea and exporting scallops to New York.

'Aye, it is. I've been working the boats since I was fourteen and left school. I didn't have your education.'

Edward knew he was a good fisherman, one of the best, but being an entrepreneur, like Bryn Clovelly, was beyond him. Behenna's Boats had provided a good living for many families up to now, but carrying on as a lone operation was looking like an increasingly risky option. Clovelly would love nothing more than to add a big share in the Behenna fleet to his portfolio and Edward was finding his offer harder and harder to resist. He knew there were men with fewer scruples than he who would bite Clovelly's hand off for a deal such as the one he was offering.

'I'm only staying on to do O levels,' Jesse reminded Edward. 'Then I'm full time working at sea on the fleet.

But when I'm a bit older and I've saved up a bit, I'm off travelling.'

His father looked at him as if he'd just said he was off to buy a Ferrari. 'Go travelling? Travelling? There's more to find in your own home town than you'd ever find travelling.'

'Oh, that's right. I'd forgotten. There're the Hanging Gardens of Bodmin, The Pyramids of Porthleven, The Colossus of St Columb . . . Cleopatra's Needle up Wadebridge. Silly me.'

Edward scowled at his son. 'That's enough of yorn lip, boy. You're the next generation. Greer Clovelly is a lovely girl and the only child Bryn and his lah-di-dah wife ever managed. Poor sod, never 'ad a son. Poor me, I got two and neither of them any bleddy good.'

'Leave off mithering the poor lad. He's only sixteen. He's got ideas of his own,' Jan said.

'I knew by his age that you were the one for me,' Edward told her, and Jan groaned inwardly as Edward played his familiar riff. 'As soon as I saw you, twelve and lookin' like an angel, I said to my mate, "There's the girl I'm gonna marry".'

'Yeah and, more fool me, I did marry you.'

Edward caught Jan's hand as she walked from the Aga to the sink. 'No regrets though, maid? No regrets?'

Jan felt the warmth of her husband's rough and calloused hand on hers and wondered. She'd had plans to travel to the Greek Islands and sleep on the beach under the stars, like the character she'd read about in a book once. The last book she'd read. Must be more than twenty years ago. But Edward had wooed her into submission and she never did send off the passport application form that had sat on her mother's dresser for two years after she'd married. For their honeymoon, Edward had taken her to Exeter and they'd seen a rep production of *The Mousetrap*. Edward had promised her that the next show they'd see would be in Paris. Almost twenty years on and they still hadn't made that trip.

She stooped and dropped a kiss on her husband's weatherbeaten forehead, feeling the spikes of his overgrown eyebrows tickling her chin. Edward Behenna would now be more likely to see the surface of the moon than the insides of the Folies Bergère. She smiled. 'No regrets my 'andsome.' She straightened up. 'But that don't mean to say you can dictate what Jesse's future is going to be.'

Edward let go of her hand and turned his attention back to Jesse. 'Greer is a lovely girl. Clever, beautiful, and comes from a good family.'

Jesse gave his father a glare. 'I'm not marrying someone so that you can do a business deal.'

'What are you talking about? Business deal? Who said anything about business? I'm just saying she's a lovely girl.' Edward looked at his son with a patient, innocent smile. Bryn Clovelly was a sharp operator. For all of his talk about a merger, Edward knew that selling a share of the business to him was a risk. However, Bryn had no boys of his own. Like Edward himself, and most vain men, Bryn was desperate for his business not to die with him. If Jesse and Greer were married, it would ensure that Behenna's Boats was safe and Bryn would have himself a son-in-law from one of Trevay's oldest fishing families. They were building a dynasty. But Jesse seemed to have other ideas. Edward got a hot itch on the back of his thinning scalp when he thought about selling his son's future off to the highest bidder.

'She may be, but I'm not marrying her. If you want to

do business with old man Clovelly, do it yourself, but leave me out of it.'

'An' what's the matter with lookin' to the future?' Edward spread his hands, fingers splayed, on the old table, his extraordinary eyebrows raised in innocence.

'Plenty.' Jesse dropped his head and stared at his lap.

'Oh, now,' cajoled his father. 'You're not bleating about that other girl, whatshername . . .'

Jesse's mother took her hands out of the sink and wiped the suds on her apron.

'Edward, leave him alone. Loveday Carter is a really nice girl. Jesse would be happy with her. Let the boy fall in love with whoever he wants.'

'Her mother hasn't got a pot to piss in, and anyway, what's love got to do with it? He doesn't know what love is.' Edward was exasperated.

'But you did, or so you say,' Jan threw back. 'And stopped me from having a bit of life in the bargain.'

'Oh, you and your life.' Jesse recognised the brewing of a row and his father didn't disappoint him. 'You didn't have a life till I took you on. You've wanted for nothing since we married. I'm a good man. I'm not a drinker or a womaniser.'

'And I'm supposed to be grateful for the fact that life now starts and ends at Trevay harbour sheds, am I?'

Edward stood up. 'There's no talking to you when you get in one of your moods like this. You sound like your mother, and she was a miserable old cow. I'm going back to work.'

'But the pasties'll be ready in a minute.'

'I'm not hungry.'

In the simmering silence that remained after Edward had stomped out of the door and into the spring sunshine of Fish Lane, Jan stood for a moment in powerless frustration. Edward had set his mind on securing the future of the fishing fleet, and if that meant arranging a marriage between Jesse and Greer Clovelly, heiress to the Clovelly Fisheries Company, then that would be it, no matter what Jesse wanted.

She ran her thin hands through her short hair and bent to get the pasties out of the oven.

'They're hot,' she said needlessly, serving one to Jesse.

'Thanks, Mum.'

She put one onto a plate for herself and, wiping her hands on the tea towel that was perpetually tucked into her apron, sat opposite her son.

'Eat,' she told him. Jesse did so. After a couple of mouthfuls, she asked. 'So . . . is it Loveday?'

Jesse shuffled a bit in his seat. With a full mouth he said, 'I dunno.'

'But it's not Greer?'

'How do I know? I'm sixteen. I want to see the world before I decide on anything. I've got my own mind and my own life.'

Jan nodded in understanding. It was one thing encouraging Jesse in a particular direction, but quite another thing to put all this pressure on the poor lad.

'I'll ask your dad to back off.'

*

'Bloody ungrateful kids.' Edward was on his boat, *The Lobster Pot*, checking the trawl nets with his old friend and ship's mechanic, Spencer. 'He doesn't know his arse from his elbow. Does he think I wanted to take on the fleet from my dad? No I bloody didn't. But it was the best thing that ever happened to me.' He looked up from his work and surveyed the harbour around him. 'Look at this place.' He swept an arm dramatically across the view. 'Trevay is the most beautiful place on earth. What's he think he's going to find anywhere else? Answer me that.'

Spencer moved his stained and smouldering hand-rolled cigarette from one corner of his gnarled mouth to another and made a noise that sounded as if he was in agreement. Edward continued: 'Fifteen boats we've got in the fleet now. Fifteen! If my dad hadn't been so canny after the war and bought them first few cheap from those poor fishing widows whose husbands had never come home from the Navy, we'd still have the arses hanging out of our trousers.'

Spencer gave another grunt.

'You and me, Spencer, you and me, we know how the world works. Hard work brings good things. Not nancying around doing yer O levels and packing yer spotted hand-kerchief to go travelling. What's that about?'

As inscrutable as ever, Spencer peeled the damp cigarette from his lips and revealed a handful of tobacco-stained teeth. 'Want a brew, Skip?'

Edward stopped what he was doing and looked at his old friend as if for the first time.

'See. You've seen it all, haven't you, Spence? I'll have a cup of tea with you and then, when we've finished here, I'll take you for a pint. How does that sound?'

Spencer went below decks to the galley and Edward could hear the comforting sounds of the pop as the gas was lit and the rattle of the old kettle as Spencer banged it on the hob. Edward took another look at the fishing village that had been his home from birth. The gulls were cackling above him and the May sunshine made mirrors of the water on the mudflats. 'Bloody kids,' he muttered to himself. 'Bloody women.' He rubbed the thick gold wedding band on his finger. 'Bloody Jan.'

He took a deep breath of the salty Cornish air and thought about his boys. Grant a bloody liability, and Jesse a dreamer. What had he done to deserve them? He loved them. Of course he did, but why didn't they do what he told them? When his dad had told him to jump, he'd asked how high. When his dad got ill and Edward had had to take on the fleet aged only eighteen, he'd had no choice. Sink or swim. He'd chosen to swim. He'd shut the door on the dreams he'd had to go to America. He'd taken on his responsibilities. He'd swallowed his resentment and done the right thing. Why the hell wouldn't Jesse?

*

Jesse knew he should be in his room revising for the imminent O levels, but he couldn't see the point. He'd be leaving school in June and joining his dad at sea. He knew how lucky he was to have a job, and he loved the sea but . . . oh, there were so many buts. He took his Levi denim jacket off one of the pegs by the back door and kissed his mum, who was now setting up the ironing board.

'You going out, son?'

'Yeah.'

'Where are you going?'

'Up the sheds.'

'Shouldn't you be doing some school work?'

'What's the point, Mum?' He bent and kissed her cheek to stop her from asking any more. 'See ya.'

He was out of the back door leaving his mother to watch him, shrugging on his beloved denim jacket, slipping his Sony Walkman headphones on his ears and retreating down the short front garden path. She heard the little gate click shut for the nth time in her life; on her own, again. She worried about her boys and their future. Grant was in the Royal Marines now, stationed in Plymouth. Last time he called he said he was going for Commando Training at Lympstone. Ever since he was 16, fuelled by the nightly bulletins reporting the Falklands War, he'd wanted to wear the Green Beret of a commando. Now, at 21, this was his chance to earn it. Grant had been a handful from the off. His unpredictable mood swings had always marked him out. It could be like treading on eggshells living under the same roof as him, and school had been one long round of visits to successive heads. He'd left school with only one exam pass to his name, in metalwork. He was lucky that the army recruiting officer had seen something in him beyond the defensive, edgy character that he conveyed.

'We'll smooth the rough edges off him, Mrs Behenna,' he told her.

She was proud of him, of course, but fearful about the dangers he would face in any war, and of those dark moods which had got him into trouble with the police already. He was such a contrast to Jesse, who was calm and steady, but still waters ran deep with Jesse – Jan knew that there was much more to him than his father gave him credit for. At least Jesse would be safe at home, working with his dad and groomed to take over the business. But what if Edward's plans to marry him off to Greer Clovelly came about? Jesse would be stuck in a loveless marriage, burdened with the responsibility of a very big business and no chance to see the world and enjoy his freedom. Just like she'd been.

'Stop it, Jan,' she said into the silence. 'Just stop it.' She plugged in the old iron, turning on the radio for her daily infusion of *The Archers* as she waited for it to warm up.

Jesse was still just a boy. Let him have his dreams; there was time enough to be a man.

*

Jesse left the cool of the narrow lane of terraced fisherman's cottages, and was walking up the hill away from Trevay and towards St Peter's, the fishermen's church. The graveyard slumbered in the warm sun and delicate white cow parsley heads shuddered in the light breeze, making shadow patterns over the cushions of forget-me-nots growing beneath them. He always glanced at his grandfather's grave as he passed. Today its granite headstone glittered like a smile. Jesse touched his brow and saluted his grandfather before carrying on up the hill towards the sheds.

The sheds were a series of around thirty to forty home-built wooden structures, owned by the people of the town who had no garages attached to their houses, which, since most of the houses were built long before the motor car was invented, was the majority. The sheds had started as makeshift stables and boat-houses but now contained all the detritus of modern living. It was a kind of shanty town sited on a two-acre plot of flattened mud and sand. Opposite the sheds, some of which were now two storeys, stood a long line of boats of all kinds. Dinghies, clinker boats, fishing boats, rotting hulks, along with trailers of varying sizes on which the boats could be towed down the hill, through the town and down the harbour slipway into the water. At the entrance to the sheds was the second of only two public phone boxes in Trevay. The other box was down on the quay. Every resident knew the number of these boxes and regular calls were made between the two to give a shout to the lifeboat crew or call a man home for his tea.

Jesse walked past the phone box, kicking up a little sandy dust as he did so. He looked over to his father's shed, which had expanded over the years and was now a run of four sheds linked together. On the upper floor were the words Behenna Boat Yard est. 1936, painted in fading blue and white letters.

He saw Mickey before Mickey saw him. His best friend since nursery school, Mickey Chandler was the person Jesse shared everything with. Mickey was standing outside his own family's smaller shed, unlocked now with its doors wide open to the sun, and was polishing the chrome of his pride and joy: a two-year-old Honda moped, a present from his family and friends for his recent sixteenth birthday.

Jesse lengthened his stride, taking the headphones from his ears and calling, 'Hey.' Mickey stood up and shielded his eyes with the hand holding the stockinet duster; Jesse could smell the metal cleaner on it.

'Hey,' he replied.

Jesse was now close enough to give his best mate a punch on the arm, which was returned with equal force and affection.

'I thought you were revising,' Mickey said, returning to his polishing.

'I thought you were too.'

'Waste of fuckin' time, isn't it?'

'Yeah. Want a snout?'

'Please.'

Jesse pulled a crumpled packet of Player's No. 6 out of his pocket and offered one to Mickey.

'Ta.'

'You got a light?'

'No. Have you?'

'No.'

'Shit.'

Both boys pondered on the dilemma of having cigarettes but no means of smoking them. Mickey laughed first. 'You're bloody useless, Behenna.'

Jesse grabbed his friend in a headlock and they scuffled contentedly for several minutes.

Eventually they stopped

'Bike's looking good,' Jesse told him.

'Got my test next week.'

'Gonna pass?'

'Of course.'

'Can I come out with you?'

'Sure. I'm gonna ask Loveday out when I've got me licence.'

Jesse's heart flipped at the sound of Loveday's name. Mickey was in love with Loveday and had never made any secret of it. Jesse had never admitted to Mickey that the mention of her name, let alone the sight of her, was enough to shoot a flame of desire and longing coursing through his body.

'Her arse is too big for the seat,' he observed.

Mickey smiled. 'Yeah. And what an arse. Imagine having her arms around you, holding tight, pressing those big boobs against your shoulder blades.'

Jesse could imagine all too clearly, but said only, 'Fill your boots, boy.'

3

'How do I look in these?' Loveday had struggled into a pair of lime-green leggings, her face flushed and perspiring.

Greer, sitting neatly on the edge of Loveday's unmade bed, wondered what to say. Should she tell her friend that she looked embarrassing? That the hideous leggings were pulling at the seams and clearly revealing the revolting cellulite clinging to her thighs. Could she tell her that she needed to lose a lot of weight and learn how to dress properly? Though on the plus side – and Greer did feel slightly guilty about this – Loveday did make Greer look great by comparison.

'You look like Loveday Carter,' she managed.

Loveday turned back to her reflection in the mirror that hung off the back of her bedroom door. 'I like the colour. They didn't 'ave 'em in the next size, but I'm gonna lose a bit of weight before the summer comes.' She turned sideways and looked at herself from right and left. 'If I put on my orange T-shirt, that'll cover me bum.'

Greer looked down at her own slim legs in their perfectly fitting Pepe jeans. The orange T-shirt might cover Loveday's bottom, but it wasn't going to disguise the two rolls of fat wobbling between the bottom edge of her bra and the elastic waist of the leggings.

'There. What d'ya think?' Loveday asked a few moments later. Greer looked up.

She wanted to say, 'Loveday. You look ghastly. You couldn't be wearing a less flattering outfit. Your breasts are too big, your stomach is enormous and your derrière huge.'

Instead, she said, 'It's very you.' She stood up and smoothed her hands over her own trim derrière, brushing off imaginary flecks. Loveday was now at her dressing-table mirror. The dressing table itself was strewn with several used cotton wool balls and a large amount of ancient make-up; a cold, half-drunk cup of tea and an empty Diet Coke tin. Hanging from a glass hand with curved upright fingers were strings of gaudy beads and a worn pair of knickers.

Greer pulled the collar of her crisp white shirt up at the nape of her neck and checked that the cuffs of her sleeves were turned back as the models in her mother's monthly *Vogue* magazine did. She wanted to get out and see Jesse. 'Come on. The boys will be waiting for us.'

Loveday took one last look in the mirror and smacked her matte red lips together. Recently she'd been copying Madonna's make-up, even adding the beauty spot above her lip with an eye pencil. 'I can't find my black pencil so I've used the green one. I rather like it. What do you think?' she said, turning to Greer. 'It shows off me green eyes, don't it?'

Greer blew her cheeks out and thought for a moment. 'I think you look . . . unique.'

Loveday hugged her uptight friend. 'You are so sweet. Unique? Really?'

'Really.' Greer extricated herself from the miasma of

Giorgio Armani's Beverly Hills rip-off scent, bought in Truro's pannier market.

'And what does that mean? Sounds posh,' bounced back Loveday, reaching for her heavily fringed and studded, stone-washed denim jacket.

'It means you are a one-off.'

*

Jesse was first to spot the girls walking up towards the sheds. Loveday's marmalade hair with its wash-and-wear perm gleamed in the sunshine; her beautiful body was gently undulating towards him in skin-tight green leggings, her large breasts swinging to the rhythm of the fringes on her jacket. He thought often about those breasts. Sometimes, when she wore her white T-shirt, he could see the outline of her nipples. He turned his back on the girls, feigning disinterest, and called over to Mickey, who was checking his quiff in the wing mirror of the Honda moped. 'The girls are coming.'

Mickey smiled in the mirror at his own cheeky face. 'I'm going to give Loveday a night to remember.'

'Oh, yeah? When's that then?'

'Tonight.'

'Never. She won't touch you with a barge pole.'

'She won't need to. I've got me own barge pole to touch her with.' Mickey ducked swiftly out of reach of Jesse's punch and together they locked the precious motorbike in its shed.

'All right?' Mickey raced to get ahead of Jesse and be first to walk by Loveday's side.

'Yeah.' She smiled at him and, for him, the sun seemed suddenly to be shining extra bright. Then he frowned.

'You've got something on your lip.' He lifted a finger to wipe at the mark on her face. She grabbed his wrist before it got to her.

'It's me beauty spot. Like Madonna's. It's unique.'

'Oh. Looks like you've drawn on yourself.'

Loveday stopped and waited for Greer, who was a couple of steps behind with Jesse.

'How does my beauty spot look?'

Greer and Jesse both looked at the green blob on Loveday's sweating lip.

'Well, it's smeared a bit,' said Greer.

'Oh shit. Badly?'

'A bit.'

Jesse looked through his pockets and found an old, dried-up tissue. 'Shall I wipe it off for you?' he offered.

'Yes, please. Get it all off.'

He lifted the tissue to Loveday's mouth. 'Spit.'

She did so and, tenderly, he wiped all trace of the green pencil away. Standing so close to her, Jesse could sense the rise and fall of her chest, and smell the heady scent that emanated from her. Her dewy golden skin glistened in the sunlight and her emerald eyes were like those of an exotic cat. The combination was suddenly overwhelming.

'There. All done.'

'Thanks.' Loveday gave her rescuer a hug, leaving him breathless on many counts.

She turned to Greer. 'Has it all gone?'

'Yes.'

'Maybe I'll try an indelible ink next time.'

'Best not,' murmured Greer.

Mickey muscled in and grabbed Loveday's arm. 'Have you eaten your tea?'

'Only a bit. Mum did shepherd's pie earlier. But I could do with some chips.'

'Come on then.' And, taking her hand he ran down the hill, forcing Jesse and then Greer to run after them.

*

Edward Behenna had been in the Golden Hind since he and Spencer had finished on the boat. Edward was full of beer and the memory of the row with Jan was disappearing as fast as a sea mist on a warm morning. The beer had warmed his heart and his humour. 'Spence, you'll 'ave another before 'e go.'

Spencer removed a battered tin of tobacco from the front of his canvas smock and nodded. 'Aye.'

'Good man, Spence. Good man.' Edward lumbered heavily to his feet and clapped his friend on the back, dislodging the scanty twigs of tobacco from the near transparent cigarette paper that Spencer was balancing between thumb and grimy index finger. He hailed the landlord. 'Same again, Pete.'

Pete, a very tall man with a stomach straining against the buttons and belt of his shirt and trousers, bent down so that he could see through the forest of pint tankards hanging from hooks on a shelf above the bar. 'Skinner's?' he asked, reaching for the empties Edward had placed on the damp counter.

'Aye.'

Without anyone taking much notice, the door of the pub opened and a slim man in his early forties entered. His quick, bright blue eyes skimmed the familiar faces and he nodded at those who acknowledged his arrival. His prey was at the bar, delving into a handful of change to pay for the two waiting pints. He walked lightly and quickly towards him. 'I'll get those, Pete, and a Scotch for me, please.'

Edward turned to see who was buying his pint. 'Bryn Clovelly, you're a gentleman.' He turned his eyes to where Spencer was sitting. 'Spence, Mr Clovelly bought you a pint.'

Spencer had rolled his cigarette; its smoking fragrance drifted towards the bar. 'Thank 'ee, Mr Clovelly.'

Bryn ignored him and spoke to Edward. 'So, Edward, when are we going to do business?'

Edward looked down at his feet, uncomfortably aware that Clovelly was completely sober.

'Bryn, I've 'ad a drink. Me 'ead's not straight for talking business.'

Bryn pulled up an empty bar stool and indicated for Edward to do the same. 'It's not business as such, is it?' He unhooked the casual blue jumper he had knotted round his shoulders and draped it on the back of the stool. 'We've known each other a long time, haven't we, Edward?'

Edward rubbed a hand over his mouth and chin. 'You've gone up in the world since we were nippers though, ain't you, Bryn?' Edward looked at Bryn's clean hands. 'Look at you. Smart clothes, smart way of talkin', smart car outside. You're different now, Bryn.'

Bryn placed his right hand on his chest. 'Not 'ere. Not in my 'eart. I can still talk as Cornish as you, boy, and don't 'e forget it. There's nothin' wrong in doing well and earning a little cash, is there?'

'No,' Edward agreed reluctantly. He had given more thought to Bryn's continued insistence that their businesses were stronger together than he wanted to let on, but it didn't do to show your hand too early where Bryn was concerned. Besides, what Jan and Jesse had said also nagged at his thoughts. Now that Bryn was sitting here in front of him, in his flash clothes and with a conceited look on his face, Edward's doubts had once more risen to the surface.

'I don't know whether I want more. I'm happy with the boats and passing them on to Jesse.'

'Not Grant then?'

'No. 'E's happy in the Marines. Best place for him.'

'Is he settling well?'

'Think so. Better to get all that anger out of 'im in hard training than 'ere in Trevay.'

Bryn placed his hand on Edward's shoulder. He knew that Grant was a worry. A drinker with a short fuse and handy fists. 'Maybe the discipline is just what he needs,' he said.

'Aye.'

Bryn remained silent, watching as Edward took a long mouthful of beer. Then he asked, 'What does Jan think?'

'With women you've got to pick your moment.'

'So you haven't told her about the offer that I've put on the table?' Bryn leant closer to Edward. ''Tis a good offer, Edward. You know that these EU quotas could be the death of the Cornish fishing industry. We need to diversify and open up our markets if we're to survive. We're better together – you'll never get an offer like this one again. The future of Behenna and Clovelly will be settled.'

'But you getting fifty-one per cent: you'd have the controlling interest then. You might leave me high and dry.'

'Look, Edward,' Bryn leant in closer. Edward could smell the scent of cigars on his beautifully laundered Pierre Cardin shirt. 'I'm prepared to sell you a share in the fish market, if that would sweeten the deal. We'd both sit on the board of Behenna and Clovelly and each have a fair shout on how the business is managed.'

Edward frowned and rubbed his chin. Bryn looked appraisingly at him.

'When did you and Jan last have a holiday?'

'What do we need an 'oliday for?'

'You'll need a holiday from all the hard work we'll be putting in running the new business together. Imagine. You could go up country and see the sights of London. Catch a plane to Italy or Greece. Or maybe have a week in New York.'

'Who'll look after the boats while I'm away?'

'Me. And you'll look after the fish market and the refrigeration factory for me when I'm away with my missus.'

Edward shook his head. He'd been thinking about Bryn's 'business' plan since the idea had first been floated. It was all very well for Bryn to talk about them joining forces but, as the months had gone by and Bryn had kept on about Jesse and Greer getting married, it felt more and more like Bryn was leading them all down a road that led in one direction, where there was no turning back. As a reality, he knew where his moral compass was pointing.

'No, no. The boy has his own life to lead, and that's with me at Behenna's Boats. The fishing fleet was built up by my dad and I'm building it now for Jesse. 'Tis enough.'

'And I'm building the fish market business for Greer. But when she's married she won't want to work. She needs a man to run it all . . .'

Edward looked at Bryn sharply. 'I've told you before.

Jesse has to make his own decisions. I could no more make Jesse marry Greer than I could get Spencer over there to stick on a tutu and pirouette off Trevay harbour wall.'

Bryn laughed and picked up his Scotch to take a sip. 'I was going to say partner, not husband. Someone bright. Someone we can trust and – yes – Jesse would be ideal.' He took another deeper draught of his whisky. 'It ain't a case of forcing anyone. My Greer's going to grow up to be a fine wife and mother. She's refined; a good catch. Anyone can see that – your Jesse just needs a bit of encouragement.'

Bryn Clovelly reached into his pocket and took out a brown envelope and placed it on the table between them.

'You've been blessed with two strapping boys, Edward. Greer is a daughter to make any man proud but . . . she's not a man, with a man's head for business. Imagine, Clovelly Fisheries and Behenna's Boats becoming one big company. Your boats supply my market. We squeeze the opposition and supply the hotels and London restaurants at the best possible prices. Finally, when our rivals are no more, we call the shots and demand the best prices we can get whilst giving the best-quality fish and customer service. When you and I are retired, my Greer and your Jesse could run the business themselves. We will have created a really lasting legacy. The icing on the cake would be for them to marry and merge two great family businesses into one. A fairy-tale ending.' Bryn swallowed the final mouthful of Scotch, pushed the envelope towards Edward and stood up, retrieving his jumper from the back of the stool. 'Just think about it, Edward. A fairy tale. That's all.'

Edward eyed the brown envelope warily.

'Saw your Jan yesterday about Trevay. Looks like she

needs that break, Edward.' With this parting shot, Bryn slung his jumper over his shoulders and headed towards the exit. For a moment, Edward was filled with the urge to run after him and stuff the envelope into Bryn's self-satisfied, smug face.

But he didn't. Instead, he picked up the envelope and looked inside. A careful observer would have seen his eyes widen momentarily, then he opened his jacket and put it quickly in the inside pocket.

He nodded to the barman. 'Another pint for me and Spence, Pete.'

*

The pain in Greer's heart was real and tangible. She didn't know how to make Jesse see her. Want her. She was slim, spoke nicely, dressed with style and had impeccable manners. A miniature of her mother who lived in the fantasy film-star world of the 1950s and 1960s. 'Greer Garson was the most beautiful and gracious actress of her day. That's why you have her name. If you'd had a sister, I should have called her Audrey after Audrey Hepburn. But your father and I were not to be blessed.' Greer was happy to be an only child. Spoilt and petted and treated to anything she wanted. The one thing she wanted now, though, was Jesse, and not even her parents could fix that.

Jesse and Mickey were sitting either side of Loveday on the harbour wall. Greer glanced across at Loveday. They were best friends, of course, but Greer felt sorry for her, really. Loveday, with her ample frame, a face full of freckles and her yokelish ways. She was pretending to read Mickey's palm. 'Ooh, now, Mickey. You're going to 'ave three children and a long life.' With his hand in hers she traced a line across his palm. 'There may be some unhappiness in your thirties, but you'll travel to faraway places and live to be an old man.'

''Ow old will I be when I die?'

She held his hand up to her face and squinted. 'At least sixty-five.'

Jesse was getting impatient. 'Do me now, Loveday. What do you see?'

'Well now, let's 'ave a look.' She held his hand softly in hers and looked into his sea-green eyes. Without looking at his palm she said, 'I feel you 'ave met the woman you will marry. There'll be two beautiful boys and you'll have lots of money.'

Jesse looked down into Loveday's mischievous green eyes; it took all of his restraint not to reach out to her and kiss her like he longed to.

'Is that right?' They held each other's gaze steadily and, for a moment, Mickey and Greer faded out and it was as if they were alone on the quay.

'Aye.' Loveday wanted more than anything for Jesse to kiss her, but not here in front of Mickey. She adored Mickey and he made no bones about his feelings for her. She'd do anything not to break his heart, but Jesse was the boy she loved and he was looking at her now with such a look . . .

Greer stepped forward from the cold metal railing she'd been leaning against. 'Let me read yours, Loveday.'

The spell was broken and Jesse pulled away.

Loveday laughed good-naturedly, 'OK, Greer. What do you see?' and stretched her hand towards her friend.

Greer had no idea what she 'saw' but she said, 'Hmm. I see you married to a really nice man. I see the initials

C and M and . . .' She folded Loveday's hand into a fist and examined the creases that her palm made by her little finger. 'I see three children.'

Loveday was impressed. 'Really? I'd love three children. I wish I had brothers and sisters, but when Dad died . . . Mum would love to have lots of grandchildren.'

Mickey was thinking who they knew whose initials were CM. 'Who's this CM bloke?'

'Dunno,' said Loveday, thinking that Jesse's initials were JB.

Greer helped them to figure it out. 'Well, it might be MC, I suppose.'

Mickey's face lit up. 'Those are my initials!' He looked as pleased as punch and Greer felt, for the second time that evening, a pang of guilt.

'Read my palm, Greer.' Jesse opened his hand to her.

She took it happily, touching his warm, dry skin and smoothing her fingertips over the calluses caused from helping his father on the boats.

'Well, I see a very happy marriage for you and lots of children. Your wife will love you with all her heart.'

'Can you see any initials?' Jesse asked. Greer thought for a moment; she knew she couldn't say her own so she truthfully said, 'No. I can't see any letters this time.'

Mickey let out a big laugh and started to play-fight with Jesse. 'No letters for you! And French letters don't count.'

Across the harbour car park, the door of the Golden Hind opened and Bryn Clovelly stepped out. He looked across to see where the laughter was coming from.

'Greer? Is that you?'

'Yes, Dad.'

'Come on then. Time you were home. Your mother'll be mithering me else.'

The pain in Greer's heart seared again. The last thing she wanted to do was go home now. Why wasn't she allowed to stay out, like her friends were?

'I can walk up later.'

'Get in the car now.'

Greer was far too well behaved to either make a scene or to defy her father, no matter how crestfallen she felt at having to leave. 'OK, Dad,' she acquiesced.

She hugged Loveday, who clung onto her dramatically. 'Bye, Greer, and thanks for helping me get ready tonight.'

'Night, G,' said the boys.

'Night, Mickey, goodnight, Jesse.'

Greer lingered momentarily and cast a meaningful glance at Jesse, but he was looking beyond her and watching her father as he walked towards his new BMW, casually pointing the automatic key fob at it. Four orange lights flickered twice as the car made a beeping sound and the locks clunked open.

'That's frickin' awesome,' declared Mickey.

'Gonna get some on the Honda, are you, Mick?' laughed Jesse.

Greer walked towards the car and heard more laughter from her friends, knowing that they had already closed the gap that she had occupied. She climbed into the car.

Her father started the engine, steering the car away from the harbour towards home. From the depths of the leather front seat, Greer craned her neck to wave at her friends, but they weren't looking at her now. Loveday was walking on the sharp upturned stones of a low wall and flapping her arms to keep her balance. Jesse went to help her but, to Greer's satisfaction, Mickey beat him to it.

As both Mickey and Loveday lost their balance and

slipped off the wall, Greer couldn't help but notice Loveday's ample bum and bosom wobble as she clumsily tried to regain her balance. Greer looked down at her own slim thighs and taut stomach, feeling pleased with what she saw and vowing that she was never, ever going to let herself end up like poor Loveday. But as the threesome slipped out of view, Greer wondered again what it would take to capture Jesse's undivided attention once and for all.

4

June 1987

'Mickey, you want to come fishing with me tonight? Celebrate the last of the exams?'

Jesse was pulling off his school tie as he walked out of the school gates for the last time. It was a momentous day; along with many others he had finished his final O level, and the occasion was marked by the usual flour and egg fight, ended only when the deputy head raged at the rabble-rousers for covering her car in cake ingredients and escorted them off the school grounds. The long hot summer lay, full of promise, ahead of Jesse.

Mickey shook his head disappointedly. 'I've got to help my dad on the boat.'

Jesse put his arm round his friend. 'Tell you what, I'll help you and we'll go out later.'

'Would you?' Mickey said gratefully, picking bits of batter off his shirt.

'Yeah. Donna at the Spar shop fancies me. She might sell us some tins of cider with our pasties.'

Mickey smiled gratefully at his best and oldest friend. They'd navigated school life pretty well together. Football, detentions and girls. He was still hopelessly in love with Loveday, but she never seemed to take him seriously. He'd found comfort with females who were more than willing.

And now school was over and out. He didn't have to worry himself with further education. He had no need. He'd been offered a job as deckhand on *Our Mermaid*, one of the newest boats on the Behenna fleet and skippered by his dad.

Meanwhile, Jesse was being groomed to take over the fleet when his own father eventually retired. He had to start at the bottom, though, and was to be deckhand on *The Lobster Pot*, the flagship of the fleet, skippered by Edward Behenna himself.

As the boys loped down the hill from school towards the harbour, they heard Loveday's voice calling to them breathlessly.

'Boys. Wait up!' Loveday was galloping towards them, her school skirt covered in flour and rolled up at the waistband to reveal wobbly thighs, her white shirt pulling at the buttons as her bosoms jiggled invitingly with every pace. A little way ahead of her, Greer was jogging effortlessly in her spotless school uniform.

'Where are you two off to?' panted Loveday.

Mickey put his arms out to catch the girl he adored. His hands caught her waist and he felt the warmth from under her breasts. She turned her smiling freckled face up to the two boys. Mickey could smell the sweetness of her breath as she asked again, 'Where are you two going?'

'Mickey and I have got stuff to do,' said Jesse, staring into the middle distance with feigned nonchalance.

'What sort of stuff?'

'The sort of stuff that don't need girls,' Jesse grunted.

Loveday looked crushed. 'Greer and me thought we

could do something together with you two. You know.
Celebrate the end of school.'

Greer narrowed her eyes astutely. 'You're going fishing,
aren't you?'

Jesse ignored her and said to Mickey over the top of both
girls' heads, 'You bring the bait and I'll bring the food.'

'We can come with you,' Loveday told him, not prepared
to brook any objections. 'Greer and I'll be good company
for you.'

Jesse shook his head. 'No. Blokes only.'

Loveday pulled a face. 'Blokes only? You arrogant arse.'

Mickey laughed and turned to Jesse pleadingly. 'They
can come, can't they?'

Jesse, who was trying to wean himself off his desirous
want for Loveday, thought he might be in with a chance
with Donna from the Spar shop later that night. Loveday
was a no-go area while Mickey still had the hots for her.
But maybe it would be nice to hang out with the girls
– they hadn't all been together for a while.

Damnit, Donna could wait.

'OK. Seven o'clock at *Our Mermaid*,' he agreed reluctantly.

Loveday took Greer's arm and pulled her away excitedly. 'What are you going to wear?' she asked.

'Jeans, I think,' said Greer.

'Me too,' smiled Loveday.

*

Greer left Loveday at the cobbled corner where her mum
had a tiny cottage. Then she walked on past the harbour
and out onto the road that led towards the better end
of Trevay.

When her father had sold the two trawlers his dad had left him, and bought the small fish market on the quay, he'd quickly turned the ailing business round. He'd taken a small selection of the best of his fresh catches up the M5 and the M4 to London's swankier restaurants and hotels, persuading the chefs that he could undercut any of their other suppliers and provide better fish. He had worked hard. As soon as the fishing boats unloaded at his market, he paid the skippers the least he could get away with and then jumped in his refrigerated van and personally drove the lobster, plaice, turbot and crab to the back door of the poshest kitchens in the United Kingdom. Gradually he could afford to pay better prices to the fishermen, and that enticed boats from around the Cornish coast to land their catches with him. As business grew he expanded the old fish market, taking up at least three times more quayside and landing space. Now he had three vans every night ploughing the motorways and bringing home the money.

Naturally, the cramped house in the back lanes of Trevay had given way to a modern and airy executive bungalow, and this was where Greer was headed now.

Greer's mother opened the front door as soon as she saw her turn into the drive.

'How did it go?' She took the proffered, and now redundant, blazer from Greer and hung it for the last time on a padded hanger in the coat cupboard, next to her husband's golf clubs.

'The English paper was fine and the history paper was everything I'd revised, so I think I'll have done OK.'

'You are a clever girl.' Elizabeth kissed her. 'I've got crab salad for tea.'

'Actually, I was hoping to go out.'

'Where?'

'Fishing with Loveday and Mickey.'

'Just Mickey and Loveday?'

'Erm, I think Jesse will be there too.'

'I see.' Elizabeth knew all about Bryn's plan for Greer and Jesse. There had never been any other children after Greer and no doctor could ever tell them why. Elizabeth was not really sorry. Childbirth was messy and dangerous, and once had been enough for her, but she knew how much it unsettled Bryn to think about what was going to happen to the company. Women were taking the reins in business more and more these days, but Greer had never shown the slightest interest – and quite right too, thought Elizabeth. Fishing was a man's world and women had no place in it. Part of her wanted Greer to marry someone outside Trevay, someone with a bit of breeding; but she supposed that Jesse Behenna was as close as it came to old money in Trevay. Besides, look at Bryn, he'd been just like all the other coarse Trevay fishermen when he'd courted her, but she could sense his ambition and together they had come far. All men could be moulded by a strong woman who knew what she wanted.

'Mum, there's nothing to worry about,' said Greer, interpreting her mother's interest as concern for her morals. 'He has tons of girlfriends and I'm not one of them.'

'But you'd like to be.'

'*Muuum*. Don't. You sound like Dad.'

Elizabeth turned and walked towards the kitchen. Greer followed her.

'Can I take the crab salad with me?' She tried to appease her mother. 'I don't want to waste it.'

Her mother nodded. 'Yes. I'll make a little picnic up. Don't want you getting hungry and eating chips or you'll get as fat as Loveday.' Mother and daughter exchanged knowing smirks.

*

Greer heard Loveday thumping down the stairs before she pulled the front door open. She had teased her hair into a big, orange, candy-floss ball and was wearing a low-cut, sleeveless, fashionably ripped T-shirt, her pink bra partly on show. She was pulling at a fringed ra-ra skirt that was at least two sizes too small for her.

'Ha!' she crowed, taking in Greer's tight white shorts, blue and white striped top and long, tanned legs. 'I knew you wouldn't wear jeans so I've pulled all the stops out. Hang on while I get my shoes.'

Greer watched as Loveday bounded back up the stairs, her ra-ra skirt lifting with every step and exposing tiny black knickers stretched over her generous bottom.

'Wait till you see these,' Loveday called from upstairs, 'They arrived from the catalogue this morning.'

A few seconds later and Loveday came down the stairs, with as much grace as a jolly pig in electric blue stilettos, gripping the banisters for balance.

'What do you think to these beauties?' She bounced off the last stair and posed like a stripper.

Greer couldn't help but smile. 'They are very eye-catching.'

Loveday looked at Greer's flat ballet pumps with sympathy. 'A word to the wise. You'll never pull Mickey in those.'

Down on the quay, the warm evening sunshine had

brought out the couples with pushchairs and people with dogs. The holiday-makers wouldn't be down in force for another six weeks so at the moment Trevay still belonged to its locals. The tide was out and the inner harbour was littered with boats lying on their keels, green fronds of seaweed hanging from their mooring ropes.

Greer couldn't help but always remember the first time she saw Jesse down here when they were both so young. His skinny brown legs hanging from his shorts and his blond hair falling over his eyes. Now he was a man. Six foot four, broad and muscular. Greer's feelings for him had intensified over the years. She dreamt about him, he lit up her life when she was with him, but he treated her like a sister. Greer his friend. Not Greer his girlfriend.

Sometimes she wondered whether he had feelings for Loveday. He certainly seemed to enjoy her company, and she knew that Loveday had a crush on him. But he always seemed careful not to encourage her, from what Greer could see. Anyway, how could he fancy someone as chaotic as Loveday? No. Jesse couldn't fancy Loveday, he probably just felt sorry for her. Mickey fancied Loveday and, one day, Greer hoped, he'd land her. Loveday would be a fool not to go for Mickey. And one day, Jesse would see that Greer was the woman for him.

Loveday jolted Greer from her musings. 'There they are!' She pointed at Jesse and Mickey, who were strolling about a hundred yards ahead with fishing rods over their shoulders. 'Jesse! Mickey!' she shouted. 'Come and give us a hand with this.' She hefted the weighty picnic basket, which Greer had asked her to carry, from one hand to the other, then waved extravagantly to the boys. Mickey, of course, came to help Loveday. His lanky frame, dark hair and sweet face with its slightly large nose and eyes that drooped at the corners a little, reminded Greer of a lovesick greyhound. As soon as Loveday had loaded him up with the picnic basket, she raced off to walk beside Jesse.

At that moment, Greer felt enormous compassion for Mickey. 'Here. Let me help.' She took his fishing rod and put it across her left shoulder, then looped her right arm through Mickey's free one and walked with him.

'Don't worry about Loveday. I know how you feel about her. She'll see sense one day,' she told him.

Mickey blushed and quickly brushed her off. 'Loveday's all right but I'm playing the field.'

Greer raised an eyebrow, unconvinced. 'Are you, Mickey?'

'Sure. I'm a fisherman and there's plenty more fish in the sea.'

'Oh, Mickey,' Greer laughed, 'you're fooling no one.' Mickey looked at her ruefully but then laughed too.

Loveday looked back over her shoulder and saw Greer and Mickey walking arm in arm. Heads together and laughing.

'Jesse, look, I knew it. Mickey and Greer are a match made in heaven.'

Jesse turned to look too, but said nothing. He was trying not to think about the lace bra that was showing through Loveday's T-shirt, which was only serving to accentuate her generous cleavage, while also trying to keep in check the dangerous sensations that threatened to overwhelm him whenever he was in close proximity to Loveday Carter.

*

Our Mermaid was a good-sized trawler painted in the traditional local colours of sky blue, chalk white and clotted cream yellow. The hull had streaks of rust coming from the holes where the anchor chain fed, but she was in good condition and well maintained. She was tied up alongside the deepest part of the harbour wall where the boys hoped to fish from.

'Hey, Dad,' called Mickey as they approached.

An older version of Mickey was standing on the fore-deck drinking a mug of tea. ''Ello, son! Where the 'ell 'ave you bin? You're too late to help me. I'm all finished.'

'Sorry, Dad.'

Mr Chandler put down his mug and helped Loveday onto the boat. 'Thank you, Mr Chandler.'

''Tis all right, maid.' Alfie Chandler was very fond of Loveday. She was warm, down to earth and undeniably sexy. A girl he'd be happy to call daughter-in-law. He hoped that Mickey would make his move before someone else came on the scene; there were many young lads who would bite their own arms off to get close to Loveday – he certainly would've done at Mickey's age.

'Hello, Mr Chandler.' Greer was holding out her hand to him. 'Would you help me aboard?'

'Certainly.' Alfie offered her his grimy and calloused hand. He couldn't deny that she was a looker, but she was too bony and prim for his taste. Poor Jesse Behenna. He was caught in a net, whether he knew it or not. Bryn Clovelly and Ed Behenna would make sure of that.

Alfie leant into the wheelhouse and put his mug on a wooden ledge. 'Right, you young 'uns. Tide's flooding in now and you should get some good mackerel off the side.'

'Cheers, Dad.' Mickey gave him a short embrace.

'Don't be home too late or your ma will be worried.'

'We won't.'

Alfie stepped off the boat. Without a backward glance he walked off along the harbour wall that led straight to the Golden Hind and its welcoming bar.

'What you got in the picnic basket, Loveday?' asked Mickey, rubbing his hands.

'You're always hungry!' Loveday swatted him away. 'How do you stay so skinny?'

Greer and Loveday unpacked a checked tablecloth that Elizabeth had thoughtfully put in, and placed the Tupperware boxes of crab, potato salad and tomatoes on the cloth.

Jesse pulled out of his fishing bag four pasties and six tins of cider; certain proof that Donna from the Spar shop might be two years older than Jesse but that she definitely fancied him rotten.

After they'd eaten (Greer had picked at the salad and declined her pasty so Loveday had had it instead), the boys set up their fishing rods. The sun slowly dropped towards the horizon and gave a final fiery blaze before sinking into the sea. Greer, who was watching Jesse bait the large hook on his line, shivered at the sudden chill. He looked up.

'You cold, Greer?'

'I am a bit.'

'Come here.' Amiably, he opened an arm up to her and she tentatively let him put it around her. She was enclosed between his arms as he held the fishing rod. She could feel his chest moving in and out as he breathed. Conversely, she held her breath, in fear of actually touching him more closely.

A tug on the line disturbed the moment and he lifted

an arm over her head, letting her out of the enclosure. 'Want to reel this one in?' he asked.

'Show me how.'

He handed her the rod and instructed her gently on how to wind in the reel. The flapping mackerel broke the surface. 'I don't like this bit,' she said.

'And you a fisherman's daughter!' He laughed kindly. 'You'd never make a fisherman's wife.'

5

The summer they left school was a good one. The sun shone, the sea remained calm and the beaches were inviting. The holiday-makers came down in their droves, so there was plenty of work for the school-leavers, waiting tables or taking money in dusty beach-side car parks.

Jesse worked on his father's flagship, *The Lobster Pot*. Being a Behenna and heir to the business made no difference: he was not given an easy ride. He had to learn the business from the bottom up.

Like most Cornish trawlers, *The Lobster Pot* had five crew members. Edward was the skipper, the toothless Spencer was his mate. In charge of the engines was the mechanic, Josh, a Kiwi of about 35 who'd landed in Cornwall as a student, years earlier, and never gone home. The cook was Hamish, a Scotsman with a surprisingly good palate, and the two deckhands were Jesse and another young school-leaver, Aaron.

The boat went out for up to seven days at a time, with two and a half days back on dry land before going to sea once more. It was a steep learning curve for Jesse, who'd not been allowed to join his father on these trips before, but he had the sea in his soul. Not only did he enjoy the work, he enjoyed the money that was divvied up at the end of each trip.

Once a catch was landed and sold at market, the money was used to pay for the diesel, food and other essentials, then the largest share of what was left over went to the owner – in this case Edward. The rest was split between the crew. The skipper Edward (again), Spencer, Josh, Hamish and then the deckies Jesse and Aaron.

It was not just a good summer for the visitors, the fish seemed to like it too; they were swimming in their droves to the Cornish fishing grounds.

The Lobster Pot would glide out of Trevay harbour with most of the Behenna fleet behind her, ready to make their fortunes. For Jesse, released from the classroom and still weighing up life's possibilities, these were halcyon days. He found he was loving life at sea: the sound of the engine chugging below his feet, the cry of the gulls performing stall turns above him, and the instinct he was starting to develop from his father as they sat poring over the charts, determining where the next good catch might be waiting for them.

On one particular warm August night, Edward and Jesse were in their usual seats in the galley, having had a supper of poached cod and bacon with new potatoes coated in bacon fat. Edward was drinking a large mug of powerfully strong tea.

'I'm reckoning we aim for Tring Fallows. Word is they'm the best fishing grounds just now.' He tapped the chart, then leant back to stretch tension out of his lower back.

Jesse remained hunched over the charts, studying the distance between where they were now and where they were going. 'How long will it take to get there?'

'Should be there in about four hours.'

Jesse glanced at the time. 'I'm on watch at midnight.'

'I recommend you get some shuteye now then,' his father said.

Jesse heaved himself a little off the leatherette bench seat and craned his head to see out of the starboard porthole. '*Our Mermaid* is still with us. She coming to Tring Fallows too?'

'Aye. We'll need both of us to haul the buggers in. This'll be a good catch if we get it right.'

The ship's radio came to life and the familiar voice of Alfie Chandler, Mickey's dad, spoke.

'*Lobster Pot, Lobster Pot, Lobster Pot.* This is *Mermaid.* Over.'

Edward unhooked the small receiver/mouthpiece from the radio set and put his thumb on the talk button.

'*Mermaid.* This is *Lobster Pot.* Wass on? Over.'

'*Mermaid, Lobster Pot.* We still headin' for Tring Fallows? Over.'

'*Lobster Pot, Mermaid.* Can you switch to channel nine? Over.'

Edward waited a minute for Alfie to swap to a channel that they could use just between themselves.

'*Lobster Pot, Mermaid.* Over.'

'Yeah, Alfie. Tring Fallows it is.'

Jesse, desperate to talk to his mate Mickey, held his hand out to his father, opening and closing his fingers in the universal code for 'hand it over.' Edward kept talking. 'Is your Mickey there, Alf? Only 'is mate wants to 'ave a word.'

'I'll get 'im.' They heard Alfie shout for his son as Edward passed the mouthpiece to Jesse.

Mickey's voice came over the airwaves. ''Ello?'

'Mickey, 'tis Jesse. You sleepin' before we get to the fishin' ground, or no?'

'Gonna have a snout up top then I'm going to grab some zeds. You?'

'Same. Give us a minute and I'll be out too.'

Edward reached forward and snatched the radio from Jesse. 'That's enough. It ain't for you two to make your social engagements on.' He pressed the talk button. 'Mickey, you still there, you great long streak of piss?'

'Yes, Mr Behenna,' came Mickey's nervous voice.

'Well fuck off and 'and me back to your dad.'

On deck the moon, although not full, was bright; its face looked down at the two trawlers as they slipped through the benign waves. Jesse, now standing in the stern of the boat, put his face to the cool wind and closed his eyes. He felt secure and peaceful. He was increasingly realising that the sea was his home; as long as he had it in his life, he knew all would be well.

Looking to starboard, and travelling at the same speed, was *Our Mermaid*. Jesse listened to the thrum of the engines together with the swish of the wash that they churned behind them. He could make out the tall, thin silhouette of Mickey appearing from a hatch and sparking up a cigarette.

'Hey, Mickey,' Jesse called over to him.

'Hey, Jess,' called back Mickey.

'Can you think of anywhere else you'd rather be?' Jesse asked his friend.

'Inside Loveday's knickers?' answered Mickey truthfully.

Jesse frowned at Mickey, knowing that – at this distance and in the dark – Mickey wouldn't be able to read his face. He didn't like Mickey talking about Loveday like that.

Loveday was under Jesse's skin. He'd known her since

. . . well, forever. And he hated to hear Mickey discuss her in such crude terms. He felt protective towards Loveday. He wanted to look after her and treat her well. He felt something that he couldn't describe; something, maybe, close to love? He pulled himself up. Love? No, not love. Not for Loveday. Loveday was Mickey's and he'd never hurt Mickey. He was like a brother to her. He just liked her. A lot. That was all. God, no, he didn't love her. He was going to see the world. Not settle down with the first girl he'd ever known, right here on his doorstep. Bugger that.

'Where would you rather be then, Jesse?' asked Mickey, sucking on his cigarette and exhaling a long plume of smoke to trail behind him.

'I told you. Nowhere other than here.' There was a splash behind him. He turned and shouted, 'Look, Mick. Dolphins!' And, sure enough, in the wake between the boats, two dolphins slipped out of the water in perfect arcs, the moonlight glistening on their skins.

'There's two more!' shouted Mickey. He bent down to the open hatch on the deck and shouted, 'Dad. Come up. Dolphins.'

Any crew member on both boats who wasn't already sleeping, or didn't have a drop of romance in his soul, came on deck to watch the display that the dolphins put on for them. They counted up to fifteen, although it was hard to tell if some had been counted twice. Both Alfie and Edward cut their engines and, for maybe five or ten minutes, fisherman and dolphin enjoyed each other's company. Finally the creatures slid beneath the waves and disappeared.

A thought dawned on Edward.

'The little fuckers'll have our catch if we don't get a

move on.' He moved quickly towards the wheelhouse. 'Full steam ahead, lads.'

Jesse was nudged awake at just before midnight. He'd been dreaming of swimming with the dolphins. One of them was swimming alongside him and he reached out to stroke its side. The dolphin turned to look at him and smiled. The smile grew wider and more familiar and Jesse became aware that this was not a dolphin but Loveday. Her red hair was streaming behind her as she swam above and below him, twisting and looping in the simple joy of being with him. Streams of air bubbles danced from her as she swam, always just a little bit faster and a little bit further out of reach. 'Come on, Jesse. Come on,' she spoke from beneath the waves, smiling up at him. 'Come on. Before you lose me.'

'Wake up, mate. It's your watch. Come on. Get up.' Jesse opened his eyes and slowly became aware of the familiar heat and smell of the *The Lobster Pot*'s cramped cabin. The tired face of Aaron, who'd just finished the first watch, loomed over Jesse's bunk. 'Wake up, you bugger. I need some kip before we start the trawl. Get out and let me in.' Jesse flipped back the blankets, lifted his head from the pillow and swung his legs onto the floor. Apart from taking off his boots, he hadn't bothered to get undressed before he slept so, apart from a quick rub of his eyes, there was no time wasted. Aaron was already crawling into the warm bunk and gave Jesse a shove as he reached for the blankets. 'Get out and let me 'ave me beauty sleep.'

'And what time would Sir like his wake-up call?' a yawning Jesse asked sarcastically.

'Bugger off.'

'As Sir wishes.' Jesse bent down and whispered in Aaron's ear, 'Would Sir like a goodnight kiss?' Aaron produced a two-fingered salute and turned over. He was already asleep by the time Jesse closed the door.

Jesse reported to his father in the wheelhouse. 'Any news?' he asked him.

'Aaron spotted some boats off to starboard about half a kilometre away. Spanish, by looks of it.'

'Shit.'

'Aye. Seeing more and more of 'em out here. Bastards are depleting our stocks and using up the quotas. Go and make us a brew, will you?'

Jesse gladly did; he was in need of one himself to wake him up. The next two hours went quietly and they saw no more foreign boats.

On the horizon he watched the occasional tanker as it headed off for who-knew-where with its lights shining in the gloom. The hypnotic throb of the engine and the rhythmic slosh of the sea water brought on an almost meditative state. He sipped his tea and thought about his future. The places he would go, the people he would meet, the money he would earn. Once he'd done all that, if Loveday were still free, he'd come back to her and marry her. Maybe Mickey would meet someone else; marry the first girl he got up the duff, like the soft bugger he was. Yes, that's what he'd do. He smiled, contented with his plan.

Gradually he grew aware of the engine note changing and the boat slowing. Edward leant out of the wheelhouse window and said, 'Get the lads up and prepare the trawl.'

*

Edward looked down from his vantage point in the wheelhouse and watched as the two derricks holding the beam trawls on either side of the boat swung out from the deck and over the water. He could hear the shackles and chain links of the trawl nets rattle as they went into the water. The rubber wheels at the bottom of the nets would allow the trawl to travel smoothly on the sea bed and gather their precious haul. He'd set the engine to a gentle towing pace of around two knots. He watched Jesse, in his yellow oilskin trousers and boots, working alongside the rest of the crew. He was a good lad. A born fisherman. He wished there was another way he could ensure the survival of Behenna's Boats, but these were dangerous times for the fishing industry – in Cornwall in particular – and no one could predict what was going to happen. The mood in the harbour was one of doom and gloom, and every week it seemed as if more boats were being decommissioned after desperate fishermen had taken the EU grant and allowed their boats to be broken up in the name of keeping the UK's quotas. It defied belief, and he knew that his own father would be turning in his grave to see the parlous state that things had reached.

But, if Behenna's Boats and Clovelly's Fisheries merged, his father's legacy would be secured, for now at least, and Jesse would have a future. But was he condemning Jesse to a life with that skinny Greer? He shook his head – it was the 1980s, for God's sake, not the 1580s and he had no power to make Jesse do anything. He felt a flash of anger at his own indecision. Damn it – why did all of this make him feel like he was selling Jesse to the bloody Clovellys?

'You'm a bleddy old fool,' he told himself. The envelope of cash was also preying on his mind. He could still give it back, couldn't he?

He'd get this haul home and tell Bryn Clovelly to get

stuffed, that's what he'd do. Relieved to have made a decision at last, he turned his concentration to the job in hand.

It was a good night. Each haul on both boats was teeming with good fish. Sole and Dover sole, mostly. These would sell like hot cakes to London chefs, who fed them to their overstuffed clients for a fortune.

Down in the hold, in the fish room, the crew were working in well-drilled harmony. The fish were sorted, gutted, washed and placed in boxes of ice ready to be landed for the market. The smell of fish guts was usurped by the gleam in every man's eye. This was a good haul, and they knew they would be well rewarded when they got it back to Trevay.

*

Bryn Clovelly caught the mooring rope that Edward threw over to him. 'I hear you had a good trip,' Bryn called, tying the rope to an ancient metal ring set into the harbour wall.

'Aye.'

'What have you got for me?'

'Some good Dover sole and plaice.'

'Not so much call for either at the moment,' shrugged Bryn, giving a hand to Edward as he stepped off the boat and onto the first dry land he'd seen for seven long days. Edward was not in the mood for haggling.

'Don't give me any of that old shit, Bryn. There's always call for Dover sole from those lah-di-bleddy-dah London types.'

Bryn shrugged again. 'I'll make my mind up when I see the catch.'

The crews of *The Lobster Pot* and *Our Mermaid* hoisted the fish boxes out of the hold and onto the quayside. There were plenty of them, and Edward could see Bryn's eyes darting over them and making calculations. He held out his hand to Edward and gave him a figure. 'Shake on it. You'll not get a better price.'

Bryn had not mentioned the sweetener and neither had Edward, but it hung there between the two men.

Edward was no fool and he held his nerve; he'd agreed to nothing as yet. Keeping his hands in his pockets, he started the negotiations.

At last a figure was agreed on and they shook hands, each man regarding the other steadily. 'I'd have given you more,' said Bryn wryly, 'if I knew that Clovelly and Behenna were destined to be one company.'

Edward pursed his lips and thought for a moment. 'If I knew that the deal was only between you and me and that it had nothing to do with your Greer and my Jesse, I might just say yes. Jesse is his own man, Bryn. He'll do as he likes.'

'You're a good negotiator, Edward, with strong powers of persuasion. You'll sway him.'

Edward said nothing, but he saw a glint in Bryn Clovelly's eyes – and it looked worryingly like victory.

'I need to know that Clovelly's has a future,' said Bryn. 'I need to know that I am passing it onto the next generation of my bloodline. I want my grandchildren to carry on the name of Clovelly. If Greer and Jesse were to marry, that would happen. But if you can't see your way to giving your son a helping hand in the world, then there are plenty of boat owners – with unmarried sons – on this coast who will.'

6

The postman, never knowingly uninterested in people's business, was enjoying his morning. It was that day in August when, around the country, exam results were dropping through letterboxes, anxious pupils waiting on the other side, braced for what news they might bring. The postman always took it upon himself to hand-deliver the envelopes in Trevay – whether he was conveying good news or bad, he wanted to pass it to the addressee personally.

Today he'd witnessed four people in tears (three of them mothers) and received two hugs of joy. No one had yet offered him a brew, and he could do with one. He was driving from the small modern housing estate at the top of Trevay, down the hill towards the old town and the sea. He pulled on the plastic sun visor to shield his eyes from the glare of the early morning light glinting off the water in the estuary. He turned right onto the posh road where the white stucco executive bungalows sat with their unfettered view of the river, the harbour and the open sea beyond. Each home was surrounded by a generous plot of land, either planted with palm trees, china-blue hydrangeas, large mounds of pampas grass or a selection of all three.

He stopped his van at Bryn and Elizabeth Clovelly's conspicuously expensive bungalow, unimaginatively named

Brybeth. He sorted through the bundles of post. He was looking for one with Greer Clovelly's name on it. He found an electricity bill, a Cellophaned edition of *Golfer's Monthly* and a letter from the DVLA (all addressed to Mr B. Clovelly), a postcard from Scotland (addressed to Mrs E. Clovelly) and finally a plain envelope addressed to Miss Greer Clovelly with a Truro postmark. He got out of his van and walked with dignified purpose towards their front door.

Greer was lying in bed listening to the radio. Kim Wilde was singing 'You Keep Me Hangin' On'. As usual Greer was thinking about Jesse. She didn't hear the doorbell ring or the bustle of her mother coming from the rear kitchen to the front door. But she did hear her mother calling her name.

'Greer. The postman has a delivery for you.'

'What is it?' she called back.

'Something you've been waiting for.' Her mother was using her singsong voice.

Greer sat up quickly. 'Is it my exam results?' She didn't listen for the answer as she leapt out of bed, grabbed her Snoopy dressing gown, a cherished Christmas present from Loveday, Mickey and more especially Jesse, and dashed down the hall to the open front door.

She thanked the postman and slid her thumb under the flap of the envelope. Her hands shook a little as she took out the letter inside and unfolded it.

The look on her face told the postman all he needed to know. He hung about briefly in case there was a congratulatory cup of coffee to be offered, but when it wasn't he set off, desperate to spread the news.

Bryn stood at the kitchen table and read the letter through again. 'You passed! Ten O levels. My God, Greer, I'm proud of you.'

'Thank you, Daddy.'

'Ten! That's ten more than you and me, eh, Elizabeth?'

'It certainly is. Oh, Greer, we are proud of you.'

'This means I can go to sixth-form college and do my art and design A level.'

Her father sat down opposite her and, pushing his reading glasses onto the top of his head, adopted a patient tone. 'How about getting a good secretarial qualification? Hmm? Secretaries are always needed. Good ones, anyway. They are the oil of the engine in any business. And when you get married, you won't need to work. You'll be looked after by your husband, while you look after your home and your family. Like Mum.'

Greer looked at her father in exasperation.

'I want to be an interior designer, and a wife and mum.'

'Well, I'd like to be a professional golfer, but we all have to be realistic.'

'I am being realistic. Lots of women have jobs these days and bring up a family.'

'You're talking about those lah-di-dah city types with posh nannies and banker husbands. It's different here.'

'And who says I can't be a lah-di-dah city type?' she countered mutinously.

Her father glowered at her. Greer chewed her lip and there was a strained silence. She knew it was pointless to provoke her father, but she consoled herself with the thought that he'd have to stop treating her like a child one day.

Her mother went to the bread bin and sliced two pieces of granary bread before popping them in the toaster. She was thinking of how best to back Greer without antagonising her dinosaur, chauvinist husband.

'I think she'd make a very good interior designer, Bryn,'

she said quietly. 'Look what she's done with her bedroom. And interior designers can charge the earth for their services. She has good taste, and people are prepared to pay for good taste.'

Bryn shook his head dismissively. 'A fool and his money are easily parted.'

*

'Mum!' Loveday was bouncing uncontrollably round the tiny stone-flagged hall of the cottage she shared with her mother. 'Mum! I got seven! And an A for maths!' She flung herself into her mother's arms and jigged them both up and down on the spot. 'Can you believe it, Mum?'

Beryl Carter managed to extricate herself from her daughter and, panting, said, 'Oh, my darlin' girl, you done so well! Your dad would be proud of you and no mistake. Seven! You'll be going to university at this rate.'

Loveday stopped jumping and pulled her mother into a giant bear hug. 'Mum, I'm not leaving you. I'm going to get a job and bring some good money into the house. I'm going to look after you properly. The way Dad would've.'

'No,' Beryl told her firmly, pulling herself out of Loveday's grip again. 'You'm not giving up your future for me. I can look after myself. You get out and see the world. You could be a doctor or . . . or . . . a professor or something.'

'Not with only seven O levels,' laughed Loveday. 'And what do I want to see the world for? I'm happy in Trevay with you and Greer and Jesse and Mickey.' A thought suddenly struck her. 'I'll ask if there's a job going at

Jesse's dad's or Greer's dad's. I'll work as hard as they like. Harder than anyone they know.'

*

Jan Behenna took the envelope from the odious postman and propped it against the teapot on the kitchen table. She prayed Jesse had done well. She wanted him to be happy and fulfil his dreams, whatever they were. If that meant emigrating to Australia, so be it. She'd barely left Cornwall herself, let alone the United Kingdom. If Jesse went to Australia, Jan could apply for a passport and fly on an aeroplane. She'd have the chance to see the Sydney Harbour Bridge. She sighed as she dreamt of Jesse's future. The one thing she didn't want for him was to be pushed into a marriage of convenience to Greer bloody Clovelly and her jumped-up family.

'Morning, Ma.' Grant came into the kitchen; he'd come home for the weekend and looked better than he had for ages. His hair was shaved close and neat and, despite being out last night drinking with his old Trevay mates, he was up bright and early this morning and looked none the worse for it. It was early days, but Jan hoped that life in the army was giving the boy the discipline he sorely needed. She fervently prayed that he'd turned a corner and was putting his old ways behind him.

Movement upstairs signalled that Jesse was awake. He and Edward had come home from a long fishing trip the night before and he was only now stirring, the smell of eggs and bacon wafting up from the kitchen as good as any alarm clock.

Jesse entered, naked except for his boxers. He hadn't known Grant was due a visit home, and the sight of his brother grinning at him from the breakfast table wasn't an entirely welcome one.

'All right, Grant.'

'Hello, little brother.' Grant ruffled Jesse's hair roughly and Jesse jerked his head away quickly.

'Get off.'

'Oo-er, someone's a bit touchy today. That Loveday Carter not let you 'ave a feel of 'er big tits yet?'

Jesse stiffened. Jan could sense the tension between them and tried to head it off at the pass.

'Grant, leave Jesse be, he doesn't need your teasing this morning. Here, Jesse.' She handed him the envelope.

Jesse could have done without Grant being there while he opened the letter. Whether the news was good or bad, his brother would find some way of goading or mocking him for it.

'Go on, son, open it,' his mother said encouragingly.

Jesse looked from her to the letter. Would any of the contents make the blindest bit of difference to his future? He doubted it. Behenna's Boats beckoned and there wasn't much in this letter could change that.

He ripped open the envelope and eyed the contents.

'Well?' Jan asked anxiously.

A grin spread across Jesse's face. Six O levels. He'd failed at geography and a couple of others, but all of the key subjects were there.

'I got six!'

'Oh, well done, son!' Jan embraced him warmly and Jesse tried not to squirm. 'Enough for college, are they?'

Grant sneered. 'College? What – our Jesse a college boy, with all those other little stuck-up snivellers.'

'Fuck off, Grant. Just because you were too busy getting in trouble and never got anything.'

'College is just for nancy boys too shit-scared to do a proper man's job.' He shovelled a mouthful of bacon and eggs into his mouth.

'Grant, stop winding Jesse up and, Jesse, mind your language at the table, please.'

'I'm going out on the boats with Dad,' Jesse announced, in a bid to put an end to both his mother and Grant's speculation.

'You don't have to decide now, Jesse,' his mother told him. 'Wait until after the summer and see how you feel then.'

'Anyway,' said Grant, talking through his mouthful of food, 'Dad's got Jesse's future all sewn up, ain't that right? You're going to be the family whore!' He let out a snort of laughter and continued to shovel in the last few fork-fuls of his breakfast.

Jesse felt the urge to get as far and as fast away from Grant as possible. He stood and headed towards the kitchen door.

'But, Jesse, your breakfast?' his mother called after him.

'Not hungry, Mum.' Jesse leapt up the hallway stairs two at a time, still with Grant's spiteful laughter ringing in his ears.

*

Mickey wasn't surprised by his results. He sat up in bed as his mum brought the envelope to him with a mug of tea.

'B for technical drawing and physics, C for maths, English and history, and the rest I failed.'

His mum was thrilled, and said so. 'How many is that you got, then?'

'Five.'

'Five,' she said with relish. 'Five O levels. You'm bleddy Einstein, boy.'

The phone in the hall started to ring. Annie Chandler gave her son a last pat on the leg and went downstairs to answer it. Mickey listened, still looking at his results letter with satisfaction.

''Ello? . . .'Ello, Jesse. How did you do in your . . . Did you? Well done, boy . . . yes, Mickey's got his . . . five, yeah . . . shall I put 'im on? . . . Just a minute.'

Mickey didn't need to be called; he was already coming down the stairs two at a time and took the phone receiver from his mother.

'What you got, Jesse?'

'Six. I can't believe it!'

'You bleddy swot.'

Jesse laughed. 'You did all right, didn't you? Five!'

'Yeah.' Mickey couldn't help smiling to himself. 'Yeah. Bleddy five O levels.'

*

'Mum. Please,' Greer was pleading. 'I know it's kind of Dad, but I don't want to go out to dinner tonight.'

'You're not going to the Golden Hind and that's an end to it.' Her mother's voice was muffled as she dragged the vacuum cleaner out of the understairs cupboard.

'But everyone's going and I want to be with my friends.'

'No.' Her mother unwound the cable from the back of the cleaner's handle. 'Your dad and I want to celebrate as a family.' She handed Greer the plug end. 'Put this in, would you?'

Greer did as she was told but wouldn't give up. 'Well, can we go out early? So that I can finish and get down to see everybody after we've eaten?'

But her mother had already drowned her out with the roar of the machine.

Greer went to her room seething with frustration. She'd been everything a daughter should be to her family. She was thoughtful, obedient, clever. She always looked her best and watched her figure. She never asked for anything. Well, she didn't need to; her parents gave her everything before she asked. And now, here she was, almost 17, and they wouldn't let her go out on the most important night of her life.

Loveday had phoned an hour ago and told her her results. Greer was pleased for her, but even happier that she had done better. Loveday had asked her to come down to Figgotty's – a locals' beach. No holiday-maker ventured there; it had such a steep descent that no buggy or grandma would be able to get down to it or, if they did, up from it again.

'We're taking some pasties,' Loveday had told her.

'Who's we?' Greer had asked.

'About eight of us.'

'Is Jesse going?' Greer had hated herself for asking, so she added hastily, 'And Mickey?'

'Course they are. It was Jesse's idea. He told me to call you.'

'Did he?' Greer hugged herself. 'Hang on, I'll just ask Mum.' A few moments later she was back on the line, almost in tears. 'My mum won't let me. She wants me to go into Truro with her.'

'Never mind.' Loveday had suddenly felt sorry for her friend. 'Maybe you can come tonight?' she'd suggested.

'The pub's doing an "exam result special" night. There's a hog roast in the beer garden and a DJ.'

But now Greer's mum had categorically said no.

*

'*Buona sera*, Signor Clovelly.' Antonio, chef proprietor of the eponymously named Italian restaurant greeted Bryn with his arms wide and a dusting of pizza flour on his cheek.

'Good to see you, Antonio. How's the golf?' Bryn and Antonio were cronies both at the golf club and in the local Masonic Lodge.

Antonio was taking Elizabeth's wrap from her shoulders and replied in his heavily accented English, 'I am playing offa sixteen.' He shrugged. 'But if I had more time, I could be closer to you. What you playing offa now?'

'Twelve.'

'Twelve? My God, you musta never be at work? *Sì?*'

The two men laughed and then Antonio saw Greer standing hunched and miserable in the doorway. He stepped towards her, holding his arms out wide again. 'Look at leetle Greer! All-a grown up.' He inclined his head to one side and brought his hands together as if in prayer. 'But you are a beautiful young woman now!'

Elizabeth beamed with pride and said, 'She got her exam results today. She did very well, so we're here to celebrate.'

'Why she not look so happy?' asked Antonio, staring at Greer as if it was he who had upset her.

'I am happy,' Greer said, trying to smile, but desperately wishing that Antonio would leave her alone.

'Thank God!' Antonio boomed. 'And now, Antonio make you even more happy with his food.' He walked them to a pretty table overlooking the inner harbour, where they could watch the visiting yachts bob on their hired moorings. The tide was high that night and Greer could see it lapping almost to the top of the wall. She heard laughter from the pavement and saw several schoolfriends walking towards the Golden Hind . . . and the party she wasn't allowed to go to.

'Well, this is nice,' Bryn smiled, once Antonio had lit the red candle in the centre of the table and left them to get drinks and menus.

'Isn't it?' smiled Elizabeth. Greer said nothing. Knowing that all of her friends were out enjoying themselves – and she was stuck here – was like a slow death.

'What's the matter with you?' asked her father.

Greer put on a bright, tight little smile. 'Nothing.'

Elizabeth turned to Bryn and explained. 'There's a do at the pub. Pete's doing a hog roast and a disco for the school-leavers. Her friends are celebrating over there.' Bryn turned his head and looked over at the Golden Hind. 'That sounds fun. Why aren't you invited, Greer?'

'I was, but Mum said I couldn't go as we're having a family dinner, so . . .' Greer shrugged and looked at her hands, trying not to cry.

Bryn winked at Elizabeth. 'You can go over after we've eaten.'

Greer immediately brightened. 'Can I?'

'Of course you can. I like a bit of a bop.'

Greer's face dropped. 'You're coming?' She couldn't think what was worse. Not being allowed to go, or going but being saddled with her parents, who were bound to embarrass her.

'Yeah. Me and your mum haven't had a night out for ages.' Bryn put his hand on top of Elizabeth's, which was resting on the table. He turned to her. 'We'll show the youngsters some of our jive moves.'

Elizabeth, who had been looking forward to an early night with her new Jackie Collins book, hid her dismay. 'What a lovely idea.'

'Yes,' murmured Greer. 'Lovely idea.' Really just wishing that the ground would open and swallow her parents up.

7

The air in the beer garden was heavy with the smoke of the hog roast. Long chains of coloured lights were swung in a zigzag from fence to wall and back again, above the dusty grass. The DJ Ricky and 'his Roadshow from Liskeard', was playing 'Walk Like an Egyptian' and blowing bubbles over a couple of girls who were vying for his attention. The centre of the garden was a heaving mass of dancing, sweating teens.

Greer arrived and stood on the periphery. She was on her own. Her mother had nipped to the Ladies and her father was at the bar chatting. Loveday spotted her and came bowling over, wreathed in smiles. 'You made it! How did you manage it?'

Greer briefly explained and Loveday handed her a glass of punch. 'My mum's here too, see.' Loveday pointed over to the bar area where her mum was laughing and joking loudly over a large vodka and orange with a group of fishermen and their women. Her cheeks were flushed, and when Loveday waved over to her, she blew her daughter an ostentatious kiss. Greer couldn't understand why Loveday wasn't more embarrassed by her mother. She dressed in clothes more appropriate for a girl half her age; her own mother would have said that she was mutton dressed as lamb.

'Here, try this. It's mostly fruit juice, with some sort of wine in it.'

Greer took a sip. It seemed innocuous enough. 'I Wanna Dance with Somebody' was playing now. 'I love Whitney!' Loveday shouted above the noise. 'Come on, Greer. Let's dance.' Greer was not the dancing type but she took another mouthful of punch and, looking around for Jesse, reluctantly followed Loveday into the throng.

Jesse was in the pub kitchen with Mickey, making another industrial-sized bowl of punch. The landlord, Pete, told them to help themselves to the cartons of fruit juice that he'd put into the huge fridge, and to add half a bottle of Lambrusco to each batch. 'No more, mind! I don't want to lose my licence.'

Mickey and Jesse had assured him they wouldn't overdo it but, as soon as they were on their own, Mickey stepped outside the kitchen door and fetched the bottle of vodka he'd hidden in the hedge and he and Jesse took a swig each from it before pouring a good slug into the punch. 'Well, Pete never said nothing about vodka, did he?'

'No,' agreed Jesse, assiduously measuring only half a bottle of Lambrusco into the deep container. The two boys took another mouthful of vodka each before hiding the bottle back under the hedge.

*

Loveday was hot. The music was getting faster and louder and she was getting thirsty. She spotted the boys lugging the punch tureen towards a trestle table. 'Want a drink, Greer?' she shouted.

Greer nodded and gently dabbed at her forehead with

the back of her hand. She was glad to stop, and gladder still to see Jesse.

Mickey saw the girls approaching and, emboldened by the vodka, nudged Jesse and slurred, 'I'm going to make sure I give Loveday a big one.'

Jesse giggled. 'You ain't got a big one.'

Mickey snorted with laughter, 'I don't mean give her my big one.' He creased over with hysteria.

'Well, I'll help you out and give her my big one if you like,' hooted Jesse.

Mickey stopped laughing and squared up to his friend. 'What did you say?'

Jesse was shocked that he'd said anything at all. The drink was muddling his thinking, but thoughts of Loveday were always bubbling just beneath the surface these days.

'It was a joke. Just a joke. That's all.' He put his hands up in surrender. 'Sorry, mate.'

Mickey looked stony faced. 'Loveday means the world to me and one day I'll marry her, so no more talking that way about her. She's my girl, you got that?'

For a brief moment, Jesse wanted to push back at Mickey, to ask him who said that Loveday was his girl. Why should he have her?

Mickey stood his ground, staring hard into Jesse's eyes. Jesse saw the fierce possession that burned there and instead of challenging Mickey, the words that came from his mouth were ones of appeasement.

'Of course, mate. I'm so sorry. I just . . . I don't know . . . must be the booze.'

Then suddenly Mickey began to giggle again. 'Yours is just a little chipolata anyway.' Jesse, relieved, started to laugh too.

'Oh, yeah?' said Loveday as she arrived at the table. 'What you two bollock-heads laughing at?'

The boys gave each other sidelong glances and started giggling again.

Loveday shook her head, dismissing their silliness. 'Honest, Greer, how these two ever managed to get any O levels is beyond me. Bleddy idiots.' She reached for the industrial catering ladle lying in a sticky pool on the paper tablecloth and dipped it into the punch.

'Give it a good stir, Loveday,' hiccuped Mickey, putting his arm round her fleshy waist and giving it a squeeze. 'All the good stuff is at the bottom.' She looked at him suspiciously. "Ave you been drinking?'

'No.'

She turned to Jesse. 'Has he?'

Jesse attempted to focus his eyes on Loveday. 'No.'

Loveday shook Mickey's arm off her and leant forward to sniff his breath. 'I can smell alcohol.'

Mickey was affronted. 'You can't smell vodka, 'tis a well-known fact.'

She opened her eyes in disbelief. 'Yes you can, and where the bleddy hell did you get vodka?'

Jesse owned up. 'Grant got us two litre bottles to celebrate. He's home for the weekend.'

'Your Grant is trouble – and now he's going to get you into trouble.' She stood with her hands on her hips, frowning at both boys. 'Where is he now?'

Greer, who'd been listening to all of this, looked around the garden and pointed to Grant, who was dancing with a couple of girls. He was in a skintight T-shirt which enhanced his muscular shoulders and tattooed pecs. The girls looked very pleased with themselves for having netted the handsomest man at the party. DJ Ricky was not looking happy – it looked as if he'd be going home alone . . . again. 'He's over there,' Greer said.

Jesse was unimpressed. 'Janine and Heather? Is that the best he can do? Anyone can pull them.'

Grant was now bumping and grinding his hips, bum and crotch towards the girls as 'Le Freak' by Chic was blaring out over the speakers. The girls willingly followed his moves.

Loveday leaned towards Jesse's ear and – above the noise – managed to ask him to dance with her.

'No thanks,' he answered, pouring himself another glass of punch. 'Not in the mood.'

'What are you in the mood for?' she asked, putting her hand on his chest. She was wearing a low-cut baby-pink vest and the skimpiest of denim skirts. Her hair was tied in a side ponytail with a pink scrunchie, and her lips were parted seductively as she gazed up at Jesse.

He felt the warmth of her skin through his shirt and wanted more than anything to drop his mouth to hers and kiss her deeply. They were so close, with barely a hair's breadth between them; all he'd have to do would be to lean in . . . but all at once Jesse became aware of Mickey standing right next to them. He took a step back, knocking the table as he did so. Loveday let her hand drop back by her side.

'I'll dance with you, Loveday,' grinned Mickey. He grabbed her elbow, guiding her erratically onto the dance floor as she looked disappointedly over her shoulder at Jesse.

He and Greer were left to watch as Mickey and Loveday were swallowed by the crowd.

'Want another drink, Greer?' asked Jesse.

Greer drank very little, but the last glass of punch had

left her feeling a little woolly around the edges, and she was enjoying the sensation. 'Yes, please.' She handed her empty glass to him. Carefully he dipped the ladle into the bowl and filled their glasses to the brim.

'Cheers, Big Ears,' Greer surprised herself by saying; the punch was definitely kicking in.

'Cheers, Greers,' he replied solemnly.

They clinked and drank.

'Why aren't you dancing?' he asked.

'No one's asked me. Except Loveday, and she doesn't count.'

'Loveday's a good girl,' Jesse said quietly.

'Mickey thinks so.'

Jesse pulled his mouth down at the corners. 'Yeah.'

'They're well suited, don't you think?'

'I s'pose.'

Greer, powered by the warmth of vodka, elucidated. 'I mean they're two of a kind. Loveday has no ambition to leave Trevay. Mickey's future is mapped out for him on the boats. Whereas you and I . . .' She took a step closer to him. 'We're lucky. We come from families who have made something of themselves.'

Jesse was now feeling very drunk but also – and this surprised him – he suddenly felt attracted to Greer. She wasn't sexy and exuberant like Loveday, but her shiny, blunt-cut bob and neat, even teeth were fascinating him. He wasn't sure what she was saying exactly, but whatever it was, she was saying it very sweetly.

'You're all right really, aren't you, Greer?' he managed. 'I don't think you're a snob. Like some of them say. You're just a bit different. That's all. Want a top-up?'

Greer frowned slightly. 'Yes, please, and I'm not a snob. Who said that?'

'Janine and Heather.'

Greer drank some more punch and enjoyed its zing as it ran down her throat and hit her stomach. 'They are a pair of bitches.' She put her glass down. 'I'm going to sort them out.' She took a step forward but her knees sank a little. Jesse caught her. 'No you don't.' He pulled her closer to him. 'You're staying with me.' Her slender frame felt surprisingly good – firm, but there was a softness there too, not soft like Loveday, but . . . He felt a shot of desire stir in his groin.

She relaxed into his arms and raised her face to his. She giggled. 'You've got strong arms, Jesse Behenna.'

He demonstrated his strength by pulling her closer to him. 'You'd better believe it.'

She snuggled into his arms. She could feel his warm breath on her hair as he rested his cheek on the top of her head. She closed her eyes and allowed herself to melt into him, to feel the heat of his body against hers. Greer felt a heady thrill at being in Jesse's arms. This was it. This was their moment.

The pounding beat of Jackie Wilson giving his all to 'Reet Petite' broke through the moment as Greer heard a familiar voice.

'Scuse us, you two,' said her father. 'Your mum and I are going to show you young 'uns some real dancing.' Her parents pushed past them and cleared a space on the dance floor before going into an incredible jive routine.

Bryn spun Elizabeth under his arm and towards him, then spun her out and away from him. They were good. They rocked back on their heels at arms' length and pinged back together with their arms round each other. Pushing Elizabeth a little away from him, Bryn caught her by the waist and bounced her high above his head then swept her down and between his legs. Elizabeth had enjoyed two large gin and tonics and was unembarrassed as her skirt slid up her thighs to reveal comfy mum knickers.

Greer was mortified. The spell was broken and she extricated herself from the bliss of Jesse's embrace to take in the full horrific embarrassment of her parents. Couldn't they see how ridiculous they looked? How could they do this to her? In front of all her friends. On tonight of all nights. She turned and ran to the Ladies where the combination of alcohol, her yearning for Jesse and the grimness of her parents' behaviour made her vomit violently.

After a while, she felt a bit better. She closed the loo lid and flushed, then sat down on the seat and dabbed at her perspiring face with a wad of loo paper. She had never had so much to drink. She stayed put, with her head in her hands, praying that the room would just slow down for a moment.

A timid knock on the cubicle door made her jolt.

'Is anyone in there?' It was Loveday's mother.

Greer got to her feet and flushed the loo again to make it look as if she hadn't been sitting there trying to sober up. She opened the door and Mrs Carter smiled kindly at her.

'You all right?' she asked.

'Fine, Mrs Carter. Thank you.'

'I saw you run in here and wondered if you might like a glass of water or something, darling?'

Greer wondered how much Mrs Carter had seen and understood.

'No, thank you. I'm fine, really.'

'That's good.' Mrs Carter made no move to go into the cubicle. Instead she put her hand comfortingly on Greer's shoulder and leant in closer. She smelt of alcohol mixed with Dior Poison.

'Seeing your mam and dad dancing like that has taken me back.' She shifted unsteadily and her eyes seemed glazed over.

Greer wanted to sit down or go home or both, but this wretched woman wouldn't leave her alone. She made an attempt at good manners. 'Taken you back to when?'

'When we was all at school together. Your dad was so handsome. All we girls wanted to dance with him. He's still got it, hasn't he? I haven't seen him dance like that since he married your mum.' Mrs Carter had a faraway look in her eye that Greer didn't like.

'He used to dance like that with me, you know.'

Greer was feeling queasy again. 'What do you mean?'

'He and I went out with each other for a little while, but your mum took dancing lessons and before long they were a couple on the dance floor . . .' Mrs Carter sighed again. 'And in life.'

Beads of sweat popped out on Greer's top lip and forehead. She didn't want to hear any more. 'Excuse me, Mrs Carter, but I must get some fresh air.' She made a dash for the door and just heard Mrs Carter's imploring, 'Don't tell Loveday, will you? She thinks her dad was my one and only boyfriend.'

God, what was going on with these adults? What kind of role models were they? She slipped through the pub bar and out to the front where she found an empty bench tucked into the shadows. She breathed the cool night air. It was tinged with the familiar smell of salt, seaweed, diesel and fish and chips. She took stock of her evening.

Her parents were some kind of dancing nuts, and her best friend's mother had gone out with her dad. She didn't want to imagine how intimate they might or might not have been. Her world seemed to have turned upside down. Then she thought of Jesse and the way he had held her tonight. She was sure she'd seen a flicker of real emotion in his eye. Until her parents had shown themselves up. What would he think of her now? She buried her face in her hands for the second time that evening.

After a while she sensed that she wasn't alone. Someone sat on the bench next to her and the wooden slats gave way a little, making her bounce slightly.

'All right, are you, Greer?' asked Jesse.

She stayed hunched but took her hands from her face. 'Yes.'

'Loveday's mum's worried about you. She thought you might not be feeling well.'

'I'm fine.'

'Sure?'

'Sure.'

Jesse stretched his long legs out in front of him and stretched his arms over his head. She turned to look at him. He was staring at the stars. She drank in his wonderful profile. His always tousled blond hair was carelessly sticking out in all directions. His eyebrows framed his honest sea-green eyes. His lashes were fair but long and his nose straight and strong. His lips, slightly parted, were on the thin side but they framed his teeth perfectly.

He spoke. 'Satellite. Look.' She tilted her head up and followed his pointing finger. Sure enough, across the heavens a bright light was moving at speed. 'I wanted to be an astronaut when I was young.'

She smiled. 'You are young.'

Now he turned those sea-green eyes to her. 'Greer, I've got six O levels and I'm leaving school to work with my dad. I'm already old.'

'You're only sixteen. You can go to college, get some more qualifications.'

'That's for people like you. You want to go to college, don't you?'

'Art school. But my dad wants me to do a secretarial course.'

'Sensible.'

'I don't want sensible. I want to be an interior designer. To make beautiful houses for beautiful people, and . . .' She looked down at her feet in their pretty pink suede court shoes, 'and I want to be married and have children.'

Jesse lifted his arm and put it round her shoulders, aware of what he was doing, thinking again of her smooth skin and her firm thighs. He couldn't seem to stop himself: the mix of alcohol, the heat of the pub and his raging hormones had put his body and his mind at odds with each other. 'Do you now? And who have you got your eye on?'

It was now or never, under the starry night sky, and still slightly drunk she looked him full in the eye and breathed, 'You.'

His father's words – *you'd do a lot worse than to marry that girl* – drifted through Jesse's alcoholic haze.

Greer felt his arm lift a little away from her and he was silent for a moment before he started to laugh. Now his arm was back by his side, searching for his other arm to cross defensively over his chest, his heart.

'You're a funny one when you're drunk, aren't you?' He stood up. 'Let's go back. The others will be wondering where we are. We don't want to start any rumours, do we?'

She stayed where she was, horrified and ashamed that she'd played her hand so openly.

'I'll join you in a minute.'

He looked down at her and held out a large hand. 'Come on, you. We all say silly things when we're pissed. I promise not to tell. Now take my hand and let's go back.'

*

The party had degenerated into several couples clinging to each other in a slow dance. Around the edges sat groups of people chatting or snogging. The fire pit for the hog roast had died down to a mellow glow and the hog itself was just a charred carcass. Greer glanced around to find her parents. She saw them through a window sitting inside in the bar.

Her feeling of relief was swiftly abated when a breathless Loveday ran up to them in distress.

'Jesse, your brother's challenged Ricky the DJ to an arm-wrestling match. He's ever so drunk and I'm frightened he's going to hurt him.'

'Oh shit,' said Jesse, and he sprinted off into the pub.

A crowd had gathered around Grant and Ricky. Ricky was a big lad with strong arms and a beer belly, and he was holding his own. Grant's tattooed muscles, though, were as dense and hard as granite. He was staring into the DJ's pudgy face and through bared teeth said, 'Come on, fat boy. You can do better than this, can't you?'

Ricky dug deep and strengthened his grip. 'You don't scare me, soldier boy. I was in the Falklands. I've killed people.'

'Yeah?' grimaced Grant, pushing his muscles till they quivered. 'Well, you're a tub of lard now, aren't you?'

There was a sudden parting of the crowd as Mickey and Jesse pushed through. Their arrival momentarily broke Grant's concentration and Ricky, seeing his chance, slammed Grant's arm down. The crowd cheered but quickly quietened as they saw Grant smash his fist into Ricky's face. There was the sickening sound of crunching bone and a splatter of blood arced from the DJ's nose across the crowd.

Someone must have dialled 999 because within minutes two police cars and an ambulance had arrived, their sirens and blue lights strobing the peace of the harbour.

A few of the more drunken and troublesome teens lingered on the harbour, looking for trouble, before they were herded away by the police; the party quickly broke up, with only the hardened rubberneckers lingering. Ricky the DJ was put in the ambulance with a police officer and driven off to Truro and Treliske Hospital.

Grant was handcuffed after attempting to resist arrest and was being questioned in the bar. It wasn't long before a Royal Marines Police vehicle arrived and he was locked in the back for the return journey to his Plymouth barracks. Jesse could only watch helplessly as Grant was driven away. Thanks to him, the night had ended on a downer and all the excitement and expectation that had been flowing through the crowd had now drained away, just like the remains of the punch that Pete was pouring down the sink.

Jesse was left with the difficult of job of going home to tell his parents that Grant was, once again, in trouble.

8

1989

Greer stepped off the train at Bodmin and walked out to the pavement, where cars were parking ready to collect her fellow travellers. She shielded her eyes against the dazzling June sunshine and stood her suitcase and two canvas 'overspill' bags at her feet, face turned to the sun, inhaling the scent of clean Cornish air.

'Greer darling!' Her mother's voice carried on the breeze. Elizabeth was stepping half in and half out of the passenger seat of Bryn's latest car. Her left leg was still in the footwell, her right on the tarmac, and both hands holding onto the top of the open car door. She was beaming and waving frantically.

Greer could see her father pushing his sunglasses to the top of his head and then opening the heavy door of the big BMW. He got out and walked to the boot. He opened it and then strolled towards her, giving Greer a chance to admire how fit and tanned and successful he looked. 'Darling, welcome home.' He kissed her and picked up the suitcase and one of the canvas bags. 'You can manage that one, can't you?' He nodded his head to the remaining bag.

'I've managed all of them from London, Dad.'

'Hope you haven't gone all women's lib on us?' He laughed.

Greer was thinking that her dad was being as embarrassing as usual and was struggling to come up with a
suitable retort when her mother bustled up. 'Darling
Greer. You look so lovely! So slim in that dress. But what
have you done with your hair?'

Greer's free hand flew to the back of her neck where
perfect feathers of hair lay short. 'I got bored with the
bob.'

'But it was a classic cut. You've had it since you were
three.'

'Exactly. I'm eighteen years old. I needed a change.'

Her mother sniffed disapprovingly before saying,
'Never mind. It will grow.'

Her father loaded her bags into the boot and Greer
stepped into the back seat. As with all her father's cars
it was the best he could afford. Top of the range, walnut,
soft leather and deep-pile carpet.

'I like your new car, Dad.'

'Only picked it up two days ago. Wanted to collect
you in style.' He put the gearstick into drive mode and
pulled away from the kerb. Her mother craned round to
chat to her daughter.

'Congratulations on your typing speed and shorthand.
And how you've mastered the word processor, I've no
idea. Your father has two in the office. The girls were
showing them to me but it's all so complicated.' Her
mother turned back to face the road.

'Not when you know how, Mum.' Greer was looking
out of the window, enjoying the sights she hadn't seen
for two long years. The valley to her right held woodland
and fields. To her left were the steep lanes leading to
Lanhydrock House.

'There's a job for a secretary in the office at the

moment.' Her father caught her gaze in the rear-view mirror. 'Tessa's going off on maternity leave in a couple of weeks. She says she'll be back, but she won't. Women don't come back once they've started a family. But I have to pay her while she's away. It's a government con.'

Greer tried to let her father's misogynistic stream flow over her. She had got what she'd wanted. She'd done a two-year course in interior design at a smart private college in Surrey, and, to keep her father happy, studied for a secretarial course in London during the holidays. That had left her no time to return to Cornwall while she focused on gaining her qualifications, but it meant she'd achieved them as quickly as possible.

'I got a distinction in my design course.'

There was a tight silence from the front seats.

'Good,' her mother finally said.

Greer persevered. 'Actually, I have a surprise for you.'

Silence.

'I got Student of the Year.'

She saw her father raise his eyebrows in a look that said, 'What's the bloody use of that?' before her mother managed: 'That's nice.'

Greer said nothing more. She knew that she'd done extremely well, despite their dismissive attitude. They could ignore it if they liked, but Greer had worked hard for that distinction and it wouldn't go to waste, no matter what her father might think. She continued to look out of the window, content to watch the familiar landmarks slide by. Trelawney Garden Centre, the bridge over the river at Wadebridge, and the Royal Cornwall Showground. They continued along the dramatic and romantically named Atlantic Highway until the first sign to Trevay came into view.

'Nearly home now, Greer.' Her mum turned back to smile at her.

Greer's heart was starting to pound and butterflies were battering away inside her stomach. Nearly home. Nearly. She opened her mouth and asked the question she'd been burning to ask since she got off the train. 'How's Jesse?'

*

Loveday was forking a chip into her mouth and lapping up everything Greer was telling her about her two years up country. The girls had stayed in touch with occasional letters and postcards, but Greer hadn't come home for the entire two years that she'd been away at college. She had been determined to get her head down and finish the course as soon as she possibly could. She'd asked Loveday to come and see her, in the hope that Mickey and Jesse might tag along too, but Loveday never seemed to have enough money or time to make what she appeared to regard as an epic journey.

Greer had vaguely entertained the thought of staying on, but when she'd tried to find a position in one of the interior design companies up there, she never seemed to have the right connections. Despite the Clovelly name meaning something in Trevay, she had quickly become aware it stood for nothing in Guildford or Woking. The Surrey set she'd mixed with had all been very sophisticated and well-to-do; the girls who had found positions all had posh dads with serious connections. Greer realised she missed that feeling of being part of an influential and wealthy family, getting what she wanted when she wanted; being envied by people around her for her style and wealth. In short, she missed being in Trevay.

'I shared a flat with another girl, Laura, who was on the same design course. You should have seen how we did the place up! We painted the kitchen warm terracotta and hung garlands of fresh hops around the top of the wall units. Our landlord had never seen anything like it. He said he'd get twice the rent for it now. Laura taught me how to make curtains and we bought yards and yards of ticking fabric in the market and made the longest drapes you've ever seen. Really theatrical with swags and tie-backs.'

'What's a tie-back?'

Greer got out a little notebook which held her sketches for ideas and showed it to her friend. It was about time Trevay had its own interior designer and Greer knew her mother had lots of wealthy friends who would jump at the chance to have their houses improved by someone with her talents and training.

'Bleddy hell. No wonder you got Top Student,' Loveday said with real wonder. 'I bet the boys loved you.'

Greer put the notebook back in her bag. 'It was a virtually all-girl course and the boys we did have were gay.'

Loveday's eyes virtually popped out of her head. 'Gay? You mean like they had boyfriends?'

'Yes. Don't be so parochial.' Greer frowned, taking a sip of her coffee. There had been a few casual boyfriends and nights out, but nothing serious, and there was no one who could give her the same thrill of excitement as she felt when she thought about Jesse. 'Do you want my biscuit?' She pushed her saucer with its small round of shortbread on it towards Loveday.

Loveday had finished her fish and chips and shook her head. 'No, thank you, I'm on a diet.'

'Are you?' Greer said archly. 'I thought Mickey liked you just the way you are.'

'Mickey's just Mickey. There's never going to be anything between him and me.'

'Is he seeing someone else?'

Loveday absentmindedly picked up the shortbread biscuit and popped it in her mouth. 'I know he wants to go out with me but, as I keep saying no, Jesse and he are playing the field. Every spare minute they're in Newquay or St Ives, doing the clubs, picking up girls. We don't hang out like we used to.'

Greer clutched her coffee cup and hoped that Loveday didn't notice her hand shaking at the mention of Jesse.

'Is he seeing anyone special?'

'No, they're just being idiots.' Loveday hoped that Greer didn't see how much it hurt to know that Jesse had become a bit of a wanker, 'making hay while the sun shone', as he called it. That was one way of making it sound nicer than it was, she thought darkly.

Both girls stared out of the window of the little café in one of Trevay's side streets. Across the road, in the window of the dress shop, Doreen's, a woman was dressing a dummy, pulling up the elasticated waist of a pair of white trousers, and adding a short-sleeved nautical T-shirt.

'Talk of the bleddy devil.' Loveday banged on the glass café window. 'Jesse!' she shouted in a voice that carried around the restaurant, out of the open door and onto the pavement.

Greer saw him as he looked around, trying to work out who was calling him and from where.

'In here!' Loveday was banging and shouting until he

saw her. He gave a small wave but kept walking. 'Greer's home, look!' she shouted again, embarrassing Greer and eliciting tuts from customers who merely wanted to eat their lunch in peace. Loveday pushed her chair back with a screech and ran out onto the pavement, physically stopping Jesse. Greer couldn't bear to watch in case Jesse shrugged and walked on. She'd seen him only twice, briefly, since the night of the hog roast, and whenever she thought about how she'd virtually proposed to him a cold river of shame poured over her.

In spite of herself, she took a quick glance through the window and out to the scene on the pavement. Oh my God, he was walking towards the café with Loveday grinning and chatting by his side.

He came in and walked up to her table. He looked taller; his muscles had filled out and he was a ton more handsome, if that were possible. Suntanned, with a chiselled jaw and his unruly blond hair just a little longer, he stood over her, smiling, making her insides do funny things.

'Hello, Greer. It's been a long time. I wouldn't have recognised you with your short hair.'

Again her hand flew to her head. 'Do you like it?' Oh God, what kind of question was that?

He appraised her steadily before saying, 'It's all right. Do you girls want a cup of tea?'

'I'd like a milkshake,' Loveday announced, noisily pulling her chair back up to the table.

'Flavour?'

'Banana.'

'Right. You, Greer?'

'No, thank you.'

'You'm skin and bone, maid.'

Greer looked at her narrow thighs in their tight black jeans. 'Oh, OK. I'll have another coffee. Thanks.'

Jesse laughed and showed his good teeth. 'Black no sugar?'

Greer hated him laughing at her. 'White coffee with sugar,' she said defiantly, even though he'd been right in the first place.

The waitress brought the order to the table.

'So, how have you been?' Greer asked stiffly.

'Brilliant,' said Jesse. 'I'm on the boats full time now. Hard work, but the pay is good. I've bought a car.'

'Gosh. How grown-up.' Greer was seething with jealousy. A car meant he could pick up as many girls as he wanted. 'What sort?'

'Ford Capri. I'm doin' it up right now. Want to come and see it?'

'Maybe.'

'Well, don't if you don't want to.' He looked rather crestfallen. 'I expect you saw plenty of nice cars up country.'

'No, I would,' she said quickly, afraid of losing this chance to be with him. 'I'd love to. Where is it?'

'Up the sheds.' He spooned three sugars into his tan-coloured mug of tea. 'What's new with you then, Greer? Been a long time since we clapped eyes on you. How was it at college?'

'It was good. Quite fun.'

'Only got Student of the Decade and all her secretarial stuff too,' interjected Loveday, proudly.

Jesse raised a blond eyebrow appraisingly and nodded slowly. 'Right, well, when I get my house I might let you do it up for me, then.' He looked at her with a smile playing around his lips.

Greer felt he was trying to bait her. And was irritated by his attitude. 'I'm very expensive.'

He smirked. 'Oh, really? How much?'

'It would depend on what you wanted.'

Loveday jumped in. 'Tell him about the curtains.'

'Well, I could do a set of curtains at about three hundred a window.'

He roared with laughter. 'No. How much really?'

'Three hundred.'

'Straight up?' He looked amazed.

'Or flounced and tied back,' joked Loveday.

Her joke flew over his head and he looked at Greer with fresh interest. 'Three hundred? Fools and their money are easily parted!' He drained his tea, pushed his chair back and stood up. 'Anyway, I gotta go back to work. Dad wants me.' He walked to the door. Greer refused to turn and watch him. At the last moment he said, 'Mick and me will be up at the sheds about half six if you want to see my car.' And he left.

*

Mickey looked the same but even taller, if that were possible. He gave her a huge bear hug.

'Greer, you've gone all posh an' that, 'aven't you?'

Greer smiled. 'Have I?'

'Yeah, look at you. London clothes and haircut and that.'

Greer looked down at her jumpsuit with its padded shoulders and wide belt and supposed that she was rather more on trend than the rest of Trevay. 'Oh, it's only Chelsea Girl.'

Loveday had already quizzed her friend on her new

wardrobe and was planning a trip to Plymouth to update her own clothes. 'Don't she look good? And what about her hair?'

Mickey took in the urchin cut but said nothing other than: 'It's good to see you. I thought you'd dumped your old mates.'

The thing was, once Greer had left Trevay, she hadn't really missed her friends that much; there was too much going on and the thought of going back home and being treated as a kid by her father was unappealing. Besides, her mother loved the shopping in Guildford, and even at Christmas they'd been quite happy to come and have their Christmas lunch at a posh hotel in Surrey. She smiled. 'I know I haven't been home for two years but I was busy, and Mum came up to see me all the time. She kept me up to date with all the Trevay news, though.'

Jesse walked over to the Behenna's Boats shed and pulled at the big doors. ''Ave a look to this beauty.' The doors opened and behind them in the workshop was Jesse's Ford Capri. Bright blue with the Cornish flag painted on the roof.

'Wow!' Greer said sarcastically. 'Who did the paint-work?'

'Me and Dad.'

'It's lovely.'

'Want a ride?'

Greer caught her breath. The thought of sitting next to Jesse after two years of dreaming about him made her giddy. She managed to say, 'Sure.'

'Right,' said Jesse. 'You two girls hop in the back and we'll all go for a ride.'

The roar and rumble of the throaty engine bounced

off the shed walls. Greer and Loveday, squished into the
back, were forced backwards as Jesse put his foot to the
floor and shot the little car out of the shed and off down
the lane towards the harbour.

*

'Cheers, Edward.'

'Cheers, Bryn.' The two men clinked their glasses of
ale at the pub and supped contemplatively for a moment
before Bryn spoke.

'My Greer's back from up country today. Got her exams
and 'ome for good now.'

'She done well up there. I 'eard from Jan. What she
planning on doing now?' Edward asked cautiously.

Edward knew what Bryn was likely to say, but there
was still a part of him that hoped Greer Clovelly would
decide that the bright lights of Surrey had more to offer
her than her home town of Trevay.

Edward Behenna and Bryn Clovelly eyed each other
along the bar of the pub.

'Like I said, she'll be 'ome for good now, be ready to
settle down and start a family, I reckon.'

'What about her qualifications? She'll want to put
them to good use, won't she?'

Bryn blew out a cloud of smoke dismissively and gave
a firm shake of his head. 'That decorating course is just
a Mickey Mouse qualification. Kept 'er happy for a couple
of years and she got to see a bit of life, but it's kids and
family that will be the making of her.'

Edward stroked his chin thoughtfully. 'She might 'ave
ideas of her own.'

'All she wants is to marry your Jesse, and that's what

I want for her as well. Don't you think it's time you told 'im about our little arrangement?'

Edward had been dreading this moment. He and Bryn had put the final touches of their merger together and all the papers had been drawn up and signed in triplicate. It was a done deal. The Clovelly Fisheries Company now owned a controlling share in Behenna's Boats. The future of the company was secured and Edward Behenna had a seat on the board. But there was one clause that didn't appear in the reams of papers that he'd read through in the offices of his Trevay solicitors, Penrose and Trewin: what would happen to Jesse's inheritance – the one that both he and his father had spent their lives trying to ensure? One fail-safe way that Jesse could guarantee his share and carry the Behenna name into the future was by marrying into the Clovelly family.

He rubbed his chin and creased his brow, anxious about how he was going to break the news to Jesse.

'Come on, Edward. Your Jesse will see sense – he'll have money in his pocket and a beautiful girl for 'is wife. For God's sake, what's to decide? Come on, here's to our future and that of our grandkids!' He clanked his pint against Edward's again. But Edward found it hard to raise a smile, let alone his glass.

*

When Greer got home that evening her parents were waiting up for her.

'Can I get you anything before bed?' asked her mother.

'No, thank you, Mum.'

Bryn folded his paper and got out of his armchair. 'How was Jesse?'

Greer, already pinkened by two glasses of white wine, coloured a deeper shade. 'Fine,' she told him, before kissing her parents goodnight.

Bryn gave his wife a knowing look, which she returned as they watched their daughter retreat to the childhood bedroom she hadn't slept in for two whole years.

*

'How was Greer?' asked Jesse's father.

'Fine, I think.'

Jesse stepped over his father's outstretched legs in an attempt to get to the stairs and the safety of his bedroom before Edward could ask any more questions.

No luck.

'Hold on, boy. I want to talk to you.'

Jesse's shoulders dropped but he put on an innocent smile and said, 'What's that then, Dad?'

'Come and 'ave a seat, lad. Want a snifter?'

Jesse's father indicated the bottle of whisky from which he'd just poured himself a generous measure.

'Not really, Dad.' Jesse thought his dad had already had enough.

'I want to 'ave a proper talk with you, it's about your future.'

Jesse knew his father was about to launch into his usual sermon about the future of Behenna's Boats and him marrying Greer Clovelly. If he'd heard it once, he'd heard it a million times – especially when his dad was in his cups, like now.

'Dad, can we talk about this tomorrow? It's late and we've an early tide.'

Jesse made another attempt to get to the stairs but

his father was out of his seat and put his hand out to hold Jesse back.

'Dad?'

'Sit down, son,' his dad said firmly.

Jesse could see something in his father's eyes that he hadn't seen before. It stopped him short.

'What's happened, Dad?' Jesse asked, taking a seat opposite his father.

Edward steeled himself and took another mouthful of whisky. 'I've sold Clovelly Fisheries a share of Behenna's Boats. We're now one company.'

'What?' Jesse felt the news wash over him like a bucket of cold water. 'But what does that mean? Are we out of a job?'

'No!' Edward almost shouted. Then more calmly, for fear that he was losing control of the conversation, 'No, son, this is a good thing. I had to make sure you had a business to inherit. Things have been more of a struggle than you realise over the last few years. Bryn's paid a good price and we're out of the danger zone. Clovelly Fisheries will open up new markets for our fish and all of our jobs are safe. The company will carry on as we always have – for now, anyway.'

'What do you mean "for now"?' Jesse asked stiffly. He couldn't believe that his father had actually gone ahead and done this. He knew that his father and Bryn Clovelly had been cooking up some stupid plan between them, but for his father to actually sell some of their assets off . . . 'How much 'ave you sold him?' he asked coldly.

Edward paused. 'Fifty-one per cent.'

'Fifty-one per cent?' Jesse exploded out of his chair. 'But that means they own more than half – Behenna's

Boats isn't yours any more – isn't ours. They can do whatever they want with us.'

Edward held his hands out to Jesse in a placating gesture. 'Of course they can't. I'll sit on the board with the other members. And as part of the deal, I've acquired a small share in the Clovelly Fisheries. I'll have a say, like all the other members, and we can't be railroaded into anything.'

Jesse felt a well of emotion rise up in his throat. All his life he knew that his future lay with his dad on the boats. It had been his granddad's, then his dad's, and one day it was going to be his. Of course he wanted to see the world, but he always knew he'd come back for the boats one day. But now . . . now they belonged to the Clovellys.

'You've sold our birthright.'

This time, Edward was out of his chair again, his face almost purple with emotion. 'No, no! It's the opposite! I've *saved* your birthright. If things had carried on as before, there might have been precious little to leave you, and what would you have said about me then? I've done this for you, Jesse, for you and for your kids. I can't rely on Grant, can I? I have to do what I think is right for *you*.'

Father and son faced each other across the living room, their chests heaving with emotion. Edward rubbed his hands across his face.

'Listen, Jesse, this is the way to survive. We're bigger and better like this . . . believe me.'

Jesse slumped down in his chair, unable to look his father in the eye. 'What will happen to the business when you're gone?'

'Well, my share will go to you.' Edward hesitated. 'But

there is one way you can guarantee that the business will stay in the family . . .'

Jesse looked at his father, knowing exactly what he was going to say, but this time the words took on a whole new meaning.

9

December 1992

It was the Tuesday after Christmas and Truro was in the grip of the coldest winter in years.

'I'm gonna feel a right prat dressed up like a tailor's dummy.' Mickey was standing in the changing room of the gents' outfitters in just his boxer shorts and socks.

Jesse, in the cubicle next door, agreed. 'But it keeps the girls happy.'

'Aye,' sighed Mickey. 'You sure that's what you want, Jesse?' Jesse never talked of it, but anyone with an ear to listen and eyes to see couldn't but notice how much Edward Behenna had interfered in his son's life. Not for the first time, Mickey felt relief that his own father seemed to want only his son's happiness, rather than talk of dynasties and building the future.

Jesse didn't answer for a moment and Mickey heard only the rustling of clothing as Jesse undressed.

'I've got everything I've ever wanted,' Jesse replied flatly.

The dapper sales assistant returned with an armful of garments on hangers.

'Now then, sirs, here we are.' He passed over matching pinstriped trousers and tailcoats to the young men. 'If you'll just slip those on for size.'

After quite a lot of fitting and twirling, even Jesse and Mickey liked what they saw in the mirrors.

'Now have you thought about what collar you'll be wearing? Wing or regular? Of course it would depend on the neckwear – cravat or the traditional tie? Also, would you be wanting a handkerchief in the pocket or would that be too much if you are sporting a bloom in your buttonhole?'

What seemed like hours later, Jesse and Mickey emerged from the shop carrying their hired finery. 'Goodbye, gentlemen, and may I extend every good wish for the future.' The shop assistant smiled benignly and closed the door behind them, with a last admiring glance of their tightly muscled backs as he did so.

*

It was already dark outside and the Christmas lights swagged across the street were blinking merrily. Jesse and Mickey pushed open the door of the nearest pub. It smelled comfortingly of tobacco and beer, accumulated over many years. Large paper snowballs dangled from the ceiling, paper chains connecting them in a maze of loops. Only one other customer was in the bar and he was playing the fruit machine; a bored barmaid sat on a stool smoking. She stubbed out the cigarette and walked round behind the bar as Jesse and Mickey ordered two pints.

'I didn't know what to say when he asked if we were sporting a bloom in our buttonholes!' Jesse laughed as the two propped up the bar.

Mickey started sniggering. 'I didn't dare look at you. But 'e knows his stuff, though. You can't deny 'e's made a couple of silk purses out of our sow's ears.'

Jesse cupped his hands round his crotch. "E's not touching my sow's ears.'

Mickey grinned, then started mincing up and down the bar, imitating the salesman's melodious voice. 'Would sirs prefer a stiff or soft one? Tie that is . . .' as Jesse brushed away tears of laughter.

'Stop it, Mickey, you idiot!'

Jesse grabbed his pint and turned to see that the salesman had entered the pub; his face made it clear that he'd seen Mickey's imitation. Jesse and Mickey stood stock-still, horrified.

'I saw that you sirs had come for refreshment. I had forgotten to give you the receipt you will require for returning the suits. This is proof of your hire agreement.' He handed over the receipt to Mickey with dignity.

Mickey didn't know what to say, so he blurted out, 'Thanks and . . . well, thanks.'

'It's been my pleasure.'

The assistant turned to leave but Jesse stepped towards him. 'Can we buy you a drink?' he said quietly.

The assistant thought for a moment then looked at his watch. 'I shut the shop in twenty minutes, after which time, if you gentlemen are still here, I should love a drink. A large gin and tonic should suffice. My name, by the way, is Bill.'

It was one of the funniest evenings Mickey and Jesse had ever spent. Bill told them stories of his life as a tailor, and of his brief marriage to a girl he had truly loved – but not in the way that either of them had wanted.

'I have a son who I dote on, and he and his mother and I have an excellent relationship. I even helped to choose her dress when she remarried. A lovely man. Just like you two young gentlemen. He laughed at me behind my back, too, but I won him round.' Mickey and Jesse felt ashamed.

'I'm really sorry . . .'

'No need to apologise. I have grown a very thick skin. Now, tell me all about the young lady you are to marry. New Year's Eve, did you say?'

*

Greer's mother was having trouble getting the zip over the gathers of the waistband. She gave it a tug.

'Ow. That's my skin.'

'It's not bleeding. Now breathe in.'

She worked the zip all the way to the top.

'There now. Turn round and let me look at you . . . oh, you look like a princess.'

'Really? It feels a bit tight.'

'Where?'

'The waist, under the arms, round my boobs.'

'That's because you've only just had lunch. No supper tonight and it'll be fine.'

'I don't know . . .'

'Once your hair's up and you've got the white silk poinsettia in, your neck will look longer and you'll look taller.'

'Really?'

'Yes.' Loveday's mother turned towards Greer, who was standing next to her. 'Greer, you've chosen her a beautiful dress for the wedding.'

Greer smiled warmly at Loveday in her bridesmaid's dress. 'You look amazing. Peach is so the right colour for you.'

Loveday lifted her arms as far as the dress would allow

and hugged her best friend. 'Thank you, Greer. I'm so proud to be your bridesmaid.'

'Loveday, who else would I ask? Now, the hairdresser is coming at nine thirty tomorrow morning. You're first, while I have my make-up done, and then we'll swap. You've got to be at the church for one forty-five and wait for me to get there at two. I've told Jesse to be there before one thirty. I don't want him hanging around the Golden Hind with Mickey getting him drunk.'

*

Jesse was at home with his mum. She was ironing her best dress.

'What you thinkin' about, young Jesse?' She turned the dress half a circle on the board and continued with a good jet of steam.

'Nothing.'

Her mouth made a firm line. 'You can tell me.'

'Nothing, honest.'

'You're getting married tomorrow. No one thinks of nothing the night before they get married.'

Jesse shifted in his chair. His mind was racing with the thought of marrying Greer tomorrow. He was 21 years old and he was getting married. He wanted to run away, or get drunk, or both.

'Nothing, Mum.'

'If you're marrying the wrong girl then it's not too late to back out,' she said, concentrating on a difficult pleat. She had decided that she wouldn't be able to sleep soundly again if she didn't speak up. Jesse kept his feelings to himself but, as his mother, she saw more than most.

Jesse shut his eyes tight for a moment. 'Greer and I

will be a good team. Dad's happy, 'er dad's happy. Greer's happy.'

'And you're not.'

Jesse didn't answer. His mum scratched her throat, then resumed her ironing as she told him quietly, 'There'll always be a bed for you here.'

The door swung open, bringing with it the chill of a frosty night and the stamping of two sets of feet.

'Bloody 'ell, it's as cold as a witch's tit out there. 'Ello, Ma.' Grant Behenna stood in the small kitchen in the full uniform of a Royal Marine, proudly wearing his green beret.

His mum put the iron down and gasped. 'You got it. The beret. You're a commando?'

'Yes, Ma. Proud of me?'

She went to him and put her hands on his shoulders. 'Yes.'

'Hello, little brother.' Grant looked at Jesse. 'Ready like a lamb for the slaughter?'

Ed Behenna finished hanging his coat up on the pegs by the door and went to the kettle.

'Don't start on him. Commando or no, you're not too old for me to give you a good hiding.'

Grant smirked, 'Wanna take me on, do you, Dad? I'm trained to kill a man with my bare hands.'

Jan let go of her elder son and gave him a stern look. 'We don't want any more trouble, Grant. Promise me.'

He laughed and hugged her. 'Why would I give my old mum any trouble? I'm a changed man. I'm one of the Queen's élite soldiers now. I fight only for her and my country. No one else.' He looked over at Jesse. 'The condemned man's allowed a last drink, isn't he? Why don't I take my little brother down to the pub?'

Jesse had known his brother would be coming back for his wedding and there had been precious little he could do about it. You could hardly *not* invite your brother to your wedding, though he had resisted pressure from his mother to ask Grant to be his best man. Grant hadn't ever been a brother he could rely on; Mickey was his best man and that was that.

'Cheer up, little brother.' He attempted to grab Jesse in a headlock, which Jesse deftly sidestepped.

'Watch it, Grant,' he warned.

Grant laughed, a little too loudly. 'Just messing, little brother. I know you didn't want me to be your best man, but I'm over it! Let me look after you tonight.'

Jesse couldn't think of a worse person to spend his last night of freedom with, but he was struggling to say no in a way that wouldn't offend his mother, his brother – or both.

Ed was pouring boiling water into an old brown teapot. 'You'll stay in and have a cup of tea and an early night if you know what's good for you.'

Grant turned towards his dad with a familiar air of menace. 'You got what you wanted when you sold the poor beggar down the Swanee. It's the night before he gets married, 'is last happy night and I'm taking him for a drink. Any objections?'

Ed took a step towards Grant but Jan stood between them. 'One drink won't do no harm. Let them go, Ed.'

*

The Golden Hind was as welcoming as it had always been for the centuries of fishermen it had served. Grant was greeted with respect, but no warmth, as he shouldered his way through in his uniform.

He nodded at the familiar faces. People he'd grown up with, gone to school with – and fought with.

He stopped to chat with a group of them, forcing Jesse to go to the bar and pay for the drinks. A pint of Skinner's for Grant and a St Clement's for himself. He'd promised Greer he wouldn't drink tonight. He saw Mickey and Loveday sitting in a corner by the Ladies and made his way over to them. Mickey shook his hand and Loveday kissed him on the cheek. 'Didn't think you were allowed out tonight,' she smiled.

'Grant's home.' Jesse looked over his shoulder as he pulled up a low stool. 'He kind of insisted.'

'He looks smart in his uniform, don't 'e?' said Mickey.

'S'pose so.' Jesse took a sip of his St Clement's. 'Don't do nothing for me.'

'Or me,' agreed Loveday. 'When's 'e going back?'

'Dunno. He said he had a forty-eight-hour pass or something. Dad picked him up off the Plymouth train just now.'

They all sipped their drinks thoughtfully. Grant was unpredictable, especially when he'd had a drink. Jesse, already nervous, had an extra strand of anxiety plugged straight into his stomach.

Mickey broke the tension. 'Loveday had 'er final dress fitting tonight.'

'Did you?' asked Jesse, glad to talk of anything but Grant. 'What's it like?'

'Well I can't tell you, can I? It's unlucky.'

'I thought it was only the wedding dress that I wasn't supposed to know about.'

'You're not supposed to know about anything.'

'Oh, right.'

'Wait till you see us in our suits,' Mickey grinned, taking Loveday's hand. 'You won't be able to keep your hands off me.'

Loveday looked down at her drink and gave what passed for a smile. 'You always look good to me, Mickey boy.'

Mickey put his arm round her and squeezed her awkwardly; her shoulder crunched up into her ear.

'Ow.'

'So,' said Jesse, putting down his drink and trying to squash his desperation for a proper drink and the chance to swap places with Mickey, 'when are you two gonna get hitched?'

Before they could answer, Grant loomed over the threesome, a pint in one hand and a large whisky chaser in the other. His eyes were brighter than they had been half an hour ago, his cheeks flushed.

'Well 'ere 'e is. The little shit my brother's chosen to be 'is best man. Better than 'is own brother. Let me buy you a drink.'

'We're all right, thanks,' Mickey told him in a flat tone. 'We were just going to make a move. Big day tomorrow, and all that. Want to be fresh.'

Grant's eyes wandered to Loveday's generous cleavage. 'There's only one person I want to get fresh with, and it isn't you, Mickey boy.' He sat down unsteadily next to Loveday. 'Got a boyfriend at the moment, Loveday?'

'Mickey,' she said quickly, taking Mickey's hand.

'Mickey? Mickey Mouse 'ere? You need a man not a mouse.' He swallowed the remains of his pint then downed the whisky chaser. He took her free hand and placed it under the table onto the front of his trousers. 'That's what a man feels like.' He held her hand against him; his grip was brutal and she couldn't pull away.

'Oi!' Mickey yelled, standing up and squaring up to Grant. 'Get your filthy hands off my girlfriend.'

'Oooh, little mousey's got a little squeak.' He leered over at Mickey.

'Let her go, Grant,' Jesse ordered, putting himself between Grant and Mickey.

'Get me another pint and a chaser and I'll let her go. But I think she likes it.' He squeezed Loveday's hand more tightly against him. 'Don't you, Loveday?'

Loveday's face was white with fear and disgust. She glanced up in mute distress at her friends. She was terrified of Grant, but petrified too at the thought of either of them getting into a fight with him.

Mickey lunged towards Grant, his face contorted in anger, while Grant threw his head back and laughed cruelly.

'Well, well, little mousey's gonna have a go with a commando? That's the funniest thing I've ever seen – little Mickey Mouse!'

With a momentous effort, Loveday managed to yank her hand away and hurl herself away from Grant. She moved quickly to Mickey's side, desperate to get him away. 'Come on, love,' she barely managed to whisper. Her voice was shaking. ''Bout time we was leaving.'

*

Jesse walked out of the pub with Mickey and Loveday, leaving his troublesome brother to tell anyone who would listen how hard it was to win a green beret. Jesse had rarely seen Mickey so fired up, but he gradually seemed to be calming down as they left the source of his fury behind.

Jesse couldn't face his parents' anxious faces if he went home without Grant, so he'd left Mickey and Loveday with promises of seeing them tomorrow, and now found himself walking towards St Peter's Church. It was the church where all the Behennas, going back three hundred years, had been married, baptised and buried.

He didn't give his usual salute to his granddad lying in the churchyard. His thoughts were absorbed by the life mapped out before him. Husband to Greer, a father, the boss of 'Behenna and Clovelly'. What had happened to his dreams? Had he ever been allowed to have any? That night when his father had told him about the merger with Clovelly, he had pushed him to marry Greer.

'She's a lovely girl. You'll want for nothing. You'll be the boss of the biggest fishing fleet and fishmongery business this side of Plymouth.'

Jesse had resisted, thinking of his feelings for Loveday and his dreams of travelling the world.

'Loveday's all right but she's got no prospects,' his father had reminded him. 'You're better than that.'

Jesse hated himself for being persuaded and, for a while, had been blinded by the riches that Greer's father had told him he would earn. And it had been easy to start a relationship with Greer. She was mad about him. She looked good. She was an heiress. The thing was, he did fancy Greer and she adored him. She was elegant and cultured; they looked good together and turned heads in Trevay. They'd become a couple.

It pained him to see Loveday. Jesse thought he had resigned himself to being with Greer and to pushing all thoughts of Loveday from his mind, but the more he tried, the more she intruded on his thoughts. Loveday would come to him in dreams, her tumbling red hair flowing over her milky-white breasts, asking Jesse, 'What are you in the mood for?' and Jesse would wake, remembering Greer and the expectations forced on him.

His engagement to Greer was a *fait accompli*. Once they'd become an item, whispers of weddings seemed to follow him everywhere. Greer dropped subtle hints, flicking through the pages of *Bride* magazine while his father urged him on. 'No time like the present, boy.'

On his twenty-first birthday, his father had handed him a wad of cash and told him he was promoted to second mate.

'Enough money there for a ring, boy,' he'd told Jesse, who had taken the money but felt like he'd sold his dreams.

The engagement had been the talk of the town. Both sets of parents had thrown a big party at the golf club, and Greer had revelled in the attention, wearing a stunning new outfit by Bruce Oldfield that she had bought in Debenhams on a special trip back to Guildford. Greer preened, showing off the diamond solitaire that Jesse could never have afforded before Behenna and Clovelly had merged. Jesse remembered little of the event, except for the strain of trying to avoid Loveday, and the sadness that he thought he saw reflected when they caught each other's eye.

Shortly after the engagement, Loveday and Mickey started to go out with each other. That had hurt Jesse, even though he had no reason to expect anything different, and he struggled to keep on top of his jealousy. To compensate he became ever more attentive to Greer, which only served to make Loveday ever more attentive towards Mickey.

He'd once asked Mickey, when they'd both been drinking,

what Loveday was like in bed. Mickey told him. That hurt too. Mickey asked what Greer was like. Jesse said that a gentleman never tells. The truth was that there was nothing to tell. Greer had never let him get further than a snog and a hand in her shirt. Her breasts felt small and pert. Nothing like the way he imagined Loveday's felt.

He'd left the church behind him and was now up at the sheds. A northerly wind was blowing and it rattled the tarpaulins tied to the boats lying against the far edge of the yard. Jesse turned his face from the wind and pulled up the collar of his parka. He wanted to be alone for a while. He fished in a pocket for his key ring and found his key to the Behenna's Boats shed.

Inside, whilst not exactly warm, it was at least windproof. He went into the small makeshift office made of plywood that he and his dad had built a few summers ago. He switched a light on and found his father's bottle of Scotch. He pulled the cork and took a sip. The burning in his throat felt good. He took another sip before hearing the creak of the outside door opening.

10

'Is that you, Mickey?' Jesse called out tentatively. He peered round the office door and nearly choked on his whisky.

'Hello,' said Loveday in a quiet voice. 'I just wanted to see you, you know, make sure you were all right an' that.'

'I'm fine.' He stood and wiped his suddenly sweating hands on his jeans. 'Do you want a drink?' He watched her as she closed the main door. The sound of the flapping tarpaulins in the yard was instantly silenced.

''Tis windy outside,' she said. 'And ever so cold.'

'I can make you tea? No milk, though. That would warm you up.'

'What are you drinking?'

Jesse looked sheepish. 'Me dad's whisky.'

'I'll 'ave one of those then.'

'Right.' Jesse found a cleanish mug and poured her a decent measure. She had walked closer to him now. 'Come in and make yourself comfortable. My dad's chair is the best.' He pointed at an ageing armchair.

'Lovely. Thanks,' said Loveday, taking the drink he handed her and settling herself. 'I thought you might be up 'ere. Are you nervous about tomorrow? Mickey's like a flea on a trampoline about his speech.'

'Is he?' smiled Jesse, plonking himself on the only

other seat, the part-time accounts secretary's swivel chair. 'He won't tell me nothing about what he's going to say.'

'He's told me some of it. It's good. Nothing too embarrassing. He doesn't want to upset Greer's family, them being so proper an' all.' She raised her mug. 'So, cheers then. 'Ere's to you and Greer.'

'Cheers,' said Jesse, and they both drank.

'Is your dress all right then?' asked Jesse.

'No.'

'What's wrong with it?'

'Everything.' Loveday began to laugh. 'It's truly 'orrible. Greer calls it peach but it's more like orange – not my kind of colour at all. It makes me look like a really fat milkmaid and I can't move my arms in it.'

Jesse frowned. 'Have you told Greer?'

Loveday waved a hand airily. 'Oh, well, it's Greer's day and it's what she wants. I can't tell her I hate it, can I?'

'I bet you look lovely in it, really.'

'No, really I don't. I mean, my mum likes it and Mickey will like it because he likes whatever I wear but . . .' She looked down at her drink, the smile gone. 'I look awful in it and I feel awful in it and I know what people will be saying behind my back.' Jesse heard the catch in her voice.

'Hey.' He leant forward and looked up into her eyes. 'I'll punch anybody who says you don't look beautiful. You always look beautiful to me.'

She wiped a burgeoning tear away and tried a smile. 'Shut up, you idiot.'

Jesse tilted back into his chair. 'I'm a bit nervous too.'

'Whatever for?'

'Well, getting married is a big step.'

'But you and Greer are made for each other.' She looked at him carefully. 'Aren't you?'

'Oh, yes, of course we are. She's great you know, we're mates. Known each other for ever, almost as long as I've known Mickey, and you.'

'I used to have a crush on you when I was little.' The whisky had gone to her head.

Jesse laughed. 'I know.'

Loveday stuck her tongue out at him. 'Don't laugh! 'Twas awful. All you ever did was go off with Mickey and play football.'

'What did you want me to do?'

'Play with me.'

'And do what? Talk about Barbie and work on dance routines?'

'You're a shit dancer, Behenna.'

'So are you.'

She stuck her leg out and kicked his shin. ''Ow dare you! I was disco champion one Christmas at school.'

'The boys voted for you because your bottom wobbled so nicely in your costume.'

She gave him another kick in the shins. 'Got any more of that whisky?'

Jesse reached for the bottle and poured each of them a generous slug.

'D'you remember the school poetry competition?' said Loveday. 'The one when Greer wrote that soppy thing about the universe and the animals.'

Jesse started to giggle. 'I didn't understand a single bleddy word.'

'Her face when she was up there reading it.' Loveday

put on a holier-than-thou expression. 'All serious like and putting on a posh voice.'

'She won, though,' said Jesse loyally.

'Yeah, but only because the bleddy teachers didn't understand it either. They only gave her first prize 'cos they couldn't face her mother complaining.'

''Er mum's all right, really,' Jesse said.

'Yeah. Course she is,' Loveday added quickly. She hadn't meant to be so mean about her friend. She blamed it on the whisky and being made to wear a dress that looked horrid.

'No . . . it's just that, well, that's my new family we're laughing about.'

They sat in silence, absorbing this reality.

Loveday moved to stand up. 'Well, I only came to see if you were all right, that's all, and you look fine to me.'

Jesse put his hand up and stopped her. 'Don't go. I like you being here.'

Loveday touched his blond hair and stroked it. 'Do you?'

'Yes.'

Loveday sat down slowly. 'How nervous are you about tomorrow?'

Jesse stretched up, leaned back and blew a long breath out of his mouth. 'To be honest, I'm shit scared. Am I doing the right thing, Loveday?'

'Course you are, Jesse.' She gave him a reassuring smile. 'You're marrying Greer. How can that be wrong? You're going to be part of a new company. You'll make money and drive a flash car and have holidays in Spain. Of course you're doing the right thing.'

'Then why does it feel so wrong?'

'What are you talking about?'

'It feels wrong. I'm only twenty-one and I'm not sure if I want to marry anyone . . . not just Greer. It's not her fault.' He stuck the heels of his hands over his eyes and almost soundlessly said, 'The truth is I'm scared.'

Loveday came off her chair and knelt in front of Jesse. 'Scared of what, darlin'?'

'Just plain scared.'

She hesitated, then put her arms round him and rocked him soothingly. 'It's all right, darlin'. I'm here. What you're feeling is normal for a bloke. Getting married is a big day, but that's all it is. A big day, then everything gets back to normal. You'll go on your honeymoon and when you get back we'll all still be here. Just the same. Nothing changed.'

'That's what makes it so frightening. Nothing will have changed and nothing will change till the day I die. Trevay, the boats, my family, you and Mickey. All the same. I'm stuck.'

'What nonsense is this? You're not stuck. You'll have money to go anywhere in the world, do anything you want.'

'With Greer and her money.'

'With your wife and your money.'

He took his hands from his eyes and looked desperately at Loveday. 'I've made a mistake. I'm . . . I'm marrying the wrong person.'

Loveday let go of him and sat back on her heels. The wind had picked up again and the sound of the wires on the masts of the boats in the harbour travelled up the lane, past St Peter's, and now swirled through the crack in the door of the Behenna shed. 'What are you talking about?'

'I should never have let Dad persuade me.' He looked at her in desperation. 'It's you, Loveday.'

He had crossed the Rubicon. The words were spoken. The truth was told. Loveday's heart was hammering in her chest. She felt faint and a bit sick.

'Me?'

He nodded.

Outside the first flurry of snow twisted in the wind. Inside she leant forward and kissed him.

*

'What are we going to do?' Loveday was lying on the makeshift blanket of Jesse's parka.

'We could do it again.' He traced the soft dough of her stomach from her belly button to her breasts. She shut her eyes to enjoy the pleasure of him squeezing her nipples and taking each in turn into his mouth and sucking gently on them.

'I mean about Mickey and Greer.'

He took his lips from her sweet breast and moved up her body to look into her eyes.

'I don't know.'

'I don't want to hurt Mickey.'

'Kiss me.'

'I don't want to hurt Greer.'

'Kiss me.'

His kiss was gentle and she couldn't help but kiss him back. Gently they made love again.

Outside the wind caught hold of something and the bang woke Loveday.

'Oh my God. Look at the time.' Loveday was holding her watch. 'We've been here for ages.'

Jesse, curled round her hips and thighs, woke groggily. 'Shit.'

The almost empty bottle of whisky, regarding them from the top of the dusty metal desk, stood as the sole witness to their crime.

They dressed in near silence, passing each other a stray sock or lost shoe.

Together they left the shed. It had been snowing and a small drift had built along the bottom edge of the door. Jesse struggled to push the door shut, leaning his full weight against it to fit the padlock in the hasp and lock it.

Finally it was done and, putting their arms around each other, they walked out of the yard, down the lane, past the church and on to their homes and their beds.

Watching them go, bivouacked between the hulls of two clinker boats, was Grant. He'd followed Loveday when she had slipped out of her house after Mickey had dropped her off. He had had ideas of his own about what he and she could get up to that night. When she'd headed towards the sheds it had seemed to him almost as if she wanted him to follow her. Then he'd seen that the door was already unlocked and that his shitty little brother, the golden son, was already there. He'd watched them then and he watched them now. This was a little treasure hoard that had fallen into his lap. He'd spend it wisely.

11

'It's still snowing.' Jesse's mother clattered the wooden curtain rings into each other as she ruthlessly ripped open his curtains. 'Rise and shine, young man. You're getting married today.'

Jesse clenched his eyes tightly as the blistering daylight lasered its way around his childhood bedroom.

'There's a cup of tea by your bed. By the smell in here you'll need it. Your brother's fault, I suppose.'

The memory of Loveday's softly yielding body erupted in his mind. What had Grant got to do with last night?

'Why ever did you both stay out so late?' He could picture his mother standing with her hands on her hips, frowning down at him. He gingerly lifted one eyelid and saw that he was right. 'You're a bloody idiot, Jesse. You'll look terrible in the photos, and what's Greer and your new in-laws going to think about a groom stinking of booze?' Jan sat down on the edge of the bed and the bounce made him feel sick. She put a cool hand on his forehead. 'You need a fry-up and some aspirin and you'll be fine.' She stood up, and again the movement of the mattress brought on nausea. 'This is the most important day of your life, Jesse, and I'm not going to let you let yourself down. Get showered and I'll put some sausages on.'

*

131

Greer sat up in her four-poster bed and looked around her beautiful bedroom. This was the last morning she'd ever wake up as a single woman. She closed her eyes and imagined, for the millionth time, the look on Jesse's face as he turned from the altar and watched her walking up the aisle, towards him. She was going to be the most beautiful bride Cornwall had ever seen. She looked to her left, at the oyster satin bag draped on a softly padded and pearl-beaded hanger on the door of her French armoire. Inside was the perfect dress. Not the flouncy meringue so many of her friends had chosen for their weddings. Hers was a chic column of finest silk satin, cut on the bias so that it fell narrowly at her ankles and then puddled into the perfect train. She sighed with pleasure and wriggled back under her lavender-scented sheets. It was only seven thirty and she had plenty of time to enjoy the most special day of her life.

There was a soft knock at the door. 'Come in,' she called.

Her mother nudged the door open with an elbow and came in carrying a breakfast tray with orange juice, coffee and a croissant. She'd put confetti on the tray.

As soon as she saw Greer, tears sprang from her eyes. 'Oh, my darling daughter. I can't believe this is your wedding day.' She put the tray on the blanket box at the foot of the bed and helped Greer to sit up whilst plumping her pillows for her. 'Comfortable?'

'Thanks, Mum.'

With the tray settled securely on Greer's lap, her mother went to the window. 'There's a little bit of magic to add to the day, my darling.' She pulled the cord and the curtains swept open, like in an Odeon cinema, to reveal the scene behind. Greer was expecting to see the familiar view of

Trevay and its harbour, with maybe a wedding helicopter on the front lawn. But it was better than that. Trevay had transformed itself into a snow-covered fairy kingdom.

'I ordered it, just for you,' said her mother.

*

Mickey Chandler had been up with the lark and was polishing his best brown shoes on the kitchen table.

'How's your speech?' asked his mother. She skirted awkwardly round his pulled-out chair as she negotiated the small room from larder to oven.

'I think it's all right.' He spat on a toecap and rubbed vigorously with a balding yellow duster.

'What does Loveday think?'

'She laughed in all the right places.'

Mrs Chandler cracked an egg into her gnarled frying pan. 'Well, that's a good sign, innit? Two eggs or three?'

Mickey thought for a moment. 'Three. I'll need something to drink on later. Is there any bacon?'

'Of course. Can't 'ave egg without it.'

'Cheers, Ma.' He leant back in his chair and puckered his lips for a kiss. She wiped her eggy fingers on her apron and obliged. 'You're a good lad.'

Mr Chandler ducked his head as he came through the low doorway from upstairs. 'Mornin', son. 'Ow's the best man today?'

'Bit nervous,' said Mickey as he picked up his second shoe and spat on that one as well.

'Nervous? What the 'ell have you got to be nervous for? 'Tis bleddy Jesse who should be nervous. Marrying that girl and that family. His dad has sold him down the river.'

Mrs Chandler clunked two old blue and white china plates down in front of Mickey and her husband. 'Now stop saying stuff like that. Jesse ain't no fool and he knows which side his bread is buttered. He'll be a very wealthy man. Two eggs or three?'

'Three.' Mr Chandler gave Mickey an astute look. 'You got the better girl and no mistake, son. I'd have Loveday Carter over Greer Clovelly any day.'

*

Loveday looked in her dressing-table mirror and groaned. On the side of her face, in the dip between her nose and her cheeks, was the largest spot she'd ever had. There was no head yet but it was hot and hard and she knew that as soon as she entered the church it would force its way to the surface of her skin in all its pus and glory, ready to take centre stage in the photographs. Greer would be furious.

'Fuck.' She put her head in her hands. It was the least of her problems. Greer was going to be furious anyway. As soon as Jesse told her what happened last night, there would be no photographs.

The memory of Jesse's loving words washed away the horror of the spot and filled her with a dreadful happiness. Greer and Mickey would be hurt, that was only to be expected, but they'd come round in time, hopefully. They were old friends. They would understand that it would have been a big mistake for Jesse and Greer to marry. It was always going to be Jesse and Loveday.

She looked at her bedside clock. She wondered if Jesse was awake yet. Had he been able to sleep? She'd slept for no more than a couple of hours. The combination of whisky and wonderment had kept her thoughts racing. She hoped he'd still be sleeping. He needed all the sleep he could get. Today of all days. He'd have to go round to see Greer. Explain before it got too late to let the guests know there wasn't going to be a wedding. Then he'd phone her; or maybe come and see her. Either way, she couldn't wait to be with him again.

*

'Whatever did you get Jesse drunk for?' Jan looked at her elder son with frustration and latent anger. 'You knew he had to get home early and get some sleep. Where did you two go?'

Grant looked at Jesse sitting at the other end of the table. He didn't look good. Grant had heard him throwing up under the sound of the running shower. Jesse had thought no one would hear him if he kept the shower running, but Grant had heard him. Grant knew all Jesse's sordid little secrets.

'Don't know what you're talking about, Mum. Jesse left the Hind before I did.'

Jesse looked up from his dry toast and Grant was pleased to see panic in his eyes. 'Where did you get to, little brother?'

Jesse looked at his mother and then pleadingly back at Grant, who toyed with him like a cat with a vole. 'Shall I tell our mummy what you were up to last night?'

If it were possible, Jesse grew a shade paler. His mind was in overdrive. Grant couldn't know that he had been at the sheds with Loveday. *Could he?* No. It wasn't possible. His hungover brain tried to think of an answer that would satisfy his mother's curiosity. 'I . . . I was wi—'

'It's all right, little bro.' Grant spoke over him. 'I'll explain.' Grant turned to his mother. 'He was up the sheds, drinking Dad's whisky with . . .' Grant threw a glance at Jesse's petrified face. '. . . With me. I'm sorry. I led him astray. I confess.'

Jan folded her arms and looked at her two sons as if they were no more than eight year-olds. 'I knew it. You're a pair of idiots. Grant, I can understand, but you, Jesse, I thought you had more sense. Neither of you have the brains you were born with . . . Where're you off to, Jesse Behenna?' Jesse felt the room reeling, the rancid whisky making its way up his throat. He dashed for the bathroom and made it just in time.

*

What the hell was he going to do? He rinsed his face and cleaned his teeth, then began the arduous task of shaving. His hands weren't his own. They belonged to someone who had the shakes. He nicked the bit of skin under his nose and it started to bleed and sting. He tore off a bit of loo paper and, spitting on it, stuck it on the cut. Greer wouldn't like that. She wanted him tall and strong and handsome. No blemishes or shaving nicks. He'd have to tell her. He'd phone her now. He heard the front door open and his auntie Gwen's voice calling out to his mum. The phone was there. By the front door. Everyone would hear him tell Greer that he was very sorry but he wasn't marrying her after all. He couldn't ring her. He'd have to walk up the hill and tell her. Like a man. In front of her mum and dad. How do you say something like that? 'I'm so sorry, Mr and Mrs Clovelly, but I can't marry Greer. I slept with Loveday last night. Up at the sheds.'

That was the truth, but he couldn't put it like that. How about, 'Greer, you're a wonderful girl and I've always liked you, but I can't marry you because I don't love you.'

Her father would punch him. That would hurt. He rinsed the shaving foam from his face and patted his cheeks dry. Using the mirror, he peeled off the drying loo paper and found the cut had stopped bleeding. He splashed a good deal of Paco Rabanne aftershave on his palms and slapped it on his face. The stinging made his bloodshot eyes water even more.

In his pain he heard the front door open once more and his mother call up the stairs. 'Jesse. Your best man's here. I'm sending him up to get you ready.'

*

Loveday looked at the now-redundant but still horrible, orange bridesmaid dress hanging on the back of her bedroom door. Why had she told Greer she liked it? Why had Greer chosen it for her? It hid every good feature of hers; made Loveday feel utterly frumpy and unsexy. She still hadn't been allowed to see The Wedding Dress. That was Top Secret. Loveday had more than a suspicion that it was nothing like the marmalade horror. But, she realised suddenly, she wasn't going to have to wear it after all. When she married Jesse, she'd make Greer wear a horrible dress. She laughed at the thought, then checked her bedside clock again. She'd hear from Jesse soon. He'd come round to get her after he had explained everything to Greer and her family. Perhaps they would go away for a few days until the dust settled. That would probably be best.

She heard a heavy knock on the front door. This was

him, it was Jesse! She ran out of her room, taking the stairs on the narrow staircase two at a time. Her mother got there a split second ahead of her and opened the door, revealing Greer's father. She stood a little way behind her mother. Mr Clovelly had obviously come to tell them the wedding was off. But he looked quite relaxed about it. He was kissing Loveday's mum and smiling.

He saw Loveday, breathless and expectant and said, 'Morning, Loveday. You look as excited as Greer! She's so thrilled with this snow. Are you ready? I'll take you up the hill in the BMW. Apparently the hairdresser is stuck over at St Agnes, but her mother's boyfriend has a Land Rover so he'll get her over here as soon as he's done the milking.' Loveday stood stock-still, barely able to take all this in. Where was Jesse? Why was everything still going ahead? Surely he'd say something before it was too late?

'Come on then, Loveday,' chided her mother. 'Get your dress bag and shoes. And don't forget the silk poinsettia for your hair.'

*

Mickey was preening himself in the mirrored wardrobe door of Jesse's room. 'I look all right in this, don't I? Loveday won't be able to keep her hands off me.'

Jesse was fumbling with the buttons of his shirt. His heart was beating way too fast and his breathing was more like a pant. Mickey turned away from his own reflection to look at Jesse. 'You'm real nervous, eh, boy? You shouldn't have had a skinful with Grant last night. Bad move.'

'I'm not doing this right.' Jesse looked at Mickey, trying to find the words. 'I am not doing the right thing.'

'I tell 'e you're not. You're doing those buttons up all wrong. Let me do them for you.' Jesse stood shaky but compliant as Mickey did up his shirt buttons, fixed his collar, got him into his pinstriped trousers and pinned the cravat. 'We'll put our tailcoats on at the church. Don't want to crease them.'

Jan came in with two mugs of tea. 'Don't you boys look smart?' She gave each of them a once-over, straightening their cravats. 'You're as white as a ghost still, Jesse. Get this tea down you. Mickey, you look after him at the altar and make sure he don't faint.'

'I need to speak to Greer,' said Jesse. 'I must go and see her.'

His mother laughed. 'You'll be seeing plenty of her after the wedding. You'll see her every day for the rest of your life.'

Jesse was desperate, his voice catching. 'I have things I need to talk to her about. It'll be too late if I don't go now.'

'You're staying here, even if I have to get Grant to hold you down.' His mother took his hand. ''Tis nerves, that's all.' She turned to Mickey. 'Come on, Best Man. What does it say in the book about nervous grooms?'

Before Mickey could think of an answer, the bedroom door was thrown open and Grant stood in the doorway in full uniform. He saluted the groom and said: 'Escort Party for Mr Jesse Behenna ready and waiting. It is the brother of the groom's duty to get a hair of the dog down his neck before he bottles it. And a Marine always does his duty.'

The little party of Grant, Mickey and Jesse prepared to leave the house. Mickey and Jesse had their tailcoats safely in protective bags to put on at the last minute. A light flurry of snow danced through the air; Jesse reached for his parka. The scent of Loveday clung to it and he immediately visualised her lying on it as he made love to her. It took all his willpower not to bury his face in it and drink her in once more. Then he saw it. On the lining by the fishtail back was the unmistakable stain of their passion, and it was red with blood.

12

Greer looked wonderful. Her hair had grown in the last six months and was styled into a glossy 1920s bob. Her make-up was natural and glowing, her dress exquisite. Her high pert bust, nipped-in waist and slender bottom were celebrated and worshipped by it. Greer was a vision of serenity and fulfilment.

Loveday, on the other hand, was not. She was having her hair pulled and backcombed by the hairdresser's sister who had come to lend a hand, seeing as the snow had made them almost two hours late. The blowdry had left Loveday's face scarlet. Her make-up lay thick on her young skin and she could feel her spot fighting vigorously to break its way through the crowd of concealer, foundation and powder. She felt sick, hungover and horribly emotional. Where was Jesse? Tears threatened yet again and she reached forward to grab a tissue from the box in front her.

'Feeling sweaty, are you?' asked the hated hairdresser, yanking the hair on the back of her neck and pinning to her head, with unnecessary ferocity, the ghastly silk poinsettia.

A tear fled down Loveday's face and she mopped it quickly with the tissue. 'No.'

'You're feeling very hot. Crying always gets me hot too.'

'I'm not crying.'

'Are you crying, Loveday?' asked Greer, looking like a cool breeze in front of her French cheval mirror.

'No.'

'Ah, Loveday, you're such a softie. It is emotional watching your best friend get married to the boy of her dreams, but don't cry off all that make-up. You'll have that spot popping up again.'

'I'm not crying.' Loveday brushed the vestige of another tear away.

'I know what will make you smile. Look at this.'

Loveday watched in the mirror's reflection as Greer opened a satin drawstring bag and took out a delicate garter made of gauze and swan's-down with tiny glittering crystals. The two hairdressers gasped in wonder, their mouths forming perfect Os.

'That's beautiful, that is,' said the older one. 'Put it on.'

Loveday watched as Greer shucked off her bridal slippers and pointed one perfect ballerina foot inside the garter. Then her slender, manicured fingers teased it up over her calf and her knee. Finally it whispered to a halt and lay perfectly in the middle of her slender thigh. It clung just below the lacy top of her sheer ivory stockings.

'My God, that'll drive Jesse Behenna mad,' screeched the hairdresser, grinning.

Greer let the satin folds of her dress fall perfectly back to the floor and smiled a secretive smile.

Loveday was being given the last squirt of hairspray and looked at herself in the mirror. Her natural curls had been tortured into a regiment of ringlets. Her young, open face was now made hard with darkened eyebrows and peach lipstick. Her throat and chest were covered in nerve-induced red blotches and the hated dress was digging into her. Where on earth was Jesse? Why hadn't he come?

*

Jesse was being helped up the snowy lane towards St Peter's. The lads in the Golden Hind had given him more than a hair of the dog. He'd had the entire pelt.

'Come on, little bro,' said Grant, pulling him up the lane. 'Your destiny awaits.'

'I don't wanta get married today,' he slurred, trying to pull away from them both. 'I can't.'

'Don't be silly,' Mickey said firmly, taking Jesse's weight as he slid on an icy cobble. He looked over at Grant on the other side. 'You shouldn't have let 'im drink so much.'

Grant laughed unpleasantly. 'He'll be all right. He's only getting married. It's nothing serious, is it?'

'But Greer's going to kill me. I'm the best man. I'm supposed to be looking after him.'

'And I'm helping you, aren't I?'

*

The Reverend Rowena Davies was immensely under-standing and compassionate. She had been an army chaplain and knew the frailties of men. She sat Jesse down on a rickety wooden ladder-backed chair and unlocked the vestry cupboard that was used by the mothers' and toddlers' group, raiding their refreshments shelf.

'There's a biscuit tin,' she said in triumph. 'Please God, let it not be empty.' Her prayer was answered. 'Oh dear.

Ginger nuts. Still, needs must. Sit down here, Jesse, and eat these. We've got about twenty minutes to get you shipshape.'

From under a curtained shelf she then produced a kettle and a jar of instant coffee. 'Only black, I'm afraid. No milk but there's sugar. Make him a strong one, Mickey. Plenty of sugar. I'm going to nip out front and greet any early-comers.'

Mickey could have kissed her. 'Thanks, Vicar.'

'All in a day's work. See you shortly.'

*

Jesse drank the coffee, ate the biscuits and swallowed a couple of pills that Grant had in his pocket. 'They give us commandos these when we're on ops. Keeps us alert.'

'Speed?' asked Mickey, shocked.

Grant tapped the side of his nose. 'No name no pack drill.'

Whatever it was that Grant had given him, Jesse began to feel a little less drunk and a little more alert very quickly. Grant crouched over him, hands on his uniformed knees, and examined his brother's face. 'You're coming back to us, Jesse boy, you're coming back.'

'Grant, I . . .' Jesse started to speak.

'Now don't do nothing stupid. We're going to walk into the church now and you and Mickey are going to look happy and sober. Got it? You're taking one for the team, ain't you now, boy? Can't let Daddy down.'

Terror gripped Jesse's heart again, but he nodded. 'How long have we got?'

Mickey checked his watch. 'About five minutes if she's on time.'

Edward Behenna burst into the vestry. 'What the hell's going on?' He took one look at Jesse, who felt his resolve stiffen. He gulped back some more of the coffee and shook himself. He knew what he had to do.

*

Loveday had been brought to the church in one of Greer's cousin's cars. She was finding it hard to absorb what was actually going on around her. She found herself squashed into the back seat of an ancient Hillman Imp, with the cousin's husband driving gingerly over the compacted snow and the cousin twisting round in the front seat to talk nonstop at her. At least she left no space for replies. Loveday's brain was left to wonder how on earth Jesse was going to stop this wedding.

The Hillman Imp couldn't make it up the lane to the church, so Loveday struggled over the front tip-up seat and out into the snow. It was cold but at least it had stopped snowing. Her pinching satin slippers might as well have been made from blotting paper as she trudged on up the road, the sound of the bells pealing in her ears, the cousin yakking by her side.

*

'You look beautiful.' Bryn Clovelly stood in awe as his only daughter stepped from her bedroom and stood in front of him. 'Give us a twirl.'

Greer obliged. 'Will I do, Daddy?'

'My darling, you'd do for a prince, never mind Jesse Behenna.'

They were alone in the house. Greer's mother had

already left with her brother, Uncle Alan, and his wife, Auntie Lou, with a handbag stuffed full of tissues.

'You do like Jesse, don't you, Daddy? You do think he is going to be a good husband?' Greer felt suddenly nervous that maybe her father didn't want her to marry Jesse.

The truth was that Bryn was delighted at the thought of the merger with the Behenna fishing fleet, and about all the money they were going to make now that the two families were one. A small gust of guilt hit him. Was this really the right thing to do?

'I'll marmalise him if he hurts you.' Greer's innocent smile of relief made him pity her, so he added, 'But he won't.'

There was the honk of a car horn outside.

'Your carriage awaits, my lady.' Smiling, Bryn proffered his arm. Greer slipped her hand through the crook of his elbow and took a deep breath. 'Ready?'

*

The 1955 cream Bentley with its wedding ribbons drew lots of attention. Its slowly negotiating the snow on the road down to Trevay meant that the locals could get a good look at Greer Clovelly on her way to marry Jesse Behenna. Greer made the most of it, smiling and offering little waves to the children through the big glass windows. She felt like a princess. At the bottom of the lane to the church, the Bentley stopped. The driver in his dove-grey peaked cap turned and said to Bryn, 'I'll 'ave to let 'e out 'ere. She'll never make it up to the church.'

Greer looked horrified. 'I can't walk up. My dress will be ruined.'

'I thought this might happen, so I've organised a little help,' smiled Bryn. 'Look over there.' He pointed towards the harbour. Sitting on the wall were two of the Trevay lifeboat crew in yellow wellies and thick navy wool jumpers. One was the coxswain, the other a strapping younger crewman. They got off the wall and came towards the car.

Bryn stepped out and shook their hands. 'Morning, lads. This is very good of you.'

The coxswain of the lifeboat, a wily old seaman who'd seen just about anything there was to see in life said, 'Our pleasure, Mr Clovelly. Can't 'ave this beautiful maid getting 'er feet wet, can we?'

Bryn walked to the other side of the car and opened Greer's door. The young lifeboat man stepped forward and smiled an appreciative smile at Greer. 'You look lovely,' he said, before sliding one strong arm under her bottom and the other around her back. He lifted her easily out of the car and began the short climb up the lane towards St Peter's.

At the church door, a damp-footed and shivering Loveday watched Greer draped in the arms of the hand-some Stevie (everyone at school had fancied him), looking for all the world like a bloody poster for *An Officer and a Gentleman*. Loveday felt trapped in a nightmare that she wasn't about to wake up from any time soon. She hadn't seen Jesse or Mickey, but the Reverend Rowena had whispered something about having to sober the groom up, which had sent Loveday's brain into meltdown. Was Jesse going to leave it right till the last moment to drunkenly jilt Greer in front of everyone? This was not how it should be. Loveday's feet grew colder and wetter.

Greer was now two paces away from Loveday and

smiling happily in the arms of the handsome Stevie. 'Isn't this romantic, Loveday?'

The wedding photographer took a couple of shots of Greer in Stevie's arms before Stevie put Greer down gently inside the church porch, which was more or less dry.

Loveday tried a bright smile, but inside her thoughts were tumbling around; a terrible confusion of guilt and fear and an over-riding yearning for Jesse to come and sort everything out. Knowing that this radiant bride was about to have her bubble burst tore at her insides. Still, better now than a few months down the line when a messy divorce would be on the cards. 'You look wonderful, Greer.'

'Would you sort my veil out for me?' Greer asked her.

'Sure.' With hands that were shaking from cold and apprehension, Loveday lifted the froth of soft tulle over Greer's face.

'Daddy,' called Greer.

'Just coming, my love.' Bryn replied, palming fifty pounds to the coxswain and saying *sotto voce*, 'Cheers, mate.'

'Come on, Loveday. Stand behind me and Daddy and let's go. I can't wait to see Jesse's face when he sees me.' Greer watched as Loveday got into position and then she took her father's arm. The church bells had stopped pealing and there was a moment's silence before the organ struck up Mendelssohn's 'Wedding March'.

*

Jesse's heart was hammering in his throat. He felt dizzy. Mickey touched his arm. 'You OK?'

The organ's swelling notes were increasing the panic he felt. He started breathing loudly through his mouth.

'Here she comes,' nudged Mickey. 'Look at 'er.'

Jesse held the back of his pew for support as he turned. Greer was coming towards him as if on a cloud. He wanted to shout 'stop', but instead his eyes slid to Loveday walking behind, her eyes glued desperately to Jesse's. His brain was telling his mouth to open and speak, but when he tried it would not obey. He turned quickly back to the altar. Behind him he could hear his mum sniffing into her hanky.

The Reverend Rowena had seen nervous grooms before, but never as stricken as Jesse. She smiled at him and offered a prayer to bring him peace.

Greer arrived at Jesse's side. She looked up at him adoringly. He couldn't move.

Greer turned to Loveday and handed her the bouquet. Loveday took it and stood rooted to the spot, staring at Jesse, who looked as if he might faint. Greer was whispering to her, 'My veil. Lift my veil.' Loveday looked at her hands, each holding a bouquet, her own and the bride's. 'Give them to my mother,' Greer hissed.

'Dearly beloved, we are gathered together here, in the sight of God, and in the face of this congregation, to join together this Man and this Woman in holy Matrimony, which is an honourable state . . .'

13

'I can't believe we've been married for almost three weeks already.' Greer stretched out her left hand and wiggled the fourth finger to allow the two shiny rings, one a diamond solitaire set in gold, the other a matching gold band, to twinkle in the sunshine.

'Are you happy, Jesse?'

Jesse, at that particular moment, was happy. He was lying on a comfortable sun lounger, by a sparkling azure pool with a cold glass of beer by his side, hundreds of miles away from the mess he'd left behind in Trevay. He was almost starting to believe he'd got away with the biggest mistake of his life. That's not to say that several times a day he didn't break out in a cold sweat thinking of his betrayal. Last night he'd dreamt of making love to Loveday in his parents' bed. Neither he nor Loveday had heard the footsteps coming up the stairs or the turn of the door handle. They hadn't seen the faces of his mother, his father, Mickey and Greer contorted in grief and horror until Mickey had pulled out a fish-gutting knife and had stabbed himself in the heart. His blood had pumped in a perfect arc over Loveday's face and into Jesse's eyes. His mother was screaming. Greer was shouting, 'Jesse, Jesse, stop it, stop it!' She was tapping at his face and shaking his shoulders. 'Jesse, wake up. Wake up! What's the matter?'

He'd opened his eyes, knowing that he would see Loveday's blood-covered face staring at him accusingly, Mickey's body lying across her. But all he saw was the concerned face of Greer gently shaking him. 'Jesse, it's OK. I'm here. It was a dream.'

His eyes slowly took in the hotel bedroom and its whitewashed walls. The early light was twinkling through the shutters and he heard the clatter of a woman in heels walk across the floor of the room above.

His heart was thudding more gently now and his breathing was returning to normal.

'You were shouting Mickey's name.' Greer's face was full of concern.

He hated himself. 'Was I?' Guilt swept through him. 'Did I say anything else?'

'You were mumbling and pushing your arms out in front of you, and you kept saying, "Mickey".'

He sat up and rubbed the sweat from his top lip. 'I must be missing the bugger.'

'Can you remember what the dream was about?' asked Greer.

'No. Funny how dreams just vanish like that.' He rubbed a hand over his bleary eyes.

Greer pushed the thin sheet off herself and padded over the marble-tiled floor towards the bathroom.

He heard her pee and wash her hands. When she came back there was just enough light in the room to penetrate her gauzy nightdress. He saw the flatness of her stomach and her small, high breasts. He hadn't been a virgin when he married Greer. There had been nights out in Newquay with Mickey and other mates where they'd all succumbed to sexual experiences of varying satisfaction and success.

He had been gentler with Greer on their wedding

night than he'd been with Loveday. He knew for sure that this was Greer's first time. He wished he'd known it had been Loveday's. He wished many things. The seething guilt rose in him again.

Greer moved gracefully to her side of the king-size bed and got under the sheet next to him. He was still getting used to the novelty of asking for sex at any time – and getting it. He rolled towards her and put his hand on her thigh, pushing the nightie over her hips and up to her stomach.

'Why do you wear this thing?'

'I always wear a nightie.' He felt the tension – or was it reluctance? – in her body.

'I like you naked.' He moved himself on top of her and eased his legs between hers.

She kept her eyes closed as he kissed her. As he pushed into her she tensed again but made no noise.

'Does it still hurt?' he asked, slowly pushing in and out of her.

'A bit.'

'You just need a bit more practice, that's all.'

Afterwards she got out of bed and had a long shower before getting dressed and organising her bag of poolside essentials. He watched her. He was fond of her. She had a good heart and loved him, he knew. She wasn't Loveday but she was his wife.

And now, here they were, lying in the January sun by a sparkling pool in Gran Canaria.

'I still can't believe how Mummy and Daddy managed to keep this whole honeymoon a secret from us,' sighed Greer. 'Hasn't it been dreamy?'

Jesse took a mouthful of the cold Spanish beer and nodded.

He still couldn't think with any clarity about his wedding day. He remembered Loveday's flow of silent tears as she stood behind them at the altar, Mickey's concern for her, and the congregation applauding when the vicar pronounced them man and wife.

In the vestry, as they had signed the register, he had tried to catch Loveday's eye, but she had kept as far away from him as she could. Then, once the signing and the photos were done and Greer had taken his arm possessively in order to walk triumphantly down the aisle, showing off her new husband, he had felt something being stuffed into his jacket pocket by Bryn, his new father-in-law. He was saying, 'It's your honeymoon, lad. Treat her well. The flight goes from Bristol in five hours. Four weeks of sun in the Grand Hotel Residencia, Gran Canaria.' Jesse had looked at him stupidly. 'And,' continued Bryn, 'when you get back, no need to worry about moving in with us. I've got a little place all set up for you.' He elbowed his new son-in-law in the ribs. 'After all, you don't want the "outlaws" breathing down your neck every time you want some privacy, do you?' He winked at Jesse as Jesse allowed himself to be dragged out of the vestry and down the aisle to the triumphant organ and hearty applause.

*

The reception, held at the golf club, had been noisy and boozy. Mickey's speech, nervously delivered, had gone down well, and Jesse managed the thank yous and the toasts he was obliged to give. 'And, finally,' he said, putting his crib notes down on the tablecloth, 'I'd like to thank my two best friends for sharing this day with me. Best man, Mickey Chandler, and bridesmaid . . .' He swallowed pushing down the terrible but wonderful thoughts of what had happened between them. '. . . Loveday Carter.' The crowd applauded and a few wolf-whistled as Loveday left her seat and took a mock bow. Smiling and waving, she smoothed down the hideous dress and walked sedately to the ladies to cry in the peace of a cubicle.

Jesse watched her go. With a cowardice that shocked him, he stayed put and continued, 'And, finally, my greatest thanks go to . . . Greer, who I've known since we were both five and who is now . . . my wife.' He raised his glass. 'Ladies and gentlemen. The bride.'

*

A few minutes later, Jesse had made his way to the lavatories. Instead of going into the Gents, he dived into the Ladies, praying no one would catch him. Instead of a row of urinals he was met with a dully lit lobby, a full-length mirror and a dressing table with stool. On the dressing table was a tissue box festooned in lilac lace and a clothes brush. He couldn't face looking at his reflection as he found the second door leading to the inner sanctuary of the women's stalls. Five in a row and only one door closed.

'Loveday, I know you're in there. Let me in.'

Loveday, sitting on the closed seat, was crying as quietly as she could. She stopped and sat still.

'Loveday. I want to talk to you.'

'Go away.'

He heard the outer door – the one that led to the small lobby – opening, and two women talking. 'She looks lovely, don't she?' remarked one.

'Aye, she does that, but her mother was always a looker and 'er dad weren't so bad when 'e was a young 'un.' As they pushed the inner door, Jesse dived into the empty cubicle next to Loveday's.

To make things sound authentic he thought he might as well have a pee while he was there. Giving himself a shake as he finished, he listened as the two strangers peed like camels, keeping up a stream of gossip about their opinions on the various outfits on display. Finally he heard their flushes and the two women washed their hands, still talking, before the hand driers drowned them out and they finally left.

He felt a hand tickling the top of his head. It was Loveday, standing on the loo seat next door. He looked up at her and a smile flooded her face. He opened his mouth to say something but she put a finger to her lips.

'Loveday,' said Jesse. 'I love you.'

'Don't, please don't say that.' Loveday's eyes welled with unspent tears. 'You're Greer's husband now and I wish you all the happiness in the world.'

He reached up and took hold of her hand.

'I mean it, Loveday. I love you and I'll never regret what happened last night.'

'Nor me. I'll never forget it and I'll never tell anyone neither.' Loveday looked so pitiful.

'Come out of there and let me hold you,' he begged.

'Someone will see.'

'No they won't.'

'They will.'

They looked at each other in a tragic impasse over the partition wall. Tentatively he asked, 'Loveday, am I . . . was I the first to . . .? Have you ever done . . . that with Mickey . . . or anyone?'

She shook her head. 'I've never let Mickey touch me.'

Jesse was surprised. 'But he told me that you had.'

'Well, he would, wouldn't he? But I couldn't. Not with Mickey and not while I was waiting for you.'

They stood in their tragic tableau, neither knowing what to say.

'You've got to go,' said Loveday with finality. 'You've got a plane to catch, haven't you?'

They heard the outer door opening again and Loveday jumped down so that she wouldn't be seen. A familiar voice called out, 'Loveday? Are you in there? I'm going to change into my going-away outfit and I need my bridesmaid to help.'

Loveday flushed her loo and came out, smoothing down the hated dress over her curves.

'Here I am.'

*

It had started to snow heavily again. The taxi company had sent a big white Range Rover to make sure that it would get out of Trevay and up the hill towards the A30 safely. Jesse helped Greer into the back seat before climbing in next to the driver. Greer opened her electric window and immediately a flurry of snow and a handful of pink and blue confetti flew into her face, landing prettily on her eyelashes and the lace of her suit jacket.

'Catch!' she shouted, throwing her bouquet towards Loveday.

Loveday tried hard not to catch it. She closed her eyes tight as the beautiful flowers arced through the snow-filled air. But the fates had decreed that it land in the centre of Loveday's chest, scraping the skin, and she had no option but to let the flowers fall into her arms. Mickey slid his arm around her waist and gave her a beerily passionate kiss on the lips.

The crowd ooh'd and aah'd and someone shouted, 'Run Mickey, run!' to a burst of laughter.

*

Jesse, sitting on his sun bed, shivered with the dreadful memory and took another swig of his cold beer.

'Yeah. It all seems unreal.'

Greer leant over and kissed her husband. 'I can't wait to get home and show off this tan. A tan in January seems so luxurious. Loveday will be so jealous.'

Jesse shifted away from her. 'She's not like that.'

'Yes, she is. She'd love Mickey to bring her on a holiday like this.' Greer sniggered. 'Not that he'd know how to leave Cornwall. Has he ever crossed the Tamar?'

Jesse hated it when Greer ran Mickey down. 'Leave it, Greer. I couldn't afford to bring you here if your dad hadn't paid.'

Greer reached her hand to his face and stroked his cheek. 'Don't be angry. I was teasing. I know how lucky we are.' She sat up and pushed her sunglasses on to her head. 'Aren't you excited about our new house, though?'

'Yeah.'

'Well, don't sound too enthusiastic.' Greer looked down at her manicured toes. 'Are you cross that Mum and Dad have done it and we don't even know what it looks like?'

Jesse frowned. 'A bit.'

'Ah, my poor caveman. Did you want to go out with your club and bash the other troglodytes on the head to steal the best cave?' She ran her fingers down his chest and tickled his stomach. He pushed her hand away.

She was apologetic. 'I was just teasing.'

'Well, don't. Your parents have been very generous. The wedding, this holiday—'

'Honeymoon.'

'. . . honeymoon. Somewhere for us to live . . .'

'And an important new job.'

Jesse rubbed his hand over his face. 'Yes, and the new job.' Suddenly the latent anxiety lapped at the base of his throat. 'It's all too much. I . . . we . . . should be making our own lives. Our own decisions.'

Greer saw the anxiety in Jesse's face and misread its reason.

'It's a dream come true for me, Jesse, and I know you'll be wonderful. Don't ever think you could let me down. I know how hard you work and what the business means to your dad as well as mine. I'm so proud of you.' She took his hand in hers. 'And, one day, you'll pass it all on to our children. It's exciting.'

Jesse felt a tightening round his chest. He was like a mackerel, caught in one of his father's trawl nets.

14

Elizabeth Clovelly couldn't stop herself from turning the loo paper roll the 'right' way round on its holder. Jan Behenna watched her.

'What did you turn it round for?'

'The loose edge mustn't rest against the wall. It must hang out into the room.'

'Why?'

'Well, over time, a grease mark will appear on the new paint, from where people's hands have to touch the wall to pull at the roll.'

'Oh, I see,' said Jan, who didn't.

'It's something my mother did; once you know about it, you can't stop doing it.' Elizabeth smiled. 'Sometimes I do it when I'm out. At other people's houses. Or restaurants. Silly, I know, but it makes sense.'

Jan wondered if this woman had done it in her house. She'd have to check the bloody thing whenever she came round.

Elizabeth was straightening the towels now. 'Sweet bathroom,' she managed to say, whilst thinking the exact opposite.

Jan looked round with pride at the room she'd lovingly decorated. She couldn't wait for Jesse and Greer to see it. The bath, basin and toilet were in aqua blue and she'd chosen dear little tiles to put around the sink, each with a picture of a penguin at his ablutions. One cleaning his teeth, one having a shave and one – her favourite – lying in a bubble bath with a shower hat on his head.

'Isn't it?' She smiled with satisfaction. 'I never had an indoor bathroom when we first got married. Outdoor privy and a wash in the old Belfast sink in the kitchen. Used to put the boys in there too when they were babies.'

'That must have been . . . difficult.'

'Well, it was fun really. We'd all dry off in front of the fire and Edward would dry my hair by brushing it till it gleamed.' Jan reached up to her short crop. 'It used to be thick and had a wave but . . . 'Tis more practical to have it short, isn't it?'

Elizabeth thought of the monthly bill to have her expensively blond hair cut and coloured and said, 'Yes, it must be.'

Jan was on the tiny landing now and peeking into the master bedroom. ''Tis proper cosy. I love the colour. I'd never have thought of mushroom.'

'It's called Drizzle,' said Elizabeth, pushing past Jan and stepping into the small but light room.

'Drizzle!' Jan laughed. 'How they come up with these names! I'd have done something like blue. Edward says bedrooms need to be blue. Calm, see. And in a marriage you need to stay calm.'

Elizabeth was twitching the duvet and smoothing it straight for the umpteenth time. 'This has a warm feel, don't you think?'

'Oh, definitely.'

Elizabeth checked her slim gold watch. 'They'll be here soon. It's nearly time.'

*

Jesse and Greer were met at the airport by the same driver who'd dropped them off four weeks before. 'Welcome home, Mr and Mrs Behenna. How was the trip?' he asked as he stowed the suitcases into the large boot.

Greer clutched at Jesse's arm. 'Wonderful, thank you. I can't believe we've been away for such a long time.'

'The sun's come out for you,' he told them, jumping into the front seat and starting the engine. 'The snow has all gone.'

Jesse felt the need to take charge. 'Would you drop us off at my parents' house, please, Fish Lane at the top of Fore Street?'

'Ah, no, sir. I have another address I have been asked to take you to.'

Greer clapped her hands with glee. 'Is it our new home?'

'Can't possibly say, Mrs Behenna,' the driver said, looking at her in his rear-view mirror.

'It is! How exciting.' Greer took Jesse's arm and snuggled in. 'We're going to our new home.'

The yellow of the early February sun lit the moors as they drove west towards Trevay and the sea. Driving down the hill and into the village, past the peeling grandeur of the old Great Western Hotel, the newlyweds wondered whether the driver would turn left or right along the estuary road. He turned left towards the heart of Trevay. Greer clutched one hand to her chest and the other to Jesse's arm. 'I wonder where it is? Will it overlook the harbour, do you think?'

Jesse frowned. The creeping, suffocating certainty that his life was not his own any more was seeping into his psyche. He was in the control of others. He wanted to order the driver to stop the car and let him out so that he could run as fast as he could away from Trevay.

'Dunno,' he muttered.

The car went past Fore Street and followed the harbour road round towards the Golden Hind. The driver indicated left and turned into Cobb Lane. Greer leant forward and pointed saying, 'Look, look!' On the right Jesse saw a house with ribbons and balloons on the gate. Both sets of parents were waving.

Greer was bouncing on the seat with excitement. 'It's Pencil Cottage! I've wanted to live here since I was a little girl! Look, Jesse, isn't it wonderful?'

Jesse looked at the house he'd walked past, and never given a thought to, for almost twenty years. Pencil thin and squeezed between two regular-sized Trevay fishermen's cottages, this was his new home.

The car rolled to a halt and the faces of Elizabeth and Jan peered in through the back windows, grinning. The driver jumped out and opened Greer's door for her. She fell into her parents' arms, where she was showered with hugs and kisses and questions about the honeymoon.

Jesse climbed out and walked to the boot of the Range Rover to help with the bags. 'I'll do that, sir,' said the driver. 'I think you're needed to carry something else over the threshold.'

Jesse looked over his shoulder and saw Greer and both sets of parents waiting expectantly for him.

*

Standing in the front room, Bryn spoke first. 'Now then, young Jesse, please accept Pencil Cottage as a wedding present. It'll keep you both warm till you can afford your own place. The company has paid for it and it should be a nice little asset for us. When the time comes for you to need a bigger house, the company will sell this and I'll split the profit with you. That way you'll have a tidy deposit for a proper family home.'

Jesse experienced three emotions. One, gratitude that this should be happening to him; two, fury that this man had, in one fell swoop, totally emasculated him, and three, the feeling that his balls were being squeezed in an ever-tighter vice.

His father stepped towards him wearing a tight smile. 'Welcome home, son. Your mother and I couldn't be more proud of the both of you.'

*

The house might have been thin on the outside but, inside, it went a long way back and up. The front door opened immediately into the sitting room, which was traditional, warm and inviting. Elizabeth had kept it all white with simple furnishings, knowing that her daughter would want to customise the entire house. It led into a smart galley kitchen, which in turn led out to a tiny concreted yard with raised flower beds full of prettily nodding daffodils.

Greer wriggled with joy. 'I bet this is a suntrap. It feels warm right now!'

Back in the house she pointed out the dishwasher, television, the large framed wedding photo on the mantelpiece that Jan had had printed especially, and the view from the front window.

'Wait till you see upstairs,' Jan said, longing for Jesse to see her handiwork in the bathroom.

'Yes, you'll love the bedroom, Greer,' said Elizabeth, leading the way before Jan could get ahead of her.

Jesse's muscles were beginning to tire where he was

attempting to smile with genuine pleasure. Greer kissed his nose and galloped up the stairs ahead of him.

'Oh, Mummy!' gasped Greer as she saw the bedroom. 'It's so glamorous!' She called out to the landing: 'Jesse, quick. In here.' Jesse ducked his head under the low latched door and absorbed the pinky-brown walls, frilly bed linen and heavy Austrian blind at the window. Greer gripped his arm with eyes wide. 'Isn't it stylish?'

Jesse nodded slowly, mystified.

'He's overwhelmed, Mummy.' Greer went to her mother and hugged and kissed her.

Jan, desperate for Jesse to see the bathroom, pulled at his arm. 'I've got something to show you too.'

The bathroom was much more to Jesse's taste. 'Oh, Mum. 'Tis lovely.'

Jan beamed with happiness. 'Look at the penguins!'

Jesse smiled. 'I like them.'

'I knew you would, and come here.' Jan pushed the loo lid shut. 'Sit here and look at the view!'

He sat. Through the tiny square of the tiny window straight ahead of him, Jesse could just make out his father's flagship, *The Lobster Pot*, bobbing gently at anchor in the harbour. Jesse laughed then and shouted out to his father on the landing, 'Dad, I'll be able to make sure you're working hard from here.' Edward laughed too. 'Aye. But I've checked it out and I can see you doing your business on that toilet if I get my binoculars out.'

Everyone but Greer and Elizabeth laughed heartily.

'Well, now. I've got tea and sandwiches ready, if you want some,' said Elizabeth, heading back downstairs. 'There might even be a bottle of bubbly in the fridge.'

*

'What's that bleddy 'orrible paint Betty's put on your bedroom walls?'

Edward had taken his shoes off and was sitting in his favourite armchair back at the family home in Fish Lane. The three Behennas had left Pencil Cottage on the pretext of collecting Jesse's bits and pieces.

'Edward.' Jan looked at her husband sternly. 'That's the latest, most stylish colour. And don't call her Betty. She prefers to be called Elizabeth, as you well know.'

Edward made a grumbling noise. 'She was Betty when we was all at school together.'

Jan ignored him. 'So, son, we missed you. What was Gran Canaria like?'

'Hot. Nice.'

'Food good?'

'Not bad. Mind you, I could have murdered a pasty.'

Jan brightened up. 'I've got some ready to heat up if you want one.'

'Go on then.' Jesse smiled at his mum as she went to the kitchen.

Edward, making sure she'd left the room before he spoke, asked under his breath, 'So, everything all right in the bedroom department?'

Jesse squirmed a little. 'Fine.'

'Ah. Good. Only some women—'

'Dad. Please. It's fine. She's fine . . . and that's all.'

'Well, that's all right then.'

'Yes.'

*

At Pencil Cottage, Greer and her mother were unpacking her suitcases in the bedroom.

'How was the honeymoon, darling? Was he kind to you?' asked Elizabeth delicately and without making eye contact with her daughter.

Greer was embarrassed. 'Yes. He was lovely.'

'He . . . didn't make things uncomfortable for you?'

Greer folded a bikini and put it into one of the new drawers, then sat on the bed. 'A bit. I think I just have to . . . get used to it.'

Elizabeth moved a pile of underwear and sat next to her daughter. 'It's not easy at first, but it gets better. It makes men happy. And in time it'll make you happy too.'

Greer looked into her mother's eyes. 'I do love him.'

Elizabeth patted her hand. 'That's all you need.'

Downstairs the phone rang and they could hear Bryn answer. ''Ello, Mickey . . . yeah, they're home safe and sound . . . right, yeah, we'll meet you there. Ten minutes? Rightyo.' He called up the stairs. 'Get your coats on, that was Mickey. He and Loveday are going down the Hind. They want to welcome you home with a couple of drinks.'

*

The Golden Hind was thick with tobacco smoke and the heady scent of Cornish beer.

Loveday really hadn't wanted to come. 'Let them have their first night in their new home by themselves, Mick,' she'd pleaded.

Mickey was incredulous. 'They've just spent four weeks on their own. If I know Jesse, he'll be desperate for a beer or two and some male company.' He added as an afterthought, 'And Greer will want to see you as well. She'll want to tell you all about her posh hotel and that.'

'That's what I'm afraid of,' replied Loveday gloomily.

'That's my girl.' Mickey put his arm around her. 'We'll have a great night.'

*

Mickey and Loveday got to the pub before anyone else and Loveday stationed herself on one of the Dralon banquettes on the far wall. From there she could see who was coming in and out of the bar. As the place filled up, it would be harder for anyone coming in to spot her first.

Mickey got her a cider shandy and a bag of pork scratchings. 'There you are. I'm going to wait at the bar. I'll send Greer over as soon as she arrives.'

Gee, thanks, thought Loveday. Her heart was beating so fast that she could feel the pulse in her neck. Waves of perspiration hit her every few minutes. She felt sick. Had Jesse told Greer what had happened between them? Was he filled with the same longing to see her as she was to see him?

She jumped as the pub door opened, but it was a group of locals trooping in to fill the space with laughter and a blast of cool February air.

Her nerves were raw. What would she say to him? What would he say to her?

The pub door opened again, and again it wasn't Jesse or Greer. At least the bar was filling up and she'd be very hard to find when – if – he came in.

She pulled at the opening of the bag of pork scratchings. Her hands were slippery with sweat and she couldn't get a good grip. She put the bag to her mouth and ripped it open with her teeth. The entire bag split from top to bottom and its greasy contents spilt itself all down her good T-shirt. She almost cried. 'Shit shit shit,' she said under her breath as she tried to pick the larger lumps up and brush the powdery residue off her clothes and onto the floor.

'All right, Loveday?' Jesse was standing over her. Smiling his warm, familiar smile. His eyes shining in a very tanned face, his good looks were almost blinding.

'I've just tipped bloody pork scratchings all over me,' she said helplessly.

'Do you want me to lick 'em off for you?' Her eyes darted to his face to see if he was laughing at her. He wasn't, but there was a look in his eyes that she couldn't read. Something she had never seen there before. A hardness.

'Do you want a drink?'

'Yes, please, darling.' Greer appeared from behind Jesse and plonked herself neatly on the bench next to Loveday. 'White wine spritzer, please.'

15

'The house is just adorable. Mum and Jan worked so hard setting it up for us. Dad's bought all new carpets and appliances. I've got such plans for the interior. I think I'm going for modern with a twist of "olde worlde". We're going to save up for bits as we go along. You must come and see it.' Greer was on a roll. The boys had left the girls to it and were now standing at the bar with a group of male pals. How Loveday longed to be with them.

'I'd love to,' said Loveday, feeling horrible but trying to sound normal. 'How was the honeymoon? Was the hotel nice?'

'It was *sooo* luxurious. Our room was huge with a balcony overlooking the pool and our own table and chairs out on it. One day we had breakfast out there. Room service. Just a continental breakfast, croissants, black coffee, freshly squeezed orange juice. I loved it, but Jesse didn't want to do it again. You know what these boys are like. He wanted the full English in the dining room. Most nights we ate in the English bar in the marina, but once or twice I made him eat local stuff. He liked the paella . . . and the calamari, until I told him it was baby octopus.'

Loveday grimaced. 'Octopus?'

'Yes. He's a fishermen! I thought he ate anything that came out of the sea.'

Loveday had been around the fishing boats all her life, and enjoyed cod and chips as well as the next woman, but octopus was going too far. She kept smiling, but as Greer went on and on, about the weather and the pool and the waiters round the pool, and the one waiter that Jesse got really jealous about because he was paying so much attention to her, and how being married gave her such a feeling of enormous security, and on and on and bloody on, Loveday fought the desire to tell her best and oldest friend to shut up.

Here, with Greer sitting right in front of her, she was struggling with the conflicting and terrible feelings she felt crashing around within her: jealousy that Greer had been alone with Jesse for so long; overwhelming guilt about sleeping with Jesse; horror at how she'd betrayed her best friend, betrayed Mickey. The last four weeks had been hell for her. She'd been dreaming of Jesse coming home. Stealing away with him, up to the sheds, to talk and make love and disentangle themselves from the mistake he'd made in marrying Greer. In her most optimistic moments, she'd imagined him coming back and explaining to Mickey and Greer what had happened and, after a while, in due course, after the divorce, Jesse would marry Loveday and Mickey and Greer would be happy for them. Everyone would understand what a mistake it had been for Greer and Jesse to marry and they'd be glad that a mistake had been rectified. They'd see that, and they'd all be so much happier. In the meantime Greer was still chuntering on, and it was seeming increasingly unlikely that was going to happen.

'Perhaps you and Mickey would like to come over to Pencil Cottage tomorrow night? Just kitchen sups. Spaghetti Bolognese?'

Loveday flicked a glance over to Mickey at the bar and saw Jesse heave himself off a well-worn bar stool and begin to walk towards them. She answered Greer with a vague, 'Erm . . . yeah, I'll ask Mickey.' She was so alert to Jesse getting closer to them that every atom in her body started to shake. He reached their table and took a seat on a low stool opposite Greer, who immediately took his hand. 'Hello, husband!' She glowed. 'I've just been telling Loveday all about our honeymoon.'

'Not everything, I hope,' he said, looking at the floor, finding a beer mat to pick up.

Greer blushed a little. 'No. Stop it. What are men like?' She looked at Loveday and raised her eyebrows. 'Honestly! Boys have one-track minds, don't they?'

Loveday picked up her pint of shandy and tried to look world-weary. 'Gosh, don't they?'

Greer twittered on, 'I've just asked Loveday and Mickey round for tea tomorrow. Loveday wants to see the house.' Jesse looked sharply at Loveday, who gave her head the slightest of shakes. Greer cantered on oblivious, 'And I know you've missed Mickey. I thought I'd do spag bol.'

Jesse was still looking at Loveday, but with an expression she couldn't interpret. Why was he being so cold towards her?

She blurted hurriedly, 'I didn't say I wanted to see the house . . . well, not the day after you come home. You need to get settled.'

Jesse turned to Greer. 'Yeah, we've only just got home, love. Let's get ourselves sorted out first.'

Mickey ambled over and put his hand on Jesse's shoulder. 'Come on, big man. I've got a hot game of bar billiards to play with you.'

Jesse stood up and, putting his hand in his back pocket,

pulled out his wallet and took out a ten-pound note. 'You girls get yourselves a drink and maybe something to eat. Mickey and I have some serious cueing to do.'

Both young women were silenced. Greer felt slighted, abandoned by her husband on her first night home, and Loveday felt, without having the right to feel it, dumped.

Just before ten thirty, Pete the landlord rang the old ship's bell behind the bar. 'Last orders, ladies and gentlemen. Last orders, please.'

*

Greer and Loveday were sitting where the boys had left them almost two hours before. In front of them was a barely touched prawn sandwich (Greer's) and the last crumbs of scampi and chips in the basket (Loveday's). They were each nursing a drink and had run out of conversation. The bar was thinning out and, across the floor, they could see into the games room, where Mickey and Jesse, more than tipsy, were whooping with jeers and laughter after each cue shot.

Pete was calling out to the stragglers, 'Drink up now, ladies and gents. Time to get home.' He was moving between the bar and the tables, collecting up the dirty glasses and ashtrays. He stopped by Loveday and Greer. 'Welcome home, Mrs Behennna. 'Ow was the honeymoon?'

'Lovely, thank you,' said Greer with an automatic politeness.

'Glad to have your mate back, aren't you, Loveday?'

'Yes,' said Loveday dully. 'Yes. Very glad.'

'I'll round those two lads up for you,' Pete assured them. 'You'm ladies need your beauty sleep.'

Pete was as good as his word and within a couple of

minutes Jesse and Mickey appeared, still giggling with each other.

'Get my coat, would you, Jesse?' Greer was irritated and impatient to get back to Pencil Cottage.

Jesse took the long black coat off one of the row of pegs by the pub door and handed it to her. 'I mean, can you help me into it?' asked Greer with an edge to her voice.

'Since when couldn't you put your own coat on for yourself?' he asked her.

'It's what husbands do for wives,' she told him, handing the coat back to him.

Loveday zipped up her scarlet padded Puffa jacket and opened the pub door. A wall of now icy February air hit her and she was glad to breathe in the freshness of it after the fug of the Hind.

Mickey stepped out behind her and put his arm through hers. His eyes were glassy with beer and he smiled soppily at her. 'That was a nice evening. Did you have a good time catching up with Greer?'

'Hmm,' said Loveday tersely. 'I know all about bloody Gran Canaria anyway.'

The pub door opened again and a coated Greer and a sloshed Jesse appeared. 'Gosh, it's cold,' shivered Greer. 'But of course after a month of winter sun we'd feel it, wouldn't we, Jesse?'

'You would 'cos you ain't got enough meat on your bones. Not like Loveday. I bet she's warm as toast, eh, Loveday?' Loveday couldn't believe that Jesse could be so heartless towards her and felt tears stinging her eyes.

Mickey grabbed at Loveday's bum and gave it a good squeeze. 'Yeah. She's got enough flesh on her to keep her warm.' Jesse laughed with him, and Loveday, feeling like a heifer, turned towards home.

'By the way, Mickey,' she heard Greer saying, 'I've invited you and Loveday round for kitchen sups tomorrow. Spag bol. Six o'clock?'

Before Loveday could warn Mickey not to accept the invitation, he had, with great bonhomie, replied, 'Lovely. That'd be just the ticket, eh, Loveday?'

'That's sorted then,' smiled Greer, before taking Jesse's arm and looking up into his eyes in a way that made Loveday feel sick. 'My husband and I are to give our first dinner party to our best friends.' She stood on her tiptoes and gave Jesse a slow kiss. 'Excited?'

To Loveday's horror, Jesse returned the kiss with warmth. 'Let's get you home, Mrs Behenna.'

He wheeled Greer round and walked her off towards Pencil Cottage. Mickey pulled Loveday towards him. 'Must be nice to be married. Jesse was telling me they had a great honeymoon.'

'Did he?' Loveday felt empty.

They started walking towards Loveday's house. She said, 'My mum's not back till tomorrow. She's gone over to Auntie Sheila's.'

'Will you be all right on your own?' asked Mickey, not understanding what she was saying to him.

She spelt it out. 'I thought you might like to stay over and keep me company?'

'What? You mean like . . . ?'

'Yes, Mickey, that's exactly what I mean.'

'Loveday,' Mickey said thickly, and Loveday returned his overjoyed smile with one of her own. She may not have Jesse, but she had the power to make Mickey the happiest man in the world.

*

Jesse and Greer were lying in their new bed in their new bedroom in their new house. Greer was listening to the old place talking to itself as it settled its eaves onto its ancient rafters and cob walls. She couldn't have felt happier. Pencil Cottage was her home. Growing up, this had been the one house in the whole of Trevay that she had dreamt of owning. And now she did. Well, OK, her dad's company owned it, but it was hers to live in and love.

She turned and snuggled into her husband, who was recovering after a short, sharp, drunken but satisfying – for him – five minutes of lovemaking.

'Are you happy?' she asked.

He was getting fed up with her always asking if he was happy.

What would she do if he told her the truth? If he just opened his mouth right now and said:

'No, as a matter of fact I'm not particularly happy. I only agreed to marry you because my father and your father persuaded me that it would be good for me, for them and for the whole financial health of Trevay. Our boats would get a better deal with the fish market; we'd freeze out the boats from further up and down the coast. They told me that you were the best catch in Cornwall and I'd be a lucky man to have you as my wife. And I am so thick, and so greedy, that I went along with it and sold my soul to the devil.

'I am no longer my own man. I married you and received a house, a job and a honeymoon as payment. I am a whore; I don't want to be lying next to you tonight, I want to be with Loveday. Yes, fat Loveday with no prospects. She has been a loyal friend to you and you despise her.

'I made love to her once, the night before our wedding,

if you want to hear the gory details, but now I'm married to you. It was cruel of me to talk about her flesh keeping her warm and to kiss you in front of her, but I was cruel tonight because I wanted her to get the message that I cannot give her anything. She deserves to be with a good man like Mickey. And you don't deserve to be with a shit like me. I'll try to be the best husband I can to you and to make you happy, but am I happy? You're happy, your dad's happy, my dad's happy, so who cares if I'm happy or not? Only Loveday, and she's as miserable as I am.'

He shifted a little so that Greer could rest her head on his shoulder. 'Yes, I'm happy, maid,' he said, and lay still, staring into the unfamiliar darkness of his new home.

*

Mickey couldn't believe that, at last, Loveday was his. She had led him up her narrow stairs and taken him into her bedroom, which looked the same as it always had. The grey carpet with swags of spring flowers woven into it was the same one that the four friends had played endless games of Monopoly on. He remembered that he and Jesse had had a huge fight, one Christmas, over paying the bill for a Monopoly hotel he'd put on Park Lane. Jesse had refused to hand over the money and they'd ended up brawling on the floor. Loveday had ended the fight by getting in between them and forcing them apart. Greer had quietly and carefully simply folded the board and put all the pieces back in their little boxed compartments.

The wallpaper was the same too, but now the A-ha posters that had littered it had come down. He'd been so jealous that Loveday had fancied Morten Harket. 'He's a poof,' he'd told her, and got a whack for his trouble.

Her single bed with the old satin eiderdown was still pushed up against the wall, and her teddy, Annabel, was still sitting on the pillow.

Loveday didn't put the bedroom light on. Instead she let the light from the landing spill softly into the room. She took his hand and knew he was nervous. 'Come on. Sit on the bed with me.'

He sat next to her and watched as she put Annabel down on the carpet. Then he kissed her more deeply than he'd ever dared before.

She felt for the buttons of her denim shirt and began undoing them, before shrugging it off to expose a large black bra, straining against the flesh and weight of her breasts. Mickey stopped kissing her and looked in wonder at her. 'You're so beautiful,' he breathed.

She helped him with the tricky clasp of her bra and, after that, he needed no help in easing both of them out of their clothes and in between the cool sheets. As inexperienced as Loveday was, she knew that where Jesse had been a lover with passion and force, Mickey was altogether different. He was tender and careful. She closed her eyes and gave herself up to the pleasure he was giving her. He wasn't Jesse. He was Mickey, and she prayed he would never, ever find out about her and Jesse.

16

The 'Sunday night sups', as Greer insisted on calling their get-together (apparently because she'd read somewhere that that's what Princess Diana called her informal evening meals), was endured and enjoyed in equal measure.

On the way there, Loveday steeled herself, determined not to let the situation get to her, or to let her emotions show through. But it was so hard. It was Jesse who answered the doorbell; instantly those sea-green eyes locked with hers, sending her stomach into backflips of desire before she had even crossed the threshold. As Jesse went to take her coat, Loveday tried to shrug her way awkwardly out of it, but she was not fast enough, and she felt Jesse's strong hands close round her shoulders, seemed to feel them burning through the thick material. She shuddered, making her way quickly through to the kitchen to give Greer a hand, trying to put distance between them. Still, when Jesse handed her a drink, she saw that her hand was shaking.

Greer was a good cook, and Loveday wasn't sure if she tucked into her meal with such relish because of her discomfort or in spite of it. Once or twice she caught Jesse's eye, but when she did he would look quickly away, or disappear to the kitchen on the pretext of getting another couple of cans of beer. He must have noticed the way she'd been in the hallway, she decided, squirming inwardly: he was making certain that they were never on their own together, or sitting anywhere near each other. Well, OK, if that was how it was going to be, Loveday thought, bristling, she had her pride. As the wine flowed and her taut nerves finally began to relax, Loveday got her own back by cosying up to Mickey, who was very happy to bask in his sexy girlfriend's attention.

Inside, Loveday was finally processing the stark message that was being ruthlessly delivered to her: that their lives had settled into a new phase – and that nothing she could do or wish for was going to change that.

*

Jesse still spent long hours at sea hunting the best catches he could. He knew his father was pleased with his progress – not that he would ever hear him say so – and he was given more responsibility on the boat. At sea he could be the old Jesse. Laughing with the boys, working hard and always respecting the ocean.

Life at Pencil Cottage was surprisingly pleasant. Comfortable. Greer was a great homemaker and the little house soon took on a polished and stylish personality. Out went the colours chosen by her and Jesse's mother; in came buff and beige and cloud grey. Jesse liked coming home to a lovely home, a decent supper and clean laundry. It was like living with his parents, but with the added bonus of sex and the satisfaction of being the man of the house. The only bore was Greer's extreme standards of tidiness, and her insistence that he should remove all his smelly fishing clothes the moment he entered the house. She would place a large towel on the floor, exactly a one-metre stride from the front door, so that he could, simultaneously, step on it, close the door behind him and strip off. She would hold out the laundry basket for him to drop the ripe jeans and overalls into before putting them – rubber gloves on – into the washing machine on a boil wash. Jesse would go upstairs to find a hot scented bath waiting for him. He'd have a soak, then a shave and clean his teeth, before finding Greer and giving her the sex he thought she was as eager for as he was.

*

It was Valentine's Day when Greer met him off the boat – odd in itself – and, odder still, kissed him full on the lips, even though he stank to high heaven.

'What was that for?' he asked as they broke apart.

'I've got some news.' She put the back of her hand to her mouth, tasting the sourness of his breath and trying not to gag.

Jesse swung his kitbag over his shoulder and, taking her hand, walked quickly towards home. The surprise of her appearance and the passionate kiss was sending messages of the bedroom kind to his nether regions.

'Let's get home.'

Lying breathless by her side, his filthy overalls for once allowed upstairs and strewn on the spotless dove-grey carpet of their bedroom, Jesse smiled. 'That was nice.' He exhaled slowly and pulled her head to rest on his shoulder. 'Now, tell me your news.'

The odour from his armpits was strong and stale. Greer shifted a little in order to avoid the worst of the fumes. 'I think we're going to have a baby.'

The fingers that had been stroking her waist stopped

abruptly. The room grew a silence that became a little thicker with each second, and then so heavy that Greer felt panicky and thirsty for oxygen.

He spoke. 'You think? Have you taken a test?'

'Yes.'

'And?'

'The blue line appeared.'

'And that means?'

'I'm pregnant.'

Jesse turned to face her, moving her from his shoulder to the soft pillows. He looked down at her pale, worried face and felt a wave of fear and exultation.

'Really?'

She nodded. 'I need to see Dr Cosgrove to confirm it, but I think I am. I've been feeling really sick for about a week and this morning I actually was sick so . . .'

'Wow.' He put his hand on her flat tummy. 'Hello, you in there. It's your daddy.'

Greer giggled and the look of worry was replaced with relief and love for her husband.

*

Dr Cosgrove moved his strong brown hands over her tummy and pressed gently, feeling for a thickening of her womb. He had known Greer since her mother was pregnant with her. He stopped his probing and left Greer lying on the ancient wood and leather examination table to get a tape measure from his desk drawer. He found the yellow booklet of tide times and, checking his watch, slipped it into his pocket. He was due to have an afternoon fishing trip with his son and he didn't want to be late. He retrieved the tape measure and stepped back to

Greer, lying prone on the bed. 'Right. Let me just make some measurements and we can work out roughly when your baby is due.'

'So I am pregnant?' asked Greer, daring to hope.

'You certainly are.' He measured from her pubic bone to a point below her navel. 'You can pull your dress down now and come and sit down.' He walked to his desk and made a squiggle in pencil on her notes. 'When was your last period?'

*

Jesse hadn't been to the doctor since he was a baby and certainly didn't feel the need to sit in on the business between Dr Cosgrove and Greer. He'd made his excuses and had gone to a meeting with his father and father-in-law to discuss business.

Greer heard his key in the lock and said hurriedly into the phone, 'Mummy, Jesse's home. I've got to go . . . Granny!' She heard her mother laughing as she put the receiver down.

Jesse closed the front door and, walking past Greer, went to the kitchen to put the kettle on. Greer followed him. 'So, ask me.'

He threw a teabag into his favourite mug and wrinkled his brow. 'Ask you what?'

'Jesse!' Greer was standing looking at him in sheer disbelief. 'You've forgotten where I was today?'

He reached for the kettle and poured the steaming water into his mug. 'At your mum's?'

Her bottom lip trembled and she turned, but he caught her before she got away and spun her round. 'I'm sorry. I was teasing.'

'Not funny. I've been waiting to tell you.'

He pulled her to him. 'Is it a girl or a boy?'

She punched his chest. 'Whatever it is, it's due on October the seventeenth.' She smiled up at him dreamily, 'A honeymoon baby. That's what Mummy said.'

He let go of her and went to the fridge for some milk. 'So you've told your mother then?'

'Don't be cross. I couldn't *not* tell her.'

'So I can tell my mum and dad now, can I?' he asked, looking over his shoulder at her.

She went to him and put her arms round his waist, leaning against his back. 'Of course. Let's invite them for supper.'

Jesse knew how uncomfortable his parents felt in Pencil Cottage, and how hurt his mother had been when Greer had repainted the bathroom and chiselled off the penguin tiles in favour of plain white Italian ones. He decided that discretion was the better part of valour. 'You don't want to cook. You need to put your feet up a bit. Let's take them to the Hind.'

Greer quietly cheered inside. Her in-laws were nice, but she had very little in common with them, and Ed didn't seem to enjoy her cooking anyway. 'Good idea.'

*

It seemed the whole of Trevay were delighted with news of the baby. Greer thoroughly enjoyed the fuss that was being made of her and played it up to the hilt. On nights when Jesse was at sea, Elizabeth would come and stay in the small spare bedroom that was destined to become the nursery. She held Greer's hair from her face when she was being sick; she massaged her stick-thin ankles in case they got puffy, and she fed her exquisite morsels of goodness – but not too much, as neither of them wanted to let Greer gain more weight than was necessary.

Mickey was happiest of all. 'Jesse, mate.' He bear-hugged him when he'd got the news. 'I didn't know you had it in you!'

Jesse adopted a macho pose. 'Plenty of lead in my pencil.'

'Pencil? You mean that tiny little thing?' The young men wrestled affectionately for a moment, as they always had done. When they broke apart Mickey asked, 'Fancy a pint? Or have you got to get on home to the missus?'

'I don't have to ask her for permission, you know,' swaggered Jesse. 'Barefoot and pregnant and tied to the sink. That's the way it is in my house.'

Mickey grinned. 'Yeah, right. Just don't let Greer hear you say that!' They were walking back from a day's work on the harbour and heading towards the Golden Hind.

Settled in a favourite corner of the dim bar, they each took a sip of their pints and sighed with pleasure in unison.

'So when's Jesse Junior due?' asked Mickey, wiping the froth from his lips.

'Middle of October.'

'Were you trying for a baby this quick?'

'No. We hadn't really spoken about it. And I thought these things took a bit of trying for.'

'She wasn't on the pill?'

'With the wedding and everything, Greer said she hadn't had time to get to the doctor's and – you know – she hadn't needed anything like that before, so . . .'

'You were her first?'

'Yeah.'

Mickey took a mouthful of beer then said, 'I was Loveday's first, too.'

Jesse tried not to react to this, but he spilt his beer a little onto his jeans. 'Shit,' he said, rubbing the damp patch into the fabric. When he'd gathered himself, he looked straight into Mickey's eyes. 'Were you? When was this?'

'The night you came home from honeymoon.'

'But you always told me . . .'

Mickey looked embarrassed. 'Yeah, well, that was just talk. She never let me touch her until that night. I think seeing you two so happy tipped the balance for me, so I have a lot to thank you for, mate.'

Jesse felt shame and fear wash through him, but smiled warmly. 'Well done.'

'Yeah.' Mickey put his pint on the table and looked down at the floor as if deciding whether to say anything more. 'Truth is, Loveday thinks she might be pregnant too.'

Jesse stared hard at Mickey. 'What?'

*

Dr Cosgrove washed his hands in the small sink in his surgery and took a paper towel to dry them. 'Congratulations to you both. Now, let's work out when this baby is due. When did your last period start, Loveday?'

Loveday clutched Mickey's hand. She had two answers and fervently hoped it was the second one. She crossed her fingers and said, 'About the tenth of January.'

Dr Cosgrove consulted his diary. 'This baby is due roughly around . . . October the seventeenth.'

'That's the same day as Jesse's baby!' Mickey was thrilled and squeezed Loveday's hand tight. 'That's amazing!'

Dr Cosgrove was putting Loveday's notes back into the brown envelope to be filed. 'You feel a little bit bigger than your dates suggest.'

Loveday looked anxious.

'No need to worry, my dear.' Dr Cosgrove smiled reassuringly and turned to Mickey. 'There are twins on your side of the family, aren't there?'

Mickey and Loveday walked out of the surgery holding hands, each thinking their own thoughts. Loveday prayed she was having Mickey's baby, or babies, as the doctor had suggested. She didn't care if she was expecting quadruplets, just as long as they were Mickey's and not Jesse's.

Mickey's mind was in a whirl. He was twenty-one. The same age his dad had been when he'd had him. He had a good job and he loved Loveday so much it hurt. They could live with his mum and dad for a bit till he'd got some money together to rent a little place. He was going to be the best dad he could be to this little baby, and the best husband to Loveday.

He stopped abruptly in his tracks and Loveday with him. 'Darlin', will you marry me?'

17

Greer was lying on her bed and smoothing oil onto her flat stomach in the hope of preventing stretch marks. *The Giant Book of Babies – From conception to five years* was next to her.

'It says here that at six weeks the baby is the size of a lentil. Imagine.' She stopped her massaging and clasped both hands across her abdomen. 'A lentil.'

Jesse was cleaning his teeth in the newly painted bathroom (a nondescript colour called Pebble Putty, apparently). He stepped onto the landing and stuck his damp face round the bedroom door. 'I don't like lentils.'

Greer tutted silently and said more clearly, 'I'm saying that the baby is the size of a lentil right now. And please remember to fold the towel and hang it on the towel heater.'

Jesse, safely back in the bathroom, pulled a face and mimicked her with childlike satisfaction. However, he did as instructed and turned out the bathroom light.

'Did you put the loo seat down?' she asked as he got into bed.

'I think so.'

'Well, can you check, because I need to pee so much in the night and I can't stand the feeling of cold, probably wet, china to sit on.'

'Turn the light on if you need to go.'

'I don't like to disturb you.'

Jesse disturbed himself and got out of bed and went to the bathroom to check on the loo seat. It was up. He closed it as quietly as he could and returned to bed.

Greer had stopped massaging her tummy and was rubbing hand cream into her hands with vigour. 'Was the seat up?'

'No.'

'Well, thank you for checking.' Greer had finished emolliating herself and kissed Jesse before turning her light out.

'My pleasure.'

Jesse turned his light out and got himself comfortable.

Greer rolled towards him and snuggled in. 'By the way,' she said sleepily, 'wonderful news about Mickey and Loveday.'

Jesse was immediately on his guard. 'What news?'

'Oh, you boys! I know you know. Loveday told me.'

'Told you what?'

'That she's pregnant. It's so sweet. They've been destined for each other ever since that first day at school.'

'Oh, that. Yeah, Mickey told me.'

'And the baby's due at about the same time as this little one.' She reached for his hand and pressed it against her stomach.

Jesse was thinking about the babies arriving at the same time. 'So does that mean that she and Mickey were at it at the same time we were?'

'Yes, I suppose so.' Greer giggled. She felt Jesse's body relax against her and assumed he wanted sex. 'Now don't get any ideas. You know how worried I am about hurting the baby. Maybe we can resume games in the second trimester.'

Jesse's thoughts were far from sex, but he played along. 'When's that then?'

'About another six weeks.'

*

Jesse chose a day when he knew that Mickey was in Bodmin, on an errand to pick up an ignition coil for *Our Mermaid*, to see Loveday. She opened the door to him in a short dressing gown that was at least two sizes too small for her. She looked awful.

'Jesse,' she said anxiously. 'What are you doing here?'

'Can I come in?'

Jesse filled the space of the small front room. He didn't sit down but stood looking at her with such tenderness that it took all Loveday's strength not to reach out and hold him.

'How are you feeling?' he asked her.

'A bit shit. Sorry, I must look awful. I didn't sleep very well and I keep being sick.'

'Poor you.' He touched her arm with his hand.

She stepped away and towards the tiny kitchen. 'I was just about to put the kettle on. Want one?'

'Yeah. OK.'

'How's Greer feeling? She said she was a bit tired.'

'Yeah. She's OK. Yeah.'

Loveday busied herself with taking mugs from the old kitchen cabinet. It was the type that had a pull-down worktop and cupboard space for larder items and crockery. He saw that she'd been making toast.

'Had your breakfast then? That'll help with the sickness, my mum says.'

The blue enamel kettle was whistling on the gas stove.

Loveday poured water into her mother's ancient brown teapot. And kept her back to him. 'What are you doing here, Jesse?'

He moved towards her but she turned and stood with the hot kettle between them. 'This baby is Mickey's,' she said.

'Loveday, I'm not cross. I'd help you. If this baby is mine, no one need ever know, if that's what you want.'

He wasn't expecting her reaction to be so swift and angry. 'So you'd let Mickey think this baby was his – which it is – and you'd be the big man secretly helping me out?'

Jesse nodded, feeling scolded and confused. 'Yes. I would. Is that so bad?'

'It'd be worse than cheating on your best friend . . . which you did.'

'So did you.'

Loveday was angry. She slammed the kettle back on the metal stove. 'I know I did. Don't you think I regret it every minute? Every time I look at Mickey? Every time I look at Greer? Shit, Jesse, we did something terrible.' She looked up at him, the anger draining away to be replaced by sheer horror and sadness at what they had both done – sleeping with each other's best friend; sacrificing their own happiness. Tears started to spill from her eyes.

Jesse slowly stepped towards her and took her in his arms. 'Hey, baby. It's OK. It's over. No one will ever know. I'm here for you. Always.' She pushed him away and wiped her eyes furiously with the backs of her hands, and then tore off a sheet of kitchen roll to blow her nose.

'You're not the father,' she snuffled.

'Are you sure?'

'Yes.'

'How can you be so sure?'

'The dates.'

Jesse shoved his hands into the pockets of his yellow waterproof jacket. 'Well, in that case, congratulations . . . to you both.'

They heard the front door squeak open and Mickey's voice calling, 'Loveday, I've got a surprise for you! What are you doing on Wednesday the seventeenth?'

Mickey ducked through the doorway of the kitchen. 'Hello, Jesse. This is lucky: I can kill two birds with one stone. What are both of you doing on Wednesday the seventeenth of March?'

He looked from one to the other and back again. 'No? Can't answer? Well, I'll tell you what you are doing – you're going to a wedding! We've got an appointment at the Register Office on Monday, then we have to wait fifteen days, but then . . .' He bounced forward and squeezed Loveday into his arms. 'You're going to be Mrs Chandler, and Jesse – ' he smiled at his best friend over the top of his wife-to-be's head – 'you're going to be my best man!'

*

The Bodmin Register Office had a small and pretty marriage room. The walls were Doulton blue and the ceiling white. There was a large arrangement of silk flowers in a corner by the window, in front of which happy couples usually had their first photos taken as man and wife. There was room for only forty guests but, as neither bride nor groom could afford a large wedding, at least ten seats were empty.

Mickey and Jesse sat in front of the important-looking leather-topped table on which the registrar, a woman in her early forties with a chirpy smile and earrings to match, was laying out her various ledgers and pieces of paper.

Mickey had had a short back and sides and was wearing a new suit from Burton's.

He was nervous and couldn't keep his hands from checking his tie, his hair and eventually his pockets. The inside breast pocket yielded the washing instructions.

'Machine washable at 40°,' he read. 'That's handy.'

'Very,' said Jesse, and the two men grinned at each other, enjoying the momentary distraction.

'Do I look all right?' Mickey asked.

'You'll do.'

'Have you got the ring?'

'Yes.'

'At least I'm not pissed like you were.'

Jesse instantly flashed back to his wedding morning and the horrible secret he was keeping from Mickey. 'If I can be half the best man and best mate you've been to me, I'll be doing OK.'

Mickey shone his innocent smile at Jesse. 'I'm so happy. I can't believe that Loveday is actually going to marry me and that we have a baby on the way. This is the best day of my life.'

*

Outside, in the chilly anteroom, where brides could gather with their flotilla of bridesmaids and attendants, Loveday was taking deep breaths. Greer was rummaging in her bag for some Rescue Remedy.

'Here,' she said, holding up the small brown bottle and opening it to reveal the glass pipette. 'Three drops under the tongue. Open wide.'

Loveday did as she was told and Greer dripped in the recommended amount, with another couple of drops for luck.

Loveday grimaced. 'That's bleddy brandy!'

'It's needed to preserve the delicate flower essences.'

'We're not supposed to drink, with the babies and all.'

'This is medicinal. How are you feeling?'

'A bit better. How do I look?'

Greer gave Loveday an inspection from head to toe and back again. The charity shop wedding dress was in good condition, but clearly bought at the height of the mania to imitate Princess Diana. Oddly enough it suited Loveday, who had the bust to fill it.

'Have you lost weight?' asked Greer who, in spite of being careful with what she was eating, had put on four pounds.

'I have. I think it's all that sickness.'

'How much have you lost?'

'About ten pounds.'

'Well,' Greer smiled thinly, 'it suits you.' Then, knowing that had sounded mean she added, 'You look very nice. Very nice indeed.'

Loveday beamed. 'Thank you. You look amazing in that dress too.'

'Thank you. Can you see my bump? I feel huge.' Greer stood sideways to let Loveday get a proper view.

'No. But your bosoms are blossoming!' Loveday gave an earthy laugh.

Greer pulled at the top of her stylish shift dress. 'Oh God. I'm hoping they don't droop.'

Loveday hoiked up her own breasts with gusto. 'Mine were drooping when I was born.'

There was a knock at the door. The assistant registrar, a middle-aged man wearing glasses, popped his head round the door. 'We are ready for the bride.'

Greer collected up her tiny clutch bag and a box of confetti and held out her hand to Loveday.

'Are you ready to become Mrs Chandler, Miss Carter?' she said before adding, 'It's not too late to say no, you know. In my capacity as best woman, it's my duty to ask you.'

Loveday looked at her closest friend. So many people found Greer to be a bit cold, rather too pleased with herself and – to be frank – a snob, but Loveday knew Greer had a good heart and she felt such guilt that she could have betrayed her as she had. She had chosen Greer to give her away as a way of exorcising that night with Jesse and of consolidating their friendship again. She reached for Greer's hand. 'Bless you for taking my dad's place and giving me away. Mum's really chuffed too.' This wasn't true. Loveday's mother had wanted to give her daughter away herself, but had deferred to Loveday's wishes.

'My pleasure,' smiled Greer, swelling with importance. 'Now pick up that bouquet and go get your man.'

*

The two women walked hand in hand down the short aisle. There were oohs and aahs from the small congregation as they pulled unruly toddlers onto laps and fished for tissues in their pockets. Loveday was well loved in Trevay and they were thrilled that she was marrying the man who adored her. This was true romance. A budget shotgun wedding with heart and a guaranteed happy ending.

Mickey gulped with emotion as he saw his bride in all her lacy finery. Loveday's mother leant out into the aisle with a disposable camera and took two shots, winding each one on carefully, before starting to sniffle. Jesse stared straight ahead until Greer, who had delivered Loveday to Mickey's side, slipped in next to him. She reached for his hand. He took hers as a drowning man would grasp at a life raft.

The registrar started. 'Welcome, everybody, to the marriage of Michael and Loveday.'

Loveday took her vows and meant them. She was determined to do her best by Mickey and be the best wife to him that she could, no matter what had gone before.

*

The reception was a boozy, smoke-filled affair at the Golden Hind. As best man, Jesse had put plenty of money behind the bar as his wedding present to the couple. The buffet table was groaning under pasties and sausage rolls, and a good time was had by all.

Jesse's speech was well judged, if short, and everyone agreed the day couldn't have gone more smoothly. At least that was until the time for the reading of the telegrams.

Jesse had had a couple of pints and was relaxing. His best friend was married. Loveday was expecting her husband's baby, and Greer was expecting his. The sky was not going to fall in, after all.

There were four telegrams. One from Mickey's godmother, who now lived in New Zealand, and two from old friends of Loveday's mother. It was the final one that struck like a sniper's bullet. He started reading it before he'd checked who it was from. It was from his brother, Grant. 42 Commando had been deployed to Northern Iraq to ensure the security of Kurdish refugees. Somehow, Grant had managed to get a telegram out. It said: CONGRATULATIONS STOP HOPE THE BABY DOESN'T LOOK LIKE HIS DADDY STOP DRINKS WHEN I GET HOME STOP REGARDS BIG G STOP

Jesse couldn't help flicking his eyes towards Loveday, who looked as if she might faint. Did Grant know what they had done? Why had he put that?

Mickey was on his – unsteady – feet now and was clapping Jesse on the back. 'Typical of your fucking brother. What a wind-up merchant.' Mickey was laughing and so was the rest of the pub. Jesse laughed nervously and again looked over at Loveday, who had been collared by a tipsy auntie. Jesse did the only thing he could think of and hauled Mickey to the bar to get smashed.

18

The following months were kind to Mickey and Loveday. Her mum welcomed the newlyweds into her tiny cottage and Mickey got a pay rise on the boat. He'd also started an apprenticeship to be the ship's mechanic and was away at sea a lot, but the fishing was good and now that the Behenna and Clovelly Fish Company was established, the prices at market were steady.

Loveday worked shifts at the bakery where she'd been a Saturday girl since she was at school. She liked the work and the banter between her colleagues and customers. She also liked the fact that her pregnancy had driven her hunger for pasties and sausage rolls right out of the door. Her weight was dropping and her midwife was pleased.

'Good girl. That's another two pounds off.' Loveday was worried.

'Will the baby be OK?'

'Baby is fine. Growing well. Don't worry, just keep listening to your body and eating healthily.'

Loveday stepped back into her shoes. 'It's funny 'cos before I was pregnant I craved chips and chocolate; now I crave salad and fish.'

The midwife was writing in her records book and laughed. 'You'll make my other ladies jealous. Just promise me you're not going on any fad diets.'

'Oh, I promise. My mum and Mickey would never let me. Mickey worries more than I do.'

The midwife handed Loveday her records card and said, 'I wish all dads were the same. See you in four weeks.'

*

If everything was going well for Loveday, things were not as easy for Greer. Her first three months were marred by extreme exhaustion and a chest infection. The second three months by heartburn and headaches. Also, she was putting weight on; she'd noticed her wedding ring feeling tighter on her finger.

During a routine visit to the antenatal clinic, in her twenty-seventh week, the midwife looked concerned. 'Greer, your blood pressure is a bit too high for my liking. You need to rest more. In fact, I am telling you to get as much rest as you can.'

Greer shifted her bulk on the uncomfortable plastic chair and felt tears burning her eyes. 'I'm so huge. I need to take exercise, don't I?'

'It depends what sort of exercise.'

'A little walk.'

'How little is little?'

'I go up the hill to The Pavilions and along the cliffs to Shellsand Bay.'

'Absolutely not. That's a good forty-minute round trip!'

'But I'm getting so fat.'

'Let's weigh you.'

The scales registered a considerable weight gain since the last visit.

The midwife smiled a poker-face smile. 'Let's get a

urine sample done and I'll get Mr Cunningham in to see you. You're lucky he's got his clinic here this morning.'

Greer went to the Ladies and duly peed into the small plastic tube. Her arm was only just long enough to get round her bump and to the required position. Naturally the first try splashed on her hand and onto the outside of the pot. 'Oh shit shit shit,' she said to the cubicle walls. 'Just what I bloody well needed.' Eventually the pot was filled and the lid screwed down. She just about managed to get her knickers up with her one dry hand and then washed the pot and her hands under hot water with lots of soap.

In the mirror above the sink she hardly recognised the pale and bloated face staring back at her.

The midwife took the pot and said nothing about the damp label. 'Mr Cunningham will pop in in a moment. Would you like a cup of tea?'

Greer was grateful for the kindness and accepted the tea without any sense that she should have warning bells ringing.

She was quietly enjoying her hot drink when there was a sharp knock on the door.

'Hello, Mrs Behenna.' A tall handsome man of about fifty entered the room and closed the door quietly behind him. Mr Cunningham was a consultant gynaecologist of extreme experience and fame among the women of the area. He had a suntanned face and wore a well-tailored navy-blue suit, both of which said, 'I'm a professional. You are in good hands.' Greer felt safe. 'Hello, Mr Cunningham. I wasn't expecting to see you until nearer the delivery.'

'Ah, yes, but Midwife Yvonne is rather worried about you.' He pulled a chair out and sat opposite her, taking her hands into his. He carefully pressed her finger joints and gave a gentle tug of her wedding ring. 'Have you noticed your wedding band getting a little tight?'

'Yes. I'm getting so fat.'

He let go of her hands and asked to see her ankles. 'They look a bit swollen too.'

'Horrible, aren't they?' She felt deeply unattractive.

The midwife entered with the results of the urine test and handed them to Mr Cunningham. 'Thank you, Yvonne. Now let me see . . . Protein is present. Tell me, Mrs Behenna, how are you feeling generally? A bit grotty?'

'A bit. I'm just tired, I think.'

Mr Cunningham thought for a moment then said, 'Yvonne, help Mrs Behenna up onto the couch. I just want to check on baby.'

Mr Cunningham examined her thoroughly. He listened to the baby's heartbeat and measured the size of her bump. When he had finished, he offered a strong arm to help her sit up and step off the couch. 'Come and sit down and I'll explain what I think is going on.'

*

Greer was advised not to walk home, but to phone her mother to come and collect her. Elizabeth had arrived looking distraught; her car was left parked rather messily in a disabled bay.

She listened intently to what the midwife had to say and together they got a frightened-looking Greer to the car. An elderly man was pacing angrily, waiting for them.

'Are you entitled to park in a disabled bay?' He jabbed his finger at Elizabeth, who ignored him. He came closer and stuck his face into Elizabeth's, flecks of spittle flying through his dentures and onto her cheek. 'Are you deaf? Do you have a blue badge?'

Midwife Yvonne put an arm out to fend him off. 'Please. This lady is a patient of mine. She can't walk too far. Just a couple of minutes and you can have this space.'

'So she doesn't have a badge.' The man was triumphant. 'I'm taking your registration number and using it as evidence. You have parked unlawfully.'

The pugnacious little man had found a pen and a tatty envelope and was scribbling down the number plate. 'I want your name,' he snarled at Elizabeth as she walked round the car to get into the driver's seat. Still she ignored him.

'I said, I want your name,' he shrieked.

Elizabeth got into the driving seat and turned on the ignition. Putting the car into reverse she backed out of the space. From within the car she could see the man in the rear-view mirror; she reversed a little further until he was forced to step aside. He was still ranting. As he ran to the front of the car to check her tax disc, Elizabeth calmly opened her electric window and said, in her most polite voice: 'Piss off, you odious little berk.'

*

Greer was settled in their bed by the time Jesse got home. Elizabeth had phoned him as soon as they'd arrived, thanking God that he wasn't away at sea.

'Darlin',' he said, taking her hand. 'What the 'ell's going on?'

Greer looked pale and puffy but comfortable on the pillows that her mother had so lovingly arranged. Her swollen feet were raised on more cushions. 'I'm fine. It's all going to be fine. I just need to rest. They're worried I've got pre-eclampsia.'

'What the 'ell's that?'

'Something to do with my blood pressure being high and I've got protein in my wee, whatever that means. I just need to rest and get this puffiness down.'

'Is the baby all right?'

Greer looked at Jesse's face, full of concern for her and their child, and was overwhelmed with compassion and love for him. 'Yes. The baby's fine. As long as I rest and take things easy. The gynaecologist said that he'll keep an eye on me and as long as I don't get worse, everything will be fine.'

'And if it does get worse?'

Elizabeth elbowed the door open, carrying in a tray of tea with tiny cucumber sandwiches on a plate. She answered for Greer. 'She'll have to have the baby a bit earlier than planned, that's all.'

Jesse looked panicked. 'Have the baby early? That's not good, is it?'

Greer reached up and touched his cheek. 'Darling, it just means I'll have a Caesarean and the baby will be fine and I will be fine.'

'Sure?'

'Sure.'

Jesse watched as Greer sipped her cup of tea and nibbled a cucumber sandwich. Was this his fault? His punishment? He would rather die himself than let anything happen to the baby or Greer. In a sudden guilt-ridden moment he knew that he loved her. The sudden realisation of what he had to lose if anyone found out about how despicable he had been, the lie he was keeping, hit him like a sledgehammer. Oh God, he said to himself, if you exist, please *please* let everything be all right. I promise I'll be true to Greer for the rest of my living days.

*

Loveday was bouncing with energy and good health. The fat from her hips and arms had melted away and her tummy stood round and proud in front of her. Most days, after her shift at the bakery finished, she'd walk up to Pencil Cottage with a little posy of sweet peas or an individual apple crumble or a small but interesting piece of gossip to entertain her housebound friend.

Greer was always pleased to see her. 'Mummy is driving me mad! I can't have five minutes' peace without her checking on me. I managed to dig out my sketchbook and pencils without her noticing. I wanted to do work on some design ideas for the nursery, but in she came and took them away from me. Said I had to sleep. It's like being a toddler again. Can you root about downstairs and see if you can find where she put them?'

Loveday laughed. ''Tis only because she loves you. She's worried for you and the baby. Not long now,' she consoled her.

*

By the third week of September, Loveday was feeling ready to pop. At the antenatal clinic she was asked if she had got her dates wrong. The baby looked to be full term.

'I'm sure I'm right. End of January this one got started.' The midwife gave her an old-fashioned look and a card with the maternity ward's phone number on it in case the baby came sooner than she expected.

It was the morning of 3 October at 7.45 when Loveday's waters broke. Mickey had been given some shore leave so that he could be on hand if anything happened.

'Mickey,' called Loveday urgently from the bathroom. 'Mickey, help.'

Mickey had been dreaming of his old scooter and how he missed it, but the anguish in Loveday's voice soon roused him. Seeing she wasn't next to him, he leapt out of bed calling, 'Loveday, where are you?'

'I'm in bathroom, you div. I think the baby's coming.'

He ran to the bathroom to find her on all fours with a large puddle around her.

'Oh my good God. What do I do?'

'Call the maternity unit and tell them we're coming in. Pick up my bag – it's packed and under my dressing table – and get me to the bloody hospital.'

*

In twenty minutes she was sitting in a warm birthing pool and feeling a ton less scared than she had been on the floor of the bathroom – or, for that matter, in the front seat of Mickey's crappy Austin Allegro, whose suspension had clearly collapsed.

Two hours later, both mother and father were besotted with their wailing, nine-and-half-pound son, who they named Hal.

19

Mickey sat in the softly lit gloom of Loveday's curtained bay on the maternity ward, holding his son and watching with fascination the dear and oddly familiar face. Phantom dreams twitched Baby Hal's lips and wrinkled his nose. Mickey lifted the swaddled body to his face and nuzzled the soft red hair, sitting like a halo on the fragile head. Hal looked like Loveday but he smelled of his own unique perfume. Warm, new and precious.

He whispered in his son's ear: 'I love you, Hal. I'll always be here for you. You can come to me for anything, 'cos I'm your dad.'

Hal wriggled and stretched, a beatific smile spreading over his face. His eyelids fluttered and opened a little. Man and boy stared at each other. 'Hello. I'm your daddy,' said Mickey.

'And I'm the mummy,' said Loveday, rustling the waterproof mattress and cotton sheets as she hauled herself upright from her sleep.

'Hello, Mummy,' grinned Mickey. 'We were just having a little chat while you were grabbing a few zeds.' He held Hal up, in front of his own lips, and said in a squeaky voice, 'Hello, Mummy. Daddy and I were just thinking of going for a pint.'

'Lucky you. I could murder a cider,' Loveday smiled.

'No luck, love, but I can get a cup of tea if you want?'

Mickey carefully handed his precious bundle to Loveday then went in search of refreshment. Loveday held Hal and stared at him. Examining every inch looking for similarities. After a few moments, she grunted with satisfaction. He looked like her. Same hair colouring. Same chin . . . but whose eyes did he have? Mickey's. Definitely Mickey's. Yes, Mickey's.

She analysed again her beautiful son's face; she couldn't find a trace of Jesse.

But a voice in her head began to whisper insidious doubts.

He's a big boy for being two weeks early. But he's the right size for being ten days overdue. Are you sure that little bleed – spotting really – in January was an actual period?

She bent her face to her innocent child and drank in the scent of him. Her lips feeling the wrinkles of his neck as she mouthed softly, 'You're mine and that's the important thing.'

The curtains around her bed swished on their plastic track and Mickey appeared with two cups of tea on rattling saucers. 'Here you go, my bird. Just saw the nurse. She's asking about breast-feeding. I said yes please.'

Loveday laughed, in spite of herself. 'Daddy's a cheeky monkey, isn't he, Hal?'

As if on cue, Hal started to whimper. His little face screwing up in pink confusion as he thought about what he really wanted. Then came the full-blown cry of a hungry baby.

By the time the nurse, an efficient woman of about thirty with short blond hair, got to him, he was happily clamped onto Loveday and suckling drowsily.

'Well done, Mum!' congratulated the nurse. 'You're a

natural. Now then, I think we'll keep you in tonight and . . .' She turned to look at Mickey. 'Daddy, if everything is all right, you can come back in the morning and take your lovely little family home.'

'Ideal,' smiled Mickey happily.

The nurse turned back to Loveday. 'I'll check on you both later, but first I've got to check on a lady who's on her way in as an emergency.'

They heard the sound of wheels on the rubber floor and the noise of anxious voices approaching.

The nurse stopped and listened. 'That'll be them.' And with another swish of the curtain, back and forward on its rail, the nurse left.

'Have you phoned home yet and told the grand-parents?' asked Loveday, who had happily lost track of all time and all responsibility for the outside world. Her focus had shrunk to her son.

'Yeah. Did that when you two were having a kip. They're all delighted and your mum sends her love. She wanted to come in tonight but I told her you were knackered.'

'Thank you, darlin'.' Loveday did feel a bit knackered now she thought about it. 'Do I look all right?'

'You look bleddy beautiful.' He got up from the armchair and bent to kiss his wife. 'Who's a clever girl?'

'I am.'

'All right, big head!' he joked, ducking before she cuffed him.

'I think I might make tracks. I want to tell Jesse all about fatherhood. It'll be the first time I've ever had anything before he has.'

Loveday felt the wound of her betrayal split open a little.

'Bye, Hal.' Mickey was bending to kiss his son. 'Be a good boy for Mummy.'

*

Beyond the curtains, a man's voice started to shout, sounding panicked. 'Nurse. Nurse. My wife is unwell. Help. Nurse.'

Mickey and Loveday listened, stock-still, as at least two sets of footsteps walked quickly towards the man's voice.

'She's shaking. She's blue. What's happening, Nurse?' asked the man, his voice trembling with panic.

'She's having a seizure,' said a female voice, who they recognised as the nurse who had just left them. She was using a calm, professional voice, which became more urgent as she issued sharp instructions to her colleague. 'Call theatre. Tell them we're on the way down.'

'Will she be OK? Will my baby be OK?' The man was beyond anguished.

'Mr Behenna, we will do everything we can to safely deliver your child. Now please . . .' Mickey and Loveday heard the metal sides of a hospital bed clang. 'I must get your wife to theatre.'

'Can I come with her?'

'The best thing you can do is wait here and I'll bring news as soon as possible.'

They listened as the bed rattled from the ward and went down some unknown corridor.

They listened as the man tried to quieten his frightened sobs.

Mickey knew what he had to do. He stepped out of the cubicle and put his arms around his best friend.

Jesse started. 'Mickey! They've taken Greer to theatre. She was shaking and her eyes were rolling. I'm scared. They won't let me go down to be with her. I've got to wait here.' He looked at the empty bay that had just held Greer's bed. 'Will you wait with me?'

'Of course I will.'

'You haven't got to get home to Loveday?'

'No.'

'Did Mum tell you we were in the ambulance up here? Is that why you came?'

'No. I was here anyway.'

'What?'

'Loveday's had a little boy. We've called him Hal.'

Jesse looked demented. 'You have a son?' He clasped at Mickey's sleeve. 'Loveday has a son?'

Mickey nodded, and steered his bewildered friend to a chair. 'Let me get you a cup of tea.'

'Can I see them? The baby and Loveday?'

Loveday, behind the safety of her curtains, gripped her sleeping son a little tighter and held her breath, hoping fervently that Mickey would say no.

'Let's see them later,' she heard him say. 'When we know Greer is all OK. Then we can meet together. Babies, mums and all.'

Jesse was slumped onto his chair. 'Yes. Yes. Of course.'

'Right, let me get you that cup of tea.'

*

Greer's son, Freddie, was delivered at 9.38 that night, by Caesarean section. He weighed five pounds six ounces and, despite being two weeks early, was pronounced healthy. Greer, on the other hand, knew nothing of the birth, or that she had a son. The severe pre-eclampsia had developed very rapidly that afternoon. That morning she had woken with a painful headache, which she couldn't budge. By teatime she had blurred vision with flashing lights and her hands, feet and face were getting increasingly swollen. It was Elizabeth who had called the ambulance.

*

Jesse, pale and exhausted, was finally allowed to see her some time after midnight. She was asleep in a quiet side room. Drips and monitors surrounded her. 'How is she?' he asked the young nurse who was writing something on the clipboard that hooked onto the foot of the bed.

'She's stable but needs complete rest.'

'Can I sit with her?'

'Of course, but she needs to sleep. I'll be back in fifteen minutes to do her checks again.'

Jesse nodded his understanding and pulled up a small plastic chair that was nearest to the bed. He sat and took her hand. There was a cannula taped to the back of it with a tube leading to a stand with a bag of fluid on it. Like a metronome, it dripped its regular drip into her body.

'Greer?' he whispered. 'Can you hear me?' She gave no response. 'We have a little boy. Freddie has arrived! We did agree on Freddie, didn't we?' He wrinkled his eyebrows anxiously. 'If you want to change it when you wake up, that's no problem.' The quiet hiss of the oxygen tube under her nostrils was the only response. He carried on regardless, the sound of his voice in the silence reassuring him, soothing his frayed nerves.

'I've been to see him. Handsome boy. Ten fingers and ten toes. He's in special care at the moment. They're keeping an eye on him till you're able to.' He felt the prick of tears and bowed his head, resting it on her hand 'Darlin', you'm gonna get better soon. The doctor says your liver, or did he say kidneys, I always get them mixed up; anyway, they might be affected, but you're in good hands. You've got to rest, take it easy.'

The nurse entered the room. 'I think you should go home now, Mr Behenna. We've given your wife a sedative that should keep her sleeping for the next few hours. Get some rest. Come back in the morning. Your wife is going to need you to be fit to take care of her and . . .' She raised her eyebrows questioningly.

'Freddie,' he said.

'Freddie. What a lovely name. So yes, you go home and we'll see you in the morning. Any change and we'll call you.'

*

Mr Cunningham sat reassuringly and handsomely at the desk in his consulting room. Greer's father was insistent that this should be a private appointment rather than NHS.

Greer and Jesse were shown in by the cool secretary, who looked like Miss Moneypenny and had clearly also been in love with her employer for years.

Mr Cunningham stood up and greeted the couple.

'Do take a seat.' He gestured to the comfortable upholstered chairs facing his desk.

'How are you, Greer?'

'A lot better, thank you.'

'And young Freddie? Not keeping you awake too much?'

'Oh, you know. He's not a great sleeper, but my mother is doing the night feeds and being back at my parents' house is nice.'

'All those home-cooked meals?' smiled Mr Cunningham. He turned to Jesse.

'And how's Dad doing – you've had quite a lot to deal with, haven't you.' It was a statement, not a question.

Jesse took his eyes off the silver-framed photos of Mrs Cunningham and offspring and tried to shake the tiredness from his brain. God, he was exhausted. Freddie was noisy, angry and impossible. Greer was fragile, and distanced from him, now that she was back at her parents' house.

'Sorry . . . what did you say?'

Mr Cunningham gave a benign professional smile. 'You've had a lot to deal with. Greer's illness. A new baby.'

'No, I'm fine. Just want to know how Greer is.'

'Ah, yes.' The consultant opened a leather folder on his desk and took out a more modest buff folder. Inside were several sheets of paper: Greer's medical notes. Mr Cunningham cleared his throat. 'Greer has had an episode of severe pre-eclampsia which developed into eclampsia. If we hadn't operated on her and delivered Freddie, you might have lost them both.'

The consultation took thirty minutes. Mr Cunningham explained that the condition was little understood, but that it needn't necessarily stop the majority of women from having normal pregnancies in the future. Mr Cunningham paused and arranged his features sombrely. 'Unfortunately, Greer falls into the minority group of women who I wouldn't recommend trying for another baby. It could be dangerous for her and the child. This is only my recommendation and you must do as you think best – but, truthfully, I do believe you shouldn't contemplate adding to your family. I'm sorry.'

20

Greer absorbed the news with a quiet acceptance. Jesse was devastated. But as neither of them was able to talk to each other with anything other than superficial stoicism, they didn't know how each of them truly felt.

When Freddie was almost six weeks old, Jesse made his regular nightly trip to his in-laws' house to see his wife and son.

Freddie was in the arms of his grandmother, drinking greedily from his bottle of formula.

Greer was taking a bath.

In the silence of the beige and cream sitting room, with its sateen sofas and Tiffany lamps, Jesse felt a stranger. Foreign. His presence neither understood nor recognised.

'How is Greer doing?' he asked Elizabeth. He wanted to ask his mother-in-law specifically when Greer could come home, but he felt awkward. He didn't want Elizabeth to accuse him of pushing Greer before she was ready.

Freddie released the teat from his mouth and Elizabeth expertly lifted him upright and forward so that she could rub his back. Freddie obliged with a deep burp.

'Good boy,' said his grandmother. 'Who's a good boy for Nanny? Want some more? Still hungry?' She stroked the teat against Freddie's lips until he took it in his mouth and closed his eyes, sucking sleepily.

Jesse asked again. 'Is she feeling better?'

Elizabeth didn't look at him as she answered. 'She's still very weak.'

Jesse tried again. 'You've been wonderful. Looking after her and Freddie. I can't wait to have them home.'

'Yes, well, Greer will know when she's well enough.' Freddie was now asleep. His head lolling in the crook of his grandmother's elbow. A small stream of creamy dribble was escaping from his lips. 'Now then, young man. It's the Moses basket for you,' said Elizabeth, putting the bottle on the table at her side and preparing to stand up.

Jesse jumped up from his chair, hoping that he might be able to help. He hadn't had many chances to hold Freddie in the last six weeks. He had not yet been allowed to give him his bottle. 'Can I hold him?'

Elizabeth hesitated before saying, 'I think he needs to sleep. He likes it. It's better that we keep his little routine going.'

Greer came in wearing her old Snoopy dressing gown and with her hair wound into a towelling turban. 'Hi, Jesse. You're earlier than usual.' Her face lit up. 'Mum, you didn't tell me Jesse was here.'

'I didn't want to disturb you when you were having a nice bath.'

Greer went to Jesse and hugged him. 'Have you had a cuddle with Freddie?'

Jesse saw his chance. 'I was just asking your mum.'

'He's asleep,' said Elizabeth, still holding Freddie. 'I'm just about to put him down.'

'Mum! Jesse and Freddie haven't seen each other since

yesterday. And Jesse didn't get a cuddle then because you'd put Freddie down. Hand him over.'

'It's important to have a routine,' Elizabeth protested, but couldn't stop Greer taking Freddie.

'I know, Mum, and you've done a wonderful job, but hand him over to his daddy.' Greer turned to her husband, who gave Elizabeth a triumphant smile. 'Now, Jesse, sit down in that armchair and get comfy.' Greer took Freddie from her mother's arms and passed him into her husband's.

Elizabeth sniffed huffily as she left the room. 'I'll be in the kitchen if you need me.'

Jesse took him gently.

'Hello, Fred. Daddy's going to bring you and Mummy home soon,' he said in a comforting soft voice.

'Let's take him to my room for a proper cuddle.'

In her room and surrounded by the paraphernalia of babyhood such as boxes of Pampers, sterilising kits and bottles, Jesse sat on the bed holding their son while Greer sat at his feet, resting her chin on his knee. 'Did you get the cot built?'

'All done.'

'And the little mobile up?'

'Yes.'

'And the changing table? Is there enough room? It's such a tiny little room.'

'It's perfect. Like an efficient galley. Everything in arm's reach.'

She sighed happily. 'I'm looking forward to coming home.'

'When do you think that'll be?'

'Another couple of weeks.'

'Another two weeks! Freddie's six weeks now.'

'I know. Doesn't time go fast?'

Jesse didn't think so. 'I want you home at the weekend.'

Greer stiffened. 'I don't think I'm ready.'

'I want you back home. In our bed. I miss you.'

'You know what the doctor said.'

'He said no more children. Not no more sex.'

Greer pulled away from him. 'I'm just not ready to be on my own with Freddie. I haven't got the confidence yet.'

'You never will have if you let your mum do everything for you.'

Greer bit her bottom lip and Jesse could see tears forming. 'What's the matter?' he asked gently. 'Don't you want to come home?'

'It's not that.'

'Well, what is it?'

'I'll be lonely when you're working.'

'Loveday's just down the road. She can't wait to see you.'

Greer brightened a little. 'How is she? How's Hal?'

'Mickey says they're both doing really well.'

'Have you seen them? Loveday and Hal? I hear he's huge!'

'I haven't actually seen her or the baby since they left hospital, but I've seen pictures.'

Jesse hadn't risked seeing Hal or Loveday. He felt blessed that Freddie had survived and swore to himself that he would never be on his own with Loveday again. Mickey was like a dog with two tails with his new family, and Jesse wasn't going to jeopardise that happiness.

Greer shifted her weight and stood up, stretching. Jesse admired the slenderness of her figure through her dressing gown and felt the stirrings of desire.

'You look good, Greer. You don't look as if you've just had a baby.'

She pulled her gown closer. 'Thanks.'

'I really miss you.'

'I miss you too.'

'I mean I miss making love to you. We haven't done it for months.'

Greer took the sleeping Freddie from Jesse's arms. 'Well, we had this little one to think of, didn't we?'

Jesse got up and stood by Greer. They both looked at the sleeping Freddie. Jesse put his hand on Greer's bottom and caressed her buttock. 'I want to take you home now and have you in our bed.'

She pulled away. 'Don't. Mum might hear us.'

'To hell with her. We're married, aren't we?' He leant in and nuzzled her neck, dropping light kisses on her until he reached her mouth and tried to kiss her deeply. Greer kept her mouth shut tight.

'What's the matter, Greer?' he whispered.

'We mustn't have any more babies.' He could feel the tension in her.

'I know, darling. That's what the doctors say now, but medical advances are happening every day. We're only young. It's terrible for us both but we can still have sex and be careful.'

'It's not that.'

'What is it then?'

'I just don't feel like it.'

'Well, you will. When I've warmed you up.' He opened the front of her dressing gown and lifted her small breast out. He bent to lick her nipple.

'Don't. Please don't.' He stopped and she pulled her robe closed.

'What's the matter? We need to talk about this properly. I'm in bits. Trying to be strong and all that, but it's breaking my heart. I want to fill you and the house up with children but, like my mum says, we have got Freddie and we can give him the very best love a boy could ever have.'

Greer looked at Jesse intently and said, 'It's not that. I'm glad Freddie will be our only one. I hated being pregnant and I hate what it's done to my body. I'm fat. I have stretch marks. My breasts aren't the same. I don't think I ever want to have sex again.'

Jesse had been told by his mum that women needed a bit of love and patience after they'd had a baby, so he wasn't surprised or worried by this little speech.

'You look bloody gorgeous to me. I fancy you like mad. A few days at home and we'll get back to normal. Don't worry.'

Greer looked so frail and vulnerable, with her baggy Snoopy gown hanging off her tiny frame, that Jesse was overcome with compassion and passion. 'You need to come home. I need to have you home. You and Freddie. You're coming home tomorrow. I'll pick you up after work. Tell your mother.'

*

The next day Jesse was down on the harbour checking the gear on the boat. Greer's father, Bryn, was walking, with some purpose, towards him.

'All right, Jesse,' he called.

Jesse saw him and knew Bryn was on a mission from Elizabeth.

'Can I have a word?' Bryn asked.

'Sure. You can have a bucketful if you want, but I'll

not be dissuaded from having my wife and son home tonight.'

Bryn stepped onto *The Lobster Pot* and held his hands up in surrender. 'Am I that transparent?'

'You and Elizabeth have been wonderful, looking after Greer and Freddie. But it's six weeks now and time they came home,' said Jesse firmly.

'Well, of course you want your family home. Who wouldn't?' Bryn patted Jesse's shoulder. 'But it's a little too soon.'

'Who says?'

'We all do,' said Bryn smoothly. 'Maybe I should give you some time off. Paid leave. That way you could spend more time at our place.'

Jesse stuck his hands in the pockets of his overall and stood his ground. 'You've given me enough. Pencil Cottage, a say in the new business—'

'Yes, and you've given me a terrific grandson to carry the Clovelly name on in the business.'

'He's not a Clovelly. He's a Behenna.' Jesse was using a dangerously quiet voice.

'You know what I mean, son.' Bryn was smiling at Jesse as if he was the village idiot who needed appeasing. 'Greer is my first consideration. She needs looking after.'

Jesse had had enough. 'Bryn, with due respect, you've given Greer everything she's ever wanted. You even made sure you gave her me.'

Bryn sneered. 'Yes, and God knows why. You were happy to take the money that she came with, weren't you? The house, the pay rise, the promotion?'

Jesse felt anger burning in his gut. 'Greer is my wife. Freddie is my son, and they'm coming home tonight. I'll play the perfect son-in-law and I'll make this company a success, but you can't stop me bringing my family home. Oh, and by the way, your friendship with Monica at the golf club is common knowledge. Wouldn't take long for that to reach Elizabeth's ears.' This was a long shot. A piece of gossip that had been circulating for as long as Jesse could remember. He hadn't been sure it was true until this very moment.

Bryn went scarlet. 'What the hell are you talking about?'

'Oh, it's OK for me to tell Elizabeth about this stupid rumour, is it? If you're innocent, that's fine.'

Bryn's slick eyes were narrowed. 'You say one word of that filthy lie and I'll have your balls for shark bait.'

Jesse laughed. 'Mum's the word, then. Make sure Greer and Freddie are all packed when I get there.'

*

Jesse helped Greer and Freddie into Pencil Cottage. 'Welcome home,' he said, putting the sleeping Freddie and his car seat on the front-room carpet.

Greer looked around her. 'It looks so cosy.'

'Mum came round earlier. She's left flowers on the table for you. Look.'

A big bunch of Jan's late dahlias was sitting in a vase with a little envelope propped up next to it with Greer's name scrawled on it.

'That's sweet of her.' Greer hated blowsy dahlias and made a mental note to chuck them out the next day and get some white long-stemmed lilies which would be more in keeping with the house style. Then she sniffed. 'Can I smell cooking?'

'Oh, yeah,' grinned Jesse. 'She's popped a chicken pie

to warm in the oven and she's brought some of her frozen runner beans over too. Are you hungry?'

'Not very.'

On cue a hungry Freddie woke up and started squalling. 'Shall I make up a bottle?' asked Jesse.

'I'll do it.' Greer began rummaging in one of the copious baby bags that Freddie seemed to need.

'Well, I'll watch how you do it, then I can do the next one,' Jesse said gently.

'It might be the middle of the night.'

'I want to share it with you. I need to learn. I'm used to being up in the night, remember?'

Greer unclipped Freddie from his chair and handed him to Jesse. 'Bloody hell, he pongs,' he laughed, pulling a face.

'Well,' said Greer on her way to the kitchen, 'this will be a night of firsts. I'll teach you how to change a nappy too.'

21

Being back at home felt better than she had expected, and seeing Freddie sleeping in his cot in the tiny nursery gave her deep satisfaction. Her days were full of washing and sterilising, feeding and winding, but she coped well. Some days she even managed to grab a shower and make a simple supper for Jesse when he came home.

If she'd had any worries about resuming their sex life, she needn't have bothered. Jesse, who insisted on doing the night feeds, was too knackered to ask.

*

It was the second week after she'd returned home that Mickey rang and invited her and Jesse round for supper.

'Bring littl'un, too. Loveday and I are dying to see him. Loveday wanted to come round the other day but Jesse said you weren't up to visitors yet.'

Greer was surprised. 'Did he? I'd love to see you. I've tried to phone Loveday a couple of times but either Hal was crying or I got no answer.' Greer had wondered if Loveday was avoiding her.

Mickey laughed. 'Yeah she's never in. If she's not out with her mum, she's walking the pram. Say you can come for your tea?'

'Yes,' said Greer decisively, 'we'd love to come.'

*

Loveday was not happy. 'What did you do that for? I haven't got time to make supper and look after Hal. And what's Mum going to do? I can't ask her to leave her own house because there's no space for her round the table.'

Mickey had already thought of that. 'I asked her if it was all right and she thought it's a great idea. She's going to her sister's for the night so that we can really let our hair down.' He slid his hands round Loveday's hips and pulled her to him. 'We 'aven't seen them in ages. We'll have fun.'

*

At Pencil Cottage, Jesse looked cross. 'I don't want to go round for tea.'

'Why not? Mickey's your best mate,' Greer sighed. 'And why did you tell him I wasn't up to visitors?'

''Cos you're not.'

'Yes I am. I think it's Loveday who's not coping. I want to see her but she's always making excuses. I feel all cooped up in here.' Greer swept her perfectly cut fringe across her face. 'I miss seeing people. You see Mickey every day at work.'

'Exactly.'

'Oh, you're being silly. We're going over there and that's that.'

*

Loveday was as nervous as kitten. She'd spent all day cleaning the house and cooking an enormous fish pie and was now laying up the small kitchen table. Hal, who had been grizzling and needy since the early hours, was strapped to her chest. 'Now then, Hal my lad,' she told him as she folded some paper napkins into triangles and popped them into the empty wine glasses, 'you'm going to meet your friend Freddie tonight, so I want you on your best behaviour. Understand?' She looked down at him, seeing his little face snuggled against her breasts. 'I don't want any trouble from you.' He looked up at her and gave a smile to melt her heart. 'That's my boy.' He caught her gaze and continued to hold it, his face gradually turning from shell pink to puce. 'Oh, no. Not now. I've only just changed you,' she beseeched, but it was too late. She felt the release as a magnificent poo hit his nappy and then the unmistakable liquid warmth as it escaped through the leg holes of his baby-grow. 'Oh, Hal.' She unclipped his harness and held him at arm's length. She looked down at her last clean shirt. 'Oh, no, you've done it all over me as well.'

She heard Mickey's key in the lock and called from the kitchen, 'Darling, Hal's just shat all over me. Do you mind helping me wi—' She stopped as she saw Mickey was not alone. Greer and Jesse were with him, and a perfectly sparkling clean, sleeping Freddie too.

Loveday wanted to cry but instead she said, 'Hello. Don't come too near, I stink. Mickey, get everyone a drink. I'll be back in a minute.'

Upstairs, feeling flustered, Loveday did let a few tears flow as she undressed Hal and quickly washed him in the sink. As soon as he was clean and dry, she popped him in his cot, where he promptly fell asleep. 'I'm not surprised you're tired. A big poo like that takes it out of you, doesn't it!'

She caught sight of her reflection in the long mirror on the landing. There were unpleasant marks on the shirt she'd just changed into and her hair could do with a trip to the hairdresser's, but so what, she told herself. She was a mum and proud to bear the battle scars.

Mickey called up the stairs, 'What you having to drink, Loveday?'

'Big mug of tea.' She laughed at the sight of herself. 'I'll be two minutes.'

*

When she got downstairs, Greer was giving Freddie his bottle.

'Sorry about that,' said Loveday. 'Now let's have a proper look at you both. I've missed you.'

She bent to kiss Greer's proffered cheek and sat down next to her. 'How are you? I'm so sorry that you had such a bad time.'

Greer looked fabulous, despite having been so ill. Her hair and make-up were understated but effective, her figure trim and her clothes unsullied. 'I'm a lot better. How about you?'

'Oh, as you can see . . .' Loveday held her hands out to show off the chaos of the cottage. 'Just the same.'

Greer smiled.

Mickey came in from the kitchen. 'Glass of wine for you, Greer, and a cup of tea for my darling wife.'

Loveday took her mug gratefully. 'I think this'll be the first hot cup of tea I've managed all day.'

'Would you like a hold of Freddie?' asked Greer,

putting his bottle aside and reaching for the glass Mickey was proffering.

Jesse put a hand to his mouth involuntarily. 'Loveday's got a hot drink in her hand,' he said.

'She can put it down,' smiled Greer reasonably.

Loveday felt caught under the expectant, innocent eyes of Greer and Mickey and the unmistakably hard eyes of Jesse.

'Here you are,' said Greer, handing Freddie over. 'This is your auntie Loveday.' Loveday took Freddie in her arms and looked quickly at Jesse, who was pulling at his upper lip, his eyes on the carpet. 'In actual fact,' Greer continued, 'I want her to be more than your auntie.' She beamed at Loveday. 'I want her to be your godmummy.'

Loveday didn't know what to say, but it didn't matter because Greer was still talking. 'And, I want you, Mickey, to be goddaddy.'

Mickey was shocked with happiness at this honour. 'Oh my! Well, that's just wonderful. I accept.' He pumped Jesse's arm and then hugged him for good measure. 'Ain't that marvellous, Loveday?'

Loveday was staring into little Freddie's face and saw a look, a fleeting look, of Hal. No, no it couldn't be. They were not brothers. They weren't. She'd been mistaken. She was feeling clammy and wanted to get Freddie out of her arms. Mickey obliged. 'Come and have a cuddle with your uncle Mickey.' He took Freddie, freeing Loveday to get to her feet. 'Excuse me, I must look at the fish pie.'

'Hang on,' said Mickey, stopping her. 'I want to ask something of you, Greer, and you, Jesse.'

Loveday knew instantly what was coming.

'I haven't had a chance to run this past Loveday yet.' He put his arm round her shoulder. 'But I know she will be wanting the same thing.' He left a small but dramatic pause. 'My wife and I would be honoured if you would both be godparents to our Hal.'

'It would be our pleasure,' smiled Greer. 'Wouldn't it, Jesse?' She looked over to where he sat, motionless.

Loveday could barely breathe.

Jesse looked at Mickey, still cradling Freddie; he looked at Greer, waiting expectantly. Finally he looked into Loveday's eyes. 'Yes. It would be an honour. I am proud to accept.'

Greer took her glass in her hand and raised it. 'To our sons, who will grow together like brothers.'

Upstairs, Hal opened his eyes and his lungs and screamed.

*

Apart from Hal screaming and Freddie sleeping like an angel, Greer drinking wine because she was bottle-feeding and Loveday having to stick to tea because she wasn't, the little supper party was more or less enjoyable.

Jesse dealt with his inner turmoil by drinking too much beer and Mickey matched him out of the sheer joy at their being all together again.

The fish pie was complimented and the pudding of arctic roll and tinned peaches was welcomed as an old favourite. Even Greer had a spoonful.

Loveday told Mickey to get everyone settled in the lounge while she brewed up a pot of coffee and cleared the table. The babies were finally sleeping. Hal in his cot upstairs and Freddie in his car seat on the rug.

Alone in the kitchen, Loveday took a moment to release the tension of the evening. She stood at the sink, clutching the cold enamel and staring out into the dark of the back garden. She could see the reflection of the room behind her in the glass. Mickey so happy and so unweighted by any of the guilt that burdened her. Greer so pretty and so bloody perfect.

Jesse, so . . . fucking annoyingly gorgeous. She knew Mickey was a much better person than Jesse; she knew she was so unbelievably lucky to have him, his unconditional love, and her beautiful Hal. But her mind and her body were saying different things; she just could not help that feeling of pure desire that surged through her whenever she saw Jesse bleddy Behenna.

She saw him bend his head to hear something Greer was saying, then he stood and came towards the kitchen, towards Loveday. She didn't turn round.

'Loveday?'

She turned the taps on and squeezed a healthy stream of washing-up liquid into the bowl. 'Yeah?'

'Do you have any sweeteners . . . for Greer's coffee.'

She turned and pointed to the shelf next to the cooker. 'If I've got any they'll be on there.'

She concentrated on picking up a wine glass and washing it carefully in the suds.

'Nope. Can't see any,' he said, stepping back to stand next to her.

'Sorry.' She rinsed the glass under the cold tap.

Still he stood next to her. 'You OK?' he asked quietly.

'Yeah.' She pulled a face. 'Why wouldn't I be?'

'I looked at Hal tonight and can see only you in him,' Jesse said.

'That's because he's mine,' Loveday said firmly.

'And Mickey's?' Jesse asked.

'And Mickey's.'

He still didn't move. She picked up another glass and began washing it with a little more vigour than last time.

'Good,' he said.

'Yeah. Good.' Her hands stopped in the soapy water and she looked at Jesse intently. 'Hal is Mickey's and Freddie is yours, and that's that.'

22

Spring 1996

In the light morning mist, Jesse could see the white brick of the day marker on the cliffs cupping the entrance to Trevay's harbour. For almost two centuries it had guided the fisherman to safety.

The engine of *The Lobster Pot* chugged reassuringly at just over ten knots. The sea was choppy and a cackle of seagulls followed the churning wake, hoping for a breakfast of fish gut and titbits.

Jesse was at the wheel. Over the last two years Edward had slowly handed the role of skipper to his son and now hardly ever came out on the boat. Not that he didn't want to. He was a victim of the success of the merger between the Behenna and the Clovelly families, and spent almost all his working hours office-bound.

Jesse knew his father and father-in-law would be pleased with the latest catch. The hold was brimming with the best the sea could offer. He counted his blessings.

His own boat.

Money coming in.

A son he adored.

A marriage that was happy enough.

A secret that was safe.

The longer time went on, the more he began to feel sure that the moment of madness that he and Loveday had shared would never be discovered. He and she had buried it deeply. They never spoke of it. Anyway, Hal was a dead ringer for Loveday. Reddish hair, still plump. While blond, wiry Freddie looked every inch a Behenna. Everyone commented on it.

Loveday and Mickey were happy and were now expecting twins. Jesse had cried when he'd heard. He covered it up as joy but really it was envy. He would love more children but he couldn't risk asking Greer. Risk her health. Risk the wrath of his father-in-law, who never let him forget that he would be nothing without Greer.

The only piece of grit in the oyster was Grant. Sometimes Jesse was certain Grant knew something. Snide comments. Quips with a sting.

Once, when he and Mickey had taken the boys down to the harbour to look at the boats and to give their mums a rest, they had run into Grant. He was on leave and was on his way back from the pub. He wasn't drunk, but he'd obviously had a couple, Jesse could tell from his swagger and the taunt in his voice.

'Well, well. What a stroke of luck running into you two, out with my two little nephews – oops, sorry, just one nephew, isn't it?'

Grant bent down and ticked the chins of the two boys in their respective buggies. He pulled a face and little Hal laughed.

'Funny thing is, if you didn't know better, you might think these two little 'uns were related,' Grant said, through narrowed eyes.

Jesse stiffened but Mickey interjected and said point-edly: 'They'll be like real blood brothers – who can rely on each other – like me and Jesse.'

Grant let out a guffaw. 'Bleddy blood brothers! Be careful what you wish for, Mickey boy.'

With a raised eyebrow he went on his way, but it was the same whenever he saw Freddie and Hal toddling together. Playing together. Thank God he wasn't home very often.

The next time he'd seen Grant, Jesse had challenged him.

'Why do you keep saying stupid stuff about Hal and Freddie?'

Grant smirked. 'You tell me.'

'If you've got something to say, just say it.'

'I think it's you who's got something to say.'

'I haven't got anything to say.'

'Well that's all right then, isn't it?' Grant gave him one of his trademark sly grins and Jesse had to fight down the urge not to wipe it off his face.

Grant had been away for a few months now, somewhere in the Middle East. Apparently he was doing well and had been involved in a successful raid on insurgents. Or at least that's what he'd told their mum in one of his infrequent phone calls home.

Jesse pulled his thoughts back to the present. Nothing had been said. Nothing was going to be said. His secret was safe. Dead and buried. He concentrated on heading *The Lobster Pot* safely into Trevay.

*

Our Mermaid, Mickey's dad's boat, was already tied up alongside, its catch unloaded.

Jesse expertly manoeuvred himself next to him.

'All right, Jesse?' called Alfie Chandler.

''Andsome!' replied Jesse. 'Mickey in yet?'

'He's about an hour away. Got a cracking catch, he told me.'

'Yeah. He was gloating on the radio last night.' Jesse laughed, throwing a rope up to his deckhand on the quay. 'Ever since he started skippering *Crabline*, he's turned into the Midas of the ocean!'

'It was good of your dad to let him have a boat.'

'Mickey's like family, isn't he?' bantered Jesse.

'Aye. Like those two boys of yorn. Might as well be brothers.' Alfie chuckled cheerfully.

A thread of fear dropped into Jesse's stomach. First Grant. And now Alfie.

'What do you mean?' he said a bit too sharply.

Alfie was surprised. 'Well, born on the same day and that, and you and Mickey growing up together. He's more a brother to you than Grant, ain't he?'

Jesse pulled himself together. 'Oh, yeah, yeah. I see what you mean.' He should be less sensitive. It was only his own jitters.

Alfie remembered something. 'Oh, nearly forgot, your dad's looking for you. He's in Mr Clovelly's office. He said if I saw you to tell you to go and see him straight away.'

*

Jesse strode through the busy fish market, full now of Alfie's iced and boxed catch, shouting greetings to the customers he knew. 'Don't touch Alfie's lot. Mine's unloaded in a minute. It's the best catch Trevay's ever seen.' Laughter followed him to the small office in the corner of the market. He knocked on the door and walked in without waiting for an answer. His father was sitting clutching a cup of coffee. His face was strained but he looked relieved when he saw Jesse.

Jesse was scared. 'What's the matter, Dad? Is it Mum?'

'No. Not Mum. It's Grant.'

Jesse's mind's eye flew to a scene in a hot desert where the bodies of British soldiers lay mutilated. Blood seeping into the dust and sand. He could see his brother lying wounded, lifeless . . . and he felt a surge of relief. Grant, the only person who might know something about him and Loveday, was dead.

'What's happened, Dad?'

'He's in trouble.'

Relief left Jesse, to be replaced by guilt that he could possibly have felt so good about his brother dying.

'Trouble for what?'

'We're not sure of the details. Someone from his base is coming to see us this morning. Your mum wants you there.'

'Of course. Can I unload the boat first?'

'No. Leave it. I'll get the lads to do it. Your mum's in bits.'

*

The officer from 42 Commando spared none of the details.

'It would appear that your son formed an attachment with a local girl whilst on deployment. Her family tried to stop her from seeing him and he went to the family home where he attacked her father. Her father is currently in a British field hospital and in a coma. The medical team are deciding whether to evacuate him to a hospital here in the UK.'

Jan pulled her crumpled tissue through her fingers, too shocked to weep. 'Are you sure Grant did it?'

'We have witnesses who would appear to be reliable.'

'But Grant has wanted to be a Marine since he was little. He worked so hard for his green beret. Why would he risk everything he loved?'

The officer, looking embarrassed, pulled at the sleeves of his immaculate uniform. 'His commanding officer has had previous cause to be concerned about Private Behenna's attitude. It was only a matter of time before he was facing a lot of trouble.'

Jan stared at him from her dry eyes. 'But he had been brave, hadn't he? He told us he'd been on a raid against the bad men – he always called them the bad men – and had saved his friend's life.'

The officer coughed and crossed his feet, his gleaming boots winking like mirrors.

'Ah.'

'That's what he told us.'

'Private Behenna has not been on active duty in the field. His unpredictable behaviour caused serious concern that he might be a danger to other men; he has been confined to base for some time. There seems little veracity to the story he has told you.'

'You mean it's not true?'

'I couldn't comment; I am sure his commanding officer will be able to give you more information.'

Jan's heartbroken face spoke clearly of her pain. 'He's always been a liar. Ever since he was a little boy.'

Edward, sitting next to her at the old kitchen table,

put his arm around her. 'Jan, let's get him home and then we'll know more.'

The officer shuffled his feet again. 'When he returns to the UK he'll be held at the barracks until his court martial.'

Jan stood up so fast that she knocked the chair over behind her. Her voice rose in an ascending scale. 'Court *martial?*'

'Yes. I know this must come as a terrible shock to you.'

Now Jan's tears came thick and fast, in a torrent that made her breathing difficult. Jesse went to her and held her as tightly as he could. She pressed her face into his dirty fishing smock and allowed Jesse to absorb the shock waves of her sobs.

The officer stood. 'I very much regret having to make this visit.' He took a card from an inside pocket of his jacket and handed it to Edward. 'Here are my details if you need any more information. I'll endeavour to be of assistance in any way I can.'

Edward took the card and placed it on the kitchen table, not knowing what to do next.

'I'll see myself out,' said the officer.

*

Edward went on a bender like no other. He sat in a dark corner of the Golden Hind, rebuffing all overtures from friends and colleagues, and drank solidly and efficiently until Pete, the landlord, refused to serve him any more.

'You've had enough, mate,' he said, taking the pint glass from his hand.

'Not yet,' Edward replied thickly. 'I don't think I'll ever have had enough.' He left the pub and, after deciding that he wasn't going home, he staggered up to the sheds and let himself into his old office. It was dusty from misuse, but he quickly laid his hands on the litre-bottle of Scotch he always kept hidden for emergencies. This was an emergency.

*

Jan had gone to bed, leaving Jesse not knowing quite what to do.

He needed to go home and get his head round what was happening. If Grant was found guilty, he could go away for a few years. If he knew anything about Jesse and Loveday, that secret would be locked up with him. Despite himself, and the evident distress all of this was causing his parents, Jesse felt a shot of elation.

'Mum?' He stuck his head round her bedroom door. 'Mum. You awake?'

His mother didn't answer. Shock had closed her down and she was in a deep sleep.

Jesse wrote a note and left it by her pillow. It said

Mum,
    You're sleeping and I need to get home. Give me a call when you wake up.
    Love you
    Jesse.

The late afternoon sunshine surprised Jesse. He was expecting it to be much later. Had it been only this morning that all this had unfolded? He walked back to the harbour and hesitated outside the Golden Hind. Should he go in and join his father? He had no doubts he was in there already. He was tempted, but decided he needed a clear head to think over what had happened.

He passed the Hind and turned left into the lane where Pencil Cottage stood. The small front courtyard was merry with spring flowers, basking in the late sunshine. Greer had been doing a distance-learning certificate in garden design; she had planted up dozens of terracotta pots of differing sizes with daffodils, blue hyacinths and cherry blossom trees. Their scent, and the news of his brother's downfall, made Jesse almost cheerful.

*

'I'm sorry to say it, but your brother is a horrible person,' said Greer, swinging Freddie into his high chair and popping his pelican bib round his neck.

'Yeah, but can you believe he would hurt someone so badly that he'd put them in a coma?' asked Jesse, passing the bowl of freshly made broccoli gratin to her.

'Yes I can,' she retorted, before turning her attention to Freddie. 'Freddie, it's your favourite! Mummy's made you yummy broccoli.'

'No,' said Freddie, turning his head away. 'For Daddy.'

'Come on, Fred, it'll make you big and strong. Just like Daddy.'

Freddie pointed at Jesse. 'Daddy, for you.'

Greer pushed a spoonful of the supper into Freddie's mouth and watched as it came smoothly out again. 'Come on, Freddie. This is silly, and Mummy's not having any nonsense.'

Freddie put his pudgy hands over his eyes and blew a raspberry.

'Let me help,' said Jesse, trying not to laugh. 'You go and watch a bit of telly, or do your nails or whatever it is you'd like to do.'

'I do need to finish the last module on planting a fruit garden,' she said, looking defeated.

'Well, off you go then, and I'll look after Littl'un.'

As soon as Greer had gone, Jesse shut the kitchen door and smiled conspiratorially at Freddie. 'Want some ketchup on this?' Freddie nodded gleefully whilst putting a finger to his lips and saying, 'SShhh. Mummy no.'

'Our little secret, son. And with a bit of luck she'll never know.'

*

For the next few weeks, the local press were full of gossip about Grant, and all and sundry came out of the woodwork to sell their lurid stories about him. Local girls gave kiss-and-tells about his bedroom exploits, and so-called friends from school said how they'd always known he was a wrong 'un.

During that time, Jan was too ashamed to show her face outside of the house while Edward, by contrast, spent even more time in the pub.

One day at the Behenna and Clovelly offices, Bryn rounded on Jesse.

'When is that father of yours going to stop drowning his sorrows in the bottom of a pint glass and get back to work? We're running a business here.'

Jesse balked at the suggestion that the catches were suffering. He and Spencer had been holding the fort admirably; if anything, their yields had been up the last few weeks since Jesse had taken the helm.

'You've got no gripes with the catches, Bryn?'

Bryn looked patronisingly at his son-in-law. 'Ain't a case of gripes, but it don't look good, your dad not turning up to meetings. People are talking.'

'Then your job is to shut them up. He's your partner, ain't he?' Jesse said firmly.

Bryn pursed his lips tightly at this unwanted defiance from his son-in-law. 'Now look 'ere—'

'No, you listen to me, Bryn. You might think that you bought me and that you bought my dad too, but what you really bought is the Behenna family. And we're strong.' He took a step closer to his father-in-law. 'You're going to give my dad an official leave of absence and I'll take a seat on the board till he's better.'

'I'm not sure that the shareholders—'

Jesse lowered his voice dangerously. 'You'll tell the shareholders what I tell you to, Bryn. Otherwise, word might start getting around that not only are you knocking off Monica and Doreen from the club, but also that you've been passing off second-grade fish as premium to one of your big clients. Where would your precious shareholder confidence be then, Bryn?'

Bryn's face drained of colour and his voice was tremulous. 'Jesse, that's blackmail.'

'Come off it, Bryn, no need to be dramatic. Just call in the shareholders and we'll all get back to business. Catching and selling fish.' He gave Bryn a cocky grin and a friendly clap on the back.

The following week, Jesse was installed on the board by a unanimous vote.

Edward pulled himself together eventually, but Jesse

never relinquished his seat on the board.

It took almost six months for Grant to be found guilty of assault. He was sentenced to eight years. His mother was never the same.

23

September 1998

Greer couldn't help the tears as she bent to straighten Freddie's school tie.

'You've got your lunch box?' she asked him, pointing at his school bag, which looked enormous hanging from his narrow shoulders.

'Yes,' he said.

'I'll be waiting here when you're finished.'

'Right here? By the gate?'

'Yes, right here by the gate.'

'Will Daddy come?'

'Yes, he should be back by then. You'll have lots to tell him.'

Freddie looked so smart in his new uniform. Exactly the way she remembered Jesse on their first day at school. Sturdy legs sticking out of his grey shorts and bruises all down his shins. 'Two peas in a pod,' her father-in-law was fond of saying.

Freddie fidgeted under her gaze then pointed behind her. 'There's Hal!' Then he shouted, 'Hal!'

Hal was walking fast, his hands holding the edge of the double buggy as Loveday had taught him. 'Can I see Freddie?' he asked his mum, who was looking ragged with the stress of getting all three children dressed in time to drop Hal for the school bell.

'Just wait till we cross the road,' she said, looking both ways and then heading towards Greer.

'Morning, Loveday,' Greer said as she kissed her friend's cheek. 'How are you?'

'Knackered. The girls got me up at half five and Hal insisted on making his own lunch box.' She turned to Freddie. 'Hiya, Fred. All ready for your first day?'

'I've got houmous and crudités in my lunch box.'

'Have you?' Loveday said. 'Hal's got Dairylea Dunkers.'

'What are they?' asked Freddie.

'I'm sure Hal will share them with you,' Loveday assured him.

Greer, who spent her life trying to keep Freddie away from preservatives, E numbers and unnecessary sugar, hurriedly changed the subject.

'Auntie Loveday, Uncle Mickey, Daddy and I all became friends on our first day at school, didn't we, Auntie Loveday?'

'Oh, we did,' laughed Loveday. 'I asked your mummy if she liked Abba. I don't think she knew who Abba were.'

Greer, hating being made fun of, said quickly, 'Yes I did.'

'Well, you did once you'd listened to my tapes.'

'What are tapes?' asked Hal.

'Things we had in the olden days . . . before CDs,' chuckled Loveday. 'Now say goodbye to your sisters.'

'Bye-bye, Becca.' He reached into the pram and gave his sister a sloppy kiss. 'Bye-bye, Bea.' He leant in to kiss her too but got a smack from a chubby hand instead. 'Ow. Bea hit me.'

'She didn't mean to. Now, off you two boys go and look after each other. Be good and do what the teacher tells you.' Loveday kissed the face of her dear son and he kissed her back.

'I love you, Mummy.' He blinked a watery smile.

'I love you too. Now off you go, you little monkey.'

Greer knelt to look into Freddie's eyes. 'Be a good boy and don't forget I love you. I want to hear all about it tonight. Now give us a kiss.'

Freddie put his arms around Greer's neck and squeezed tight. 'I'll be good and you be good too, Mummy.'

'I will,' she said solemnly, 'I promise.'

Finally disentangled from their mothers, the two boys ran towards a gathering group of small children who were being summoned by a smiley female teacher called Miss Woods. 'Good morning, children. Wave goodbye to your mummys and daddys. We've got lots of lovely things to do today, so get in a nice line and follow me to the classroom.'

*

Loveday and Greer watched as their precious boys disappeared into the familiar building.

'Where has the time gone? 'Twas only yesterday they were in nappies,' sighed Loveday.

'It was only yesterday since we were coming to school,' Greer said, wryly. She checked her watch. 'Got time for a coffee?'

'Yeah. Why not?'

*

The Cockle Café was situated just off the quay in a narrow back street. It had only been open since the start of the summer season, and had been very busy with the holidaying, trendy young parents who appreciated its organic menu.

As Loveday and Greer turned the corner towards the café, they struggled with the double buggy on the cobbles; it was cumbersome and awkward to manoeuvre. Three women in their sixties were sitting outside, enjoying the September sunshine, an Ordnance Survey map spread out in front of them. They were clearly discussing their walking route for the day, but there seemed to be quite a vigorous exchange of views going on.

As Loveday and Greer drew nearer, the leader of the pack pulled her glasses onto her head, where they were anchored securely by a fierce perm. Seeming suddenly to make a decision, she barked at them, asking: 'Excuse me, are you local?'

Loveday reversed the buggy and yanked it onto the smoother pavement. She looked in the direction of women and said, 'Yes, more's the pity. The roads round here are very bumpy.' She applied the buggy's brake and straightened up. 'Can I help you?'

The leader, Ena, outlined her ambitious plans. Her idea was to get a bus to Boscastle and the start of the Smuggler's Way, continue to Rough Tor and then finish at Looe, thirty-seven miles away. Her companions voiced their concerns about the length of the trek, wondering where they would stay if they didn't reach Looe.

'Well, it's a tricky walk,' Loveday agreed. 'And are you ladies familiar with using a compass? The way isn't marked too well.'

'My sense of direction is excellent. Never needed a compass,' preened Ena.

'It's going to be the Isle of Wight all over again,' one of her companions murmured, *sotto voce*, to the other.

'I heard that.' Ena turned back to Loveday. 'You see, I am a great fan of ancient neolithic monuments. I mean to see Rough Tor and push the legendary Logan Rock to see if it really does rock back and forth.' She jerked her head towards her companions. 'These two don't harbour the same love of the magic of Cornish landscape in their souls as I do.'

'Really,' said Loveday, somewhat bemused, but also already flatly disliking this woman. She turned away. 'Greer, would you order me a strong tea and the girls a juice each. I'll get us settled on the table over there.' She waved at a table as far away from Neolithic Woman as possible.

At this safe distance, Loveday unbuckled the harnesses of both Bea and Becca. The little girls struggled out of their confinement and into the freedom of the cobbled lane. A seagull was strutting in the gutter, cocking his beady-eyed gaze from left to right, searching for a snack. Bea and Becca toddled after him, laughing as he quickened his pace until, finally, he flew to the top of a lamp-post where he opened his beak and laughed.

'Now little girls,' called Ena. 'Don't encourage the seagulls. They're dirty and spread disease.'

Loveday stopped folding Becca's anorak and said, 'I beg your pardon? What did you say?'

Ena was unabashed. 'I was just telling the little girls not to encourage the seagulls.'

'And what business is it of yours?' asked Loveday stonily, the sequence of broken nights with the girls and the emotional rush of Hal's first day at school combining to produce a spectacular red mist. Loveday gave vent.

'My girls live here. They understand seagulls and they know more about bloody Cornwall and its magic than you'll ever know.'

'Well, *really*.' Ena flared her nostrils and stood up, busying herself with folding her map and packing it into her canvas knapsack. She gave rapid instructions to her companions. 'Sylvie, it's your turn to pay the coffee bill. Babs, come with me. Let's wait for Sylvie on the quay.'

Greer came out of the shop. She was laden with a tray of teacups, teapot and juice cartons, and was just in time to see the three women scuttling off to the harbour and Loveday yelling, 'And, by the way, 'tisn't pronounced Rough Tor, except by grockles like you. It's Row Tor. Row, to rhyme with cow.'

'Loveday!' Greer was horrified. 'Shush! What's happened?'

Loveday retold the story and had the grace to be embarrassed. 'I don't know why I saw red. Tired, I suppose, but I get so fed up with these visitors thinkin' we'm got straw in our ears.'

Greer smiled. 'You get very Cornish when you're cross, don't you? Why don't you go home and get a nap? It'll do you the world of good.'

'I can't. I've got the girls.'

'Well, I'm their godmother, aren't I? And today I'm your fairy godmother too. Let me take them and we'll have a lovely day. You and I will meet up at the school to pick the boys up. What do you say?'

'Are you sure?' Loveday was feeling exhausted. 'That would be wonderful.'

Greer shrugged her shoulders. 'Well, now my little man's gone to school, I've got all the time in the world.'

Loveday put her hand out to her friend. 'Are the doctors sure you can't have any more babies?'

Greer shrugged again. 'They're not always right, are they? And it's almost five years now . . .' She chewed the inside of her cheek. 'The thing is. I know it would make Jesse so happy to have another little one. He envies Mickey and you. Three children!'

Loveday felt the old twang of guilt deep within her breast. 'Yeah, well, they'm buggers too. Run me ragged.' She tried to make Greer smile, 'And they ruined my supermodel figure.'

Greer didn't laugh. She looked ashamed. 'That's what I hated about being pregnant. I told Jesse I never wanted to be pregnant again. It was an awful thing to say. I think I was scared. But I'd do it again for Jesse.' She hesitated. 'In fact, please don't say anything to anyone . . . Promise?'

Loveday frowned, not wanting to hear what Greer was about to say. 'I hope you haven't done anything silly?'

Greer started to chew her cheek again. 'Well I . . . I've stopped taking the pill. Jesse doesn't know, but I thought, why not? Give it a try. If it's meant to be . . . and all that.'

Loveday was shocked. 'My God, Greer. It could kill you and the baby.'

'Well, it didn't last time, did it?' Greer smiled tightly. 'Please don't tell Jesse. I just want one more chance. Promise you won't say anything.'

Against her better judgement, Loveday nodded. 'I promise.'

Bea ran up and helped herself to her carton of apple juice. 'Take Becca's too, would you, darlin'?' she said as her mind whirled. She turned her attention back to Greer. 'How long you been off the pill?'

'About five months.'

'But no luck?'

Greer's face told her all she needed to know. 'Oh my God,' Loveday breathed. 'You're pregnant.'

Loveday nodded. 'I think so. I'm late. About two weeks.'

'Have you seen the doctor?'

Greer shook her head. 'He'll be cross with me.'

'Cross?' Loveday said in a voice louder than she intended. 'Cross? That's a bleddy understatement. You've got to make an appointment now. Today. And tell Jesse.'

24

Louisa Caroline was stillborn at twenty weeks.

It was one of the most difficult funerals the Reverend Rowena had ever had to conduct. What can you say to grieving parents to heal their pain?

God was merciful and loving?

He never sent more than a person could bear?

He needed Louisa as an angel?

These trite but trusted platitudes just didn't match the enormity of the situation.

Would a loving God do this?

Rowena found herself struggling with her faith these days. Too many wars. Too many deaths. Too much sadness.

*

She was standing in the porch of St Peter's Church and watched as the small funeral cortège came up the hill. It was a bright but bitterly cold December day and she was grateful for the extra clothes that were hidden under her cassock.

Jesse insisted on carrying Louisa's coffin. He held it tenderly as he entered the church, his feet echoing on the red tiles of the aisle. He walked towards the flower-strewn dais that was to be Louisa's.

Behind him walked a Greer so pale and so thin that

she was almost translucent. She walked with Freddie, gripping his hand with a determination that frightened her. He was everything to her now. Nothing and nobody would ever take him from her. For his part, Freddie was scared. His mother had been ill and nearly died. His sister, who he'd never met, had died, and his father looked so ill that it was possible he was going to die too.

They reached the front pew and watched as Jesse laid the tiny white coffin on top of the sweet-smelling lilies and ivy.

*

Afterwards Freddie went to play with Hal, who always cheered him up. He'd packed a bag with his pyjamas in. He liked going to Auntie Loveday's and Uncle Mickey's. They let him and Hal eat crisps on the sofa and watch loads of television. Freddie felt that today he'd be allowed anything he wanted.

*

Greer was still frail. She had lost a lot of blood and needed to rest.

After the burial, next to Jesse's granddad, she and Jesse turned down all offers of lunch from their parents and returned home to Pencil Cottage.

'Would you like a cup of tea, darlin'?' asked Jesse, watching as Greer took off her coat.

'No, Thank you.' Greer ran her hands through her hair. 'Can I make you one?'

'No, thanks.' Jesse felt big and awkward and out of his depth. 'Can I get you anything at all?'

Greer shook her head and headed for the stairs.

'You going to have a lie-down?' he asked.

'Yes. I'm tired.'

He was tired, too. Weary to his bones. He'd been cross with Greer when she'd told him that Louisa was on the way. But when she had explained, so tenderly, that she wanted to give him another child, maybe a daughter, he hadn't stayed cross for long. The doctors had wheeled out all the usual warnings, but Greer said that she was feeling fine. She was only twenty-eight, and strong enough to have several more babies.

That is, until her blood pressure rose, her ankles swelled and Jesse found her unconscious in the kitchen having banged her head on the corner of the stove during a sudden seizure.

That was it. Game over.

He watched her tiny frame climb the staircase and head towards their bedroom. He fought the desperate need he had to follow her and cry in her arms.

The house was as quiet as the grave. No Freddie. No Greer singing to the radio in the kitchen or telling him off for leaving his shoes by the door rather than the specially designed shoe rack in the tiny entrance.

The phone rang and gave him a start. He went to it quickly before it disturbed Greer.

'Hello?'

'Jesse? It's Mick. I thought you might like a drink.'

*

The bar of the Golden Hind was weighted down with tinsel and paper lanterns. The jukebox was playing a medley of Christmas songs and the comforting smell of tobacco smoke and beer hit Jesse like a hug. Mickey was at the bar, foot on the brass footrail, tenner in hand and two frothy pints sitting on the bar towel in front of him.

'All right, mate?' He looked at Jesse with pure love and friendship. 'Want a pasty?'

They ate their pasties and drank their pints, talking about anything but the morning they had just endured.

'Two weeks to Christmas,' said Mickey, wiping the pastry crumbs from his lips with a red paper napkin.

'Not sure I feel very Christmassy,' sighed Jesse.

'Why not come over to us? Loveday and her mum always cook for a blessed army.'

'I think Greer's mum may have something arranged.'

'Oh shit. Poor you.'

Jesse managed a smile. 'Yeah. Not a barrel of laughs over there. Lunch at one on the dot. The queen at three. Presents at six.'

'What? You can't open your presents till six? You're definitely coming over to ours. If ours aren't open by six in the morning, there's something wrong.'

'We let Freddie open his early before we go over there. But he's still got to wait for his grandparents' presents at six like everyone else. And then we all sit in a circle on those bleddy uncomfortable sofas of Elizabeth's and have to go round in turn opening our gifts and bleddy oohing and aahing over them.'

'Fuck that,' said Mickey, finishing his pint. 'Want another?'

'I should be getting back.'

The thought of Jesse's return to the sadness of Pencil House brought their mood down again.

'I'm really sorry, Jesse,' Mick said, putting his arm round his best friend and squeezing him tight. 'For both of you.'

'It's pretty shit,' said Jesse.

'Yeah,' agreed Mickey. 'It is.'

*

Walking round the corner to Pencil Cottage, Jesse could see the twinkling of fairy lights through the window into the lounge. Was Greer putting up the Christmas decorations?

Taking his key from the lock and pushing open the door, he saw her, in her old Snoopy dressing gown, sorting through a large box of baubles. There was an open bottle of champagne on the coffee table by the gas-effect fire and a champagne flute next to it.

'Hello, darling,' he said gently. 'This is a nice surprise.'

She was a bit drunk. He could see that.

'Hello, Jesse.' She showed him two baubles, one green, one blue. 'Shall we go for a green theme or a blue theme? We had green last year, but blue doesn't seem quite right. What do you think?'

'I dunno. I like the green.'

'But is it Christmassy enough? You see . . .' She delved into the box and brought out three more baubles. 'Red, gold and silver. Now that's Christmassy, isn't it?'

'Definitely.'

She put the decorations down and poured herself another glass of champagne. 'The thing is, we've got to make the house nice for Freddie and Louisa.'

Jesse saw that the champagne bottle was more than half empty. 'For Freddie, you mean?'

'Yes, of course, and Louisa.'

Jesse went to Greer and held her. 'Louisa isn't here.'

She hugged him. 'I know. I'm a bit pissed but I'm not

mad. Or maybe you'll think I am.' She pulled back from their embrace and picked up her glass. 'I'm drinking champagne to toast Louisa's short life. I want to celebrate her. I never want people to feel they can't talk about her. I want to talk about her.' Greer's eyes filled with tears and her voice cracked as she continued, 'I was asleep earlier and I had such a dream. She was in bed with me and we talked about Christmas. She wants to see what a Christmas tree looks like, with all the lights and the sparkle, and I'm going to let her see it.' Greer held her glass towards the ceiling and raised her eyes. 'Louisa, this is for you, for ever and always.' She brought the glass to her lips and drank. She turned to Jesse. 'Would you like to toast your daughter?'

'OK,' he said guardedly. He'd never seen Greer like this before.

'I'll get you a glass.' She went to the cabinet where a row of Stuart crystal champagne flutes glistened. Untouched since they'd been imprisoned there as wedding presents six years ago.

She took one and filled it with the last of the champagne. She offered it to Jesse. 'Make a toast to our daughter Louisa.'

Jesse felt the prickle of tears at the back of his eyes and a constriction at the back of his throat. He held the glass out as Greer had done. 'Louisa. If you can see us and hear us, you know that we miss you. We will always miss you. And we're sorry.' The tears of both of them were flowing now. 'We're so sorry.'

*

'I'm going to open another bottle,' said Greer. 'We need to make this a night that we'll always want to remember.'

The champagne loosened them both so that they could talk freely of their grief. Sitting on the sofa with her head on Jesse's chest, Greer asked, 'We shall always remember her, won't we, Jesse? You'll never forget.'

'We'll never forget.' He kissed the top of her head. 'I'm so glad we saw her.'

'I'm going to put her photo up next to Freddie's. Our two children.'

'Our two children.'

'Poor Freddie. Did Mickey say he was all right?'

'Yes, he's fine. He and Hal were planning to watch *Toy Story*.'

'I love that film.'

'Yeah.'

Greer tilted her head so that she could see Jesse properly. 'Jesse. Do you love me even though I can't . . . I can't . . . give you any more children?'

'Don't be silly.'

'But do you love me? You don't say it very often.'

'Well, I'm a bloke, aren't I?'

'Mickey tells Loveday all the time . . .'

'Well that's just Mickey.'

'Do you love me?'

He kissed her nose. 'Of course.'

'Say it.'

'You know I do.'

'Say it.'

He took a beat, and in the silence Greer could hear the hiss of the flame-effect fire. She waited until he said, 'I love you.'

*

In the end, Christmas was spent at Pencil Cottage, just the three of them.

Greer used all her design skills to turn their little home into a cosy and inviting grotto.

The front door sported a wreath made of preserved apples and bundles of cinnamon sticks tied with gingham ribbon.

The Christmas tree was the biggest Jesse could fit into their tiny front room. It glistened with red, green, silver and gold baubles and countless strings of bright white lights.

The fireplace was cloaked in a fresh swag of fir, pine cones, holly, and heavily berried ivy.

Freddie was helping. 'What's in this box, Mummy?'

Greer watched as Freddie shook the box, then she knelt down next to him.

'Something special. One box for you, and . . . look, there's another box for Louisa.'

Freddie stretched across the pile of tissue paper and empty boxes of fairy lights. 'This one?'

'Yes.'

'I will open it for Louisa because she can't.'

Greer's heart contracted with love for her son. 'Good idea.'

Inside lay a small and glittery pink fairy carrying a wand.

'Ooh,' said Freddie. 'She'll like this.'

'There's a little button by her wand. Can you see?'

'Yes.'

'Press it.'

His warm little fingers found the button and pressed it. The wand lit up.

'Isn't that pretty?' smiled Greer.

'What's in my box?' asked Freddie, bored already with the fairy.

Greer laughed. 'Open it.'

He opened it and inside was a small cowboy wearing a T-shirt that read, 'Happy Christmas, Freddie Behenna.'

'Is this Woody from *Toy Story*?' asked Freddie, his eyes like saucers.

'Yep.'

'Has he brought Buzz?' Freddie, with Woody in one hand, was riffling through the tissue paper to see if there was another box.

'No. Buzz is on a mission. But he might come next year.'

'OK.' Freddie stopped looking for Buzz and picked up Louisa's fairy. 'Shall we put them on the tree? Woody on the top?'

'I think the fairy should go on the top.'

'No, Woody should. Then he can look for Buzz in the sky.'

'We'll be the only people in Trevay with a cowboy on the tree and not a fairy!' said Greer.

Freddie knitted his brows and thought for a moment. 'Don't tell Louisa, but I don't really like fairies.'

Greer took a moment before she could speak.

'I don't think she'll mind.'

Part Two

25

July 2009

Jesse Behenna, managing director of Behenna and Clovelly Fish Company, surveyed the assembled faces of his staff as they lined up in the bar of the Golden Hind and waited for him to say a few words. Spencer was finally retiring after a lifetime spent working on the boats with three generations of Behenna men. There would be a retirement luncheon later on, which Jesse would be too busy to attend. But his father would be there, along with plenty of Trevay's salty old seadogs, who would regale each other with tales told a thousand times before. Scanning the expectant faces, Jesse noted that Bryn Clovelly wasn't there. Both he and Edward still held their seats on the board, in non-executive roles, but Bryn was more likely to be seen on the golf course these days, though he still enjoyed blustering pointlessly at the annual shareholder meetings.

Three years ago, Jesse had bought another stretch of the harbour, at least the length of a football pitch, and had demolished the ramshackle buildings that had been there for as long as anyone could remember. The old chandler's, the boat engine workshop, the damp and worm-riddled sail loft. All gone, to be replaced with a twenty-first-century, three-storey building made from glass and metal, with an atrium and balconies over-looking the estuary. The old fish market next door had been given a revamp and was still the money-making heart of the business, even more so now that it had its own adjoining restaurant, which had become a destina-tion in itself and attracted wealthy holiday-makers and locals alike.

Jesse looked like the epitome of the relaxed modern executive. His open-necked shirt was Paul Smith and his tan leather brogues were Church's, but his full head of blond hair still fell in boyish waves and, even though he was often stuck behind his desk, driving deals stretching from London to Madrid, he still liked nothing better than going out with the boats and crewing with Mickey. Creeping crow's feet around his eyes were the only indica-tors of the stresses and strains that came with Behenna and Clovelly.

'And so, let's raise a toast to the man who has been the beating heart and soul of Behenna and Clovelly for longer than anyone else – Spence! It won't be the same without you, but luckily we'll still get a chance to see your ugly mug every lunchtime here at the Hind, which is where I imagine you'll be spending most of your retirement.'

There was a round of cheers as Jesse gave Spencer and his wife two all-expenses-paid tickets for dinner and a show in London. Spencer's wife wiped away a tear, and Spencer, embarrassed at all the attention, looked awkward.

As the group clapped and crowded around Spencer, oohing and aahing at his gift, Lauren, Jesse's assistant, touched him on the arm to get his attention.

'Houston, we have a problem.'

Jesse was on immediate alert. 'What's up?'

'Just got a call from Bob. A lorry jack-knifed on the A30 and there's been a pile-up. His van is totalled.'

'Is Bob all right?' Jesse's brow was creased with concern.

'He is totally fine, but he won't be able to get that consignment of John Dory and sea bass where it's supposed to be.'

'They were destined for the River Café and the Dorchester, weren't they?'

'Correct.'

Jesse thought quickly. 'Has Phil left with that order for Rick in Padstow yet?'

'I think he's just loading up.'

'Right.' Jesse fished in his trousers and pulled out a pile of notes. He quickly counted out £200 and pushed it into her hand. 'Tell him change of plan. He's to take his delivery to London instead. Give him a new manifest, and I'll give Rick a call and square things with him.'

'What will you do?'

'I'll find him something even better and drive it there myself.' He took his BlackBerry out of his pocket to make a call just as Greer's number popped up on his screen. He hesitated a moment before answering.

'Hi.'

'How's Spencer's send-off going?'

'Fine, but I've got a work crisis so won't be back until later . . .'

'Jesse – I was counting on you to take Freddie to his maths tutor tonight.'

'Can't you do it?'

'No! I told you, I'm visiting clients in St Just this afternoon – that new restaurant that looks out over the headland. It's a really important commission as they're refurbishing the whole place. It needs my complete attention. I did tell you all of this already.'

'Well, it's tough, Greer. He'll just have to get on his bike and take himself there. Where is he now, anyway?

'He's managed to twist my arm to let him out on the boat with Hal, even though he should be revising.'

'You're too soft.'

'And you're not?'

'Listen, I've got to go. I'll text you later.' He sighed and rang off, running his hands irritably through his hair before heading back to his office.

*

Hal was feeding a mackerel line off the side of Freddie's solid wooden rowing boat. His hair was flame red like his mother's but, unlike her, he was as brown as a nut; he always went a deep golden brown like his dad. Freddie was pulling at the oars, his blond hair now almost bleached white in the intense heat of the Cornish summer.

The sun was hot and the sea smooth and both boys were stripped to their waists. Hal was wearing a pair of battered Converse and an old pair of cut-off jeans. Freddie, by contrast, looked as if he was out of a Ralph Lauren advert, in his tailored shorts and expensive deck shoes.

The only sound was that of the oars in the rowlocks as Freddie pulled them in and out of the water, backwards and forwards.

'I've got another,' Hal said, pulling a flapping gleam of mackerel out of the water and into a bucket that held two others. 'I'm a mackerel magnet!' He thumped his chest, Tarzan-style. 'Can't wait to get these babies over a fire.'

'Do you always think about your stomach?' Freddie laughed.

'Oh, yes,' said Hal, putting his baited line over the side again. 'That and the gorgeous Kelly Brook. Keeps me busy.'

'You're always busy, ain't yer!' and Freddie made the universal sign for wanker at his best mate.

'Oh, fuck off,' Hal replied genially. 'What you doing later?'

Freddie pulled a face. 'Mum's got me a maths tutor for the summer. Says I've got to buck up.'

'Bollocks. Can't you duck out? Dad's getting the barbecue out later and Mum will be doing some of her Chinese pork ribs.'

The idea sounded a lot more appealing to Freddie than swotting over his maths books. Didn't his mum know that it was summer?

'What's the point in maths anyway? Ain't you going out on the boats when school's finished?'

'Not if Mum has her way. Stick me in a suit and call me an accountant, she would.' Freddie frowned at the thought, but then something in the distance caught his attention. He stopped sculling and laid the oars inside the boat. 'What's that bloke doing up there?' He pointed to the headland above Tide Cove.

Hal followed his gaze and saw the outline of a man struggling to stand up straight. As the two boys watched, the man staggered, fell over, got up again and then tottered to the edge of the cliff. Trying to find his balance, he staggered forward again and then, missing his step completely, fell and slid over the side of the cliff onto a narrow shale ledge, which began to crumble at its edge.

'What the fuck's he doing?' said Freddie.

'Oh shit,' shouted Hal, and the two friends watched,

horrified, as the man tried to stand again but slipped, breaking the shale beneath him. They heard his scream as he fell the one hundred metres headfirst into the sea below.

The boys remained shocked for a split second, then Hal pulled out his mobile phone and started to dial 999.

'Shit. I haven't got a fucking signal.' He shook the phone violently, hoping that it would catch some radio waves, however small. Nothing.

Freddie had already turned the small boat round and was heading towards the spot where he thought the man had fallen.

'Can you see him?' he asked breathlessly.

'Nothing.' Hal was still waving his phone about. 'Got it. Got a signal.'

Freddie pulled with all his might on his oars as he heard Hal speaking down the phone. 'Hello? Yeah, there's a man just fallen off the cliff at Tide Cove . . . I'm in a boat . . . no, it's a rowing boat . . . about two minutes ago he fell. We're on our way to see if we can find him but I think we'll need the lifeboat . . . yeah, I'll hang on but I might lose the signal . . . Hello, hello?' He looked at the phone. 'Shit. Lost signal.'

'Are they coming?' asked Freddie breathlessly.

'She said she was going to put me through but—' His phone rang. 'Hello? Yes it was me who rang you . . . we need the lifeboat and an ambulance . . . I'm Hal Chandler . . . my dad's the mechanic on the Trevay lifeboat . . . hello ? Hello?'

Hal threw the handset into the bottom of the boat in frustration. 'The signal keeps going.'

'They'll get here,' said Freddie, his arms straining with effort. 'I know they will.'

For the next few minutes, neither boy spoke to the other.

Freddie was trying to ignore the pain in his shoulders in an effort to keep the boat moving forwards, and Hal was kneeling in the prow of the boat, scanning the rolling sea.

'I see him,' he shouted suddenly.

Freddie drew the boat alongside the man, not knowing whether he wanted to see what lay there. 'Is he breathing?' he asked Hal.

'He's face up, anyway,' said Hal.

Bravely he put his hand in the water and pulled at the man's jacket, bringing him closer to the boat. 'All right, mate?' he said fearfully. 'We got you.'

There was no response.

Freddie turned and looked over his shoulder at the man's face. It was pallid, the eyelids puffy and closed. A good week's worth of grey stubble covered his jowls and a frond of red seaweed had caught in it. 'Is he dead?'

'I don't know,' said Hal shakily.

'Keep his head out of the water until the lifeboat comes,' Freddie ordered.

'I'm trying.' But Hal didn't know how much longer he could hold on.

*

Jesse was just a minute away from the office when he felt his pager vibrate in his pocket just as he saw Mickey dashing towards him.

His face was etched with anxiety.

'We got a shout on the lifeboat, Jesse.'

'Not a boat in trouble, not in this weather – the water's as still as anything.'

'There's a body in the water. But, Jesse, it's the boys.'

Jesse's heart froze. 'What do you mean?'

'They made the call.'

All thoughts of lorries, John Dory and maths tutors fled his mind.

He and Mickey raced to the lifeboat station.

*

Freddie thought he could hear something. An engine coming fast from around the corner of the headland. He looked over his shoulder and, with a shout, said, 'It's them. They're here.' In crazy relief he stood up and started to wave and shout. 'We're over here! Dad, we're over here!'

'Sit down,' shouted Hal. 'You're tipping the boat, I can't keep hold of him.'

The Spirit of Trevay in its orange and blue livery, had never looked more wonderful as it approached the boys and the drowned man. At the helm was Jesse. 'There they are,' He slowed the powerful engines and expertly brought the boat alongside the small rowing boat.

Leaving the engines idling, and shouting orders to the crew, Jesse climbed up on deck and leant over the side. He saw the white faces of Freddie and Hal staring up from the little boat.

'Are you boys all right?' he called.

'We're fine, Dad,' said Freddie with a sob of relief. 'It's this bloke, he fell off the cliff.'

Hal was still hanging on to the man's jacket and valiantly keeping his head out of the water.

Jesse, thanking a God he wasn't sure existed that the two boys weren't harmed, took a look at the casualty. His heart skipped a beat and he involuntarily swore.

Mickey was up on deck now and scanning the rowing boat for Hal.

'Hal!' he called. 'You're OK?'

'Yes, Dad.'

'What you got there?'

'This man just fell off the cliff,' Hal called back, tears coming in shock and in the relief of seeing his father. 'I've been holding him. I don't know if he's dead.'

Mickey was first to clamber down into the wooden boat and take the weight of the man from Hal. 'It's all right. I've got 'im. You can let go now.'

When Mickey could see the man's face he frowned. 'Jesse,' he shouted. 'It's your'n brother. 'Tis Grant.'

Jesse was feeling an old sickness in his stomach, a sixth sense that the past was about to collide with the present. 'Are you sure?' he asked.

'Yeah, I'm sure.'

Mickey had a toughness that his wiry frame belied. Swinging Grant's body round in the water, he managed to get his hands under his arms and haul his dead weight into the bottom of the little boat.

'Is he dead?' asked Jesse, who as coxswain would never leave the lifeboat.

'Give me a minute,' said Mickey. He put his ear to the man's nose to see if he could hear or feel any breath. It was hard to tell with the soft breeze playing around the two boats. He put a hand inside the collar of Grant's camouflage jacket and felt the cold neck for a pulse.

Jesse and the boys waited.

'I've got it!' Mickey said. 'I've got a pulse, but it's faint. Radio for the ambulance to meet us on the harbour. Let's get him back quick.'

*

The side ward in the hospital looked over the car park and a sprawling cemetery.

Grant lay in the bed with a drip in his arm, an oxygen tube in his nostrils and a big bandage round his head. The young doctor was talking to Grant's parents and Jesse.

'He's had a pretty big bang to his head. He must have hit something when he fell. Not a rock but maybe a piece of flotsam. Piece of wood, maybe. There's not much of a cut but he has a lot of swelling. When he wakes up he's going to have quite a headache.'

'It's a miracle he didn't drown,' said Jan, his mother. She was sitting on a small chair at Grant's bedside and was holding his hand.

'Indeed,' agreed the doctor. 'He managed not to swallow much water but I think that the amount of alcohol he'd already consumed meant that he was very relaxed when he fell and therefore didn't panic when he hit the water.'

Edward was standing by the window, his back to the room. He was watching an elderly man wearing a tweed hat standing by a grave. A small girl of about twelve, maybe his granddaughter, guessed Edward, was hopping and skipping around him whilst swinging a Marks & Spencer plastic bag. The man said something to her and she stopped her skipping and opened the bag, taking out a potted plant with garish pink blooms. The old man took it and reverentially removed his tweed hat and bent to place the offering at the headstone. As he struggled to stand up, the young girl offered her arm and the two of them walked away. Edward turned his back on the comforting mundanity of the scene, and faced his own.

'It's Freddie and young Hal I'm proud of,' he said. 'Young lads. To do what they did. Bloody brave.'

Jesse nodded. 'Yeah. They'm did well.'

'What was Grant doing on those cliffs?' Edward asked. 'We haven't heard from him for years.'

'Two years,' said Jan. 'We had that letter from him. Remember? Telling us he was out of – ' she lowered her voice so that the doctor wouldn't hear – 'prison.'

Edward's mouth tightened to a thin line. 'Sorry, Doctor, but you may as well know. Grant has been a Heller all his life. Since he was a boy. If there was a fight he'd have started it, if there was trouble, he was in it.' Edward shook his head. 'When he joined the Marines we thought he was in the perfect job.'

'He got his green berct, Doctor,' said Jan, wanting the doctor not to think too badly of her son, but Edward ploughed on.

'Fat lot of good that was. He couldn't keep his fists to himself. Got court-martialled. Banged up in chokey for eight years.' Edward put his hands to his head and rubbed his temples. 'Dishonourably discharged four or five years ago. We haven't heard from him since. He couldn't even send me a note just to let me know he was all right. We had no idea he was back till today.'

Jan started to cry quietly and rummaged around in her handbag for a tissue.

Edward looked at her with pity. 'He broke his mother's heart and now look at him. I wish he'd never come back.'

Jan shouted through her tears. 'Don't say that.'

'I'll say what I like.' Edward raised his voice in return. 'He's brought us nothing but heartache and—'

Jesse stepped in. 'Dad. That's enough. We're all upset.' He turned to the doctor. 'I'm sorry, Doctor.'

*

Jesse had insisted that his parents go down to the hospital cafeteria to get something to eat and drink.

'Let me sit with him till you get back.'

On his own with Grant, Jesse wondered what his brother's dramatic reappearance would mean to the family. Did Grant know that Jesse was managing director of Behenna and Clovelly? Bryn and Edward were still nominally joint chief executives, but the day-to-day running of the company was in Jesse's control. Had Grant come back hoping to get a slice of the company? There was no way Jesse would give him one. He looked down at Grant, lying so still in the bed, so white against the pillow. How could he come back here after all this time? Jesse had seen the damage that Grant's behaviour had done to his parents, and he had worked his fingers to the bone doing fourteen-hour days to make Behenna and Clovelly the best in the business. He had clients across the globe, and a reputation that was the envy of his competitors. He was damned if Grant was going to come back and fuck it all up.

'What are you doing back here, Grant?' he asked.

Grant didn't open his eyes. But he answered, 'I missed my family.'

Jesse put his face close to his brother's. 'Well, we haven't missed you,' he said with menace.

'That's nice, little brother.' Grant slowly opened his eyes and winced. 'My head hurts.'

'It will.'

'I didn't mean to fall off the edge. I was just having a little drink when I saw the boys in the boat. Thought I'd get a better look at 'em.'

Jesse's heart started to pound. 'You're lucky we got you out.'

'You rescued me?' Grant coughed a little. 'Got any water? My throat's sore.'

Jesse looked and saw a plastic jug of water and a beaker on the bedside cabinet. He poured half a cup and handed it to Grant. 'Here. I ain't nursing you. Hold it yourself.'

'How lucky I am to have a brother so kind.' With difficulty, Grant took the cup and held it to his lips, taking a couple of mouthfuls. 'So you rescued me then.'

'Coxswain on the lifeboat, ain't I.'

Grant attempted to laugh but started to cough, spilling the water on the bedclothes.

'Lifeboat, eh? What a pillar of the community! So unlike your scallywag of a brother. How proud Mum and Dad must be,' he said with venom.

Jesse couldn't take any more of this bullshit. In a dangerous voice he said, 'Just tell me what the fuck you're doing here.'

'I told you,' Grant smiled. 'I missed my family.' He opened an eye. 'And those lovely boys.' He smiled a smile of pure evil. 'By the way, how is the gorgeous Loveday? Oh, and your uptight wife, Greer? I'd have had a go at Loveday myself, but I don't like taking sloppy seconds, especially from my little brother.'

Jesse lifted his fist and would have smashed it into Grant's face sending him spiralling back to oblivion, if it hadn't been for the door opening and the arrival of Jan and Edward.

Jan ran to Grant's side. 'Son. You're awake. It's OK. You've had a terrible fall but the doctor says you'll be fine. You're safe with your family now. We'll take you home.' She took his hand and, rubbing it, dropped a kiss on his forehead.

'Thanks, Ma,' said Grant. 'Give us a hug.'

Laughing through her tears, she bent and hugged him as best she could.

Over her shoulder Grant looked at Jesse and winked slyly. 'Yeah. I'm home, Ma. With my family. For good.'

26

Normally Jesse took enormous pleasure from arriving at the new offices of Behenna and Clovelly.

He parked his car in his reserved space. He climbed out of the new Jaguar XK V8 and breathed the clean, salty air. His head was aching. He hadn't slept well. Grant's reappearance had left him troubled.

'Morning, Jesse.' Mickey was walking towards him with Loveday. ''Ow's Grant doing?'

'Morning!' Jesse pressed the button on his key fob and the car bleeped and locked itself. 'He's all right. Coming out today. He's going to stay at Mum and Dad's for a bit, but I'm worried for them . . . they could do without a scrounger like him living off them.'

Loveday was concerned. 'Your poor mum. Last thing she needs.' She looked at her watch. 'Give us a kiss, Mick. I'm late for work.' Mickey obliged and both men watched Loveday as she walked into the Behenna and Clovelly offices.

'She loves that job, Jesse,' said Mickey.

'Well, she's very good at it.'

'Yeah. Always good with her head. Better'n me.'

'How are things with the new house?'

'Great. The girls love their room up in the attic and Hal's got space to do his school work in his room rather than on the kitchen table.' Mickey looked at Jesse's car.

'Look at us, Jesse. We ain't done too bad, 'ave we? Remember that old Ford Capri you had?'

'That was a classic.'

''Twas a heap of shit.'

'What about your bike?' said Jesse indignantly. 'That was knackered before you got it.'

'That was class, that was. With Loveday on the back of it, I felt like a king.'

The men smiled. 'Those were the days, Mick,' said Jesse fondly.

'Yeah,' nodded Mick. 'They were shit really, weren't they?' He laughed out loud. 'But look at us. Your'n all prosperous boss an' that. The car, the house, the business.'

'You haven't done so bad! Skipper of the biggest boat in our fleet.'

Mickey looked abashed. 'I wouldn't have any of it if it weren't for you.'

'Nor I if it weren't for you, Mickey.'

'Well, you got your bugger of a brother to deal with now, and I'm glad I ain't got him.'

Jesse sighed. 'I hope he'll just piss off again and never come back.'

*

Having said goodbye to each other, Mickey headed off to his boat and its waiting crew, and Jesse stepped into the air-conditioned luxury of his building. As he glided upstairs in the glass lift, he saw the whole of Trevay spread out below him. Nothing much had changed since he was a boy. The old cottages and houses in the cobbled lanes were looking better kept, though, now, owned as they were by sharp-eyed Londoners who'd bought them as holiday homes. Up on the hill, the housing estate had grown and was sprawling out over what had been farm-land, but where else could the locals afford to live? Not in the centre of highly priced Trevay, that was for sure. And they didn't want to. Cramped old houses with wonky floors and no garage? Let the ones from up country have them. Fools and their money, and all that.

The lift stopped with barely a whisper and the door opened, revealing a long, sunny room that had been partitioned into small, private offices or larger open areas, where long couches, glass tables and local art were displayed beautifully. This was Greer's handiwork. Her interiors company was now so busy that she employed three designers and a team of builders and tradesmen. Jesse's office was at the end of the building and took up the entire width of it. His secretary was at her desk, writing something in his diary.

'Morning, Mr Behenna,' she smiled.

'Good morning, Lauren.'

'Coffee? Usual?'

'Yes, please.'

Lauren stood up to go to the canteen. 'By the way, your father's in the office waiting for you. I'll bring you two coffees up.'

Jesse's pleasure at walking into his kingdom, already dissipated, dissolved entirely.

'Dad.' He wrapped a smile on his face. 'Nice surprise. How's Grant?'

Jesse noticed that Edward had aged in the three days since Grant had turned up.

'He's all right. Your mum's fussing at home, making up the bed, writing lists. He's coming out of hospital this afternoon.'

Jesse walked round his big wooden desk and sat down. 'I'd go and collect him for you but . . .' He spread his arms, indicating a day full of work, even though his desktop was clear.

'Your mum and I'll get him. No, it's not what I came to see you about. I want to get things sorted. Legally. Grant's not having what you've got.'

'Dad.' Jesse knew that his father would wash his hands of Grant if he could, but the fact that his father was of the same mind as him regarding the business was music to his ears. However, it was important that his father didn't think Jesse was trying to push Grant out.

'Dad, I'm only number two son.'

'Yeah, but you've worked hard. I am not about to see Grant try to take it from you.'

'Does Mum know about this?'

'She don't need to.'

'Are you sure about that?'

'I won't leave him empty-handed. He'll get what's right, but he ain't getting the business. It's twenty years since Bryn and I agreed that it would be yours and Greer's, and then Freddie's.'

'If he wants it.'

'Why wouldn't he?'

'Because . . . there's a world out there and he wants to see it. Just as I wanted to see it . . .'

Lauren came in, pushing the heavy door with her bottom. 'Two lattes.' She put the two chunky pottery mugs onto the coffee table. 'Anything else I can get you?'

'No, thank you, Lauren.' Jesse smiled impatiently.

Lauren took her cue and left quietly, and Jesse turned

to his father. He didn't want to look this gift horse in the mouth. 'OK. I'll get on to Penrose tomorrow and make sure that the paperwork is watertight, if that's what you want me to do.'

'I do,' his father said firmly. 'And Bryn agrees with me too.'

'So when are you going to tell Grant?' Jesse asked, stirring his coffee. 'Or will you leave it until you're gone and we're at the reading of the will?'

Edward smiled ruefully. 'I'd like to do that, but it's the coward's way out. No, I'll tell him sooner rather than later.' He took a sip of the latte. 'That way, with a bit of luck, he might not be tempted to hang around.'

*

It was a long day, made longer by the nagging thought that Grant was bound to be the bearer of trouble. Jesse was snappy and irritable. Problems heaped up. More than once, Lauren bit her lip and retreated to her desk. The final straw came late in the day when a London chef, not known for his equability, rang complaining about 'this shit you've sent me. I wouldn't give it to me cats. The lobsters aren't big enough, the skate is too expensive, and where's the sodding lemon sole? I'm not paying for this crap . . .' On and on he ranted, in his pseudo-cockney accent. Jesse put the receiver on the desk and rubbed his temples. When the man had calmed down he picked the receiver up and said, with a serenity he did not feel, 'Luigi, I am so sorry. I shall send you up a box of twelve dozen Falmouth oysters on the overnight van, on the house. And, next time you're down here, I'd like you to have dinner here at our expense. What do you say?'

*

An hour later, Jesse climbed back into the dark luxury of the Jaguar. The leather seat gave under his weight and released its hypnotic aroma. Jesse put his head on the steering wheel and closed his eyes. His headache was worse. He gave in to his exhaustion and relaxed the tension in his shoulders. 'What a shit of a day,' he said to himself.

A sharp knock on his window made his heart pound as he jerked upright. His headache shot an arrow of pain through his left eye.

Grant, still wearing his head bandage, was leering through the glass. 'First sign of madness, talking to yourself.'

Jesse turned on the engine and the dashboard glowed sweetly, but even that small pleasure was now spoilt. He opened the electric window. 'Grant. What do you want?' he asked dully.

'A bed for a bit. Ma and Pa's house is too small and Ma's driving me mad. As soon as I got home she was mithering me. I walked out while she was in the kitchen putting the kettle on. She was talking so much she didn't hear me go.'

'What about Dad?' Jesse sighed.

'He'd pissed off to the pub.'

'Why not go with him?'

'Whaaat? When my brother has a fancy new car that needs to be sat in and a beautiful new house that needs to be visited?'

Grant walked round the outside of the car and opened the passenger door. He got in. 'Not bad.' He wiped his none-too-clean hands over the walnut trim.

Jesse was not a happy man. A bad day had just got worse. 'Thank you,' he said flatly.

'Well, come on then!' smiled Grant, rubbing his hands gleefully. 'Show me what this baby can do.'

27

When they had lost Louisa, Greer's father, Bryn, had helped them to move out of Pencil Cottage, with all its sadness, and buy Tide House. Bryn had made enquiries through various solicitors and found that the cove below had passed from the previous owner to distant relatives, who lived in Canada and who had no idea of the beauty – or worth – of it. He had bought it for a song. A wooden gate and a large 'KEEP OUT PRIVATE PROPERTY' sign made sure that no wandering tourist could ever honestly say they didn't know that they were trespassing.

This evening, Freddie was home first for a change; he kicked off his shoes in the hallway. He was starving and headed straight into the kitchen and made a beeline for the fridge. He sighed as he eyed the contents. Six low-fat yogurts, a ready-made couscous salad and a packet of defrosted chicken fillets. If this was the fridge at Hal's house, it would be groaning with Dairylea, mini sausage rolls and thick-cut ham. His stomach groaned loudly as he grabbed one of the yogurts and he pulled a face as he tasted the bland goo.

He heard his mother's car pull up in the drive and made a dash for the stairs and the sanctuary of his room.

His mother's voice drifted up from the hallway. 'Freddie! How many times have I told you not to leave your trainers in the hallway? There is a perfectly good shoe store under the stairs.' He heard her tread on the stairs, heading his way.

She strode proprietorially into his room. 'And how many times have I told you not to eat in bed?'

'They eat wherever they want in Hal's house.'

'Exactly. Point proven.' She picked up the empty yogurt pot and sat on the edge of his bed.

'How was your maths tutorial?'

'Boring. A waste of time.'

'It isn't a waste of time. You've got a good head on your shoulders and all you need to do is apply yourself.'

'No point if I'm going out on the boats.'

Greer frowned. Just because Jesse had left school at 16, it didn't mean that Freddie had to as well. She was determined that Freddie was going to make something of himself. She turned and headed back downstairs towards the kitchen; catching sight of her refection on the staircase, she stopped to appraise herself. Greer now wore her hair in an elegant pixie cut. It accentuated her cheekbones. She was wearing a pair of skinny jeans from All Saints paired with a plain white T-shirt and a navy blazer from Joseph. As usual, she saw herself with a critical eye. It took work to look as good as this and, as well as running a successful interior design business, Greer also saw looking after herself as part of the package. She managed to squeeze in either a Pilates or a yoga class every day, and their basement downstairs was equipped with a state-of-the-art gym, which she made good use of.

'What's for dinner?' Freddie shouted from his room.

'Chicken, new potatoes and salad.'

There was silence above, then, after crashing down

the stairs like a herd of elephants, Freddie made an appearance at the kitchen door.

'Can I go over to Hal's tonight?'

'Freddie, that's the third night this week.'

'Well, if my mates come round here you only complain that they dirty the carpet or leave the toilet seat up. They don't care about any of that at Hal's.'

Greer raised an eyebrow. 'It's "lavatory" – and indeed.'

Freddie persisted. 'I'm doing you a favour. Besides, they're having a barbecue again tonight.'

'You'll have to ask your father. Speaking of which, he sent a text to say he's on his way. Apparently we've got a guest.' She looked out of the kitchen window to see if she could spot his Jaguar. 'I wonder who it is.'

*

It was less than a fifteen-minute drive to get to Jesse's home. At the top of Trevay, he turned right and continued along the cliff road towards the crossroads, where you could go straight on for Truro, left for Pendruggan or right towards Tide Cove. He turned right. The lane was wide enough for two cars at this point, and they were high enough up to see the sun glinting off the Atlantic. Holiday-makers, with sandy bare feet, were struggling up the hill after a long day on the beach. They hauled toddlers and dogs, pushchairs and beach trolleys. Fit young men, in surf suits peeled to their navels, jogged up with surfboards on their backs; gaggles of girls with sea-bleached hair stared after them and giggled. Jesse steered the car care-fully through them all, pulling into impossibly small passing spaces to allow camper vans and Chelsea tractors coming from the beach to get by. About two minutes from the beach itself there was a small left-hand turning, discreetly signed: 'Tide Cove. Private Property'.

Grant was impressed. 'Don't tell me you've got the big house down here?'

Jesse said nothing, but drove the car towards two large metal gates fifty yards ahead. He pulled out a small plastic fob from the ashtray and pointed it through the windscreen.

After a second or two the gates swung cleanly open, revealing a gravelled drive, a landscaped front garden and a beautiful honey-stoned house.

*

'Hello,' called Jesse, unlocking the front door.

'Hi, darling,' called Greer from the rear of the house.

'Hi, Greer,' called Grant gaily. 'Guess who's come for dinner.'

Jesse threw his keys onto the ebony console table under the large Edwardian gilt mirror in the hall. Greer popped out from behind a curved wall holding a gin and tonic and wearing an expression of dread. 'Grant?'

'Aye.' He walked towards her and embraced her. She stood stiffly, still holding her glass. He took it from her. 'Cheers. What's for supper?'

Greer's eyes slid to meet Jesse's, but he was staring resolutely at the floor.

'How's your head?' Greer managed, looking at the bandage.

'Bloody sore.' He took a big mouthful of gin and tonic.

'Should you be drinking with a head trauma?'

'Best thing for it,' said Grant, who was now opening a door to his left. 'What's in here?'

'That's the library,' said Greer automatically.

'Nice.' Grant looked into the room. 'Fancy.' He left the library and, crossing the hall, opened a door on his right. 'And what's in 'ere?'

'The drawing room,' said Greer tightly.

'I'm looking for the bleddy telly,' said Grant in exasperation. 'Don't tell me you ain't got one. Or 'ave you gone so la-di-dah that you listen only to the wireless?'

Jesse pulled himself together. 'The television is in there. In the drawing room.'

Grant looked again round the door. 'I can't bleddy see it.'

'It's behind the bookcase,' said Jesse.

Grant was impressed and then suspicious. 'You'm taking the piss out of me? I've had a bang on the 'ead but I'm still all 'ere.'

Jesse went to the bookcase – actually a fake wall with fake books – and slid it away to reveal an enormous television screen.

Grant gasped. 'Well, fuck me! You'm know how to treat yourselves, don't 'e?' He turned to Greer, who was standing in the doorway looking bewildered, if not horrified. 'Get me another drink, G,' said Grant, holding out his empty glass. 'You're not going to get rid of me now.'

*

Grant was a horrible guest.

''Twas a lovely tea that, Greer.' He belched. Greer closed her eyes. 'My compliments to the cook.' He drained his tin of Skinner's Wink beer and wiped his mouth on the sleeve of his grubby pullover. 'Where's the fridge?

I'll get another one of those. Don't want you waiting on me just because you 'aven't seen me for a long time.'

'It's that cupboard there,' said Freddie, pointing towards the integrated larder fridge/freezer with double doors painted in a colour called Sea Fret.

'Your'n a good lad.' Grant grinned at him. 'That's twice you've saved my life. Once taking me out of the drink, and twice getting the drink into me.'

Freddie was pleased to be a hero, and to have an uncle who was a real-life war veteran. All thoughts of going to Hal's were forgotten. His uncle was like no one else in the family, and the thought that he'd been a commando and had been to prison was very exciting.

'Have you killed anyone face to face?' he asked.

Grant came back with his tin of beer and farted before taking his seat again. Freddie sniggered.

'Several,' said Grant sagely. ''Tis a terrible thing to watch a man die. Even if he is the enemy. But Marines don't shirk their duty.'

Greer stood up quickly and began clearing the table.

'Don't 'e 'ave someone to do that for you?' asked Grant, scratching a scurfy scalp under his head bandage.

'I like to look after my family myself. Without too much help,' said Greer.

'Oh. Very commendable.' He winked at Jesse. 'You got a good 'un there, bro. Cook in the kitchen, angel in the living room. Whore in the bedroom, eh?'

Greer put the plates on the worktop and spun to face Grant. 'That sort of sexist talk is not welcome at our table.'

Grant tilted his chair onto its back legs and laughed. 'Don't tell me you're a feminist lesbo now, G? You weren't so picky about that sort of stuff when you had the hots for Jesse, were you? Used all your girly tricks to trap him then, eh?'

'Watch it Grant,' Jesse warned.

Greer threw her tea towel into the sink and spoke to Jesse. 'Can I speak to you in the library for a moment, please?'

'Of course,' said Jesse, pushing his chair back.

'Uh-oh. Nothing to do with me, I hope?' smirked Grant.

*

In the library, Greer shook with anger and emotion. 'Why the hell didn't you tell me he was coming for supper?'

'I didn't know myself. He's walked out of Mum and Dad's.'

'But he's going back there tonight?'

'I'm not sure.'

'Ask him.'

'It's late. If I throw him out, Mum will be in pieces. She's already a bag of nerves.'

'He's not staying here.' Jesse couldn't look her in the eye. Greer shook her head in disgust. 'I'll tell him then, shall I?' Greer pushed past Jesse and walked out into the hall, where Grant was being helped up the stairs by Freddie. 'Where are you going?' she almost shrieked.

'I'm showing Uncle Grant up to his room,' said Freddie innocently.

'It's so kind of you both to give me a roof over my head,' said Grant. 'I'll be no trouble.'

*

In their perfectly appointed master bedroom, Greer sat at her dressing table, vigorously rubbing cleanser into her face and giving Jesse chapter and verse.

'He looks awful. He drinks too much, he's filthy dirty, he has no manners and he's not staying here more than this one night. Do you understand?'

'I didn't invite him,' groaned Jesse. 'I don't want him here any more than you do.'

'Then send him back to your mother's tomorrow, or . . .' She brightened at the thought. 'Give him a fat cheque and tell him to get lost. That's the only thing he understands.' She plucked three tissues from their box and wiped the cleanser from her face.

'How much?' asked Jesse.

'Five hundred,' asserted Greer.

*

The wad of notes was waiting in a plump envelope on the kitchen table at the breakfast place laid for Grant. 'What's this then?' he asked, picking the envelope up and shaking it.

Neither Jesse nor Greer answered.

''Twouldn't be a little "piss off Grant and don't come back", would it?'

Jesse cleared his throat. 'It's something to tide you over while you find your feet. It should pay for a nice lodging and some food.'

Grant narrowed his eyes thoughtfully. 'I see.' He tapped the envelope on the table, sucking air through his teeth. 'No room at the inn. Is that it?'

They could hear Freddie coming down the stairs.

'Don't say anything to Freddie,' warned Jesse.

'Morning,' said Freddie brightly.

'Morning, boy.' Grant stashed the envelope inside his pullover, much to the relief of Jesse and Greer. 'What you up to today? No school?'

'Another week till we go back.' Freddie stretched across the table and picked up the box of Crunchy Nut Cornflakes. 'Big year this year. GCSEs.'

'GCSEs? There's posh. My education was the university of life, and I'm still learning.' He patted the wad under his jumper and looked slyly at Grant. 'In fact, starting today, your dad's going to teach me all about the family business. I've got a lot of catching up to do.'

*

'This ain't too shabby,' said Grant, as they headed up in the lift towards the top floor. He pulled at the cuffs of his borrowed shirt. ''Ow do I look?'

Jesse, who'd done his best to dissuade Grant from coming to the office with him, said, 'Cleaner.'

'Yeah, well,' said Grant, patting at the fresh jumper Jesse had found for him, 'the life of a gentlemen of the road don't stretch to hot baths and razor blades.'

Jesse looked appalled. 'You were sleeping rough?'

'Yeah. On and off over the last few years. And, after the confines of chokey, I tell 'ee, to sleep under the roof of the heavens was better'n a bed at the Starfish . . . I managed all right, a little bit of this, a little bit of that . . .'

Who knows what he had been up to in the intervening years, if his ravaged features were anything to go by, thought Jesse grimly. Prison, alcohol and those years on the street had all taken their toll.

The lift doors slid open and the scent of opulence surrounded them.

Grant took it all in, a smile of entitlement creeping across his face. He clapped Jesse on the shoulder. 'So, this is what you've been up to. I'll have a slice of this.'

Jesse couldn't bear to look at his brother and strode off towards Lauren and his office, Grant bowling insouciantly beside him.

'Two coffees, Mr Behenna?' asked Lauren, looking at Grant with a questioning arch of one eyebrow.

''Ow do?' said Grant, proffering his hand. 'I'm Grant Behenna. Jesse's older brother. I've been away for a while, but I'm here now, ready to give my all to the family firm.'

Lauren took his hand and felt the calloused, slightly greasy, palm. Grant hung on a little too long and she was afraid he was going to kiss it, but Jesse called him off. 'Grant, if I see you bothering Lauren you'll be out on your ear. Same goes for any woman employed here.'

Grant let go of Lauren's hand and grinned. ''E's jealous. No sugar in me coffee, darlin'.'

Jesse opened his office door and Grant squeezed past him. 'Very nice.' He walked to Jesse's desk and got himself settled behind it. He spun the chair round to take in the view across the estuary. 'When I see Trevay like this, it makes me wonder why I ever left.'

'Get out of my chair,' Jesse ordered. 'And you left Trevay because you went into the Marines, disgraced yourself, and got banged up for eight years for hurting an innocent old man.'

Grant, looking miffed, lifted himself out of the ergonomic chair and grudgingly settled himself in a comfy leather one by the coffee table. 'Just details, old boy.

Details. Now, where are you going to place me and what's the starting salary?'

Jesse had picked up the phone. 'Hi, Johnny? Mr Behenna here. You know that job you've got downstairs? Can I bring a potential candidate down?'

*

Grant looked down at the white overall and white rubber boots he was wearing. 'Here you are.' Johnny, the foreman of the fish market, handed him a white hairnet. 'Put that on and follow me.'

'Of course, I'm just here to learn the business from the bottom. Then I'll be moved around the rest of company to get a taste of all the departments before taking my place on the board,' blagged Grant.

'Sure,' said Johnny. 'That's what they all say.'

Grant caught Johnny's arm and spun him round, pushing him against the brick wall and winding him. 'Listen, you little fucker. I am a Behenna and you will treat me with respect . . . if you want to keep your job.'

'Let go of him immediately.' Edward Behenna, who had been up early, was glad he'd decided to drop in and see how his elder son was doing. Grant let go of Johnny.

'Just playing, Dad. Fooling around. Weren't we, Johnny?'

'Something like that,' said Johnny.

Edward was no fool. 'You have a lot to prove, Grant.'

Grant stood to attention and mock-saluted his father. 'Yessir.' He didn't like playing the lackey one little bit, but to be honest he'd had enough of roaming and he wouldn't mind a bit of what Jesse had managed to secure. Yes indeed, that would do nicely.

Edward ignored his son's sarcasm. 'The tide's running in and there are a lot of boats coming in to unload. I want to see you earning your money.'

*

Edward hadn't been wrong. Several boats chugged in together and tied up on the fish quay, each eager to unload its catch and get the best prices before the next boats came in.

Crates and crates of plastic boxes, full of ice and fish, were unloaded from the bellies of the vessels.

Monkfish, spider crab, mackerel, bass, sole, turbot – you name it, it was there.

Buyers materialised as soon as they heard the catch was in, and it wasn't long before large amounts of money was changing hands. The London chefs had got their orders in already and their boxes were being loaded onto the refrigerated vans immediately.

It was heavy work and Grant, once so fit, had lost his strength. His muscles had turned to fat and his lungs were clogged with nicotine. In a short lull, he sat at the back of the market on a pile of empty boxes, underneath a No Smoking sign. He was desperate for a nicotine hit, but he wanted this job more. Despite all his blustering, even he knew this was last orders in the last-chance saloon.

On the quayside, boats were leaving and more boats were arriving. Johnny spotted Grant. 'Grant, get over here and unload this next boat.' Grant reluctantly did as he was told, as Johnny hailed the skipper of the approaching vessel. 'All right, Mickey boy?'

Mickey threw a rope to Johnny, who tied it onto one of the ancient bollards.

'Bleddy tired,' called back Mickey. 'Good fishin' but no sleep.'

'Hi, Mickey.' Grant had wandered over and said sarcastically, 'My hero.'

Mickey jumped onto the quay. ''Twasn't me 'oo saved you.' Mickey thought that if he'd found Grant he would probably have left him to drown. Definitely would if there was a next time. ''Twas Hal.'

'Hal?' asked Grant innocently. 'Who's Hal?'

'You know – my boy.'

'Your boy? I hear him and Fred are like brothers?'

Mickey smiled fondly. 'Aye. They're like Jesse and I was growing up. 'Tis lovely to see.'

'Like brothers?' Grant feigned amazement. 'Isn't that sweet? Course, I wouldn't know what having a brother to play with was like. Jesse was so much younger – and always ran off with you.'

Mickey was remembering how much he disliked Grant. 'What you doin' here?'

'Learning the business, boy. Learning the business.'

A tall and skinny boy came out of the ship's hold. 'Dad, you ready to unload?'

'Hal, this is Freddie's Uncle Grant.' Mickey nodded towards Grant. 'He'm got something to say to you.'

Grant took his cue and smiled at the boy warmly. 'So you're Hal? I got to thank you for saving my life. You're like a superhero to me.'

Hal blushed. ''Twas nothin'.'

'That's not what I heard. You kept me from going under, didn't you?'

'Yeah.'

'That must have been frightening. Did you think I was dead?'

The memory flashed through Hal's mind and brought the horror back to him. 'Sort of.'

'Takes more'n a dip in the sea to kill off your uncle Grant.' Grant laughed unpleasantly, then said, 'Oh, no, I'm not your uncle, am I? I get mixed up.' He put his hand up to his now bandage-free head. 'I had quite a bang on the old noggin'.'

'Yeah,' said Hal uncertainly, and he turned to Mickey. 'Anyway, Dad. All the boxes are ready . . .'

*

Just as the last boxes were coming off Mickey's boat, Grant heard a familiar female voice call, 'Hiya, Mick. Good trip?' It was Loveday. She was just as sexy as Grant remembered her.

'Well, well, if ain't luscious Loveday Carter,' said Grant, sidling up to her.

She looked at him, recognition dawning. She was shocked at how different he looked. His once muscular frame was now skin and bone. He had never been her cup of tea in the looks department, but he'd always been able to pick up girls. Now his features were gaunt and sallow and he looked ancient. He could only be early forties, by Loveday's calculations.

'Grant. I 'eard you were back.'

Mickey came to join them. 'She's Loveday Chandler now. My missus.' Mickey put his arm protectively around Loveday and squeezed her.

'Oh, yeah,' said Grant, nodding slowly. 'You were up the duff, weren't you?'

Loveday was annoyed. 'Trust you to remember that. Yeah, I was. I was expecting Hal.'

'Oh, that's right.' Grant's voice held a hint of malevolence. 'Trouble with me is, I remember some funny things. I remember the night before Jesse got married. Do you?'

Loveday nervously put a hand to her hair, brushing away an invisible strand. 'Not really.'

'Course you do.' He insisted. 'It was snowing.'

Johnny shouted over to Mickey. 'Mick, come in the office and sign this paperwork, would 'e?'

'Back in a minute, darlin',' said Mick, leaving Grant and Loveday by themselves.

Grant watched Mickey till he was safely out of earshot, then he said slowly and with no small pleasure. 'You went up to the sheds. Why you were there I couldn't say. Maybe you were cold and needed warming up by something . . . or someone?'

Loveday looked at Grant with fear. 'I don't know what you're talking about.'

'I think you do. You see, I was . . .' He stopped and quickly changed the subject as he saw Mickey and Hal coming towards them. 'I was wondering what you do for Jesse now.'

'What?' she said, feeling panicked.

'I was just saying to your missus, Mickey,' Grant raised his voice as Mickey and Hal approached, 'what's she doing here for Jesse?'

Mickey smiled proudly. 'She'm in accounts. Always good with her 'ead.'

Grant suppressed a snigger. 'I'm sure that's true.'

Loveday was desperate to get away from this loathsome man. 'You'm ready to go home, boys?' she asked her son and husband.

'Aye,' they said in unison.

'Then I'll get my things. Hang on a minute.'

As Loveday scurried off, Jesse appeared. 'Had a good day, Grant?'

'Smashing,' said Grant. 'Just catching up with old friends, ain't we, Mickey?'

Loveday came back holding a handbag and a cardigan. 'We're off home now, Jesse,' she said. 'See you tomorrow.'

As the family walked away, Grant couldn't resist sprinkling a little agitant in their brains. 'Cheerio! And thanks again, Hal, for saving my life. Your dad must be so proud of you? Eh, Jesse?'

28

August 2009

Grant moved out of Tide House with the five hundred pounds in his pocket and the promise of wages, into one of the letting rooms above the Golden Hind. Living in the pub suited him – and Jesse – perfectly.

Grant had settled into his job on the fish market too. He did it well enough, even with a hangover, and over the next few weeks he stopped mithering Jesse about a bigger, better position in the company. At the moment he couldn't really face the extra responsibilities a higher position would entail; he was sure he would take his rightful place at the top of the tree in due course. 'I'm in clover,' he said to himself. 'Living in a pub, all the beer I can drink and a job that I can't be sacked from. Grant, lad, you landed on your arse in butter all right.'

For his part, Jesse was relieved that Grant had apparently settled for his lot. Yes, he drank too much and was sometimes late for work – or didn't turn up at all – but, all in all, it was the best of a bad situation.

*

Greer had been very upset by Grant's reappearance, and Jesse's weakness in dealing with him. She had sanitised the house from top to bottom. 'This room needs fumigating,' she said, stomping around the beautiful *lit bateau* bed in the spare room that Grant had slept in.

'He's only been here a night,' said Jesse testily.

'But where was he the previous nights? Eh?' she'd demanded, snapping on a pair of rubber gloves and stripping the duvet and mattress protector off.

'He was in hospital.'

'Yes, and we all know how filthy hospitals are nowadays, don't we?' She handed Jesse a black bin liner. 'Open that and hold it while I put this bedding in.' Jesse did as he was told. He watched Greer as she moved around the room picking up the towels that Grant had left in a damp heap on the beautiful suede chair by the window; finding three empty tins of Skinner's Wink behind the curtains, and curling her lips as she saw a pair of very dirty, rather stiff socks spread out on the radiator. Greer had been a good wife to him and a great mother to Freddie. When they had lost Louisa, he had made a promise to himself that he would be the best husband and father Greer and Freddie could hope for. And he'd held to that promise.

If there had been any vestige of longing for Loveday, he made sure he'd killed it. Smothering the thoughts till there was no breath left in them. He loved Greer in his own way and he knew she loved him.

'I do love you, Greer,' he said suddenly.

She stopped fussing with the clean sheets and looked at him. 'Don't try to get round me.'

'I'm not.' He put the stuffed bin liner down and came towards her. He put his arms around her waist and pulled her into him. 'I'm sorry about Grant. He won't come back here again.'

She tried to wriggle out of his embrace, saying, 'Too right he won't be coming back here again,' but he held her tighter. He kissed her neck the way she used to like it and he felt her relax just a little.

'What are you doing?' she asked quietly.

'What do you think?' He nibbled her ear.

'I haven't got time for this,' she said after a pause. 'I've got to get this room sorted, then I'm meeting a client over in Liskeard after lunch.'

He persisted with the nibbling. 'We've got plenty of time.'

Greer weighed up all she had to do, versus having sex with her husband. 'OK. But we'll have to be quick.'

*

The summer turned slowly into autumn and Jesse was feeling confident that life was back under his control. Grant was behaving himself. Greer had secured a very lucrative job doing up a huge country house just outside Liskeard. Freddie was back at school and on track to do well in his GCSEs. And the business had just had its best summer profits for three years.

So nothing could have prepared him for the entrance, one afternoon, of Loveday into his office. Her face was blotched and her make-up dislodged by tears.

'What's happened?' he asked, getting up and closing the office door behind her. He glimpsed Lauren looking curiously at him. 'It's OK, Lauren.' He smiled.

'Would you like a tea? Coffee?' Lauren asked, desperate to know what was going on.

'I'll let you know.' He smiled again and closed the door firmly.

He turned to Loveday, his smile replaced with concern. 'What's happened? Is it Mickey? The kids?'

'It's Grant.' She was shaking.

Jesse sat Loveday on one of the comfy chairs by the coffee table. 'What's he done?'

'Nothing . . . n-not yet . . . It's what he's been saying.'

'Tell me.' Jesse was feeling the old dread in his stomach.

'He was overheard in the Hind last night, saying . . .' Loveday's voice broke and she wiped at her tears angrily, '. . . saying that Hal's not Mickey's son. He said that he had a good idea who the father is.'

'Did he give a name?'

Loveday looked at Jesse coldly, 'Of course not. There's no other bloody name but Mickey's.'

Jesse bit his lip. 'Loveday, I don't want to get you cross but . . . are you sure – you know – that Hal is Mickey's?'

She jumped up, looking as if he'd slapped her. 'I've told you. You are nothing to do with Hal.' She was shouting now. 'Get that into your thick bleddy head, will you?'

'All right. All right. Come and sit back down.' He spoke calmly and she returned to her seat. 'So why have you come to tell me this?' he asked gently.

She wiped her eyes and blew her nose. 'Because Grant's your brother and you need to shut him up before Mickey hears anything.'

'OK,' he said slowly. 'Who was he talking to in the pub?'

'Peter the landlord. A few of the boat crews and some of the lads who work downstairs. I heard it from Johnny. He said no one believed a word of it and it was all a load of shit, but he thought I should know.'

'Oh shit,' said Jesse.

'Yeah,' replied a crumpled Loveday.

*

On the upstairs landing of the Hind, Jesse peered at the nameplates on each of the four letting rooms. He walked past Francis Drake, The Armada Room and The Good Queen Bess Suite. When he got to The Pelican he stopped, took a deep breath and knocked with what he hoped was authority.

He heard a shuffling and the creak of a bedspring. He knocked again.

'Piss off,' came Grant's voice.

'It's me. Jesse. Let me in.'

'If it's about me not coming in to work today, I've got the flu. See you tomorrow.'

'It's not that. Let me in.'

Jesse heard a few muttered curses then the sound of approaching feet. The bolt was drawn back and the door opened. Grant looked terrible and smelt as ripe as a whisky distillery.

'I told you. I've got the flu. If I were you I wouldn't come near me.'

Jesse ignored this and pushed his way into the room.

'Good God, Grant. Look at the state of your room. Does no one come in and clean for you?'

Grant looked sheepish. 'I don't like to put the girls to any bother.'

Jesse, with years of the training that Greer had instilled in him, crossed the room and opened the sagging curtains. He pushed at the sash window to let the cool October night air in. It wouldn't budge. Giving up, he picked his way across the floor and its patchwork of beer cans and improvised ashtrays. 'You and I need a little talk.'

'I don't feel very well.'

'Beer and fags tend to make people feel like shit,' glowered Jesse. 'Get downstairs in five minutes.'

Jesse must have looked more threatening than he felt because Grant did appear downstairs without keeping him waiting more than a couple of minutes.

'I'll have a pint, please,' Grant said, walking towards the bar.

'Oh, no.' Jesse pulled his brother towards the door. 'You and I are having a little chat where flapping ears can't hear us.'

*

There was a keen wind whistling over the water as Jesse dragged a reluctant Grant past the public toilets and towards a covered shelter with benches for weary tourists. 'Sit down,' Jesse ordered Grant.

Grant sat and whimpered, 'I ain't done nothing wrong.'

'You shouted your mouth off in the bar last night about Hal Chandler not being Mickey's son.'

Grant looked sly and licked his lips. 'Well, maybe I did and maybe I didn't, and maybe he is and maybe he isn't.'

'You are going to go into the Hind tonight and you'll put the record straight,' said Jesse with impressive menace. 'You will tell them that you are a hopeless piss-head and that you talk all sorts of shit when you've had a drink. What you said was not only untrue, it was hurtful to people who have been good friends to you.'

Grant pulled a wry smile. 'Well, I would say that if it were a lie.'

Jesse looked at his brother coldly. 'It was a lie.'

'I don't think so. The night before you got married to the oh-so-wealthy Greer, I saw you with Loveday. Lying on your old parka on the floor of Dad's old office up at the sheds.'

Jesse pushed his face close to Grant's unshaven, alcohol-ravaged face. 'No you didn't.'

Grant pushed his face into Jesse's and laughed. 'Oh, yes I did. You were giving her a hell of a going-over.'

Jesse could feel something building inside him. Hatred, resentment, anger.

'How dare you? All I've ever done is the right thing, while you . . . you're just a dirty little disappointment who has thrown his life away and broken Mum and Dad's hearts in the process.'

Grant sneered. 'You think you're so much better than me, Daddy's Number One son, but one day we'll be the same. You won't be able to keep me from my rightful inheritance. We'll see who's the "Number One" then.'

Now it was Jesse's turn to laugh. 'You'll never get a penny, Grant. Dad's cut you out and I'll get the business – all of it. We made sure.'

The sneer faded from Grant's face. 'You fucker. I was right about you. Dad would never do this, but you would. You shafted Loveday, you shafted your best friend and now you're going to shaft me.' He pushed his face close to Jesse's and Jesse could smell the sour stench of alcohol, cigarettes and decay on his breath. 'You might fool other people – all respectable with your la-di-dah wife and house – but I know it's just a front. Underneath you're a lying little shit bag – just like me.'

Neither Grant – nor Jesse himself, imprisoned in a red mist – expected the punch that smashed into Grant's jaw, sending teeth and a fine mist of blood in an arc to his left. Jesse, once he'd let loose the first fist, couldn't stop himself. He pummelled his brother until Grant's body slid to the floor, and then didn't stop, kicking him until exhaustion halted him and he stood, dazed and panting, over Grant's prone body.

It was Mickey, on his way for a quick pint, who found them.

'What's happened, Jesse?' he shouted urgently. 'What's happened to Grant?'

Jesse turned his eyes to Mickey and looked at him as if he'd never seen him before.

'Jesse,' said Mickey, reaching out to touch his arm. 'It's me, Mick.'

'Mickey?' Jesse breathed. 'Grant's hurt.'

'Just stay there, Jesse. Don't do anything.' Mickey held his hands out in a pacifying gesture. He pulled his mobile from his pocket. He pressed the 9 button three times. When he'd finished, he put the phone back in his pocket and walked over to Grant, who was lying awkwardly on the cold concrete floor. His breathing didn't sound good. There was a clear greyish-looking liquid coming from his left ear. Mickey took his coat off and rolled it up. He put it under Grant's head.

'Jesse. I want you to take your coat off too and put it over Grant like a blanket. It's got Grant's blood on it anyway.'

Jesse, meek as a child, did as he was told.

'And now, Jesse, you're going to go to the public toilets and wash your face and hands.' Jesse looked at his hands and saw they were stained with blood. 'OK?'

Jesse nodded.

'Good. Be quick because the police and ambulance will be here very soon.'

An efficient constable assessed the situation and, taking his notebook from his top pocket, started to question Jesse and Mickey. 'Do either of you know the injured man?'

'Yes,' said Jesse. 'He's my brother.'

'And can you tell me what happened to him, sir?'

'I . . .' The horror and realisation of what he'd done stole across him. His breathing became shallow and ragged, 'He . . . I . . . we . . .'

Mickey took charge. 'This is Jesse Behenna. My name is Mickey Chandler and he,' he motioned towards Grant who was being loaded onto a stretcher and moaning, 'is Grant Behenna. Jesse's brother.'

Jesse looked helplessly into Mickey's eyes and said, 'It was me, I . . .'

Mickey once more took over. 'That's right, Jesse. You found him.' He turned to the policeman. 'Jesse must have heard something in the shelter. I was walking past, just on my way to the pub and saw him. I saw a man come running out of the shelter as Jesse got there. Must've been the bloke who did it. I called after him but he didn't stop, then I heard Jesse saying Grant's name and I came to see what I could do. I saw Jesse kneeling over Grant and putting his coat over him.'

Jesse grasped Mickey's arm and began to cry with fear and gratitude.

'He's barely recognisable, but we know Grant Behenna. In fact, his name has come up recently in an investigation we're conducting into a drug gang.' The policeman addressed Jesse. 'Is this what happened, sir?' asked the constable.

Jesse nodded; out of the corner of his eye he watched as Grant's battered body was loaded into the ambulance.

'Can I go with Grant to the hospital?' he asked.

'I don't think you're in a fit state, sir. In fact, I recommend you go home and rest. You're in shock. You need a nice cup of tea. We'll drive you home.'

'No,' said Mickey, 'I'll take him home.'

The policeman took down Jesse's address and phone number and also that of Mickey. 'I'll be round to see Mr Behenna tomorrow to complete the paperwork. Get some sleep. Grant Behenna has been in trouble quite a few times and mixes with an unsavoury lot. I'll go down to the hospital now and see if your brother can tell me anything about his assailant, if, I mean – ' he gave an embarrassed cough – '*when* he wakes up.'

29

October 2009

The soft blue of the lights around Grant's intensive care bed threw ghoulish shadows onto his parents' faces. They had come to the hospital as soon as they had heard, which was fourteen hours ago.

Jesse stood back from the scene. He stayed out of the glow around the bed and waited at the dark outer reaches of the room. Through the window he could see that the sun was rising.

The door opened with a slight suction of air and a young female doctor, slender with long dark hair, entered.

'Hello, Mr and Mrs Behenna.' She offered her hand. 'My name is Dr Shawna Dhaliwal. I'm part of the care team for your son.'

'How is he, Doctor?' asked Jan.

'As you know, he has broken ribs, a punctured lung, a broken jaw and a broken nose. But it's the scan we did on his brain that is worrying us.'

Jan closed her eyes and reached out for Edward's hand.

'What do you mean?' asked Edward, his voice cracking.

'We need to get inside and take a look. He hasn't fractured the skull but we believe he may have a substantial bleed and we need to get that fixed as soon as possible. It's imperative we release the pressure on his brain.'

Jan wiped her eyes with the tissue clutched in her shaking hands. 'An operation?'

'Yes,' said Dr Dhaliwal. 'And we need to do it sooner rather than later. Your son is very poorly. Theatre are getting prepared now.'

*

Six hours they waited. Jan trying to keep cheerful. Getting fresh cups of thin milky tea. Edward fretting about the car park ticket. Jesse unable to look either of them in the eye.

Eventually the ward sister came to see them. 'Grant is in recovery. The operation went as well as we could have hoped.'

Jan's hands grasped hers. 'Oh, thank God. He's OK?'

'Dr Dhaliwal is coming to talk to you as soon as she's changed.' The sister wore an unreadable expression. 'Although the operation has gone well, I can't tell you more than that. Would you like some tea?'

At last, Dr Dhaliwal came. 'We found the bleed and we've stopped it, which has released some pressure on Grant's brain. However, his brain is bruised and rather swollen. It has some lacerations which may have been caused when he fell during the attack, or maybe . . . when the attacker had already got him on the floor and had kicked him.'

Edward couldn't contain himself. 'The police had better find this coward before I do.'

Jesse felt sick. 'Dad, the police will do all they can.'

'They'm better 'ad do, or by God I swear I'll kill 'em myself.'

'Edward,' said Jan. 'Let's hear everything the doctor

has to tell us first.' She turned to Dr Dhaliwal. 'What happens next? When can he come home?'

Dr Dhaliwal frowned in a practised, professional and concerned way. 'I'm afraid I can't tell you that. It's a waiting game. We will monitor his progress. It may be a few days or,' she swallowed, 'or maybe weeks, maybe months, before he wakes up.'

Jesse looked at her sharply. 'Will he ever wake up?'

'It's possible that he won't.'

The sound of Jan's anguished wail filled the room.

*

'Live by the sword, die by the sword,' said Greer, handing Jesse a whisky. She settled herself into the depths of their elephant-grey velvet sofa.

Jesse rubbed his forehead. 'Don't say that.'

'I'm just saying he chose to live recklessly and that's what happens.'

'He might never recover.'

'Yes, and that's awful, of course, but it's not your responsibility.'

There was a knock at the front door. 'I'll get it,' said Greer, unfolding her slim legs from underneath her.

Moments later she arrived back in the room with the policeman Jesse remembered from the night before.

The constable stepped awkwardly into the room, his hat under one arm, his radio burbling indecipherable messages. Jesse stood up. 'Hello, I'm sorry, I don't think I got your name last night.'

The policeman held out his hand. 'Constable Steve Durrell. Steve.'

'Sit down, sit down. Would you like a drink?' asked Jesse.

'A soft drink, please.'

Greer disappeared to the kitchen. Steve watched her go.

'I'm afraid I have bad news.'

Jesse felt his stomach twist. 'What?'

'Your brother, Grant . . . He died an hour ago.'

Jesse could hear the rushing of his own blood in his ears. 'He can't have. I've been at the hospital all day. He had his operation. I saw him, on his bed, being wheeled back into his room.'

'I'm sorry.'

Greer came back in with a beautiful tray laid stylishly with a linen napkin, a small jug of orange juice, a glass and a ceramic dish containing olives. 'Here we are,' she said.

*

Grant's body was released after a post mortem. The police investigation had been unable to turn up any leads for the actual attack, but all their enquiries led them to the unsavoury characters and unfortunates with whom he had spent those lost years after he had left prison. Jan was tortured anew as details came out of his years of drug dealing and a drug habit that he had picked up in prison. It seemed that in the last months he had taken up dealing again and his life was starting to spiral out of control. The paraphernalia of a drug habit had been found in his rooms and the general consensus seemed to be that things were heading in only one direction for Grant.

Despite all this, Jesse made sure that the funeral befitted a Behenna. Grant hadn't many friends in Trevay, but the town turned out to honour Edward and Jan. Reverend Rowena gave a suitable tribute to Grant. She didn't go into his army career or his violent and often drunken personality. But she carefully described him as a son of Trevay. One who had had the joy of growing up in a tight community and loving family. 'The choices he made in this life were never the easy ones, but we trust in our heavenly father to take Grant's soul and heal it. We pray too that his murderer will one day be revealed and that the grace of God be with his parents, Edward and Jan, and his brother, Jesse. Let us pray.'

Jesse looked at the hunched figure of his mother, clinging on to her husband like a child as tortured sobs racked her body.

Jesse sat bolt upright in his pew and stared at the stained-glass window of Jesus calling the fishermen to be his disciples. He was glad that no one could hear the conversation in his head. 'Forgive me but I'm glad he's dead,' he said to the sunlit face of Christ. 'I'm glad. He hurt us all. And he's not going to hurt us again. I didn't mean him to die. But he did. Finally he did the right thing.'

The vicar ended her prayer and the congregation intoned 'Amen'.

Greer got up from the embroidered hassock she'd been kneeling on and squeezed Jesse's knee. 'All right?' she whispered.

He nodded.

The organist started to play 'The day Thou gavest, Lord, is ended'. Everyone stood and began to sing. Jesse, Mickey, Hal and Freddie went to the coffin with two of the funeral directors and lifted it onto their shoulders.

Outside the sun shone and a flock of seagulls cast their shadows as they flew over the churchyard cackling into the wind.

The freshly dug grave accepted Grant into its red earth, allowing him to rest on the slate beneath.

Jesse stepped back and bowed his head with a respect he did not feel. Greer slipped her arm through his elbow. 'It's over,' she said to him quietly.

He looked at her sharply. 'What did you say?'

'I said: It's over.'

He looked at her intently to see what, if anything, she knew. He examined the expression in her eyes, the turn of her mouth, the colour of her cheeks, but there was nothing.

'Yes.' He dropped a kiss on her dry lips. 'You're right. It's over.'

30

New Year's Eve 2012

Jesse was woken by the weight of four paws kneading the duvet around his chin.

'Bugger off, Tom.' He pushed the fat rescue cat – which Greer had brought home without asking him – off the bed. Tom sat on the floor twitching his tail and looking astonished, before jumping up again, and this time wiping his wet whiskers across Jesse's lips.

'I said bugger off.' Jesse took his arm from under the covers and caught Tom by the scruff of his neck, throwing him back onto the floor.

The bedroom door opened and Greer came in with a chink of mugs on the morning tea tray.

'Is Tom up here?'

'Yes,' Jesse grunted with his eyes closed and his face pressed into the pillow.

'Did he wake you up?'

'Yes.'

Geer put the tray down and Jesse heard tea being poured. 'Did you wake Daddy up? You naughty puss,' she said to Tom, who was mewing loudly and pushing himself around Greer's legs. 'And did he throw you off the bed?'

'He jumped off of his own accord,' mumbled Jesse.

'I think Daddy's lying,' said Greer, walking round to Jesse's side of the bed and putting his mug of tea on the coaster on the mahogany bedside table. She bent down and kissed his bristly cheek. 'Happy Anniversary, darling.'

He opened his eyes and squinted at her. 'Happy Anniversary.' He sat and yawned, rubbing a hand across his face. 'Twenty years. That's some bleddy time, in't it?' Jesse found it hard to believe that it was twenty years ago that he had walked down the aisle with Greer. Twenty years since he and Loveday . . .

'Yes, it is,' said Greer, getting into her side of the bed and pulling the covers up. She took a sip of tea thoughtfully and said, 'I think we're just about all ready for the party.'

Jesse groaned. 'I 'ate bleddy parties.' He already felt that his house was barely his own. It looked like something from a magazine rather than a real home where a man could be himself. He'd rather be down at the boathouse on the beach at Tide Cove. It was his domain. It housed lobster pots, fishing gear, all the small things that Freddie had made at school, which Greer did not want cluttering her pristine house, but which made Jesse's heart swell with pride and love for his son.

Greer couldn't hide her irritation. 'Well, you only have to come and enjoy it. Everything else has been done for you.'

Tom jumped back onto the bed and nudged Greer's hand. 'Tom, you nearly spilt my tea. Be careful.' She reached out a hand and stroked Tom's ears. He began purring loudly.

'That bleddy animal oughtn't be allowed on the bed. 'Tis unhygienic,' moaned Jesse.

'He's spotless. Besides, he's been out all night in the

cold and needs to warm up.' Tom dribbled with ecstasy and, opening one yellow eye, gave Jesse a look of pure disdain. 'He just wants a little affection.' Greer held Tom to her and nuzzled him against her cheek. 'Don't you, Mr Tom?'

'Mr Jesse could do with a little affection too,' Jesse said, turning to Greer and giving her what he assumed was an alluring look. He put his hand on her thigh and slowly ran it upwards.

Greer was not in the mood. 'Mind Tom. You'll squash him.'

'I don't care.' Jesse began his well-worn foreplay routine and started to nibble Greer's ear. Tom, totally affronted, jumped off the bed and left the room, tail high.

'I've got a mug of hot tea in my hands,' said Greer pathetically, pulling away from her husband.

Jesse stopped the nibbling and took the tea from her. He put it on his side table and turned back to her. 'There. No tea. No Tom. Just you and me.' He restarted his nuzzling.

Greer attempted another diversion. 'The florist is coming at ten. I haven't got time for this.'

'Don't 'ee worry about that. I'll be coming before him.'

'Her. And don't be crude. It puts me off,' she scowled.

'Come on, Greer. It's been a while.' He was on top of her now, whether she liked it or not. 'And it is our anniversary.'

Greer went through the motions. Sex had never really been her thing. Her sex drive had always been at odds with Jesse's. But she'd been dutiful. Nowadays she'd do anything to avoid it. It wasn't that she didn't love Jesse. She did. Very much. But all this physical stuff was, frankly, a bit of a bore. A chore. She'd asked Loveday once when they'd had a couple of glasses of wine on one of their infrequent girls' nights out: 'Do you and Mickey still, you know, fancy each other?'

Loveday had answered with passion. 'Course! It's the glue that keeps a marriage together.'

'Oh. Yes. Absolutely.' Greer had felt a deep sense of inadequacy and a feeling that she really must try harder.

*

'That was lovely, wasn't it?' asked a satisfied Jesse, as he hoicked himself back onto his side of the bed.

'Uha,' Greer replied.

'What's the matter with you? Come, on, give me a cuddle.' He put an arm around her and she was obliged to settle into his shoulder. She waited until his breathing became shallow and even, and then made her escape.

Without disturbing his slumber, she tiptoed to her new pride and joy. The en-suite wet room. This was what turned her on. Her interior design work. Her natural sense of style and feel for colour. The wet room was an oasis of Zen beauty. From the fat alabaster Buddha sitting beneath the waterfall shower, to the underheated Delabole slate on the floor. There was a mirror covering one entire wall and she glanced at herself. The light from the adjacent window, with plantation blinds providing moody shadows, played across her skin. She took off her silk Elle Macpherson chemise and carefully hung it on the padded hanger on the hook on the back of the door.

She looked intently at her still slender body from all angles. The pain she felt at Louisa's death still had the power to take her breath away. It would creep up on her suddenly when she wasn't expecting it. But, looking at her slim outline, she thanked God that she hadn't ended up looking like Loveday. Loveday was fatter than ever and the size of her humungous breasts was just embarrassing. Greer had once asked her if she hadn't thought of a breast reduction. Loveday, hurt and embarrassed, had said something about leaving alone things that God had intended.

Now, Greer switched on the daylight lamp surrounding the circular and magnified mirror above the basin. She checked her wrinkles and the tautness of her neck. She was satisfied. Finally she reached for the tweezers and plucked a couple of stray hairs from her brows and, horror of horrors, a wiry one from her chin.

Job done, she stepped back and took a last pleasing look at herself. Yes, the self-denial over Christmas had paid off. Her Donna Karan evening dress, all four thousand pounds of it, would fit like a glove.

*

The house was busy all day long. The florist, the cleaners and the caterers were finally all done by four o'clock.

At five o'clock, Loveday drove over with the twins, Becca and Bea, who had made the celebration cake as their gift.

'Oh my goodness,' exclaimed Greer, who had to admit that the confection looked rather good. 'When did you girls get so clever?'

'It is good, isn't it!' said Loveday proudly. 'They'm loving their baking. I blame that Mary Berry and Mr Blue Eyes.'

'Paul Hollywood,' sighed the girls in unison. 'We done what you asked for, Auntie Greer. Top tier white chocolate. Bottom tier dark with brandy-soaked cherries.'

'And,' said Loveday, grinning from ear to ear, 'we found you something special to go on the top. Show her, girls.'

From out of one of the many shopping bags they'd brought with them, Becca pulled a smallish cardboard box. She thrust it towards Greer. 'Open it!'

Loveday and her girls stood in harnessed excitement as Greer removed the rubber band then opened the lid, pulling away at some scruffy pink tissue paper. Resting inside were two hideous china figures.

''Tis a bride and a groom,' squealed Bea.

'It's you and Uncle Jesse!' panted Becca. 'We got them in the charity shop over St Mawgan.'

'It's shabby chic. Just your thing!' breathed Bea.

'We washed them in a drop of Milton, so they'm clean,' Loveday told Greer, thrilled with herself and her girls.

Greer didn't know what to say. 'It's . . . the last thing I expected,' she managed to blurt out, and kissed the girls, wondering how she could possibly avoid spoiling the beautiful cake by putting this worst bit of kitsch on the top.

'Right,' said Loveday, gathering up the various bits of baggage that she'd sprawled all over Greer's immaculate kitchen table. 'We'm off home to get ready. Kick-off is at eight o'clock, right?'

'Right,' confirmed Greer. 'Drinks at eight, dinner at nine.'

*

Greer was dressed and looking perfect by seven thirty. She went downstairs to admire her beautiful home. Tide House always scrubbed up well. The candles, the Christmas tree, the flowers. It all looked ravishing. In the library and the drawing room the fires were lit, giving out a subtle and pervasive scent of pine. In the dining room the table, set for twenty friends and immediate family, shimmered with crystal and silver.

One of the four waiting staff stepped into the dining room as Greer was straightening an errant napkin. 'Good evening, Mrs Behenna. You look very nice this evening. Can I get you a drink?'

Greer gave the young man a quick once-over, satisfied to see he was wearing the black linen shirt and trousers with long white apron that she had specified for all the waiting staff. 'Thank you. You look very smart too . . . and yes, please, I'd like a cranberry juice.'

'Of course, Mrs Behenna. Would you like a vodka in that?' He gave her a cheeky glint.

'No, thank you.' She smiled. What a charming young man. 'Too early for me.'

'Not too early for me, though.' Jesse stood in the doorway dressed in black tie. 'Get me a large Scotch, would you, before the hordes arrive?'

'Certainly, Mr Behenna,' said the young man, gliding out of the room.

'He'm bloody gay, ain't 'im?' remarked Jesse.

'You sound just like your father.' Greer tutted. 'Please keep your sexist, racist opinions to yourself.'

Jesse walked into the hall and stood before the large gilt mirror that greeted all guests. He was fiddling with his bow tie. 'Have I tied this thing right? Why you won't let me have one on elastic, I don't know. And this shirt collar is choking me, it's so tight.'

Greer went to him and smoothed his tie and eased his collar. She looked at both their reflections. 'We look OK after twenty years, don't we?'

Freddie came down the stairs in an open-necked white

shirt and tight blue jeans. 'I'd say you look pretty good for a pair of wrinklies.' He kissed Greer and hugged his father.

'How come he got away with jeans and I'm dressed up like next year's turkey?'

'Because he's young and he can get away with anything,' replied Greer, gazing fondly at her son. 'Freddie, would you get my camera for me? It's in the drawing room on the ottoman. I think we need a family photo.'

*

Dinner was delicious. Seared scallops in lemon chilli butter, rib of beef with all the trimmings and a light syllabub with fruit salad and a cheese board to follow.

Greer excused herself from her father-in-law on her right and Mickey on her left and went to the kitchen to congratulate the staff, who were busy stacking the dish-washer.

'Well done, everyone. Superb work.'

'When do you want the cake served?' asked the young chef, Danny.

'Oh, I think mulled wine and cake in the conservatory after the fireworks, don't you?'

'Right-oh, Mrs B.'

'Thank God it's not raining!'

*

At five minutes to midnight, everyone had their coats found for them and they were ushered out, through the conservatory, into the front garden overlooking Tide Cove.

Freddie and Hal found Radio Four on the house sound system and wound up the volume so that everyone in the garden could hear the countdown to Big Ben.

'. . . Three, two, one . . . BONG! Happy New Year!'

Mickey gave his wife a kiss and a cuddle. She still looked beautiful to him and Loveday hugged him back tightly.

'They've put on a good show tonight, don't you think?' He nodded towards Greer and Jesse.

'They always do, don't they? Greer knows how to throw a good party,' Loveday agreed.

'Even Jesse looks like he's enjoying himself.'

Loveday knitted her brow thoughtfully. 'Mmmm.' She hadn't said anything, but she thought Jesse had been drinking a bit more than usual of late. He often worked long hours, but more often than not these days he seemed to have a bottle of whisky to keep him company as he pored over the figures.

'It'll be our anniversary soon,' Mickey said. 'Shall we throw a party?'

Loveday hugged him tighter. 'Let's just do something with the kids, shall we?'

'Whatever you want, darling.'

As the kissing and the singing of 'Auld Lang Syne' gathered strength, a fusillade of rockets went up from the Cove. They were followed by Roman candles, flying lanterns, barrages and brilliant showers of diamond sparks.

*

Greer, tottering slightly after two glasses of very good Pinotage on very high L.K. Bennett heels, slipped her arm through Jesse's. He smelled of whisky and fresh air and she surprised herself by finding him very attractive. More attractive than she had this morning, anyway.

'Do you want to know what your anniversary present is?' she asked him, resting her cheek on his lapel.

'Go on then,' he said. 'I thought you'd forgotten.'

'Well, you've forgotten mine,' she said in a mock huff.

'Ah well. That's where you're wrong. You had so much on today that I thought I'd surprise you tomorrow.'

'Really?' She looked up at him with the excitement of a little girl. 'What have you got me?' she wheedled.

'Not telling.'

'Give me a clue?'

'No. But I'm getting it in the morning.' He kissed the top of her head. 'So, what you got for me?'

'We are going to get on the Whatsit Express and go to . . . Venice!'

'Bloody 'ell, maid. That's some bleddy 'oliday.'

'Yes it is. Romance. Art. Museums. Architecture.'

'Have they got any booze?'

'Plenty.'

'Well, that's all right then.'

'When are we going?'

'The weekend after next.'

Jesse frowned. 'You'll 'ave to put it off until after the end of the financial year. We've got too much on, and I'll have to pull all the stops out if we're to make the numbers.'

'Oh, rubbish,' Greer said. 'You can manage a few days off, surely?'

'I can't. You'll just have to give them a call and re-arrange the dates.'

The drink had made Greer argumentative. 'I will not.

I'm always making sacrifices for you and that company. For once, can't you put me first?'

Jesse felt a dangerous darkness descend. 'Put you first? I've always put you first, Greer. You, your family, the bloody business – and I've never complained.'

'You have no right to complain.' Greer was fired up now. 'My daddy gave you everything you've ever had. If it wasn't for him, you'd be just like any other fisherman down at the harbour: small time. Clovelly Fisheries have given you everything.'

As soon as the words left her mouth, Greer regretted saying them. The look on Jesse's face was like nothing she had seen before.

He regarded her coldly. 'Small time, was I, Greer? Not so small that you didn't follow me around like a dog, grateful for any scraps that I threw in your direction.'

Greer drew a gasp at the words and put her hand to her mouth, but Jesse couldn't stop himself. 'Where would you be if it weren't for me, Greer? Who would have married a stuck-up self-important frigid cow like you – you weren't my first choice, you know that, don't you?'

Greer rallied. 'Oh, that's right, Jesse Behenna, babe magnet. You'd screw any old scrubber down at the sheds. You're lucky to have someone like me. You couldn't even boil an egg without a mother or a wife to do it for you!'

Jesse was just about to let rip in response when Mickey and Loveday came up to say goodbye and thank them for a nice evening. Both Greer and Jesse clammed up immediately and Loveday and Mickey couldn't help but sense the tense atmosphere.

'We're just off now, but wanted to say thanks for a lovely evening.' Loveday gave her friend a huge hug and Greer responded with a tight smile.

'Yeah, thanks, mate – here's to the next twenty years!' laughed Mickey, and drunkenly clapped Jesse on the back.

Jesse shook Mickey's hand as Greer went off to find another drink.

'Bye, Jesse,' said Loveday, and gave him a peck on the cheek.

'Twenty years,' said Jesse, and held onto her for just a moment too long before they departed.

31

A week later

'**O**h, Greer, it's lovely.'
      Loveday was sitting in the passenger seat of
the new 4x4 that Jesse had given Greer as her anniversary
present. 'I could've done with one of these when the kids
were small.'

Greer was reversing down the steep hill where Loveday
and Mickey lived. 'Have I got enough room your side?'

Loveday checked the wing mirror. 'You're fine.'

Greer got to the bottom of the hill without a scrape
and put the car into drive. 'Here we go.'

The big car was cumbersome and Greer didn't really
like it, but Jesse had meant well when he bought it for
her.

The morning after the row, nothing had been said.
Jesse was up early and Greer heard him call from the
bathroom, 'Where are the paracetamol?'

Smiling to herself she called back, 'On the third shelf
of the cabinet.' She paused, then added, 'Would you
bring me some, please?'

Greer wasn't much of a drinker, she didn't like losing
control, and she and Jesse's argument had left her feeling
very churned up and emotionally exhausted, but all of
that seemed to be forgotten when Jesse presented her

with the 4x4. She'd thanked him and spoken to the travel company, and now she and Jesse would be going to Venice in April. They'd never had such a bad row before, and Greer thought the break would do them both good; they'd had a lot on their plates and tensions were bound to be high.

She had nodded and smiled appreciatively as he had shown off the walnut dashboard and in-car entertainment system. 'Even has a reversing camera, so you can't have any excuses for kerbing the wheels.' She laughed dutifully and spared a thought for Loveday; Mickey would probably take Loveday and the kids to Wetherspoon's for their anniversary. Mind you, Loveday would probably love it, Greer smiled to herself.

Jesse was still talking. 'I thought it would be useful when you're carting all that stuff about to your houses.'

'Carting my stuff?'

'All those fancy cushions and books of wallpaper that your rich people like to look at. And your scrapbooks.'

'Mood albums,' she corrected.

'Whatever. Anyhow, I thought a nice big car would be useful . . . and when you're not using it I can borrow it for fishing or—'

'So you bought it for yourself?' The old resentment started to flourish.

'You didn't buy a trip to Venice solely for me, did you?'

He had her there, and so she kissed him and neutralised the negative turn the conversation had taken and thanked him for such a perfect present.

Today, she and Loveday were making use of the car for a trip to the sales in Bristol.

'I feel so high up,' Loveday said, settling into her leather seat. 'We'll be in Bristol in no time.'

'I'm glad of your company.'

'I like a bargain. The girls have given me a list of stuff they want me to get. As if they didn't have enough already at Christmas!'

'I'm hoping to pick up a lovely little Turkish Kelim for a client and also get some curtain fabric for the Liskeard people.'

'Ain't that job finished yet?'

'I got most of it done in time for Christmas, but now they've decided they want the tall window on the stairs to have curtains. They don't need them. The light it throws onto the panelled walls is a clever piece of design by the architect back in the 1680s, but they think the sun is too bright and, if they want to have curtains, they shall have curtains. At least I talked them out of Venetian blinds.'

'You'm clever, Greer.'

'Well, I can't do what you do.'

'It's only tallying the books,' said Loveday self-deprecatingly.

'Oh, yes, that's easy enough, what I mean is, I couldn't sit in that soulless building that Jesse loves so much, with all those dull people, doing the same thing day in day out.'

Loveday frowned. 'They'm not dull people. They're my friends. And if it wasn't for them you wouldn't have a car like this.'

'I didn't mean it like that,' Greer said. 'I think it's wonderful that some people enjoy mundanity. Whereas I have to be creative.' She glanced at her friend and smiled. 'How are your upholstery classes going?'

Loveday had turned her face to look out of the window so that Greer couldn't see her annoyance. 'OK.'

Greer sensed that she had gone too far. 'Good.'

She drove on for a few minutes, neither speaking. Then, to ease the tension she said, 'Shall I put the radio on?'

*

'What a day.' Greer was in her kitchen and shrugging out of her coat. 'Loveday insisted we went into Ikea. God, what a dreadful place. Nothing in there will stand the test of time. Put the kettle on, would you?'

Jesse did as he was asked. 'How did the car go?'

'Lovely. The boot is full. I bought much too much but some of the fabric was at such a good price, and classic patterns, that I thought it was an investment, really.'

'Where would you like your tea?'

'Shall we sit in the library?'

'You can, I've got to go back to the office. Got some stuff to finish off for the accountants.'

'Will you be home for dinner?'

'Probably not.'

*

The building was warm and silent. He made himself a mug of coffee in the tiny office kitchen and went to his office. Lauren, as always, had prepared his desk for the next day. His bin was empty and his laptop was charging.

He logged on and opened the files he wanted. He read the first page and then the next. He found it brutally boring. He tried again. But again he could not concentrate.

He gave up and spun his chair so that he could look at the view through the glass. Trevay lay peacefully beneath him. His mind wandered as he looked at the familiar streets and buildings. There was his old school, with its memories of Greer, Mickey and Loveday. The church where he'd got married and where Louisa lay next to his grandfather.

The sheds where he and Loveday had made love.

The harbour where his boats were bobbing, tied up against the wall.

The shelter where Grant had died.

No, he mustn't think about Grant. He looked again over the rooftops of Trevay. Now he could see Grant smoking at the school gate.

Grant hiding in the yard outside the sheds watching him and Loveday.

Grant lying in the churchyard.

Grant sitting in this office.

Jesse hated these thoughts. He'd had them on and off since Grant had died. If he was strong enough, he could make them go away. And they would go away, but tonight they were real and sharp. *Why didn't bloody Grant leave him in peace?*

Jesse went to the office kitchen and filled the kettle to make another cup of coffee.

He heard what sounded like the lift, whirring its way up to his floor.

Was that the lift he heard?

He stepped out of the kitchen and listened.

Yes. The lift, definitely.

Who would come into the office at this time?

Had he locked the front door?

He couldn't remember.

He stepped back into the kitchen, turned the light off and stood very still.

The lift stopped.

The doors opened.

He heard the rustle of clothing as someone got out and started walking towards his office.

He could hear his breathing.

He could hear their breathing.

When he judged that they were almost adjacent to the kitchen doorway, he leapt out, shouting a huge roar.

The woman screamed, dropped her bag and ran back to the lift.

'Loveday,' said Jesse, running after her. 'Loveday. 'Tis only me.'

She stopped running and he could see the fear on her face. 'Jesse.' She was breathless. 'What the bleddy 'ell you do that for?'

'I thought you was a burglar.'

'Well, I'm not.' She started to giggle. 'You'm bleddy frightening when you shout like that.'

'I meant to be. Anyhow, serves you right for sneaking up on me.'

'I was not sneaking. I came in to make sure I had all the documents you'll need for the accountant tomorrow and found the front door unlocked. I thought it would be you. I saw your office lights on, so I came up to say hello. Got the bleddy fright of my life instead!'

'Sorry. Want a coffee?'

'I need a bleddy brandy.'

'I've got some whisky?'

'No, you're all right. Give us a coffee, I'll get the papers you need and I'll be off home.'

*

Loveday took her coffee down to her ground-floor office and soon became absorbed in answering emails and checking her diary for the week ahead. The phone on her desk rang, startling her. She looked at her watch and saw that an hour and a half had gone by. It must be Mickey.

'Hi, Mick. Sorry I've been so long. I'm on my way now. Shall I pick up some fish and chips or have you and the kids eaten?'

Jesse's voice replied, 'No, I haven't eaten yet, but I'd love fish and chips with you.'

Loveday laughed. 'Oh, sorry, Jesse. I'm just emailing the stuff up to you now.

'What would I do without you? Did you put the spreadsheets in?'

'Of course.'

'Thank you. The accountants always love a spreadsheet.'

Loveday had the receiver between her shoulder and her chin as she tried to put one arm into the sleeve of her coat. 'Well, I'll be off, if there's nothing else you need.'

'No, that's fine,' said Jesse. 'See you tomorrow.'

'Yeah, see you tomorrow.'

'Oh . . . er, Loveday?'

'Yeah?'

'Fancy that glass of whisky before we shut up shop for the night?'

'Erm . . .' Loveday looked at her watch again. 'As long as I'm home in the next hour.'

'Just ten minutes. Come up to my office.'

*

'What a view you have from up here. Never seen it at night before. You must be almost as high as St Peter's steeple.'

'Not quite.' He handed her a tumbler of Scotch. Loveday noticed that inroads had definitely been made into the bottle, and she thought that Jesse looked a little flushed. 'Sorry, no ice. Cheers.' They clinked glasses.

'Cheers,' said Loveday.

Jesse continued. 'The planners were very strict with us. They made it clear they didn't want us to "impede the view". Which is why we made it pretty much entirely of glass.'

He sat down behind his desk and Loveday sat opposite him. Two old friends comfortable in each other's company.

'I like your Greer's new car.'

'I don't think she does.'

'Yes, she does. She was loving filling it with all her knick-knacks.'

'By knick-knacks do you mean the very latest on the front line of the style war that is raging across the land, in houses that are too big and too expensive, lived in by people who have more money than sense?'

Loveday giggled. It had been a long time since she had had her sushi lunch with Greer and the whisky was leaking warmly into her veins. 'That's very unkind of you.'

'But true.' Jesse motioned at the bottle of Scotch. 'Just a little one for the road?'

'Just a little one.' She watched as Jesse poured. 'But your house is beautiful, ain't it? Greer has done a wonderful job. It's so welcoming and comfortable. I'm not house-proud like that,' said Loveday, taking her shoes off and rubbing one foot against the other. 'With my three and Mickey it'd be like King Canute trying to keep the tide from flooding in.'

Jesse leant forward on the desk. 'How is Mickey?'

'He's great. Loving his job. Loving working with Hal and teaching him the ropes like his dad taught him. I tell you, we Chandlers have got a lot to thank you Behennas for.'

Jesse leant back again and relaxed into his chair. 'Our dads were all mates, weren't they. It's keeping up tradition. Mickey is my best mate. Hal is Freddie's best mate. And so it will go on, as long as Trevay has a fishing industry.'

Loveday nodded her agreement. 'And don't forget the Clovellys. Without Greer's side, neither of us would be sitting in this office drinking whisky.'

Jesse turned his chair to look at Trevay again. 'You're right. Mick and I would be working our arses off up at the sheds.' He sat thinking for a few moments. Loveday shut her eyes, giving in to the whisky, but not to her memory of her and Jesse in the sheds.

Jesse broke the silence. 'I miss those days. Just me and Mickey. You and Greer. No kids. No responsibilities.' She heard the faintest squeak as he spun his chair back to her. Her eyelids were heavy and she didn't have the energy to open them.

'I wish I'd have married you.' He said the words boldly into the still air between them.

She sat still, eyes still shut.

'Did you hear me?'

'Yes.'

'We'd have been happy.'

'Stop it.'

'I know we'd have been happy. That night. In the sheds. When it was snowing. You made me so very happy.'

She opened her eyes and looked at her hand holding the whisky glass. 'Don't talk about it. I don't even think about it.'

'Don't you?' He leant forward again across the desk.
'No.'

'I don't believe you. I was your first and you and I were happy that night.'

'We were pissed. And I think you may be a bit pissed now.' Loveday stood up and put her glass down. 'I'm off home. To Mickey.'

Jesse stood up and walked round the desk, blocking her path. 'I've never stopped loving you, Loveday.'

'You love Greer.' She sidestepped him but he was too quick for her.

'Kiss me,' he begged.

She leant forward and kissed his cheek. 'Night night, Jesse. See you tomorrow.'

She collected up her coat and bag and walked out of the office without a backward glance.

32

Early spring 2014

Lifeboat training was always on a Wednesday night and, on this particular evening, the boat-house was crowded.

The star of the show was, as always, the boat herself. Sitting in the centre of the spotless boat-house, her paintwork gleaming, *The Spirit of Trevay* sat on the runners that sent her through the doors, down the slipway and into the waiting sea. All around her were railings to keep her fans close, but not close enough. Small boys, starstruck mums and men who could only dream of being one of the élite hung over these railings in wonder.

Jesse, in his capacity as coxswain, was speaking from the deck of the boat.

'And so, ladies and gentlemen, it is with great pleasure we welcome our three new crew members to *The Spirit of Trevay*. Would you put your hands together for Miss Katie Farrow! Come up here, Katie.' A pretty blonde girl in her twenties stepped up and faced the crowd, smiling.

'Give us a smile, Katie.' In the middle of the crowd, Katie's mum took a photo of her daughter.

'Muuum,' said Katie, blushing, before trying to melt back into the throng. Jesse stopped her.

'Oh, no you don't. You stay right here, young lady. I

want all three of my new crew to have a picture with the lot of us.' Katie obeyed.

Jesse spoke up again. 'And 'tis with enormous pride I welcome another youngster. His dad, Mickey, has been the *Spirit*'s mechanic for as long as I've been coxswain, and his dad before him the same, so put your hands together for the third generation of Chandlers to serve on the lifeboat: Hal Chandler.' Hal loped up to Jesse. With his height and gangly limbs he towered over everyone. From the back of the room, Loveday gave a whoop and a whistle through her teeth, whilst clinging onto Mickey's arm. Becca and Bea leapt up and down with excitement and chanted Hal's name, falling into giggles when Loveday shushed them.

'And finally,' said Jesse, 'and I don't know 'ow he got on the crew, but I'd like to welcome my own son, Freddie Behenna.'

Freddie bowed his head as he made his way to the front and accepted his father's handshake. Greer, in perfectly tailored navy-blue trousers and an RNLI sweatshirt, smiled tightly but clapped loudly. She had argued with both Jesse and Freddie about joining the crew. Greer desperately wanted Freddie to get good exam results so that he had other options rather than only a life on the boats to look forward to, but because Hal wanted that life, it seemed it was what Freddie wanted too. Greer wondered if perhaps she'd taken her eye off the ball a bit with Freddie. Maybe he'd been spending too much time at the Chandlers' house, as their ways seemed to be rubbing off on him more and more these days. She felt another flutter of fear in her stomach – working on the trawler fleet was dangerous enough. Why did he have to risk his life on the lifeboat too?

'You don't stop me from going out and risking my life,' said Jesse.

'You're different. You know what you're getting your-self into. Freddie is our only child. Why put him in danger?'

But Freddie wanted to do it – and what Freddie wanted, Freddie usually got.

Loveday pushed her way towards Greer. 'Well, that's it. Our precious boys are lifeboatmen.'

'They're only twenty,' said Greer, feeling her throat tighten. 'Boys still, really.'

'But ain't you proud of them?'

Greer pushed her hair behind one ear and tried to be pleased. 'Oh, of course, I'm always proud of them, but . . . they are so young.'

'They'll be fine. They've got Mick and Jesse and the other lads.' Loveday could see that Greer was very upset about the whole thing so she said, 'What you need, Mrs Behenna, is a gin and tonic.'

Greer managed a laugh. 'I probably do, but I'm on coffee duty tonight and then there's the raffle to draw.' As in all lifeboat stations, the opportunities to raise funds were never overlooked. This evening was special because it was an open evening. Lifeboat groupies and RNLI supporters were encouraged to come into the boat-house to look around, ask questions of the crew and, if they had the lucky raffle ticket, even get the chance of going out on the boat that evening.

'Well, I'll sell the tickets, you pour the coffee, and we'll get this show on the road,' said Loveday.

*

A man of maybe sixty was talking very earnestly to Jesse about the merits of the Tamar class of boat as opposed to the Severn class. 'I see that *The Spirit of Trevay* is a Tamar class, but is it as manoeuvrable as the Severn? Although it's a metre longer, it may at first sight appear to be less nimble—' Jesse interrupted the techie flow. 'I'm so sorry, but my wife is wanting me.' He'd never been so grateful to see Greer waving at him.

He shouldered his way over to the other side of the room, to where Greer was anxiously waiting. 'Thanks, darling,' he said when he reached her. 'That bloke's a bleddy fanatic.'

'It's time to make the draw,' Greer told him. 'Loveday's been folding the tickets and putting them in the bucket for the last hour.'

'I hope he doesn't win the trip tonight,' said Jesse, rubbing a hand over his tired face. 'We'm got enough to do without him blethering.'

'Oh, him?' said Greer, spotting the man making his way towards another cup of free coffee. 'He's bought more tickets than anyone else.'

'Shit.'

Mickey reached them. 'Loveday's got the tickets ready for the draw. Who do you want to do it?'

'Get the new kids to do it,' said Jesse. 'Wherever they are.' He scanned the crowd and saw both Hal and Freddie leaning against the crew-room door chatting up Katie. All three of them were dressed in their yellow oilskins and loving it. As Jesse watched, a small boy approached Katie and asked her something. She laughed but took the pen and piece of paper he was holding and signed her name for him. The boy's mother, giggling and emboldened, then asked the lads if she could have a selfie with them.

'Becca, Bea,' called Jesse to the twins, who were just

passing, 'go and get them boys and Katie, would you? I need them for the raffle.'

*

There was a healthy assortment of raffle prizes on the table, including a box of chocolates, an RNLI T-shirt, supper for two at Antonio's Italian pizzeria, a bottle of whisky and the star prize of a trip on the boat.

The final ticket was drawn by Katie, who rummaged extravagantly in the bucket before pulling out, 'Green ticket number four-three-seven.'

A woman's voice yelled loud and clear, 'Here! Yes.'

There were many groans of disappointment from everyone else. Not least the man who'd been interrogating Jesse about the boat's specifications and performance. He screwed his tickets up and put them in his pocket, then moved to position himself in a prime spot to watch the launch.

The crew were on board in their allotted places. The boat-house doors were open, revealing the slipway and the smoky sea below. Jesse was on the open bridge.

On Jesse's command, the pin holding the boat on the slipway was pulled, and she moved swiftly down the rails, nose-first into the water. Jesse pushed the throttle forward and the twin engines drove the boat away from the boat-house and the waving, cheering fans.

'Oooh,' said the woman who'd won the raffle, 'I feel like Princess Diana on the water ride at Alton Towers!'

*

'Cheers, lads.' Jesse handed out the pints of Skinner's to Mickey, Hal and Freddie. 'You done a good job tonight.

I don't want you missing any training nights, because we don't know when the real shout will come. I want you ready. It may be tonight. It may be tomorrow or next week. But I want to know that you lads are ready.' He took a satisfying mouthful of beer and wiped his lips. 'By the way, I don't want you thinking that just 'cos Katie's a girl she's a walkover. She's had as much experience at sea as you boys. She's sailed the Atlantic single-handed – you've got to be pretty bleddy tough to do that.'

'She's nice,' said Freddie.

'A bit posh,' said Hal.

'You're punching above your weight with her, boys, so don't even think about it,' laughed Mickey. 'She'd have you for breakfast.'

'How old is she?' asked Freddie.

'Too old for you, son,' said Jesse. 'Besides, you lads need to spread your wild oats.'

'Ha, says you who got married at twenty-one,' joked Freddie.

'Oh, your uncle Mickey and I had our moments, didn't we, Mick?' said Jesse.

'One or two,' nodded Mickey. 'But I knew Loveday was always the one for me.'

'Oh, Dad.' Hal looked embarrassed. 'I don't want to hear.'

Freddie looked at Jesse. 'And was Mum always the only one for you? From school?'

Jesse stuck his chin out and scratched the stubble there. 'You could say that.'

'Granddad Behenna always says he knew he had to get you two together to ensure the future of the company. He said it was like two royal families arranging the marriage of a princess and a prince.'

'Don't pay too much attention to what your granddad says.'

'And he says that Granddad Clovelly was the man who made it all happen.'

Jesse frowned and picked up a beer mat, flipping it over and catching it. Mickey steered the conversation round. 'I was his best man on the day he married your mum, Freddie. And let me tell you, he was as hungover as a highwayman. I could barely get him dressed.' A memory slid into his mind. 'It was Grant who got you drunk, wasn't it?'

Jesse shook his head. 'No. It was me. I went up to the sheds, because I didn't want to go home. I needed to think. 'Tis a big thing getting married. I found my dad's whisky in his desk up at the sheds and . . .' He stopped talking. In the silence the others waited for him to continue. Then he picked up his beer glass and downed the remains. '. . . And I drank it,' he finished abruptly.

'But I thought Grant said he was with you?' Mickey persisted.

Jesse thought for a moment and said, 'Maybe he was. I was so pissed I can't remember.' He stood up. 'Now then, who'd like another?'

*

By the time the pool table came free, the four men were more than merry.

'Right, you lads,' said Jesse, squinting to focus on getting the coins in the slot. 'You whippersnappers against we old Turks. Yes?'

'Fine by us,' said Freddie, passing a cue to Hal and chalking his own. 'What we playing for?'

'Hmm. Let me think,' said Jesse. 'What do you think, Mick?'

'Twenty quid?' ventured Mickey, balancing his cue between his legs as he attempted to tuck his shirt into his jeans.

'Twenty?' shrugged Freddie. 'That's nothing. It's got to be something really worth playing for.'

'Right. If that's what you want,' slurred Jesse, waggling his forefinger. 'How about this. You're both twenty-one later this year, yes?'

'Yes.'

'Well, 'ow about, if you win, I'll buy you a car each for your birthday. But if we win, I don't.'

'Bleddy hell,' blurted Hal.

'We'll hold you to that,' said Freddie. 'Shake on it?'

They shook.

Mickey took Jesse to one side while the boys set the balls up on the table. 'You are joking, aren't you?'

'No. But,' Jesse tapped the side of his nose, 'they'm useless at pool and you and I were bleddy good.'

'That's a long time ago.'

'It's like riding a bike. You and I will pull out the old tricks and they won't know what's hit 'em.'

It didn't take more than seventeen minutes. Hal lined up the black eight ball and hit it cleanly into the pocket.

Jesse chucked his cue onto the baize but he was impressed. 'How the hell did you learn to play like that? You're almost as good as I was at your age. Well. A bet's a bet. You won fair and square.' Jesse walked around the table and clapped Hal on the back.

'Nice one, Dad!' The boys were jubilant. 'Can we choose our own cars?'

'Never on your life.'

Mickey looked worried. 'Boys, don't hold him to it. This was a bit of fun.'

'No it weren't,' stated Jesse firmly. 'My word is my bond, and if I can't treat my son and godson, what kind of a man am I?'

'Just think it over in the morning,' said Mickey. 'I don't want you getting the boys' hopes up.'

Jesse rounded on Mickey. 'I am buying my boys cars for their birthday and that's that.'

'Take it easy, Jesse,' said Mickey, frowning. 'You're perfectly entitled to do what you like for your boy – but me and Loveday will decide what's right for our boy.'

Jesse regarded Mickey. 'My mind's made up, and nothing is going to stop me.'

33

Loveday pushed the door of the office shut with her foot as she dialled Greer's mobile phone number. She'd tried her at Tide House but the answerphone had kicked in and she hadn't dared to leave a message in case Jesse picked it up.

Mickey had come home late last night, annoyed at Jesse's high-handed idea to give Hal and Freddie a car each for their twenty-first birthdays.

'It was the way 'e said it. "I'm buying cars for my boys' birthdays and you're not stopping me". As if we can't afford a car for our own son.'

Loveday had been in bed reading when Mickey had come upstairs and broken this news. She didn't like the sound of it. My boys? What the hell did Jesse mean by that? She put her book aside and wriggled upright. 'Well, he is Hal's godfather and it's very generous but . . . was he pissed?'

'A bit. But that's not the point. It was the way he said it. As if I don't have any say. I'm Freddie's godfather but I can't afford to buy him an expensive present. And what will he get him for a wedding present? A bleddy house?'

As Mickey spoke, he became more and more agitated. He paced the bedroom carpet, sat on the edge of the bed, then sprang up again and paced the carpet once more.

Loveday watched him, her mind trying to second-guess what Jesse was doing.

'Did he say anything else?' she asked.

Mickey stopped pacing and sat down on the bed again. 'I know he's the one with all the money now; he's the boss and all that, whereas I'm just an employee, but I thought he knew us better than this. He knows I've always paid my way, but this time it's like he's trying to get one up on me.'

Loveday got out of bed and took her dressing gown from the hook on the door. 'Want a cup of tea?'

Mickey nodded and took her hand as she opened the door to the landing. 'Thanks, darlin'. Am I overreacting?'

'Let's talk about it.'

Dowstairs, Hal was lolling on the sofa watching a police drama on the television, his long legs spilling over one arm. 'Hey, Mum. Thought you'd be asleep. We had a great night. Fred and I absolutely slaughtered Dad and Uncle Jesse at pool. Did Dad tell you what Uncle Jesse bet us if we beat him?'

'Ah. It was a bet.' Loveday relaxed. A beer-fuelled bet tonight wouldn't be worth the breath it was made with once Jesse sobered up tomorrow and, besides, Mickey and Hal had downed a fair few too by the looks of it. 'I wouldn't get too excited.' She patted Hal's size 12 feet as she went past.

'No, he meant it,' said Hal, grinning with excitement.

'Well, let's just wait and see. I'm not sure your dad and I would be comfortable about him giving you a car, anyway.'

Mickey chipped in, 'Your mum's right.'

Hal reached for the remote control and switched the television off. He stood up and stretched. 'Well, you two can think what you like, but Uncle Jesse has always been decent to me. Treated me the same way he treats Freddie, so why shouldn't I get a car out of him?'

'That's enough,' said Mickey. He took a step towards Hal and jabbed a pointed finger at him. 'Jesse is a friend, not family. If anyone's going to buy you a car, it'll be your mum and me.'

'Really?' Hal's face lit up. 'For my twenty-first?'

Loveday stepped in before Mickey could reply. 'Darlin', this all needs a bit of thinking about. Now go up to bed and don't wake the girls. They'm got their exams in the morning. We'll talk about this when we're all less tired.'

Loveday wondered about what was happening with Jesse. What with that awkward conversation they'd had at the office, plus the drinking . . . what would Greer be making of it all? Loveday tried to crush the creeping sense of anxiety, but it nagged away at her as she returned to bed and tried to get off to sleep.

*

In the morning, Loveday knew she had to speak to Greer. It took a few moments to connect to Greer's mobile, and four or five rings before she picked up.

'Greer, it's Loveday.'

'Morning, Loveday. How are you?'

'Fine. I wanted to talk to you about something.'

'Sorry, you're breaking up. I'm in the lanes on my way to Mevagissey. There's a woman there with the most wonderful antiques. She has a Victorian claw-footed bath, needs restoring and re-enamelling but that's OK, it means it'll be a bargain, and a fabulous, huge oak dresser. She reckons it's seventeenth century, but I need to look at it to be sure—'

Loveday broke into her chatter. 'Can you hear me now?' she asked.

'Sort of, but you're coming and going. Can I ring you back when I'm on my way home later? Is it anything important?'

Loveday took a deep breath and told her. 'Jesse wants to buy Hal a car.'

'What?'

'For his birthday.'

'Sorry, I'm only getting every other word. I'll call you later.'

*

It was just before lunch when the phone on Loveday's desk went.

'Hello, Loveday Chandler.'

'Darling, it's me, Greer. The dresser was a let-down. Early nineteen hundreds and pine, not oak. The bath has a crack through the middle and will leak through an entire house. Total rubbish, and I told her so. Anyway, the upshot is that I'm ten minutes away from Trevay. Shall I swing by for a coffee and you can talk to me about this car business?'

Loveday's stomach was rumbling and she needed more than coffee. 'How hungry are you?'

'Not at all. I never eat lunch nowadays.'

Loveday's heart sank. She had been considering a macaroni cheese. She tried her chances. 'The Fo'c'sle do nice coffee. They've put in a team of baristas and everything.'

'Oh, yes, I'd heard that. OK. See you there.'

*

The new owners had really turned the old place around. Where there had been lines of Formica-topped tables, striplights, and condensation-clouded windows, there were now cosy corner tables, subdued lighting and air conditioning. The hiss and gurgle of the state-of-the-art coffee machine lent the whole place an air of European sophistication. A smart young waitress dressed to look like an early American bartender, with striped waistcoat, white shirt and long apron, welcomed her.

'Where would you like to sit. Inside or out?'

The spring sunshine was bright and the tables outside in the rear courtyard were inviting with their cushioned chairs and jolly parasols. 'Outside would be lovely, thank you.'

'I'll bring you a menu in a moment.' The waitress walked back inside and Loveday perused the menu. The macaroni cheese looked so tempting but, fearful of Greer's disapproval, she settled for a starter-sized portion of smoked salmon

'Hi, Loveday. What a glorious day.' Greer, wearing sunglasses and carrying an enormous leather handbag, was heading towards her. 'So glad you chose to sit outside. I've been cooped up in that huge tank of a car for hours.' Greer sat elegantly on the chair opposite Loveday and, raising a slender arm in the air, summoned the waitress.

'Yes, Mrs Behenna, what can I get you?'

Greer looked at her over the top of her Fendi shades. 'Miri? How lovely to see you. Home from uni?'

'Yes, just for the Easter holidays.' The young waitress held her notepad in one hand and searched for her pen, stuck into her straggly bun of hair, with the other. 'How's Freddie?'

'He's fine. Working on the fishing fleet – and he's just got on the crew of the lifeboat.'

Miri gave a couple of rapids blinks. 'The lifeboat? Well done him. I bet he looks good in his uniform.'

'He certainly does,' smiled Greer. 'You should give him a bell.'

'Do you think so?'

'Of course. He'd be delighted to hear from you.'

'Well, in that case, I might . . . depends how busy I am . . . Anyway, what can I get you ladies?'

'Loveday, you first, I'm still choosing,' said Greer.

'I'd like the salmon starter and a pot of green tea, please,' Loveday said with an enthusiasm she did not feel.

The waitress wrote the order down. 'And for you, Mrs Behenna?'

'Actually I'm rather hungry. No time for breakfast this morning. I'll have the macaroni cheese, please, and a skinny latte.' Loveday couldn't believe her ears.

'Well, if you're having the macaroni, I'll join you. Thank you.'

'Great. I'll be back with the drinks in a minute.'

When Miri had gone, Loveday asked Greer how she knew her. 'She was at school with the boys. Don't you remember? Miranda? Her mother lives over at Trevone. Was an actress? I did her conservatory for her. She had a splendid divorce and has plenty of cash.'

'The one with the suede fringed jacket, blue sports car and the boob job?'

'That's the one.'

'Miri was sweet on your Freddie, wasn't she?'

'Very. He used to hide upstairs whenever she called

round. Which was frequently.' Greer laughed.

Loveday did too. 'And you've just set him up again.'

'She's turned into an attractive girl. He might thank me.'

Miri arrived with a tray bearing the drinks; as soon as she'd gone again, Greer looked at Loveday. 'I spoke to Jesse after your call and asked him about this business of giving the boys a car each. And he says he's serious. He's always treated them like they're brothers.'

'But they're not brothers,' Loveday said in a low voice. 'Mickey and I want Hal to earn his way in the world and not think that whatever Freddie gets, he'll get too. Life don't work that way.'

Greer thought for a moment. For once she agreed with Loveday. The boys weren't brothers and, fond as she was of Hal, Freddie and he were not equals in her eyes. It was all fine when they were little boys, but now they were growing up and it was time for Freddie to move on to bigger and better things. Of course, Freddie loved the relaxed rules at the Chandlers' house, but it was time that both he and his father thought more ambitiously. If he wanted to buy Hal an old banger, then fair enough, but really his own son deserved something better.

She reached across the table and put her hand on Loveday's. 'Darling, I'm sure he's only going to help Hal out a little bit. It isn't like it's a share in the business.'

'If Hal gets a car, it'll be an old banger. Remember Jesse's old Ford Capri?'

'I do. Filthy smelly thing.'

'Yeah, but he worked for it and he loved it. He had to look after it because no one was going to buy him another one for the hell of it. You give your Freddie anything you like, but let me and Mick do what's right for our son.'

Greer pulled the corners of her mouth down and shrugged. 'Well, in a way I agree with you, but once Jesse has an idea in his head it's very difficult to shake. I have to pick my battles. But I do understand, and I'll talk to him.'

*

Jesse was adamant. 'I want Hal to have the best. He's a good lad. I'm his godfather and I'm going to get him a car. There's no need for him to be a second-class citizen.'

Greer poured them each a glass of wine. 'I don't know why you feel so strongly about him. He's a lovely boy and all that, but when it comes down to it, he's just a godson. You've already done quite enough in your role as his father's best friend. More than enough. He has a good job on the fleet. You've got him on the lifeboat and in the next couple of years you'll give him his own boat to skipper.' Jesse looked up at her sharply. She raised her hand, palm facing him. 'I know you're going to give him his own boat. I do listen to what's happening in the business, you know. I'm not a fool. But where does your generosity stop?' She laughed, a light, scoffing laugh. 'I mean, what are you going to do, give him a share in the company?'

Jesse looked out of the big bay window in the drawing room of Tide House. He could see the cove and the sea beyond. He didn't answer Greer.

'Jesse! Tell me you're not seriously thinking of—'

'All I'm doing is helping a young boy get on in life.'

'As long as that's all?'

Jesse lifted his wine glass and tipped the contents down his throat. 'What's for supper?'

*

Later that night, when Greer had gone to bed, Jesse sat alone in his den. The window was open; on the fresh breeze he could hear the waves as they rolled onto the golden sand below the house. Recently he'd been having bad dreams about Grant. Sometimes Grant accused him of murder. Those dreams were the worst. But Jesse knew he hadn't murdered his own brother. Grant had had a death wish. The injury to his head he'd got when he fell off the cliff into the sea had been what had killed him. Some little weakness in his skull had killed him when they'd scuffled in the bus shelter. I'm not a murderer, Jesse told himself. But, after these dreams, Jesse would feel a tortured sadness. Grant, his own brother, hadn't been able to take his position in the company. It was Grant's own fault, of course. He was a destructive headcase. But Jesse still felt tortured with anguish for a brother who was always going to destroy himself. Dying in the shelter like that was inevitable, and Grant was always going to come to a bad end. It was sad. Tragic. But probably best all round. If only Grant had just kept his mouth shut and not said those terrible things. If he hadn't said anything about Loveday and Hal, he'd still be alive. But he wasn't, and Loveday and Hal needed protection. Hal deserved what was his by rights. Hal and Freddie were brothers, and if Grant couldn't share the company with Jesse, then Jesse would make sure that the next generation would. He'd play it carefully. Not let Mickey guess at anything. He didn't want to break his best mate's heart, after all. He'd talk to Loveday tomorrow. Tell her how he still felt about her. Tell her that he was going to make sure that he did right by Hal.

34

Lauren popped her head round Loveday's office door, tying up the soft belt of her lilac mac. 'Boss wants to see you. I'm off up to Tesco to get a sandwich – want anything?'

Loveday was in the middle of collating that month's wages, and wrote a number down on her pad so that she remembered where she was. She looked up. 'Now?'

'Yes.'

Loveday sighed, blowing her cheeks out. 'OK.' She put her hands on her desk and stood up, pushing her chair back at the same time. 'Could you get me a duck wrap and a packet of crisps?'

She knocked on Jesse's door and looked in. Jesse was at his desk, on the phone. He motioned for her to sit down. She waited while he wound the call up.

He smiled at her. 'You look nice, Loveday.'

She gave him a small frown and pulled her chin in with suspicion. 'Uh-oh. What do you want?'

'Nothing.' He gave her an appraising look which made her feel a bit uncomfortable.

'Jesse, if I've done something wrong, just say it.'

'You ain't done nothing wrong. I thank my lucky stars every day that I got you downstairs sorting out the company. Honest as the day is long, aren't you?'

'Yeeees,' she said, cocking her head to one side questioningly. 'So Lauren said you wanted to see me?'

'It's about Hal's present.'

Loveday relaxed. 'Oh, good. Has Greer spoken to you? Only Mickey and I can't accept . . .'

He held his hands up to shush her. 'I understand all your objections, but I can't accept them. I want to buy Freddie a car for his birthday and I can't do that without buying Hal one too.'

Loveday was getting fed up. 'You can and you will. Mickey and I will buy Hal a car. He won't go wanting.'

Jesse leant back in his chair with an air of one who knew he would win out in the end. 'No offence, but the car you and Mickey can afford won't be up to much, will it?'

Loveday had had enough and said so. 'When did you turn into such a pompous prick? His dad and I will buy Hal a car and he'll love it because he's not a spoilt brat.'

Jesse gave a rueful smile. 'I take it from that that you're insinuating Freddie is? I don't think Greer will be too happy to hear her best friend describe her only son like that.'

Loveday stood up, hot with anger. 'I'm not saying that. You've every right to buy your son whatever you want to buy him, but—'

Jesse's face lost its humour and he looked at Loveday with deadly earnest. 'Freddie isn't my only son, is he?'

Loveday's legs gave way and she sat down again. 'Jesse, I've told you time and again. Hal is Mickey's son. Not yours.'

'I don't believe you. I never have. I went along with your little deception for all these years, but now . . . well, Hal's his own person and he has a right to know.'

Loveday's heart was beating fast and her breathing was uneven. She said as clearly as she could: 'Hal is not your son. He is Mickey's.'

Jesse smiled. 'I don't want to upset the apple cart by telling everyone the truth. I just want you to let me help him. A car, a boat – mebbe a house when the time is right. Just the same as I'll do for Freddie. After all, he was conceived before Fred, so Hal is actually my number one son.'

'Shut up.' Loveday stood again.

'I am trying to be reasonable and do the right thing. He deserves what's rightfully his. Just as Grant did. But it was Grant's own fault that I got what should have been his.'

'Shut your mouth. Have you gone mad?' For a moment, Loveday saw something in his face, something that reminded her of Grant with his bullying and threats.

Jesse twisted his leather chair from side to side. His hands folded on his chest. 'What shall we do, then? We could get all Jeremy Kyle about it and I could demand a DNA test, or you could just keep things as they are and let me look after my boys equally.'

Loveday could feel the threat of tears stinging her eyes. She looked at him in anguish. 'Please,' she whispered, 'please don't do this. He's my son. Mickey's son.'

There was a knock on the office door and Lauren came in bearing a Tesco bag. 'There you are – duck wrap and crisps.' She handed the bag to the white-faced Loveday. 'Are you feeling all right? You're awful pale.'

'Bit of a headache,' said Loveday, her hands gripping the bag handles with ferocious tension. 'How much do I owe you?'

'Don't worry about that. My treat. I think you should get on home. Don't you, Mr Behenna?'

*

As Loveday walked home, she had a sense of dread. A feeling that she'd been delivered a fatal wound. One that would go unnoticed for months or maybe years, but that oozed the life force out of her until she became an empty shell. She stopped at a place on the harbour wall where she could lean and look out to the horizon. She wanted to be in a far, faraway place. A town where no one knew her or could judge her. The truth was she didn't know for sure who Hal's father was. With all her heart she wanted it to be Mickey, but she didn't know and she didn't want to know. Hal was theirs – hers and Mickey's – and that was all that mattered.

A local woman she knew a little was walking towards her, a small scruffy dog on a lead by her side. Loveday considered turning round and running, but she held her ground. The woman got closer and said, 'Hello, Loveday. Beautiful day.'

'Yes,' Loveday replied.

'How's your boy and the twins?'

Please go away. 'Fine.'

'I hear your boy's on the lifeboat.'

'Yes.'

'Must be so proud of him.'

'Hmm.'

'What are your twins doing now?'

Please go away. Please. 'They're doing A levels.'

'Is it uni after?'

'Depends on their grades.'

'What they going to do?'

Oh, please God stop talking at me and go away. 'Maybe nursing.'

'Nursing! Well, they need good nurses in the hospitals. My dad had a terrible time when he had his operation. They never fed him nor changed his sheets—'

'I'm so sorry, I'm not feeling very well. I'm on my way home.'

'You should have said.' The woman peered into Loveday's face. 'You'm looking peaky.'

'Yes. Thank you. Well, bye.'

'Bye then.'

The woman finally walked away with her little dog jingling on its lead.

*

Loveday struggled with the key but finally her front door opened. She shut it behind her, leaning on it in relief. After a few moments she headed to the kitchen, taking off her coat and shoes as she went. The Tesco bag, and its contents, she threw into the bin.

The hot cup of tea gave her comfort, as did the familiar surroundings of her home.

Pilot's Cottages stood in a terrace of seventeenth-century dwellings. Mickey and she had bought one cottage in a damp and unmodernised state years ago, and the next-door cottage (in much the same state) a few years later. They'd knocked through and created four bedrooms and a bathroom upstairs, and an open-plan lounge and dining room downstairs, with a good-sized kitchen off it. She loved this house and all that she and Mickey had done to it. Her favourite thing was the brick archway connecting the kitchen and the lounge. It was like something out of a magazine.

She began to feel a bit better. There was a pile of ironing on the sofa and, as Mickey and Hal were away at sea for a few days, she decided to tackle it later in front of the television. She looked at her watch. Almost time for the girls to come home. There was a half-eaten cottage pie in the fridge. She'd heat it up and that would do for the three of them. They'd eat it on their laps. Loveday took a deep breath. The sky hadn't fallen in. Life was as it always had been. Tomorrow she'd put Jesse straight once and for all.

*

The next morning, as she approached the entrance to Behenna and Clovelly, Jesse's Jaguar slid into its space. He called to her through the open window. 'Loveday. Just the girl. I'm going over to Newlyn at lunchtime. See what the opposition are up to.' He laughed as he got out of the car, still talking. 'I was wondering if you'd come with me. I'd like your professional opinion on their new computer system. See if it would work for us.'

'I don't know anything about IT. You should take Steve.'

Jesse reached into the car and grabbed his fisherman's jumper from the passenger seat. 'Steve can't make it, but he said you'd be the best person. After all, it's you who uses the thing most and knows all the ins and outs.'

'So does Lauren, and every other person who works for you.'

He locked the doors and came towards her. 'Yeah, but I don't owe them an apology, do I?'

'What are you apologising for?' she asked warily.

'Yesterday. I was heavy-handed and put you in an uncomfortable position.'

'Yes. You did.'

'So can I give you a day out in Newlyn, with lunch thrown in?'

'I thought we were going to look at the Newlyn Fish Market, not have a jolly.'

'Yes. We are. But I can throw lunch in too, can't I?'

She eyed him cautiously. 'Promise me you won't say anything more about getting Hal a car?'

'Promise.'

*

They left shortly before eleven and the conversation in the car was work-based and relaxed. Loveday began to think she wasn't going to have to have words with him after all.

The Newlyn operation was interesting, although the computer system wasn't that different from Behenna and Clovelly's. The head of accounts, a woman called April, was friendly, taking Loveday through all the systems she had. Most were familiar to Loveday, but there were one or two short cuts that she'd look into for B&C.

While she was with April, Jesse was in the fish market, looking first at the equipment in there, and later meeting his counterparts in the boardroom, where plans for a new fish-processing plant were discussed. It was clear that the Newlyn company wanted to share the facilities, and the cost, with an injection of cash from – and partnership with – Behenna and Clovelly.

It was four o'clock by the time they left.

'Are you hungry?' Jesse asked Loveday.

'Flipping starving.'

'Sorry about lunch. Fancy an early supper?'

'Sounds good, but I don't want to be home late.'

'Of course not. I know a nice little pub on our way home. We passed it. The Smuggler's Tree?'

'Perfect.'

*

The pub was old but clean. Jesse dodged the low beams as he entered.

'Hello, sir. What can I get you?' asked an elderly barman with thick spectacles and mutton-chop whiskers.

'I'll have a pint of Skinner's, please, and . . .' He turned to Loveday, raising his eyebrows in query.

'Just a lime and soda, please.'

'Coming up,' said the barman. 'Take a seat. I'll bring the drinks over. Will you be eating?'

'Yes, please.'

'I'll bring a menu too. I can recommend the steak.'

*

'That was really nice,' said Loveday, doing up her jacket as they went out into the cool evening. 'Thank you, Jesse.'

'The least I could do.'

They got into the car and Jesse turned on the CD player. Michael Bublé started to sing.

'Oh, I like him,' said Loveday, settling down in her seat. 'I think he's a nice person too.'

'He sings all right,' said Jesse.

The music filled the car and neither Jesse nor Loveday

felt the need to talk. Loveday closed her eyes and let the gentle motion of the car and Michael Bublé's voice flood through her.

*

She had lost sense of time but was aware that the car had stopped. She opened her eyes. They weren't in Trevay. Outside it was pitch black. She turned to Jesse, who was looking at her carefully.

'Where are we?' she asked.

'On the moor.'

She looked out of the window again and could just make out some hills against the moonlit skyline. 'Have we run out of petrol? Is there something wrong with the car?'

'I wanted to talk to you.'

She groaned. 'No, Jesse. We've had this conversation.'

'That's not the conversation I'm thinking of.'

She was puzzled. 'What are you talking about?'

'I love you, Loveday. Always have and always will.'

She sat upright in her seat and folded her arms across her body. 'Don't start this again.'

'It's true. I love you.'

'And Mickey and I love you and Greer as friends.'

'You broke my heart. You know that?'

Loveday felt a white-hot rush of anger. 'What the hell are you talking about? I waited for you to come to me on the morning of your wedding. I waited for you, in my bedroom, expecting the knock at the door. Imagining you telling Mr Clovelly that you couldn't marry Greer. But you didn't come and you left me feeling a fool, watching you and Greer get married. It was my heart that was broken.'

He smiled a gentle smile and put his hand to her cheek. 'I knew you still loved me.'

She pulled away from him. 'I did but I don't now. I love Mickey. He's been good and true and he's not a coward, like you were that day.'

He sat back in his seat. 'Well, that's told me, hasn't it?'

'I hope so. Now please take me home.'

He looked regretful. 'I will take you home as soon as we've sorted something out.'

'What?'

'In return for me not telling Mickey about you, me and Hal . . . I want you to be nice to me.'

'Of course. We're friends.'

'Yes, we're friends, but I'd like us to be close friends. I can be your best friend who keeps your deepest, darkest secret in return for, how shall I put this delicately, being my mistress.'

Loveday's slap came hard and fast and stung his cheek. 'You are mad,' she spat. 'I would have done anything for you. But you didn't want that. You wanted your boats, your fancy wife, your fancy life, and now you want my son. Well, it's too late.'

To her horror, Jesse started to cry and began banging his head on the side window. Loveday was filled with disgust. 'You made all the moves and all the decisions and left me feeling a fool. Now you've got the fucking cheek to cry like a baby. Let me tell you, I love my son, I love my husband. My Mickey is worth ten of you.'

Jesse wiped a string of snot from his nose and turned imploring eyes upon her. 'Please, Loveday. You don't know how hard it's been for me, seeing you and Mickey and Hal together. It breaks my heart.'

'You don't know the meaning of heartbreak. Now either get me home or I'll get out and walk.'

He pulled a clean, pressed handkerchief out of his pocket and blew his nose. 'Please don't go.' He grabbed her hand and looked at her in desperation. 'Please. I feel like I'm going mad.' His eyes filled again and he leant towards her and buried his face in her lap. She pushed him away.

'Stop feeling so sorry for yourself and grow up. Like I've had to.'

'But I killed Grant.'

She looked at him in confusion. 'What?'

'I killed Grant. I killed him. He should have had what I've got but I took it from him.'

Loveday was in no mood for this. 'This self-pity is disgusting. You didn't kill Grant. He died because he was an idiot. Like you are being right now.'

He sat up and wiped his eyes. He looked so forlorn that for a moment Loveday pitied him. 'Come on. Let's just go home. Do you want me to drive?'

'No.' He shook himself and rubbed a hand over his face. 'Let's go.'

35

'Happy Father's Day.' Becca and Bea danced into the bedroom brandishing cards and a beautifully wrapped parcel.

'Wake up, Daddy.' Bea stuck a finger in her sleeping father's ear and twisted it.

'Get off me, you stupid maid,' growled Mickey, grabbing her wrist and pushing it away from him.

'Ow-wer. That hurt.' Bea retreated in a sulk. 'I was only playing.'

'Don't be such a wuss,' said Becca, taking her sister's place and putting her hands either side of her father's pillow, squashing it up over his cheeks. 'Get. Up. Dad. We've got cards and a present.'

Loveday lay still, on her side. Her back to Mickey, as she had done for the last couple of days. She'd managed to get home with no more dramas, but today there was no avoiding him.

She felt the mattress move as Mickey sat up against his pillows and the girls settled themselves in any space on the duvet they could find.

'What's this, then?' she heard him say. 'Where are my ugly daughters and what have you two done with them?'

'Just open the cards. Mine's the funniest,' Bea said.

Loveday listened as an envelope was opened and Mickey read out the message. 'Dad, you're like an old fart, you never know when to leave. Happy Father's Day, Love from Bea.' The girls giggled. 'Well, that's charming. Lovely sentiments. Thank you Bea.'

'Open mine now,' said Becca.

There was another rip of an envelope, then, 'To my dear Daddy, you are my star to guide me home, my hug to stop my tears and my fat wallet when I haven't got any money. Love you Daddy, Becca. Well, I must say the quality of greetings cards is going up. Thank you, girls.'

'Now open the present,' the girls chorused.

Loveday opened her eyes and looked at the clock. Just after eight. How was she going to get through today? She turned over and smiled at her family. 'Morning, girls. Happy Father's Day, Mickey.'

'Thank you, darling.' He leant over and kissed her. 'Look what our special little daughters have got for me.' He shook out a T-shirt which had printed on the front the torso of a very muscly man with a six-pack and huge biceps. On the back was written the legend 'Welcome To The Gun Show'.

'It's 'cos your muscles don't show,' explained Becca.

'I'll show you muscles.' The girls shrieked as Mickey grabbed them and began a play-wrestle.

Loveday got out of bed and padded downstairs to the kitchen to make the traditional Father's Day breakfast.

The drive over to Tide House was noisy. The girls and Hal, in the back of the car, were squabbling over some shared earphones. Mickey, wearing his new T-shirt, was driving. The late June sun was warm and the hedges alive with sea pinks and foxgloves. Loveday knew each bend and dip in the lane. Here was Foxy Loxy Corner, named after the night they saw a fox sitting right there in the field. Next came Owl Stone, where most nights a tawny owl would sit, rotating its head with exorcist flexibility. And now, as they breached the hill in the lane and turned right, beneath them appeared Tide Cove. The sea sparkled and flashed in the sun. A small fishing boat with a scarlet wheelhouse was bobbing on a yellow buoy a little way off the beach. Loveday could see two figures on the sand, pushing a rowing boat into the waves. She dropped her sunglasses onto her nose and took slow, deep breaths. She needed to get this day over and done with.

*

'Hello, hello!' said Greer, greeting them at the steps of Tide House. 'The boys are taking provisions from shore to ship as we speak. Hal, would you and the girls like to take a couple more things down to them? Saves your mum and me.'

A box of Coca-Cola tins and some Tupperware containing sandwiches and cake were handed over.

Greer watched as the three trooped off and then turned to Mickey and Loveday. 'Happy Father's Day, Mickey.' She hugged him and then kissed Loveday. 'Aren't we lucky with this weather! Either of you want a cup of coffee and a pee before we set off?'

Loveday tried to pull her mood up to match Greer's relentless cheerfulness. It had been Jesse, of course, who'd suggested that they all get together for a big fishing outing on this Father's Day. The two families had never shared the day before, and Loveday was sick to her toes with anxiety.

'We'll have a coffee with you,' said Mickey, putting his arm around Loveday. 'Won't we, darlin'?'

*

Greer swallowed the last of her coffee and began filling a bag with a camera and a bottle of sunscreen. 'Got everything?'

'I'll just nip to the loo,' said Loveday.

Mickey watched her go then said quietly, 'Does she look all right to you, Greer?'

Greer thought for a moment. 'I think so. Why?'

'I dunno. She's been quiet. Not herself at all.'

Greer searched for and found her sunglasses. 'In what way?'

'Tired. Quiet. D'you think it's the menopause?'

Greer pulled a face. 'She's only in her early forties. I shouldn't think so.' She looked at Mickey more carefully and saw the anxiety in the lines around his eyes and in the slump of his shoulders. 'Maybe get her to see the doctor? She might be anaemic or need a tonic.'

They heard the flush of the downstairs loo and Mickey stood up in readiness. 'Thanks, Greer.'

*

The three of them walked down the lane and through the dappled shade towards Tide Cove. Years ago it had belonged to a syndicate of lobster fishers, long since dead. Ever since, this had been Freddie and Hal's playground. This is where they learnt to fish for bass off the beach, sail a small dinghy, and now put down their own lobster pots from the *Sand Castle*, the little boat with the red wheelhouse that Jesse had bought for family fishing trips.

Loveday saw Jesse and her heart sank. How was she going to get through this day?

'All aboard the *Skylark*,' called Jesse jauntily. Loveday

stared at him with a frown. How was this man able to change from a snivelling wreck to playing happy families? 'Hurry up. The kids will have eaten everything.' He was up to his knees in the waves, his old pink canvas shorts wet on the hem. He was holding the rowing boat for the latecomers. 'Greer, did you bring my specs?' he asked.

'No. Why, haven't you got them?'

'I wouldn't ask you if I had them, would I?'

Greer looked at Loveday and raised her eyebrows in infuriation. 'Men.' Then she called back to Jesse. 'Have you checked the pocket of your smock?'

His smock was tied round his shoulders; as he undid the arms and swung it round to check the pouch, a pair of glasses slid out and splashed gently into the light surf. 'Bugger,' he said and bent to retrieve them.

Loveday was feeling a sense of panic. 'Look, I'm really not feeling too good. Would you mind if I went home, only I think I'll be a terrible hindrance to you all.'

'What's the matter, love?' asked Mickey, all concern.

'Just a headache and a bit of flu maybe.'

Jesse had pulled the boat up and beached it. 'What's this? Not well, Loveday?'

'No. I'm so sorry.'

'You were fine on Friday.'

The memory of Friday and the car stopped on the moor came slicing through her brain.

'Friday?' said Greer.

Loveday answered hurriedly, 'I helped Jesse with that computer thing in Newlyn.'

'Oh, right.' Greer was already uninterested. 'Will you be ok to get yourself home?'

'I'll be fine. So sorry to be a party pooper.' She kissed

Mickey, who held her tight and whispered, 'You sure you're all right? I don't mind coming home with you.'

'No, darlin'. Enjoy the day.'

'Don't I get a hug and a kiss for Father's Day, Loveday?' asked Jesse, smiling innocently, with his arms held wide.

'Yes, of course. ' She stepped forward and he surprised her by picking her up in a bear hug and lifting her off her feet. The smell of him made her want to kill him. He put her down. 'That's better. See you later. You'll be having lobster for your tea if we catch any.'

*

Freddie was already in the wheelhouse when the rest of the party boarded. 'Right little fishes,' he laughed, turning on the engine, 'we'm coming to get you.'

He turned the boat away from Tide Cove and pointed the nose to the horizon. 'Hang onto your hats!' He pushed the throttle forward and the sturdy boat roared through the smooth sea, while Jesse cracked open the beers.

*

Greer was lying in the bow, face in the sunshine, relaxed in the company of her boys, enjoying a rare moment of complete indolence. Jesse and Mickey were fast asleep. Freddie was at the wheel, manoeuvring the boat into a better position from which to drop the lobster pots. The regular chug of the motor was soporific. She thought she might just close her eyes for a moment.

A changed engine note crashed suddenly into her consciousness – a strange and horrible sound that made her stomach lurch with fear. She leapt up, dashing to the stern. Freddie had stopped the boat and joined her; they shared a mutual glance of sick dread before they looked down towards the water.

It was Greer shouting for Jesse that woke Mickey.

'Jesse! Jesse! There's blood. Oh shit. Oh God. Freddie, get in the water, quick; hold his head up!'

Mickey sat up, immediately alert, and saw Greer hanging over the stern, clearly struggling to hold onto something. 'Jesse!' she screamed now in a shrill pitch that finally woke him. He and Mickey got to Greer within seconds of each other. As they too looked over the back of the boat, they saw Freddie, white faced and frightened, hanging onto the unmoving body of Hal.

'Hal!' Mickey was screaming now. 'What the fuck's happened? Hal!' His training on the lifeboat had given him the ability to assess a casualty with speed. Most of Hal's left side was submerged, but Freddie was keeping Hal's head and shoulders out of the water. Mickey could see a deep cut on the left shoulder and similar wounds to the left side of his chest.

'Pull him up!' Jesse somehow managed to lean as far over the boat as he could without falling in and got an arm around Hal's body.

'Push, Freddie,' Mickey ordered.

'I'm trying to,' Freddie sobbed. Slowly Hal's right side was lifted from the water and Freddie, with God-given strength, managed to get him to a height where Jesse and Mickey could take Hal's weight.

Then Mickey saw. 'His arm,' he cried in horror. 'His arm. Where's it gone?'

*

383

Loveday was waiting at the hospital as the air ambulance landed. Through the glass wall of the A&E department she saw several medics running with a trolley towards it. She turned to the policewoman who was waiting with her. 'Can I go to him?'.

The constable took her hand but shook her head. 'He'll be in the building any minute.'

Loveday felt nothing. Her body was standing, but she was floating near the ceiling. She saw herself wide-eyed and numb. No tears. But she was clenching and unclenching her hands. At last the double doors were pushed open and the trolley carrying Hal went past her. She followed and listened. 'Young male. Aged twenty. Left arm severed by a boat propeller. Losing blood.'

'Loveday!' It was Mickey running towards her. 'I'm so sorry.' He was crying. 'I'm so sorry. I was asleep. He was swimming. I don't know how it happened.' He collapsed into her arms and she watched from the ceiling as she comforted him, still following the trolley carrying Hal. 'It's OK, Mickey. He's still with us. He's still with us.'

They were stopped from going into the emergency room. A handsome male nurse said, 'Please take a seat in the relatives' room. The doctor will come and tell you what's happening as soon as she's had a chance to assess your son's injuries.'

Loveday crashed back into her body with a jolt and sat down, but she couldn't stay seated for long. 'I must do something or go mad. Shall I find a cup of tea?'

'I don't want anything,' said Mickey, his head in his hands.

'I'll go,' said the policewoman.

'No,' Loveday insisted. 'I need to do something.'

She left the room, desperate to move around, burn the awful energy flooding her body.

*

In the corridor she met a woman in blue scrubs who asked, 'Mrs Chandler?'

'Yes.'

'I'm looking after Hal. I'm Dr Sutton.'

'Can I see him?'

'He's not looking very good.'

'I want to see him.'

The doctor thought for a moment then relented. 'OK. Just for a few minutes. He's not conscious. He's lost a lot of blood.'

'I just want to see him.'

*

Jesse banged the door of the relatives' room open, making Mickey and the constable jump. 'Mick. How is he?'

'We're just waiting for the doctor,' Mickey said in a quiet, shocked voice. 'Loveday's gone to get tea.' He looked at the clock on the wall. 'She's been gone ages . . .'

'Where's Hal?' Jesse's anguished voice was completely at odds with Mickey's.

'With the doctor.'

'How is he?'

'We're waiting . . .'

'He lost a lot of blood.' Jesse was agitated. 'He'll need a transfusion.'

'Yes. I expect so.'

'I want you to know, Mickey, that I am going to give him my blood.'

'That's kind of you, but if they don't have enough at the hospital, he'll need some from a relative, won't he? Me or Loveday? Or the girls? Where are the girls?'

'With Greer and Freddie at home.'

'Oh, good.'

'But,' Jesse tried to be gentle, 'I might have the right blood.'

'Yes,' Mickey said kindly. 'It might be you. It might be me. It might be lots of people in this hospital, so I'm sure we'll get some.'

The doctor came in. 'Mr Chandler?' She looked from one man to the other. 'Yes,' said Mickey. 'I'm Hal's dad. How is he?'

'He's lost a lot of blood and we're going to start transfusing him before he goes to theatre.'

Jesse leapt to his feet. 'I'll be a donor.'

The doctor looked surprised. 'Are you a relative?'

'I'm his—'

Mickey stepped in. 'He's his godfather.'

The doctor had experience of dealing with shocked and confused relatives, so she smiled and carried on. 'We're always grateful for donors, but there's no need in this instance. Mrs Chandler has offered and she's a perfect match.'

36

There was a police investigation, which found that human error was the strongest factor in what had happened. Freddie hadn't known that Hal was in the water when he nudged the throttle forward to move the boat round slightly.

Mickey and Loveday refused to press charges against him, so he was left with the freedom of liberty but also the imprisonment of guilt. He was filled with remorse and suffering from sleepless nights and panic attacks; the doctor concluded that he was probably suffering from of PTSD. He was suspended from the lifeboat crew on compassionate grounds as he was unable to perform his duties. All talk of a future on the lifeboats was quietly forgotten. For now, he was given shore duties only, at Behenna and Clovelly. The unending kindness and sympathy of Hal, Mickey and Loveday served only to bury him under a dark cloak of depression.

Jesse left Loveday alone after that. In the back of their minds, both Mickey and Jesse blamed themselves for drinking on the boat; both felt that if they had been more alert and professional, the accident might never have happened. But the two sets of friends continued as they always had, albeit with an underlying strain and an overlying brightness, and kept their private thoughts to themselves.

Hal's left arm now finished just above his elbow. The scars on his stump, face and chest began to fade and, incredibly, he bore no resentment. 'I'm alive, aren't I?' he said again and again to the well-wishers who pitied him.

Before his birthday, Loveday had asked Hal what it was he wanted to do.

'Me and Freddie's having a joint party, ain't we?'

'I know that was what you wanted . . . before.' She hesitated. 'But you might feel differently now, what with your arm.'

'No way are we cancelling this party, Mum.'

'I didn't mean cancel . . . just that maybe a joint party with Freddie might be a bit upsetting for both of you,' she said kindly.

'Mum, Freddie's been to hell and back with his guilt and is suffering more than I am. I want Freddie to see that nothing has changed between us. He's my best friend and he always will be.'

Loveday felt tears sting her eyes as she nodded and hugged her brave, loyal son.

*

It was October, and the last Lifeboat Day of the season fell on the Friday Freddie and Hal turned twenty-one. There was no more talk of new cars. Instead, Loveday planned a family lunch, to include the Behennas, at Pilot's Cottages.

It was twelve thirty, and Greer squinted her eyes against the pearly autumn sun that highlighted the peeling paint surrounding the brass Piskey doorknocker and revealed the silvered timbers beneath. She shifted the plastic cake box from her right hand to her left and knocked.

Jesse had parked the car against the low dry-stone wall in front of the cottage's garden, and was walking up the slate path towards her. 'Have you knocked?'

She didn't bother to hide her irritation. 'Of course I have.'

'Try the handle. It won't be locked.'

'I don't like to.'

'Oh, for God's sake.' Jesse pushed his arm in front of her and opened the door. 'Hello!' he called cheerily.

The house released the steam of vegetables boiling on the stove and the smell of a chicken roasting in the oven. They could hear music coming from a radio.

'Mickey boy?' shouted Jesse as he walked into the comfortably loved lounge. 'Where are you, you bugger?'

Greer, standing on the threshold, looked at the surroundings with her usual judgmental eye. If it were stripped back of all the tasteless clutter, it could be so stylish. Thick and wonky stone walls. Flagstoned floor. Original fireplace and stunning views out to the harbour. But Loveday had smothered all that with her Dralon chintz four-piece suite, grim Austrian blinds and, to Greer's mind, pointless gewgaws on every available surface. The room was separated into two areas. The hideous sitting area to the left and a dining area to the right. The table was laid for six and festooned with streamers and birthday cards.

The kitchen was accessed via the worst assault on the concept of design that Greer could remember. A brick arch, a plastic vine nailed to it and raffia-covered bottles of chianti placed at odd angles. Loveday was inordinately proud of it. She had once told Greer, who had never forgotten, that it reminded her of the Greek taverna in *Shirley Valentine*. Greer hadn't the energy to tell Loveday that Greeks drank retsina and not chianti.

The kitchen itself was functional but dull, the walls the same terracotta colour that had once been so desirable in the nineties.

Greer shocked herself with this bitchy inner dialogue. Loveday had been nothing but generous to her after Hal lost his arm. Loveday could – *should* – hate her, but she didn't.

Greer took the cake box into the kitchen and found Loveday standing outside the back door having a cup of coffee.

'Oh,' said Loveday, clutching her chest. 'I didn't hear you, darlin'. I was just thinking about what you and I were doing twenty-one years ago.'

They embraced each other and Greer handed over the cake. 'What a day that was. But we've survived, more or less intact.' Realising what she'd said, she quickly apologised, feeling the heat of horror in her face. 'I'm so sorry, I didn't mean to—'

Loveday was quick with her reassurance. 'No, no, it's fine. Figure of speech. Now then.' She opened the cake box. 'What have you made for us?'

'It's not much. Chocolate sponge, as usual.'

'Tradition, that's what it is,' said Loveday, smiling. 'Imagine if one year you didn't make it? The boys would go mad.'

Greer slipped her coat off and hung it over a kitchen chair. 'How can I help?'

Jesse wandered in. 'Where's that husband of your'n?'

'Upstairs, having a shower.' Loveday handed Greer an apron. 'Can you make some gravy?'

'Yes, of course,' said Greer. 'Did the boys have a good night last night?'

'I didn't hear them come in so it must've been late. I

took them coffee this morning and they don't look too good.'

Greer felt her stomach flip with relief that Freddie was safe. She hated it when she didn't hear from him. She always asked him to text, just to let her know he was OK, but he would forget.

Jesse went to the fridge and found himself a tin of beer. 'Don't mind, do you?'

'Help yourself,' said Loveday, taking the pan of boiled potatoes off the Aga and carrying them to the sink to drain them.

Greer was looking in the larder. 'Do you have any cornflour?'

'What for?' asked Loveday, the steam from the potatoes billowing in her face.

'The gravy.'

Loveday smiled indulgently at her old friend. 'Bless you, Greer. If you look to the right there's a red tub of Bisto granules. They'll do.'

Greer found the tub and felt somehow foolish for asking for the cornflour. She read the instructions with care. 'So all I have to do is boil a kettle?'

'That's all you have to do.'

'Morning, all.' Mickey's lanky frame stood in the archway. His hair was still damp from the shower but combed smooth, and he smelt of Lynx. He spotted Jesse's beer. 'Pass me one of those, Jess.'

'Coming up.' Jesse tossed a tin to Mickey. 'You girls want a drink?'

'Gin and tonic, please,' said Loveday, pouring batter mix into a red-hot roasting tin for Yorkshire pudding.

'Same for me, Jesse, thank you,' said Greer. 'Are the boys up yet, Mickey?'

'Aye, they're showering. Can't believe they're twenty-one. Where's the time gone? Cheers.' He lifted his tin and the girls took their drinks from Jesse. 'Cheers.' They chinked and drank.

*

Greer was mixing the carefully measured gravy granules with the hot water when Freddie appeared and slid an arm round her waist and kissed her. 'All right, Mum?'

He loomed tall above her and she looked up to drink him in. Her one and only precious son. He was in yesterday's jeans and T-shirt and his breath smelt of last night's alcohol, but he looked all right. Her heart beat a little quicker knowing he was safe.

'You should have texted me.'

'Sorry, Mum. Battery went dead.'

'I should have bought you an extra big battery for your birthday.'

'Oh, yes.' He stretched himself tall, grazing his knuckles on the low ceiling. 'It's my birthday. Happy birthday to me!'

'All right, son?' Jesse passed him a tin of beer. 'Need a hair of the dog?'

'Get on then.' He took the can and opened it with a hiss. 'What you got me for my birthday then?'

'You'll have to wait.'

'What about me?' Hal came into the crowded kitchen. His stump was clearly visible under his short-sleeved shirt. He gave his mum and Greer a one-armed hug.

'Happy Birthday, Hal. I hope you had a good night last night?'

'Awesome, weren't it, Fred?'

'Legend,' Freddie agreed. 'Beer, mate?'

'Yes, please.'

'Would you boys please get out of the kitchen and let Greer and I get on?' Loveday shooed them out.

*

'So what's the plan of action today?' Jesse asked, settling himself on the sofa with half an eye on the football that Hal and Freddie had found on the television.

'The Lifeboat Parade starts at two thirty, so if we get down to the harbour around two fifteen we'll have a bit of time to form up with everyone,' said Mickey.

Loveday shouted from the kitchen. 'I've got to get the raffle tickets and collection buckets from the harbour master's office just after two.'

'Well, you can go ahead of us if you want to,' Mickey shouted back.

'I can give you a lift,' said Greer, adding a small knob of butter to the new potatoes in their dish. 'I've got to get the cream teas set up in the hall by three. I was up till one o'clock this morning making the flipping scones. Hundreds of them.' She picked up the bowl of peas and the jug of gravy and walked through to put them on the dining-room table. Loveday surreptitiously added a larger slab of butter to the potatoes. 'Greer,' she called, 'I've got a wine box in the fridge. Specially for you. Chardonnay. I know you like good wine.'

Greer inwardly winced at the notion that any wine in a box could be good, but she thanked Loveday and gamely retrieved the box from the fridge and put it on the table.

'Right,' said Loveday grandly, 'luncheon is served.'

As soon as they sat down, the phone rang. With dramatic huffs and puffs, Loveday pulled herself back out of her chair and answered it. ''Ello? . . . Becca? Hello, darlin'! Is Bea with you? How's uni? . . . yeah . . . yeah . . . sounds brilliant, yeah. Your dad's fine. We're all here having birthday lunch with the boys . . . OK, I'll put you on . . . speak later. Love you. Here's your brother. '

*

Lunch was relaxed and easy. Pudding was Loveday's signature dish: apple crumble and clotted cream. Her crumble topping was always deep and delicious. 'One-third fruit to two-thirds crumble' was her mantra.

'Oh my, look at the time. 'Tis a quarter to two,' Loveday yelped, jumping up. 'We'd better get down to the quay.'

Greer stood too and began to clear the table.

'What are you doing girl?' asked Loveday. 'Get your coat on or we'll be late.'

'I'll just clear these things,' said Greer, who couldn't bear coming home to unwashed dishes.

'No you won't, they'll keep till tomorrow. Come on.'

*

The last Lifeboat Day of the year was always a huge event in the Trevay calendar. There were still quite a few tourists about; they were always keen to watch the parade and throw their spare change into the jingling buckets.

The parade itself was always headed by the Trevay Pipe Band, followed by Trevay's serving lifeboatmen. Behind them came a succession of floats bearing a series of tableaux. This year's theme was 'The Majesty of the

Sea' and entrants included the Trevay Infant School, the WI, the Pavilions Theatre Players, the St Peter's Church Sunday School and, incongruously, a man dressed as a gorilla riding a motorbike.

Trevay quay was awash with revellers, most a little drunk and all enjoying the spectacle, the autumn sun and a day off work.

Loveday walked among them shaking her bucket and doling out sweeties to the children. Greer, having laid out her cream teas and organised the helpers into getting the tea urns on, looked down from the large windows of the Old Hall above the harbour, and watched.

Freddie and Hal were sitting outside the Golden Hind, drinking with a group of mates.

As the lifeboat crew marched past the pub, it was Freddie who saw Jesse touch his trouser pocket and pull out his pager.

Freddie nudged Hal's stump. 'They've got a shout.'

37

David, the divisional launch authority who'd taken the initial message from the coastguards in Falmouth, was waiting in the boat-house crew room.

'What we got?' Jesse asked, as he pulled on his yellow oilskin trousers, boots, jacket and life vest.

'Yacht about seventeen miles out. Broken mast. Falmouth are getting an accurate position for her. Two on board. Father and son. No casualties reported. But weather doesn't look good.'

Jesse looked over the assembled faces of the crew who'd rushed here, ready to put their lives on the line for strangers. He only needed seven of them.

'Mickey, Malcom, Si, Jeff, Kate, Brian and Don. Get your kit on. Everybody else, thanks and stand by launch.'

The chosen ones got into their kit, quietly shitting themselves.

Jesse walked from the crew room to *The Spirit of Trevay* standing shiny on her rails. The doors of the boat-house were opening and the crew boarded the boat and took their positions.

Jesse gave the command. The pin was pulled and she slid with speed down the slip, out of the boat-house and into the open air. The crowd roared its cheer of support as she hit the water and the engines powered her out of the harbour and out to sea.

The radio came to life.

'*Spirit of Trevay, Spirit of Trevay, Spirit of Trevay*, this is Falmouth Coastguard, Falmouth Coastguard. Over.'

Jesse took up the radio handset. 'Falmouth Coastguard, this is *Spirit of Trevay*. We've launched. Do you have coordinates? Over.'

Jesse made a note as the coastguard reeled them off and made some calculations. 'We should be there in about three and a half hours at our current speed of five knots. Out.'

Malcolm, the helmsman, locked the boat onto auto-pilot. Everything was going by the book. At this rate they'd be home before last orders.

*

Greer was tired as she drove through the electric gates of Tide House. The cream teas had been a huge success and the added excitement of an actual emergency launch had given the visitors a good appetite.

There wasn't a crumb left of the scones or a spoon left of the clotted cream and jam. She hadn't watched the *The Spirit* go out. She'd seen it enough times, as coxswain's wife, to know what it looked like, but she had heard about it via a text from Loveday. She'd sent up a silent prayer of thanks that Freddie was no longer on the crew.

Now, sitting in her huge car parked in front of her beautiful home, she felt drained. She took a few moments and looked up at the house she loved. It was an unusual building for this part of the coast. Not built of granite or brick, but of honey-coloured stone that now glowed in the late sunshine. The glass of the big sash windows was fiery with the first rays of sunset.

Greer opened the heavy car door and felt a breeze coming off the sea below her. It lifted the corners of her grey cashmere cardigan and made her shiver.

She couldn't see the ocean from here. That view was from the house, but she could hear it on the wind. The hiss and suck of the waves as they dragged through the sand and shingle. It was louder than this morning. A sign that the wind was changing. She turned her face to the sky. Clouds were forming on the horizon. She went round to the boot and spent some minutes trundling backwards and forwards with empty cake boxes and bags of bits, until at last she locked the car with the remote key, climbed the steps to her front door and closed it on the early evening chill.

Sanctuary. Her home was welcoming and stylish. Nothing out of place. Peaceful and harmonious. If someone gave her an ornament she disliked she ruthlessly discarded it. The charity shop in Truro, far enough away for the giver of the gift not to find it, always looked forward to her donations. Sentiment had no part to play in her décor.

One of the few rows she'd won with Jesse was that not one of Freddie's school-crafted Christmas decorations or Easter cards were to make their way onto her tree or mantelpiece. That was why Jesse's boat-house on Tide Cove was a shrine to Freddie's schoolboy art. She adored her son, but not to the extent that she was prepared to compromise the look of her home. Thank God there would be no more of it. Now he was twenty-one, he was more interested in boozing and birds than papier-mâché and macramé.

She walked through her dove-grey drawing room, turning on the well-placed lamps that gave the room an ambient glow, through the conservatory with its white orchids and cream cane sofas, and into the kitchen.

She needed a coffee. As she filled the kettle, she heard the cat-flap rattle. Tom danced in with a loud mew. 'Looking for some grub are you, Thomas?' He wound himself through her legs, then sat and curled his tail around his front legs. He gave her a wide-eyed, unblinking, stare. 'OK. OK. What do you want?' She held up two sachets and read from them. 'Prawn in jelly? Or beef casserole?' He yawned when she said casserole. 'Bored with casserole? Prawn in jelly it is, then.'

She prepared his bowl and put it on the floor for him. The kettle boiled and she opened a drawer for a teaspoon, hesitated, then shut it and went to the fridge. She needed a proper drink. She took it to the far end of the kitchen where the plasma television was surrounded by silver-grey striped sofas and a coffee table. The cushions were perfectly plumped. No imprint of previous occupants defiled them. She sat down and closed her eyes. Home. She loved these precious moments when she was alone in the house. Nobody to disturb her with their noise and mess. She opened her eyes and took in the beautiful room. The antique, scrubbed pine kitchen table, big enough to seat twelve, was the perfect foil for the huge bowl of late roses and dogwood stems sitting in the middle of it. The insanely expensive range cooker – she couldn't be doing with the original Aga, which she'd had taken out – was gleaming. She was satisfied. She took a mouthful of her wine and flicked on the TV to watch the news.

Half an hour later she took her second glass of chilled Sancerre up to her bedroom and into the en suite where she ran a deep and bubbly bath. Wallowing, almost floating, in its depths, she heard the first spatter of raindrops on the window, like gravel thrown against it by a lover. The glass of wine, with its beads of condensation, lay cool in her hand. She took another sip and lay her head back on the bath's rim. The rain was sporadic at first but gradually came in drumming gusts. She thought of Jesse and hoped that the weather wouldn't hold him up too much.

*

The heat of the bath and the wine made Greer drowsy. Wrapping a warm bath sheet round her, she lay on her bed, the deeply enveloping duvet closing over her. She hadn't closed her bedroom curtains and she could see that it was almost completely dark outside. The phone rang. She stretched to pick up the receiver. 'Hi. All safe?' she asked, expecting Jesse's voice.

It was Loveday. 'Greer, it's me. I haven't heard anything. Have you?'

'Not yet.' She looked at her clock. 'It's still early, though.'

'Yeah . . .' Loveday hesitated. 'The weather's not too good for them, is it?'

'It might be a bit lumpy out there, but nothing they can't handle.'

'Yeah,' Loveday agreed. 'If I hear anything, I'll give you a shout.'

'Me too.' Greer saw the streaks of rain on her window and heard the wind moan as it pushed itself around the corners of the house. 'Thanks for a lovely lunch, Loveday.'

'My pleasure. I'm stacking the dishwasher now.'

'I should have stayed to help.'

'Absolutely not. Gives me something to do.'

'Right, well, if you hear anything . . .'

'Yeah. Bye.'

'Bye.'

Neither woman would have dreamt of trying the men on their mobiles. It was an unwritten rule. Greer got off the bed and closed the curtains, shutting out the bleakness of the night. She pulled on a pair of soft leggings, cashmere socks and a warm sweatshirt, then padded onto the landing.

At the top of the stairs, a tall, wide window had the clearest view of the sea. On the deep window ledge stood a fat church candle and a box of matches. She shook a match from the box and lit the candle's wick. The flame sputtered before growing tall and unwavering. This was a time-honoured custom. A talisman. A light to guide the lifeboat home. When Freddie was little he was the one who lit it. 'Daddy will see the light and come home to us.'

She walked along the landing and into Freddie's room. God knows when he'd be home. The birthday celebrations could go on for days. He was a different person since the accident and was taking refuge in mates and beer. She drew his curtains and turned his bedside lamp on, just in case. Later she'd turn the corners of his duvet down and pop in a hot-water bottle. She knew he preferred a cold bed, but it was an old habit she enjoyed. He might be glad of it when he came home.

She went downstairs to light the open fire in the library. It was smaller than the formal sitting room and she could feel snug in here with a book. As the fire licked into life she stoked it with coal and a good-sized log, then went to put a chicken casserole in the oven. Something for Jesse when he got back.

*

Loveday put the phone down and spoke to her reflection in the kitchen mirror. 'Come on, girl,' she told it. 'The boys'll be back from the pub and Mickey'll be home and they need food in their bellies.' She threw five jacket potatoes into the Aga and took a packet of sausages out of the fridge. That and a couple of tins of beans would do them just right.

Upstairs she got out of her clothes and had a hot shower, enjoying the warmth on her neck and shoulders. The weather would be hampering *The Spirit* a bit and maybe the yacht was a bit bigger than expected and taking longer to tow in. She dried her hair roughly and sprayed herself with some perfume. She wanted Mickey to hold her and love her when he came home. Since the whole horrible business with Jesse had started, and then stopped so tragically, she'd been unresponsive to Mickey's affections. He'd been kind and patient, he'd even tried to get her to see the doctor, but she couldn't tell anyone about her and Jesse. Well, today was a turning point. Hal was twenty-one and Jesse was history. When Mickey came home tonight she'd show him how much she loved him.

Feeling better, she decided to phone the twins.

''Ello, darling. It's Mum. You all right?'

'Hi, Mum.' Becca pulled a face at her twin sister, Bea, who was listening in. They loved their mum, but why did she have to ring so much? 'How are you? How did the birthday lunch go?'

'Really good, and Lifeboat Day went really well. Gave the grockles something to talk about 'cos the boat went out on a real shout.'

'Oooo, *exciting*,' said Becca, rolling her eyes at her sister.

'How are you doing for money? Not overspending your allowances?'

'No, Mum. We're doing really well.' Becca looked over at the half-drunk litre bottle of vodka and giggled.

'How are your studies going?'

'I was on a geriatric ward this week.'

'Oh, poor old souls. How'd you get on?'

'Good, yeah. I wouldn't mind working in geriatrics.'

Loveday held the phone between her shoulder and her ear and started to open a tin of baked beans.

'And Bea?'

'Ask her yourself. She's right here.'

Bea shook her head wildly but it was too late, Becca had put the phone in her hand.

'Hi, Mum,' she said, balling her fist and miming a punch at her sister, who ducked out of the way, laughing.

'How's your course going?'

'Full on. Lots of work.'

'Well, of course it is, darling. Have you delivered any babies yet?'

'I was at a birth the other night. Little boy, Finlay. Really sweet.'

'Ah. Ain't that lovely? And how are you doing with your allowance? Not overspending?'

'Fine, Mum. I had to get some textbooks the other day, but they were second-hand so not too bad.' Becca heard this and, pulling a shocked face, pointed at the new super-sexy Top Shop dress that her sister was wearing. Bea gave her a playful shove.

'How's Dad?' she managed to say as Becca made her laugh by pointing at her nose and pretending it was growing, Pinocchio style.

''E's out on a shout. Not back yet.'

Bea heard the familiar worry in her mother's voice. 'You OK, Mum?'

'Yeah, I'm fine. It's just that the weather's turned a bit.'

'And where's Hal?'

'In the pub, I think. Celebrating with Freddie.'

'Dad'll be all right, Mum. He always falls on his bum in butter.'

Loveday laughed. 'Well, that's what your grandma always used to say. How's London? Grandma never got there. She'd be so proud of you. Have you seen Buckingham Palace yet?'

'Yes. I'll take you when you come up.' Bea looked over at her sister, who was tapping her watch. They were going out with a gang of mates any minute.

'Mum, I've got to go. Love to Dad and Hal and Fred. Love you.'

'Love you too.'

Loveday smiled, comforting herself with the thought of her clever girls who had chosen such exciting careers. No hanging about in Trevay waiting for life to happen to them. They could travel the world when they were qualified. Loveday felt tears and a tightening in her throat. She missed them so much and worried about them constantly. At least she still had Hal. Hal wouldn't be leaving Trevay. Not now.

She looked at the clock. If he and Mick didn't come home soon, the jacket potatoes would spoil.

38

The sun was setting and the light was dying over the roughening sea. *The Spirit of Trevay*, a sturdy, all-weather, self-righting, Tamar-class boat forged through the waves.

Malcolm, the helmsman, was on the bridge but steering manually now. The sea was getting too big for the autopilot. They'd just gone over the biggest wave of the night. He eased off the throttle as the boat surfed down the other side of it and then pushed the power back on to go up another bigger wave. The splash as he came over the top caught him broadside, filling his ears with water. He pulled the hood of his jacket up. Jesse was standing beside him, eyes scanning the sea.

'All right, Malc?' he asked.

'Yeah.'

The radio came to life. '*Spirit of Trevay*, *Spirit of Trevay*, *Spirit of Trevay*, this is Falmouth Coastguard, Falmouth Coastguard. Over.'

'Falmouth Coastguard, this is *Spirit of Trevay*. Over.'

'Yacht *Ocean Blue* is not responding to radio calls. But we've got the GPS position.'

'Right, give it to me.' Jesse made a note and checked the screen, showing their position and the yacht's last known position. 'That's a long way off the original reference, Falmouth.'

'She's probably drifted. Met Office tells us winds are gusting Force Eight.'

'Shit.' Jesse rubbed a hand over his face. 'Roger that. Setting new course. Out.' Jesse looked up in time to see a huge wave roll past on the portside. 'We need to get below, Malc.'

All crew members came to the main cabin and buckled themselves into their bouncy, shock-absorbent seats. With the hatches tightly shut, it was a bit like sitting in a people carrier, but on a very rough road. There were three seats in front of the dark windscreen. Malc sat on the far left, Jesse was in the middle taking control of the boat, then Si was to his right on radar. Behind Si was the hatch to the survivors' space.

Behind Malc was Mickey and behind him in the doctor's chair was Kate. Opposite Kate, Jeff worked at the chart table. Outside it was definitely getting worse.

Inside, the noise of the engines was deafening. The air was getting uncomfortably hot. Coming off the top of a particularly big wave, the hull dropped through thin air until it smashed onto the trough below, rattling the teeth of everyone. The adrenaline running through the crew was tangible.

Jesse looked over to Si on the radar. 'Doing OK, Si?'

Si was usually the first to get sick. 'Could do with a bucket.'

'Kate?' Jesse called back. 'Pass a bucket to Si.'

After some quiet retching, Si looked a bit better.

Malcolm was next to go. 'Pass the bucket.'

Jesse had never suffered, but he also never underestimated the courage of his crew who felt so ill but still managed to concentrate on the job.

The radio crackled again. 'Trevay, this is Falmouth. How far?'

'We should be there in about ten minutes,' Jesse said.

On the radar, Si picked up an orange blip that looked about the right size for a yacht.

He told Jesse.

Jesse reached for his binoculars. 'Turn the lamps on, Malc.' Immediately the raging sea was illuminated and everyone focused their eyes through the rain-streaked windows.

'There,' said Malcolm as they rose to the top of a wave. 'You'll see it over the top of the next one.'

Jesse saw it. The mast was hanging like a broken limb. The mainsail torn and flapping in the strong wind. He scanned the deck for any sign of the two sailors. He couldn't see them but they were probably, hopefully, tucked below and riding it out.

Jesse steered *The Spirit* towards her, throttling back as he did so. 'Malc, take over,' Jesse barked. 'Open the hatch, Kate.' Opening a locker, he took out a loud-hailer, and climbed through the open hatch.

On deck the wind was strong and he ducked his head as a sheet of water threw itself at him. His eyes stung with the salt. Hanging onto the grab rails, he pulled himself round to starboard deck and raised the loud-hailer to his lips.

'Hello. This is Trevay Lifeboat. We're going to get alongside and give you a tow.'

The wind was ripping the words from his mouth and throwing them backwards, over his shoulder, away from the stricken yacht. He tried again. 'Hello. Is there anybody on board? Can you hear me?'

It was a tiny movement, but he saw a hand raised for a moment from the stern of the vessel.

'Are you OK?' he shouted again. The hand reappeared and gave a limp thumbs-up. Brian and Kate appeared next to him.

He quickly filled them in. 'The cockpit. He must be lying on the bottom. Look. See?'

The hand came up again and gave a painful wave.

Jesse put the loud-hailer to his mouth. 'Can you get a line to us?'

The hand gave a thumbs-down.

Malcolm nudged the lifeboat closer and closer to the damaged yacht. But the waves frustrated him. Eventually he got close enough for Don to leap across a tiny gap before the sea surged them apart again. Don pulled on the lifeboat's line and got it secured to a cleat on the yacht's bow. Now the boats pulled against each other. As one went up, the other came down.

Jesse watched as Don steadied himself and walked with uneven steps to the stern to check on the casualty. He jumped down into the cockpit and knelt so that Jesse could only just see the top of his head. After a few moments, Don stood up and shouted against the wind, miming injuries as he spoke.

Jesse turned to Kate. 'Did you get that?'

'I think he's saying it's a broken arm, shoulder and ankle. Do you want me to go over?'

'Let's get that line attached to the stern first. Brian!' he shouted. 'You and Si, get a line secure on the arse end.'

Mickey appeared on deck. 'Jesse, Falmouth are asking if you need the helicopter?'

'I'll know as soon as we find the second man. Tell them to give me a couple of minutes.'

Brian and Don had at last got the two boats tied together securely. 'Brian,' shouted Jesse, 'do you need Kate to come over?'

'No, let's get him on the lifeboat. Then she can have a look at him.'

'OK. What's happened to the other bloke?'

'His dad thinks the mast hit him.'

Jesse was exasperated. 'Well, have a fucking look then.'

Brian stood up out of the cockpit and stepped onto the deck, steadying himself on the low railing and edging slowly forward. The boat was pitching and yawing and a huge wave crashed over him. He spat out the worst of it and finally got to the torn and flapping sail. The cords attached to it were snapping and flicking with lethal unpredictability. He took an armful of the tough sailcloth and slowly bundled as much as he could into his arms, the wind tugging it all the while. Every armful, he looked underneath for the second man. As he stooped, the boat tipped sharply and he lost his footing. He slid across the deck on his hip, his eyes tight shut, waiting to hit something hard.

'Arrggh.' A cleat caught the hem of his trousers. His leg stopped but the rest of his body spun one hundred and eighty degrees before his head banged something hard. Another wave breached the deck and sea water flooded up his nose and into his mouth.

'Brian!' Jesse was shouting over the loud-hailer. 'Don! Brian's hit his head. Help him.'

Brian was dazed but able enough to board the lifeboat and be sent below to the survivors' space to be seen to by Kate. Getting the injured sailor out of the yacht's cockpit and below deck to join him was harder, but they did it.

'Trevay, this is Falmouth. Will you require the helicopter?'

Jesse, who'd gone to check on Brian, answered: 'Yes. I'm a crew member down. Possible concussion. One casualty taken off yacht with suspected multiple fractures. One person still missing, presumed under the mast and mainsail. Over.'

'Understood. It's on its way. Out.'

Jesse climbed back on deck. The wind had dropped and a small moon gave the scene a silvery shine. 'Don!'

Don was crouching on the deck of the yacht, one arm stuck under the opposite armpit. He looked grey.

'Don,' Jesse said again. 'What is it?'

'I've cut my hand.'

Jesse swore under his breath. 'Badly?' he asked.

Don nodded and brought the wounded hand out from under his arm. Even from where he was standing, Jesse could see the tendons shine white through the neatly sliced flesh.

'How the fuck did you do that?'

Don bent his head towards the flapping cords on the mainsail. 'I tried to catch one.'

'Right, let's get you back over here.'

'Falmouth. This is Trevay. I'm another crew member down. What's the ETA for the chopper?'

Jesse listened as the coastguard spoke to the helicopter. 'Trevay. This is Falmouth. Helicopter is about eighteen minutes away. Over.'

'We're going to find the other casualty. Out.'

Mickey volunteered. 'I'll find him.'

Jesse hesitated. He had three crew members to choose from. Malcolm, who was at the helm; Jeff, who was eager but hadn't been on the boat very long, and Mickey, who was more than capable – but could Jesse spare him?

Jesse looked from one man to the other. He made his decision. 'OK, Mickey, it's you, but be careful.'

Jesse watched as Mickey stepped nimbly from one boat to the other.

'It's a bit calmer. Not so bad,' shouted Mickey. He arrived at the flapping mass of sail and burrowed underneath it. Jesse held his breath, then Mickey popped out.

'Got him. He's unconscious but alive. As far as I can see, the mast is lying at an angle from one hip, across his stomach and up to his shoulder. I'll see if I can get to him.'

As Jesse watched, Mickey took a knife and started to cut the mainsail loose from its rigging. The wind was picking up a little and Jesse felt some rain in his face. The sea beneath his feet started to dance, and from the blackness rolled a wave twice as big as anything they'd seen that night.

'Mickey. Get down!' shouted Jesse, as the wave crashed on top of the yacht and spilled its weight on Mickey's head. It swept Jesse off his feet, but he held a grab rail and jammed his feet against the boat's side. As the water drained away, Jesse yelled, 'Mickey? Mickey?'

'It's OK. I'm OK,' came Mickey's voice.

Jesse saw him hanging over the edge of the yacht. Gripping tight to the railing, his legs in the sea. There was, at most, a metre and a half between both boats. If they were pushed closer together, Mickey would be crushed.

'Oh Jesus,' said Jesse. 'Malc!' he screamed.

Malcolm, at the helm, had seen what had happened and he was doing all he could to keep the boats at a safe distance.

Jesse knew what he had to do. 'I'm coming over, Mickey. I'm coming.'

Mickey, the muscles in his shoulders tearing with the effort of hanging on, shook his head. 'Get Jeff. You're the bleddy coxswain. You can't leave the boat.'

'Watch me.'

Jesse looked at the sea and counted the seconds in between the swell, then jumped, landing safely on the yacht.

'I've got you, Mickey.' He lay on the deck and grabbed Mickey's lifejacket. He got his hands under the shoulders and pulled.

'Thank God you'm a fucking skinny bastard,' he said as he pulled Mickey onto the deck. They lay side by side. Breathless and exhausted.

Mickey spoke first. 'I suppose this makes us even.'

'Even?' Jesse panted.

'Yeah, you saved my life and I saved yours.'

'You've lost me, mate.'

'All those years ago. Remember? The shelter on the harbour where you and Grant had your fight?'

Jesse felt the first stirrings of unease. 'It wasn't me. I found him. You saw the bloke who did it running away.'

Mickey looked at him incredulously. 'No. I didn't see anyone run away, as well you know. But I did see you kicking shit out of your brother. You killed him.'

'No. They never found who killed him.'

'Because I lied for you and saved your life.'

Jesse sat up. 'You've had more of a bang to the head than I thought, boy.'

'I protected you to protect Loveday,' said Mickey, staring at Jesse.

'What?'

Mickey sat up. His breath was ragged and he fought

to get the words out – tears mingled with salty sea water burned his eyes.

'I knew. I always knew I was second best. Grant told me once that you and Loveday had had a fling. The night before you married Greer. He told me that Hal, my Hal, was really your son.' Mickey spoke quietly. 'So you see, I'm as guilty as you. I wanted Grant dead too. To stop him spreading those lies. And when I saw you kicking and kicking and kicking him, I could have stopped you. But I didn't because I wanted him dead so I am as guilty of his murder as you are.'

Jesse edged over to Mickey and clung to him. Shaking him. 'No. No you didn't. I did it. I hated him. I didn't want him in my life.'

Mickey wiped his running nose and looked into Jesse's eyes. 'Tell me the truth. Tell me. Did you sleep with Loveday?'

From the lifeboat, Jeff appeared and shouted: 'The chopper's here.'

Jesse turned and looked into the sky. He saw the searchlight beam coming towards them and heard the thud of the rotor blades.

'Tell me, Jesse,' Mickey pleaded. 'Tell me the truth and we'll never speak of it again.'

The helicopter was directly behind Jesse now. The noise was intense. 'Tell me!' Mickey shouted.

'I'm going to do the right thing, Mickey.' He looked up to the helicopter and gave the thumbs-up to the pilot. The side door of the Sea King opened and the winch man appeared on his wire.

Jesse turned back to his best friend, his silhouette dark against the bright light. 'I love you, Mick.' He moved his hands to his life vest and started to undo its buckles, and then the zip. He took it off and chucked it down on the deck.

'What are you doing?' shouted Mickey, jumping to his feet.

'I'm sorry,' mouthed Jesse over the beat of the thundering rotor blades.

'Jesse, what the fuck are you doing?' screamed Mickey again.

Jesse moved towards Mickey and kissed him on both cheeks.

Then he walked backwards to the edge of the boat and jumped.

39

Greer had woken with a jolt. She looked at her bedside clock. 03.27.

She put a hand out to feel Jesse's side of the bed. Empty.

Turning her sidelight on she got out of bed and went downstairs. Maybe he was in the kitchen.

He wasn't.

She saw her phone and checked for texts from Jesse or Loveday. Nothing. She wondered if she should call Loveday, then decided against it. She'd wait another hour.

She was halfway up the stairs when she realised that the candle in the window had burnt down and extinguished itself. A chill hand gripped her heart.

The buzzer from the electric gates sounded by the front door. She walked calmly back down the stairs and towards the intercom. She lifted the receiver. 'Hello?'

'Mrs Behenna?'

'Yes.'

'Devon and Cornwall police. May we come in, please?'

*

The media arrived like sharks smelling blood. The survival of the two sailors on the yacht was noted, but

417

it was the mystery of the hero coxswain who had taken off his lifejacket and drowned that caught the public's imagination.

Much was written. Little of it was truth.

*

At the inquest Mickey gave his evidence and stuck to the facts. Yes, Jesse was his normal self that day. No, there was nothing to suggest he was suicidal. Yes, he saw Jesse take off his lifejacket. No, he no idea why he had done that.

The coroner recorded an open verdict.

Jesse was never found.

*

A few months after his death, Mickey and Loveday came to see Greer. Jesse's death had hit her hard. Jesse had been everything to her, and her whole life had revolved around him. Her father had been roped in to manage the day-to-day affairs along with Mickey manning the boats. Edward Behenna and his wife were in deep shock at this unexpected blow to their family and it wasn't clear that Jan would ever recover. But both Hal and Freddie were surprising everyone with their handle on the business. Ideas of college had been forgotten for now, but she was glad that she'd encouraged Freddie with his school work. He had a good head for numbers.

Loveday had been a rock for Greer. As well as mucking in alongside everyone with Behenna and Clovelly, she had also helped Greer to keep her interior design business afloat. Greer hadn't taken on any new commissions, but in the back of her mind she hadn't quite given up on it.

Mickey and Greer took a walk down to the beach while Loveday prepared them a light lunch and sat down looking out at the *Sand Castle*, Jesse's cheerful family boat, which still lay moored, waiting for its skipper to take it out.

'Can I ask you something, Mickey?' Greer was still perfectly groomed, but her previously slim frame was now noticeably underweight, and grief and sleepless nights had all aged her in the last few months. Creases now appeared around her eyes and lips.

Mickey put his arms around his old friend. He knew Greer could be a cold fish, but he'd always felt a soft spot for her and wished he could do more to help her through this.

'Of course.'

'Do you think he killed himself?'

Mickey stared out at the big blue sea, calm today, but unpredictable and unknowable. He thought carefully about what to say for a moment. 'His mum always used to say still waters run deep with Jesse.'

'It's just . . .' Greer's voice caught and she struggled to get the words out. 'We had a big row. At our anniversary. I said some awful things that I didn't mean and he said . . . he said I wasn't his first choice.'

Mickey held her closer as sobs escaped her tiny frame.

'The thing is, Mickey . . . I've got this horrible feeling that Jesse wasn't happy. That all of this . . .' She swept her arm backwards to indicate the house and everything that went with it. '. . . Behenna and Clovelly, all of it . . . none of it was what he really wanted. There was something missing. Am I right, Mickey? Please tell me I've got it horribly wrong.'

Mickey thought about his best friend. The Jesse that he knew.

'Jesse did the right thing all his life, Greer, and deep down, I know that he wouldn't have changed a thing. We'll never really know what was in his mind that day, but I do know that he loved you and Freddie.'

Loveday's voice rang out behind them. 'Hey, you two. Lunch is up.' Loveday plonked herself down on the other side of Greer and put her arm around her too.

'I'm starving,' said Mickey. But Greer said nothing and continued to stare at the horizon, ensconced between her two friends but alone with her thoughts.

*

It was a sparkling February day and the clouds were racing across the bright Cornish sky. The small gathering of Trevay folk stood respectfully watching the handsome young man on the dais.

'And so I'd like to thank everyone who helped make this memorial to my father a reality.'

The crowd gave a round of applause and Freddie looked over his shoulder at his mother, who was standing with her hands folded over her neat navy coat. The wind had pulled a whip of hair from her neat bun and her face was expressionless.

'Mum.' Freddie held out his hand to her. 'Would you do the honours?'

She blinked away whatever memories she'd been sorting through and smiled. 'Yes.'

The blue velvet curtains opened smoothly as she pulled the cord, and revealed a simple plaque with Jesse's name and dates on it. There was a short inscription detailing his years with the RNLI and the event that led to his death.

More applause, and a few flashbulb pops as the local paper recorded the moment.

Freddie turned to face the crowd again, now joined by a smiley, petite blonde, who was holding a toddler on her hip.

'The mystery of my father's death may never be solved, but his memory lives on in Trevay. Sadly, we lost my granny, my dad's mum, at Easter, but I like to think she would be very proud of this memorial to her son. In fact, if we don't keep it polished, she'll come and haunt me.'

The crowd laughed.

'But I'm glad to say that my parents' best friends, Mickey and Loveday Chandler, have come all the way back from New Zealand to be with us today.'

The crowd swivelled, hoping to identify them.

'All right!' Mickey raised a hand and beamed at everyone. There were murmurs of recognition as the crowd spotted the tanned and smiling couple standing on the edge of the crowd.

Freddie continued, 'We had supper with Uncle Mickey and Auntie Loveday last night and they've asked me to tell you that anyone going over to New Zealand can have a free holiday with them, stay as long as you like.'

More laughter.

'But seriously . . .' Freddie quietened the crowd. 'They sound as if they're doing all right with their fishing trip business, and as soon as Jesse Junior,' he turned to the toddler on the young woman's hip and chucked him under the chin, 'and Miri and I can, we'll be coming to see you!'

Mickey put his hand up and waved, to another round of applause.

Freddie scanned the crowd. 'Hal? Where are you? Come up here.'

Hal, as tall and lanky as his father, was standing with Loveday and Mickey. He ducked his head when his name was called, hating public attention as much as Freddie loved it.

'Come on, Hal. Don't be shy,' urged Freddie.

Hal made his way through the people and stood next to Freddie, looking as uncomfortable as he felt.

Freddie put an arm round his shoulder. 'Hal Chandler is my best friend. Without him I wouldn't have coped when Dad died, or been able to learn the business without his help. He's got the brains from his mum not his dad!'

Loveday blushed and Mickey squeezed her hand.

Freddie laughed and carried on. 'We share the same birthday, Hal and I, and are brothers in all but name. Even though it's not our birthday till October, I'd like to give him an early birthday present. It's in recognition of all that your dad meant to my dad.' Freddie's voice developed a crack and he swallowed hard before managing to continue. 'Mum and I reckon this is what Dad would have done if he'd been alive, because he always treated us the same. From now on, the company formerly known as Behenna and Clovelly will be called . . .' He paused and looked into Hal's eyes. Loveday held her breath. Mickey clenched his jaw. '. . . Will be called . . . Behenna, Clovelly and Chandler.'

The End

AFTERWORD

Inspiration for stories comes from all sorts of unusual places. Last year I cycled around Sri Lanka (as you do!) and visited the ruins of the amazing Royal Palace at Sigiriya. The story of two princes – one legitimate, the other a bastard – caught my imagination and so *A Good Catch* was born.

I owe big thanks to David Flide, the Divisional Launch Authority for the Padstow Lifeboat, who arranged an unforgettable trip for me – including a launch down the slip! – and has been my expert in describing life on board. Any errors are entirely my own!

By the way, if you're in Padstow, I recommend the Basement Café where you may be lucky enough to find David cooking breakfast. He's good!

Thanks as always go to my lovely editor Kate Bradley, who just leaves me to my own devices while sending encouraging thoughts and ideas.

To the elegant Luigi Bonomi, who I am so grateful to have as my literary agent, and to the wonderful John Rush, my agent but also my great friend and sounding board.

To my darling Phil, children and cats who put up with me.

To the lovely Liz Parker, who boosts my ego to an unhealthy level (the sign of a great publicist)!

To the wonderful team at HarperCollins, who continue to have faith in me.

And finally to you, who have been generous enough to pick this book up. I hope it was worth it.

I'm a lucky woman.

With love,
Fern
November 2014

There are lots of ways to keep up-to-date with all things
Fern

Be the first to find out about Fern's latest news, competitions and events